The Shape of Snakes

12/2000   34.99

Fiction
WINDLEY, CAROL
Breathing under water

Breathing Under Water

A Novel

Carol Windley

OOLICHAN BOOKS

LANTZVILLE, BRITISH COLUMBIA, CANADA

1998

All the characters in this book are fictitious, and any resemblance to persons living or dead is purely coincidental.

Canadian Cataloguing in Publication Data

Windley, Carol, 1947-
Breathing under water

ISBN 0-88982-171-2
I. Title.
PS8595.I5926B73 1998   C813'.54   C98-910934-8
PR9199.3.W4989B73 1998

We acknowledge the support of the Canada Council for the Arts for our publishing programme.

THE CANADA COUNCIL | LE CONSEIL DES ARTS
FOR THE ARTS | DU CANADA
SINCE 1957 | DEPUIS 1957

Grateful acknowledgement is made to the BC Ministry of Tourism, Small Business and Culture for their financial support.

We acknowledge the financial support of the Government of Canada through the Book Publishing Industry Development Program for our publishing activities.

Cover image "Brothers" courtesy of Carol Evans and Dayspring Studio, Salt Spring Island, B.C.

Published by
Oolichan Books
P.O. Box 10, Lantzville
British Columbia, Canada
V0R 2H0

Printed in Canada by
Morriss Printing Company
Victoria, Britich Columbia

Acknowledgements

The author wishes to thank Ron Smith for his keen editorial advice and encouragement along the way, and Pat Smith for her excellent suggestions with an earlier version of this novel. Thanks to Cynthia Cecil for reading the entire manuscript and offering her insightful comments and her unfailing support and friendship. An invaluable resource was *Between Pacific Tides* by Edward Ricketts and Jack Calvin, with a foreword by John Steinbeck, Stanford University Press, Third Edition, 1952. Thanks also to my husband Robert and my daughter Tara for being there.

For my parents
Anthony and Mavis Guppy

1957-1966

CHAPTER ONE

"Read to me," Catherine said.

Her mother was lying on the sofa in the living room, reading a book. She was wearing her bathrobe, and her bare feet were propped up on cushions. Her toenails were painted the true pink of cotton candy.

"Read me this page," Catherine said.

"No," her mother said.

"Read me this word. Just this one word." Catherine leaned against the arm of the sofa and let her head rest on her mother's shoulder. "Please," she said.

"Oh, Catherine. The word is 'conversation,'" her mother said. "Go away. Go play with Matt."

Matt was sitting on the floor, playing with his alphabet blocks. He put two blocks side by side and gave each one a little push. One block had a blue letter A on it, the other had a red letter E. Catherine knew the alphabet off by heart, but she didn't know any real words yet.

"What does conversation mean?" she said. She dug her chin into her mother's shoulder.

"It means when two people are talking. Well, it can be more than two people. They're talking, that's all."

"Read the next word."

"No," said her mother.

"Yes," said Catherine.

"'Turned.' The next word is 'turned.' You're a pest, Catherine."

"Conversation turned?" Catherine frowned. She pulled at the edge of the book. "Let me see that," she said.

"Catherine, let go. In a minute, I'm going to put this book down, and smack you good and hard. Go play with your brother."

"What book is this, Mama?" Catherine said.

"Jesus Christ." Her mother slammed the book shut and sat up. She leaned over Catherine, who was wedged between the sofa and the coffee table. Her mother's hair, still damp from the shower, smelled of shampoo. It made a dark frame for the space between her face and Catherine's face. Her mother's arms were tanned brown, with a thin band of paler skin around her wrist, where she wore her watch.

"Okay, Catherine, if you're so interested," her mother said. "This book is called *Anna Karenina*. It was written a long time ago by a man called Tolstoy. Leo Tolstoy. He was a Russian man who understood people very well. He understood why they wanted things, and why they felt sad when it turned out they couldn't have what they wanted."

Sad, Catherine thought. She could see the word "sad" spinning slowly, a dull blue speck, far-off.

Her mother put her hand on Catherine's head and started playing with her hair, pulling a little at the tangles, saying, "Where's the hairbrush, what an old rat's nest this is." Then she took her hand away and picked up her book and said, "Now, give me ten minutes, then I'll get you and Matt some cookies and milk. Ten minutes is a short time, okay, Catherine? I promise."

Catherine crawled over to where Matt was playing. A thin line of drool from his mouth had attached itself to his bib. Matt had a lot of thick, dark reddish hair, like their mother, and brown eyes with a strange pool of dark blue light floating on the surface. Catherine's mother had the same kind of eyes. Sometimes they frightened Catherine, these eyes. She worried that her mother and Matt were able to see things that she missed out on. She worried that they could see inside her mind and tell what she was thinking, all the swear words she knew, like *damn* and *fart* and *Jesus Christ* and *holy shit*, and all her secrets.

She lay on the floor beside Matt, and looked up at the ceiling. She imagined herself up there, walking around the chandelier in the dining room, drops of glass like ice, like stars. She imagined herself dancing around the chandelier. She could feel the bumpy, crinkly, cold plaster under her toes.

Conversation turned, she said to herself. Conversation turned. She lifted up her blouse and let her hand rest on her bare tummy. The words had no meaning, and yet they must have a meaning. Her mother knew what it was. Her mother could tell her, if she wanted to. Her mother had long hair down to her waist, almost, and pink polish on her toenails, and in ten minutes, no, less than that, because some time had already gone by, she was going to stop reading and get up off the sofa and get cookies and milk for Catherine and Matt.

Catherine pushed her fingers along the hardwood floor, making a squeaking sound. She could smell the wax her mother used on the floor. It smelled like bananas and dog poop.

The blinds at the windows were closed to keep out the hot morning sun, but still the light entered, falling in narrow bands on the wall above the sofa where her mother was reading. Squeak, squeak, squeak, went Catherine's hand. She could make the sound as loud as she wanted.

Suddenly her mother banged her book down hard on the coffee table. Catherine, startled, sat up.

"All right. I give up," her mother said. She stood and drew the sash on her robe tight around her waist. "I bloody give up," she said. She scooped Matt up off the floor and carried him down the hall into the kitchen. Catherine followed. In the kitchen she climbed into a chair and rested her elbows on the table. Her mother put Matt in his blue highchair. She gave Matt his milk in a plastic bottle and she gave Catherine hers in her own glass with a pink lamb painted on it. "Hold the glass with two hands," her mother told her. Catherine drank her milk and watched Matt drooling on his oatmeal cookie. Catherine's mother waved her fingers at him.

"Hi," she said. "Hi, Mr. Bud." She was always calling Matt a strange name. Mr. Bud. Matt the Hat. Young Mister Matty-cakes. Catherine hated this. She said, "Call him Matt. Call him Matt the Brat."

The French doors were open. It was summer; there were pink and white flowers in pots outside on the patio. Catherine could see the swing under the apple tree. Her father had made it out of a piece of wood and some rope when they had first moved into this house, so that she could play out in the yard and let her mother have some peace and quiet. He made her a sandbox and filled it with sand he got from the Cayley River. Catherine went with him, in the car. She had a shovel of her own, and she helped him shovel sand into cardboard boxes. The sand was white and full of bright specks that shone like diamonds in the sun. Today her father was at work. He was in his new office at the sawmill, near the sea, and the boats.

She nibbled around the edge of her cookie, and watched her mother put the milk away in the fridge. Then her mother filled the sink with soapy hot water and began washing up the breakfast dishes. She leaned against the counter and stared out the window, as if she could see something in the yard, or farther off, above the tops of the alder trees that grew down in the ravine. As if she were watching something hidden from Catherine, something wonderful, surprising: a scene stolen from the pages of a book.

Catherine took another cookie from the plate on the table and broke it in half. She dropped a piece of cookie into her milk and watched it sink. Then she tried to fish it out, but the glass was too small for her hand. The glass tipped over and milk with soggy bits of cookie in it spilled on the table and dripped onto Catherine's skirt and onto the chair she was kneeling on, and then it went all over the floor.

Her mother flew across the kitchen and grabbed Catherine's milky wet hand and squeezed it hard. Catherine tried to pull away. "Don't, Mama," she said. Matt dropped his bottle on the highchair tray and shrieked. The sound he made was so loud Catherine started to cry.

"Darn you, Catherine," her mother said. "Shut up. I mean it. You're scaring Matt. Just shut up. Just stop that noise, would you?" She gripped Catherine's shoulders tight and said, "Honestly, I could shake you until your teeth rattle to bits in your head."

Catherine laughed. She pictured her head as a big blue rattle with a handle, like the rattle Matt played with in his crib, and she laughed until she started to cough, and then she sneezed. Her mother let go of her and said, "Oh, shit, Catherine."

Catherine thought her mother was going to laugh, but instead she sat down in the chair beside Matt's highchair and covered her face with her hands and started to cry.

CHAPTER TWO

One morning Arlene wakened to an insistent, irregular knocking that at times seemed impatient and anxious and at other times playful, teasing. The sound had begun in a dream—a dream in which Catherine was impudently banging a spoon against the table, refusing to stop or relinquish her grip, giving her mother that cold, challenging look, banging the spoon down with greater vehemence—and then the sound had moved outward until it was situated at some distant, unidentifiable point in the rooms downstairs.

It was half past four in the morning, not quite dawn, although an ashen mottled light was insinuating itself into the darkness. Arlene got out of bed and made her way along the hall to the stairs. A strip of worn carpeting ran down the centre of the staircase, and the banister was cool to the touch, polished, absolutely straight until it curved lavishly at the foot of the stairs. Whenever she came downstairs like this, her feet quick and light, as if she were in a hurry, as if an unexpected and well-beloved guest or a surprising phone call awaited her, she was reminded of the house she had lived in years ago, when she was a child. Small, urgent, glimpses of that time came to her, and she thought, I was happy, I was perfectly happy in that house, at that time, when my father was still alive and we were together, my father and Eunice and I. As I am happy now, aren't I?

Each time she descended the stairs it seemed there was something new for the eye to take note of, a richness that the house had thought to suppress, to conceal from her until it had decided the moment was right. Now, for example, an agitated sliver of light that came in through the narrow window beside the front door and fell flickering and imprecise across the last stair and a portion of the hall floor. When she looked outside, she saw that the light came not from the moon, as she had first supposed, but from the streetlight at the corner. She saw, also, that it was windy, the splendid old firs in the front yard tossing to and fro, high, thin wisps of cloud moving across the sky. She placed her fingers lightly on the cool glass as if she could touch the separate elements of the scene.

This was what she liked: to be awake in this empty, shadowed house while her husband and children were tucked safely away upstairs. To be solitary, able to find her way on her own. The strangeness of this house, even now! She was just beginning to get to know it, and the house in turn was just starting to know her. She thought it was, a little. Neither she nor the house were, as yet, willing to reveal their true selves. They were both apprehensive; skittish, it seemed to her. And there was this banging sound, which was frightening, disturbing, deliberately so, Arlene thought, although it must, surely, be nothing but the wind pulling at a window or door. What else could it be?

She went into the kitchen, her bare feet sensitive to the irregularities in the tiled floor, dried particles, crumbs, minuscule spills of milk or juice that had thickened to an unpleasantly gelatinous consistency. She swept and dampmopped and dusted and never managed to get things properly clean. It was the age of this house, and the fact that it didn't trust her, not yet, and tried to pull away, to squirm away from her, as Catherine did when Arlene tried to brush her hair and wash her face, to care for her in the way that a mother cared for a child. Surely Catherine trusted her? It couldn't be right to think that her own daughter mistrusted her, her five-year-old daughter, could it? When Catherine was born, Arlene had been so young, nineteen years old, married for no more than sixteen, seventeen months. Married to the first man she'd met. And lucky for her it was David, who was reliable and kind. He always said, Of course Catherine loves you, you're her mother, she adores you. The truth was, Catherine got along better with her father than she did with Arlene; she always had, from the time she was an infant. Between Catherine and Arlene there was mistrust, and suspicion, some form of suspicion. What it was based on, what had caused it, Arlene couldn't figure out. A firstborn child, a child who was wanted, why did she have to be so difficult? It worried Arlene, and surfaced in her dreams, those disturbing dream-images, her daughter taunting her, forcing her to lose her temper and to do or say something she was bound to feel sorry for later.

19

As an infant, only a few days, a few weeks old, Catherine's eyes had always been wide open, watching every move Arlene made. Which wasn't natural, was it? She had waved her strong little arms and legs in the air and babbled constantly, her unintelligible commentary accompanying every minute of the day. Her hair had sprung up around her head in ferocious electric little curls, like antennae that could sense every movement, every whisper. Arlene and David had been nervous with her, almost afraid of her. What kind of baby was this? they had asked each other, laughing and genuinely bewildered at the same time. She never slept; how was it possible that a baby could simply give up sleep, like giving up a pacifier, or a certain brand of orange juice? Her first words had been No, Don't, Give me, give *me, me, me*. Infant omnipotence, wasn't that what Dr. Spock called it? A perfectly natural phase, and yet wearing, exhausting, unending. After Catherine, Arlene hadn't wanted another baby. One was enough, she had said, more than enough. David wanted three, or even four children. Why, four at least! he had said. He came from a big family himself, a big, happy, high-spirited family, and besides, he'd said, he'd like to have a son as well as a daughter. And so they had had Matt, who—luckily for Arlene, and for Matt himself, for all of them—had turned out to be a good baby, sociable and easy-going, sleeping through the night from the time he was only four or five weeks old.

The French doors that led from the kitchen to the patio had not been properly latched, Arlene discovered, and the wind was catching one of the doors, banging it against the door frame. That was all it was. No mystery, and yet it puzzled her that the door had been left unlatched. She tugged at the handle, jiggled it, but nothing seemed to be broken. The wind had worked the door loose, that was the only explanation, and then the sound had echoed strangely through the house, waking her. She stood there, looking out at the back yard, and, as she watched, the highest branches of the fir trees at the edge of the lawn, near the back fence, began to be edged in the purest, deepest gold. And a delicate blue wash was transforming the sky, and the wind was dying down, as it always seemed to do at this hour. It was going to be another hot day. She leaned over the sink and pushed open the window, and then went into the dining room and opened the window there. A cool breeze came in and she shivered slightly, although it felt good, too, on her face, on the bare skin of her arms. By late afternoon the house would be uncomfortably hot again. Early summer, and already they were having an unusually long spell of hot, dry weather that showed no sign of coming to an end.

For some reason, as she stood at the dining room window, alone, the only one awake in her house, a memory came to her of a day when she'd been about ten years old. She must have been ten, because her father had been alive. She'd been in his office with him, on the third floor of a building on Burrard Street in Vancouver, and he'd been showing her a model of the solar system displayed on a rather elegant, highly polished table. The planets, in their separate orbits, their implied orbits, were poised on flexible metal rods. The planets were made of some kind of dense, solid metal, smooth as glass. The sun, she remembered, had been cold, startlingly cold, nothing like the fiery exploding mass

21

of hot gas she understood it to be. She had touched it and then had drawn her hand away. Nervously, she had clasped her hands behind her. Her father had glanced at her, amused, perhaps, and then had flicked his finger against the planet Earth and it had zinged back and forth. Earth, third planet from the sun, not the biggest planet—what was it, the fourth, or the fifth biggest planet? he had demanded, without waiting for her response—but it was the only planet capable of sustaining life. The only planet capable of sustaining intelligent life—if you could call it intelligent, he had said, with a quick, wry twist of his mouth—in the entire universe, as far as anyone could tell. Gives you a lonely feeling, doesn't it? he had said, smiling down at her, and she had shaken her head, shy, suddenly, unable to speak. How could she feel lonely when she was with him? she had wanted to say.

What, she wondered, had happened to her father's model of the solar system? She wished she had it. She had hardly anything to remember her father by, and the model of the solar system had been quite beautiful, and unusual, and certainly worth keeping. Had her mother, Eunice, disposed of it after Arlene's father had died? Arlene had asked her about it once, and, strangely, Eunice couldn't remember it, although Arlene had described it to her in detail. It was gone, evidently, like so much else from Arlene's childhood. The solar system hadn't looked like a symbol for impermanence, for a life of pulling up roots time and time again, and moving on, and yet that was what life was, it was almost all it was, Arlene had discovered. In any case, Eunice had made her feel as if she'd made it up, imagined the whole episode in that silent law office, her father setting the earth in motion. One complete revolution on its axis every twenty-four hours, he had patiently explained, although she'd learned that basic fact at school years earlier. Night and day; darkness and light. And here it was summer, the longest days, the shortest nights, the most wearying time of the year, it seemed to Arlene.

She went back into the kitchen and filled the kettle with water and put it on the stove. It was too early to be awake, she'd be sorry later, she'd be exhausted by noon, but this was simply too good to be true, being by herself, having the house to herself. She made tea and poured herself a cup. Weak, pale tea, barely sweetened with a few grains of sugar. She put the cup on the kitchen table, then went into the living room, where she found her book open on the table beside the sofa. She picked it up and carried it back with her to the kitchen, the floor creaking with every step, no matter how carefully, how lightly she moved—was there something wrong with this house, some kind of structural defect? David had already arranged the purchase, had signed the final papers and bought the house before she even saw it. She'd been up the coast, in their last house, which they'd lived in for only ten months. She'd been emptying the linen closet, transferring sheets and pillowcases into cardboard boxes, Matt balanced on her hip as she worked. She'd stopped to answer the phone; she'd listened to David's excited, enthusiastic description of the house, the wonderful house he'd managed to find all by himself. He'd described the gable windows and the tall trees in the front yard, the narrow, winding path leading from the street to the front porch, and she had said, "Yes, yes, it sounds fine to me. If you like it, I'll like it. As long as I get this move over with, I'll be happy anywhere," she had said.

In the kitchen, Arlene sat down with her book and her tea. An hour, if she was lucky, of solitude. She opened her old worn copy of *Anna Karenina*—a twenty-first birthday gift from her Grandfather Myles—at random, and began to read, and became lost, lost to everything. Except when the wind got up again and caused the French doors to rattle. She looked up, eyes wide, feeling as if she'd been dragged back to earth. She ran her hand across the open pages, as if she were reading Braille, reading the same passage over and over again. She wished she had been born then, into a world of such passion and eloquence. She wished Tolstoy would appear in front of her in her kitchen, his brow knotted, his fist raised, saying, Woman, woman, what is it you want? She was caught out, caught in an act of genuine communication between the living and the dead.

"Is that all you can do with your time, read?" Tolstoy shouted at her, and she held up the book and said, "Look, it's your book I'm reading."

"You should do something besides read," Tolstoy said, only slightly mollified. "You should love your children and bake bread every day so that they will grow strong." "Never mind," she said to him. "Never mind what I do in my own house." How was he to know it wasn't really her house, that she hadn't lived in it long enough to feel that it was her house? He stood there in a plain black garment, close-fitting, belted, his dark eyes forbidding and sparkling with humour at the same time. He looked exactly as he looked in the photograph in her book, the same long forked patriarch's beard, his hair slicked back from a thin, bony face, a big nose, big ears. His hand, which he continued to point at her, trembled.

She got up from the table and opened the drawer where she kept her cigarettes. She was out of her usual brand; she could find only a pack of Cameos, and she took one and lit it and inhaled deeply, the astringent menthol burning her throat, making her feel dizzy. "It's a beautiful book," she said, coughing a little. "I love it."

"Oh, do you, indeed? You *love* it. Of course, you would. I wrote it so that even a simpleton like you could understand it," Tolstoy said.

"I'm not a simpleton," Arlene said. "Sir."

"Ah, 'sir,' you call me," he said, laughing. She reached behind her for a clean ashtray, sliding it across the counter, and when she turned back, the kitchen was empty. It was immensely empty, the floor shining as if no one had ever stepped on it, the French doors rattling again in that discontented manner. Outside the wind was shaking the trees, bending the tops back and forth. The sky was blue, cloudless. A bird flew past. From upstairs there was a sudden, loud thump, a door slamming against a wall, and then, predictably, the sound of feet running across the floor, and then Catherine was calling to her from the head of the stairs. "Mummy, Mummy!" she called.

Yes, I'm here, Arlene said, silently. I'm here, waiting for you.

CHAPTER THREE

So here was Catherine playing alone in the sandbox and the gate in the fence at the side of the yard swung open and in walked a stranger. At first, Catherine thought this was one of the pretend people who sat on the edge of the sandbox watching her as she played. The pretend people were a little scary, because they came out of the air and had thin, stretched places where the light shone through, and fingers so skinny they could hardly hold on to Catherine's toy cups. But this person, this new person, wasn't like that. Her hair and skin were bright, and she was beautiful, she was like an angel. She wore red shorts and a blouse with a big floppy bow tied at the neck, and glittery gold sandals with high heels that sank into the grass with every step she took. She was carrying a brown suitcase. Her eyes had bright blue lids that opened and closed quickly, like a doll's.

"Is your mother at home today?" the lady asked. She put her suitcase down on the grass. Now that she was closer,

Catherine could see that her red lipstick was smudged, as if she'd wiped her hand over her mouth. She sat down on the edge of the sandbox and began to pick little clumps of grass and dirt from the heels of her sandals. She brushed the dirt off her hands and opened her suitcase. It was filled, Catherine saw, with small gold lipstick tubes, and tiny glass bottles of perfume, and miniature bottles of nail polish, and tiny gold powder compacts, like the one Catherine's mother took out of her handbag whenever they went somewhere, so that she could look in the mirror and fix her lipstick.

"Do you think your mother would like to see my line of fine cosmetics?" the lady said.

Catherine stepped out of the sandbox and wiped her hands on her overalls. Her mother was in the house reading her book. "Go outside and play," she had said, holding her book in front of her face. "Go," she kept saying. And then she became very quiet and disappeared. She went *into the book*. Catherine could see her and touch her, but she wasn't there. She was *in the book*.

Catherine started to walk toward the house. "I'll see if she can come out," she said. Then she stopped. "I'm not supposed to bother her," she said.

"Oh," said the lady. "Why is that? Is your mother busy?"

"I don't know. She'll get mad at me," Catherine said.

"Well, we don't want that, do we? We don't want her to get mad at us, do we?" the lady said. Catherine walked back to the sandbox and sat down beside the lady. "We can get by without your mother, can't we?" She looked at Catherine for a moment. Then she smiled. "What's your name, honey?" she asked.

"Catherine," said Catherine.

"That's a nice name. It's got a very classy sound. I hate my name. It's Myrtle. My mother wanted to call me Theresa, and then I could have been Terry, which I would have liked because it's short and sort of upbeat. But my Daddy liked Myrtle. You have real pretty hair, Catherine. It's all in little curls. It's sweet. Are you having a tea party? I used to have tea parties with my dollies when I was a little girl." She placed her hand under Catherine's chin and tilted her head back. "You have such pretty blue eyes," she said. "You are a very pretty little girl, did you know that? You remind me of Marilyn Monroe when she was real young and her name was Norma Jean. Before she started bleaching her hair."

Catherine shook her head, and put her hands over her face.

"Don't be shy, honey. Heavens, there's nothing in the world to be shy about. Cosmetics are just the most fun. Here, why don't you let me put some lipstick on your lips? Just a little. That's a girl."

Catherine closed her eyes and offered up her face. Her skin was tingling; her lips were dry and hot.

"Oh, don't lick your lips, honey," Myrtle said. "Here, let me blot your lipstick. And you need some rouge. You're a tiny bit pale, I think. You remind me of my sister. She takes after our mother's side of the family. She's got the most gorgeous eyes, and her face is a perfect oval, but she's so pale. There's no need to look like death warmed over, I tell her. The problem is, she's got this husband who doesn't believe in makeup. Lipstick is the most he'll go for. He's such a stuffed-shirt. Sunday dinner on the table at five o'clock exactly. Meat and potatoes. Starch in the bed sheets. No coffee allowed because he believes it's a stimulant. When what he needs is a good stimulant, something to wake him up. Want me to do your eyes? Close them for a minute, sweetheart."

All over her face, Catherine could feel soft feathery touches, and then she opened her eyes and Myrtle was smiling two inches away from her face. "Oh," Myrtle said, "this is such fun! I have two little boys, two wonderful little boys, but I would really like a little girl. When I got married I was sixteen years old and I was in this dress made of pure lace, and I believed in my heart of hearts it would be for ever, until death do us part, as they say. I never thought I'd end up a divorcée with two little boys to bring up. It's history repeating itself all over again. My mother raised me and my sister with no help from our father. Literally."

Catherine stood up and said, "I'll get my Mummy." She started to walk toward the patio doors because she wanted her mother to see her makeup, her beautiful made-up face, but Myrtle caught hold of her wrist and pulled her back.

"No, wait, honey," she said. "I'll see your mother some other time." She was laughing. She touched her finger to the tip of Catherine's nose, and said, "You just show your mother what a good job I did. You look beautiful. She's going to be so surprised."

Myrtle put two tiny gold lipstick cases and four little glass tubes filled with liquid the colour of pee in Catherine's hand. "You give these samples to your mummy with my compliments. I'll call by some other time to do a demonstration. How's that?"

She snapped her suitcase shut and stood up. She pulled at the legs of her shorts and brushed sand off her rear end.

Catherine watched Myrtle tip-toe across the grass in her gold sandals, and then slip through the gate. She disappeared just as silently and completely as the tea party people had disappeared. Catherine put the perfume and lipstick samples in the pockets of her overalls. Then she closed her eyes, which felt heavy, as if she was about to fall into a deep sleep, and held her arms out for balance, like a ballet dancer, and then she opened her eyes and began to run toward the house.

In the kitchen, her mother was standing at the open door of the refrigerator. Matt was sitting in his highchair with a baby bottle half full of milk. Catherine thought he looked disgusting, the way he held the bottle in his mouth sideways, his sharp teeth pulling on the nipple while he stared at her. Then he yanked the bottle out of his mouth with a popping sound and pointed at Catherine and laughed and shouted, "C'rine, C'rine," which was the only way he knew how to say her name.

Then her mother backed out of the refrigerator with a bowl of potato salad in her hands. "Oh, Christ," she said. She kicked the refrigerator door shut with her foot and put the salad down on the counter and then grabbed Catherine's wrists.

"Who did this to you?" she demanded.

"No one. A real lady. A real lady with a suitcase." Catherine started to cry. Every time her mother got mad, Catherine started to cry, no matter how hard she tried not to. If she cried too hard she'd wreck her makeup. She stopped, and sniffed. Her mother pulled her by the arm out of the kitchen and down the hall to the bathroom.

"Have you seen yourself? Do you have any idea what you look like?"

She put her hands under Catherine's arms and picked her up and made her look in the mirror. Catherine stared at herself. She looked like a fairy princess, a mermaid, a ballerina. Her eyes were the most amazing blue, the bright blue of the sky, the same blue as Myrtle's eyes. Her lips were bright pink. They tasted of raspberries, of sour strawberries. Her cheeks were a dull fuzzy red. She half closed her eyes so that she was looking at her reflection through a tangled forest of long black lashes.

Her mother set her down on the floor so suddenly she bit her tongue and tasted blood. "Oh," she said. Her mother said, "Quiet, quiet." She filled the sink with hot soapy water and then got a clean face cloth out of a drawer. She grabbed a handful of Catherine's hair and pulled her head back, and began washing off the makeup.

"It's too hot, it's too hot," Catherine said.

Her mother didn't say anything. She scrubbed and rinsed the face cloth under the tap and scrubbed some more. "I should leave this garbage on your face so your father can see it. He never believes the kind of things you get up to. Who would believe it? I can't trust you on your own for five minutes, can I?"

In the kitchen, Matt was crying. Catherine heard his bottle hit the floor.

"Damn," Catherine's mother said. She threw the face cloth into the sink. Some blue water splashed on the counter and ran down the cupboard door to the floor.

"Stay there," her mother said, shaking a finger at her. "Sit on the floor. I'm so angry with you, Catherine. Mummy's so angry. Just stay there."

Catherine sat on the edge of the bathtub. She stared at the bathroom floor, at the black and white tiles and the puddle of water from the sink. Her face stung. There were wet patches all over the front of her overalls. She put her hands in her pockets and felt the tiny glass perfume bottles. She pressed her scrubbed-clean lips together. She felt as if the real lady in her red shorts and her gold sandals was sitting beside her on the bathtub. Her long fingers were smoothing Catherine's hair away from her hot, sore eyes. Don't cry, she was saying. Don't cry. Her name was Myrtle. If you cry, she said, your mother is just going to get madder and madder, and you don't want that, do you? That's what happens with my little boys. They won't stop hollering and I just lose my temper, I don't mean to, but I do. Shut up, for crying out loud, I scream at them. I try to be nice, like those magazine mothers you read about, but it's an uphill job, let me tell you.

Catherine's mother appeared in the bathroom door, Matt in her arms. He was rubbing his ear with his hand and his face was wet and red. He stuck his thumb in his mouth. Such a baby, Catherine thought. Such an old sucky-baby. She wanted to put her arms around him and hug him. She wanted to sing to him.

"Come here," Catherine's mother said, holding her hand out. "Come and have a glass of apple juice and a cookie."

Catherine took her mother's hand. She walked with her mother into the kitchen, where her mother gave her juice and a chocolate chip cookie. It took Catherine a long time to finish the cookie because crumbs kept getting caught in her throat. She coughed, and cookie crumbs flew out of her mouth. Her mother said, "Catherine, if you can't eat that cookie properly, I'm taking it away from you."

Never talk to strangers, her father told her. He took her on his knee. This was in the morning, before he left for work. He was wearing a shirt and a blue tie with gold squares all over it. His suit jacket was hanging on the back of his chair. Never, ever talk to strangers, he said. Not even when they seem very nice. Not even when they walk into your own backyard. If anyone asks to see your mother or me, you run as fast as you can into the house. Say, Mummy, Daddy, someone wants to see you. That is the polite thing to do. And the best thing to do, as well.

Her father set her down, and she walked around the table and sat down at her own place. Her father said, "That poor woman. That poor Myrtle Kriskin, trying to make a living selling cosmetics door to door. Who's going to buy cosmetics from her?" Her father whirled a finger near his ear. "Well," he said. "You know what I mean. And she has two little boys, I hear, and no husband, no one to look out for her. Well, she has a husband, but he absconded, I heard. It's a real shame. People like that. You feel as if you should do something. But what? What can you do?"

Catherine was eating cereal shaped like letters of the alphabet. She scooped up a spoonful of letters and watched them floating in a sea of sugary milk. A. D. L. B. Or was that a P? She knew almost every letter. She could almost read. She put the letters in her mouth and swallowed them.

Catherine's mother was wearing her white silk bathrobe. Her hair was still damp from her shower, and she had a towel draped around her shoulders. Her feet were bare. She combed her fingers slowly through her damp hair and picked up her coffee cup and took a drink. She stared out the window over the sink. "You know, I don't care," she said. "I don't care what the lady's problems are. I don't want her sneaking around my house, pestering my children. What kind of person would walk onto someone's private property and out of the blue start plastering cheap cosmetics all over a child's face? She must be right out of her head. I think she must be. I just hope I never see her around again, not around this house, that's all I can say."

Chapter Four

The hot weather continued all through the month of July, every day hotter than the last, the air absolutely still, the leaves hanging motionless and limp, somehow even deprived of colour, pale and drab, on the apple tree in the backyard, at which Arlene was staring as she folded a stack of diapers. Every morning a great high mass of clouds rose over the mountain—David had told her its name; was it Mt. Newell?—over Mt. Newell, and towered precariously above the town, snow-white, heavy, full of pictures: lambs, and giant faces, castles, ocean waves. The clouds didn't ever amount to anything; by noon they usually got burned off by the heat of the sun. If only the heat would break; if only it would rain. If only there were a wind, a breeze. David accused her of taking the weather personally, but she couldn't help it; she couldn't help feeling as if she were being singled out and made to suffer. When she brought the diapers in off the clothesline, they were as stiff and unwieldy as cardboard.

She had to keep rubbing the cloth, trying to ease the fabric back to its normal state. By the time they were folded into a neat stack, she was worn out. She had to drag herself up the stairs to Matt's bedroom, where she put the diapers on the shelf under the changing table. Matt was too big for the changing table now; it should be sold, or given away. And then his crib would go, and the stuffed toys would be packed away—she envisioned all this happening effortlessly, while her back was turned, the infant Matt instantaneously replaced by a studious adult who would laugh with her at the improbable, already fading memories of his childhood. Catherine would be—where? Easier by far to envision Matt grown up; he was in a state of determined metamorphosis: this inconvenient, not-quite-amusing disguise would soon enough fall away, he would will see to it—an assurance he'd seemed to give Arlene from the time he was born.

When she came back downstairs, she paused and leaned on the banister, watching Matt and Catherine playing in the living room. They were actually being quite peaceable and good. Matt was sitting on the floor, wearing diapers and a little cotton vest, and Catherine was sprawled across the coffee table, a small doll clutched in her hand, singing a mournful tune to herself. *La, la, la.* Arlene was singing the same lament, inwardly. Poor kids, she thought; they were hot, too, and tired from not sleeping in this heat, and from being trapped in the house day after day, just as she was. They didn't know anyone; they didn't have any friends or relatives living close by who could visit and break up the day. This was an unfriendly town, in a way. She thought it was. Several times this week she'd found herself standing in front of the telephone, ready to call Eunice to ask her to come and stay for a few days. Which Arlene thought was a good indication of just how desperate she felt.

Then she remembered that David had been given a ride to work that morning. The car was still in the garage. She looked at her watch; it was nearly eleven.

"I'll tell you what," she said, going into the living room and picking Matt up, whirling around with him, his face broad and calm with wonderment. She stopped and rubbed noses with him and he grinned at her. He had prickly heat rash on his neck and Arrowroot cookie crumbs stuck between his fingers. "Let's go out and get ourselves some ice cream," she said. "How's that? Catherine? How's that for a good idea?"

Arlene had taken Matt and Catherine to the Turf Café several times before, when they were out for a walk, or had finished picking up their groceries at Sam Wong's Grocery Store. The Turf Café was on Ashlar Street, the main street of town. Really it was the only street. There were a few shops, an old auto court, and a restaurant out on the old Cayley Road, which led down from the Island Highway, wound its way past Cayley and then eventually joined the Island Highway again somewhere past the river. The drug store, a shoe store, a ladies' dress store, an insurance office and a hardware store were on one side of Ashlar Street, and on the other side there was a jewellery store, the post office and library, a pool hall with a soda fountain, and St. Ann's Anglican Church set back from the road in a garden surrounded by a low picket fence. Down the block there was a furniture store and the United Church, a white stucco building with a square bell tower. Cayley was a small town, a village, really, with a total population, David had told her, of something like eight or nine hundred residents. He thought it was the prettiest town he'd ever seen, and Arlene agreed, with some reservations, that it had its good points. There were proper sidewalks and rose gardens in front of some of the houses, and you could walk along the paved lanes behind the houses and admire the vegetable gardens, tidy rows of peas and carrots and summer squash. Today, however, in this heat, the whole town, the houses and gardens, the stores and churches, even the sky, looked unreal and even menacing.

She parked the Oldsmobile on the street in front of the café, and got the children out of the car. She took their hands and led them inside and took the first booth, the one closest to the open door. She sat down with Matt on her lap. Catherine kneeled on the seat opposite and fiddled with the jukebox selector. She wanted a dime, she wanted to pick a song, and Arlene said, "Wait a minute, please, Catherine," before turning to give her order to the waitress: a dish of Neapolitan ice cream for Matt and Catherine and for herself a 7-Up. "With lots of ice," she told the waitress, who jabbed her pen importantly across her order pad, as if she'd forget such a complicated order in the time it took her to walk behind the counter. Two booths down, there were some young men talking and laughing, the only people in the café besides her and the kids, on this hot, airless day. She got a dime out of her change purse and gave it to Catherine, who dropped it in the slot on the jukebox selector and then said, "What song should I pick, Mummy?" Arlene leaned forward, self-consciously, and said, "Oh, this one, this is my favourite." She punched in D-12, "Love Is a Many-Splendoured Thing," by the Four Aces. A completely inappropriate song for the Turf Café, Arlene realised, as soon as she heard the first notes, which seemed formal, even pompous, unduly sentimental. She felt conspicuous, uncomfortable. She should have taken the kids to the beach instead. She should have stayed at home. She watched Catherine dancing her fingers across the table in time to the Four Aces. Before they'd left the house, she'd had a brief tussle with Catherine over Catherine's choice of clothes. In the end Arlene had given in, and Catherine had on a blue and white striped skirt with a frill around the hem and a yellow blouse with puffed sleeves and eyelet lace trim. Where did she find these clothes? Arlene could have sworn she'd never seen them before. Catherine seemed to have at least recovered from her encounter with that odd, possibly deranged woman. Such a bizarre, unlikely occurrence! Arlene still couldn't get over it. Imagine someone walking into the yard and painting Catherine's face so grotesquely. Catherine had moped around the house for a few days afterwards, running to the windows or the door if she detected the least noise. "Will Myrtle come back?" she'd asked a number of times, and Arlene had said, "No, I don't think so. Why? Why would you want her to come back?" To which Catherine had remained silent, tugging at her hair, pouting, avoiding Arlene's eyes.

The waitress brought their order and said, "Will that be all?" and Arlene said, "For now it will." She didn't like the waitress, her snotty tone of voice and perky little green and white cap anchored with bobby pins to her permed hair.

One of the young men got up and went to the cigarette machine near the cash register. Arlene found herself staring at him. She noticed the waitress was staring at him, too. She was arranging her face in the first pleasant expression she'd had on it all day, Arlene was sure. He *was* good-looking, Arlene had to admit; slim, tall, with broad shoulders, long legs, a nice rear end. Arlene couldn't help it; she couldn't help noticing these things. He wanted to be looked at, she could tell. He had dark blond hair combed in a ducktail and waved on top, as if he was trying his best to look like James Dean in *Rebel Without A Cause*, a move Arlene had seen last summer and which had made her glad she was a married lady and not a teenager.

On his way past, James Dean stopped and actually leaned on the back of Catherine's side of the booth and smiled at Arlene, a friendly, teasing sort of smile, and she smiled back and said hello. The last notes of "Love Is a Many-Splendoured Thing" were, thankfully, fading away. James Dean looked at Matt for a moment and said, "That ice cream is about as big as you are, you know that?" Matt whacked his spoon in the ice cream and gurgled happily.

"Baby-sitting?" James Dean said to her.

She laughed. "No," she said. "No, I'm not baby-sitting."

"Don't tell me these kids belong to you?" he said. "No. You must be their big sister, right?"

"No," Arlene said, smiling. "I'm not their sister."

"These are your kids?"

"Well, yes, they are my kids." She smoothed Matt's hair with her hand. She took his spoon from him and fed him some ice cream. "I think you're trying to flatter me," she said.

"No, I'm not. You look awful young to have two kids," he said. "Mind if I sit down for a minute?"

There was a silence in the café; she could tell everyone was listening. She could tell the waitress and this young man's friends were waiting for her to tell him to get lost. Instead, she said, "Sure, have a seat."

"I have the worst luck," he said, sitting down beside Catherine, who moved herself along into the corner, where she began flipping through the jukebox selector. "The worst darned luck," he was saying. "All the pretty ones are taken. It happens to me over and over again. I have to reconcile myself to it, I guess."

Arlene scratched at a little imaginary itch on her wrist and stirred her 7-Up with the straw. "You'll meet someone nice," she said. She didn't want him to meet anyone nicer than she was, anyone better-looking. Wasn't that silly? She didn't even know his name, although that was the next thing he told her. His name was Al, short for Alvin, he said. "Al Dods. Pleased to meet you, ma'am." She shook his hand, hers cool and a little damp from holding her glass of 7-Up, and she told him her name was Arlene, and he said wasn't that a coincidence, their names sounding practically the same. He told her that his main occupation lately was wasting time. He didn't have a single thing to do these days. He worked out at Muir Creek, as a faller, and the woods had been closed since the end of May because of the hot, dry weather. "Isn't it hot?" he said. "If it gets any hotter, we'll fry." A break in the weather was coming soon, though, he said. He'd noticed first thing this morning that the wind was finally shifting around to the southeast. Although even a storm wouldn't ease the situation much, in his opinion. The forests needed a lot of rain. He didn't know when he'd be able to go back to work. He wasn't all that eager, anyway, he said. Right about now he was fed up with living in camp, living in a bunkhouse, the noise of a chain-saw in his head all day. It wasn't what he'd planned for his life, that was for sure, he said, patting the front of his waved hair.

"Your husband, does he work in the woods?" he said.

"No, he doesn't work in the woods," she said.

"He works at the mill?"

"Yes," Arlene said. "He does."

"You lived around here long? You haven't, have you? I would have noticed you before now, if you did." He had high cheekbones, a dimple in his chin, a nice smile that was obviously meant to be uncomplicated, transparent—a smile that would draw the girls to him, flies to honey. Or was it just that she wanted him to be handsome, a handsome stranger; perhaps she'd invented him and his beautiful smile, his entire aspect, his thin, worn, but spotlessly clean, carefully ironed shirt, sleeves rolled neatly to the elbows, a crescent-shaped, only recently healed gash on the side of his right hand, just below his little finger. Invented him out of whole cloth, to get her through this long silent, heavy, otherwise unendurable summer day. As perhaps she could reinvent herself, a sixteen-year-old baby-sitter, giddy and a little bored, minding these two bothersome young children to give their mother a chance to put her feet up.

"You're new to town, aren't you?" he said.

"Yes, I am," she said. "I moved here at the end of May. That is, we moved here, my husband and I." She busied herself with spooning ice cream into Matt. She wanted to indicate an end to the conversation, which had gone on long enough, which never should have started. She had to . . . *observe the proprieties*. She had to remember who she was. Arlene Greenwood, wife of David Greenwood, accountant and office supervisor with Western Forest Ventures, the company this Al—short for Alvin—also worked for, as a faller. Only daughter of the late George Francis May, who had been a partner, a senior partner, in a prestigious Vancouver law firm. Not that it mattered who she was, or where she came from; she was here now. She was this person, sitting here in the Turf Café in a cotton sun dress, a tiny silver heart on a chain around her neck, her hair tied back in a pony tail. *Who are you, ma'am? The baby sitter? The older sister?*

Catherine wanted another dime for the jukebox. She kept pushing the buttons, and the waitress, carrying burgers past on her way to the back of the café, paused and gave Catherine a dirty look.

"There goes my lunch, I guess," Al said. "Beef on the hoof. Ouch, bad joke." He laughed and pulled a dime out of his pocket and dropped it on the table in front of Catherine. "You pick a song, honey," he said to Catherine.

"What song?" Catherine said, squinting up at him, rubbing at her eye. "I don't know what song to pick."

"You want me to pick a song for you?" Al said. Arlene was trying to say, No, no, thanks very much, but there was no need to give Catherine money, no need whatsoever. "Please, take your dime back," she said firmly. But he was leaning over Catherine, looking through the music selections, reading out the song titles: "Secret Love," "Three Coins in the

Fountain," "I Walk the Line," "Be-Bop-A-Lula." He liked "Be-Bop-A Lula"; he started singing it softly.

Arlene wiped Matt's mouth with a napkin. She wished she'd never said hello to Al, Alvin Dods, alias James Dean. She had no business chatting with young men she didn't know. What would David think if he could see her? What was wrong with her? It was the weather, the heat, the temperature in the café, the stupid, noisy little electric fan the waitress had set up on the counter, near the cash register. She heard the jukebox starting and then the sound of Theresa Breuer singing "How Much is the Doggie in the Window." She told Catherine to say thank you very much to Mr. Dods, and to sit down properly and finish her ice cream, which had melted into an unappetising-looking soup.

Catherine beamed at Al. She pushed her hair behind her ears and gave him a look from under her long, dark lashes. Al said, "You're a sweet kid, aren't you? You're a real sweetie." He slid out of the booth and stood up. "Have a good day, ma'am," he said. Arlene was busy wiping ice cream off her hands, and off the table, and moving her glass of 7-Up out of Matt's reach. "Yes," she said, without looking up. "You have a nice day, too." A minute later, she heard Al saying something to the men he was with, and then there was a quick, answering burst of laughter. They were laughing at her; she knew they were. She felt ridiculously betrayed, resentful, let down. By this time there were others in the café, an older couple having sandwiches with side orders of fries, a man sitting on a stool at the counter drinking coffee, and although they looked at her, as people always did in a small town, measuring newcomers in that cold, blank way, they

44

at least provided a distraction. Arlene gathered up the children and made them wait beside her as she paid the bill. She told Catherine they had to go right now, this minute, there was no time to listen to the rest of the song, no time to finish her melted ice cream.

She walked outside, with Matt in her arms, into what felt like a solid wall of hot, humid air. The sky had a stretched, thin look, as if it might snap, and there was a high, whitish haze that made everything look flat, without dimension or lustre. The car was hot, even though it had been in the shade, and the trip home was almost unbearable. The interior of the house, when Arlene walked inside, was hotter than ever, and dark, as well, because she'd locked the doors and closed the windows and pulled the curtains before going out. What was the matter with her, she'd like to know. She couldn't seem to put a foot right these days. This unfriendly town, she'd thought, and then she'd met a friendly, talkative young man, an ordinary young man who maybe had an elevated opinion of himself, and she'd let him take advantage of her, of her kindness, her innocence. Or was it that he had attempted simple friendliness when both of them knew perfectly well that what he projected and what she perceived, by design or by sheer accident, was plain sex, sexual attraction, and that it had been to this that Arlene had instinctively responded? It was too much for her to think about. She had a headache developing as it was.

She went quickly through the house, opening curtains and windows; then she went to the kitchen sink and turned on the cold water tap, letting the water run down the drain, trying to make it cold, but it remained lukewarm and not in the least refreshing, although she drank a full glass, then filled it again and drank thirstily. There was a feeling in the air, in the very atmosphere of the house, akin to an indrawn breath, an unvoiced thought. In spite of the heat, she felt chilled, chilled through, her skin cold to the touch. She lit a cigarette and stood with her back against the kitchen counter, quietly smoking and listening to the children squabbling, their voices edging on tears, tantrums. Matt was tired; she knew what would happen. He'd start to cry over some little thing; then he'd fall asleep without having had his lunch. They hadn't had lunch, she realised. She couldn't get anything right; she couldn't get through a day respectably, it seemed. She stubbed out her cigarette and opened the fridge door, taking out the peanut butter and the jam.

It was no surprise to Arlene that when she woke during the night—awoke from a dream that featured the irrepressible Al Dods at a fairground, in a black leather jacket and cowboy boots, smiling his lovely false smile and leading Arlene and the children past the waitress from the café, who was dressed in a sequinned tuxedo and was making an elephant stand on a drum—it was to the sound of thunder, followed almost at once by a fierce flash of lightning that lit up the bedroom for one brief, unnerving second. She slipped out of bed and went to the open window. The air had that strange, sharp, almost sweet, almost burnt odour that went with electrical storms, but it didn't feel appreciably cooler. In fact, it felt muggier, more humid, than ever. David was awake, throwing off the single sheet they had on the bed, fumbling for his slippers, saying he had to find the flashlight and locate the storm candles—he had bought storm candles, hadn't he, just a few weeks ago?—in case the power went out. And then, when he went to turn on the lamp, he discovered the power was already out. They found their way downstairs together, holding hands. Arlene felt like laughing. She felt like dancing. Thunder shook the house; lightning illuminated the rooms, casting shimmering indigo-coloured shadows along the walls. In the kitchen, Arlene threw open the French doors and went outside. Wind, at last, at last, a cool, bracing wind, agitating the trees and the wind chimes in the neighbour's yard, making David's shirt on the clothesline dance as if inhabited, pulling seductively at Arlene's hair. After a while, she could see a glow in the sky, just above the trees. It looked like a sunrise, except that it was taking place in the wrong part of the sky, at the wrong hour. She called David, and he walked over to her with Catherine in his arms. She'd been wakened by the noise of the thunder and had been crying in fright. Matt, of course, slept through everything; Arlene didn't even need to worry about him. The three of them stood there, watching lightning streak against the undersides of low, billowy clouds, watching something far off burning down. "Listen," Arlene said. She could hear the fire station siren, which sounded like an air raid alarm, and then the sirens on the fire trucks. Then it started to rain, big, hard drops of rain. David ran into the house with Catherine. "Hurry up, Arlene," he said from the door, "the rain is blowing in the door. Everything's getting wet." Arlene said, "Yes, I'll be right there. I'll be there." But she couldn't move. How could she leave this? It was magical, it was terrible. The rain soaked her nightie, plastered her hair to her head. There was a taste in the air of metal. She held out her arms and received the rain in her cupped hands. Long ago, she thought, she had been outdoors in similar, equally violent, but nearly forgotten, storms. As a child. She thought she had; certainly she had. The storm carried within it the seeds of recollection and of promise, the promise of some future time in her life, undefined and unsought, that would nevertheless bring with it everything she wanted, everything she hoped for but couldn't precisely name or identify at this exact moment, no matter how hard she tried.

"Goddamn it, Arlene, get in the house," David said. "You're soaked. You're going to make yourself sick."

"I will, I am, I'm coming," Arlene said. But it was the hardest thing, to leave the elements, the wild fierce wind and the cold rain that was striking the patio floor at her feet, splattering jubilantly on the concrete, pelting the geranium blossoms, destroying, transforming, healing, making everything new again.

The fire they'd witnessed from the patio that night turned out to have been at a place called the El Rancho Restaurant. Arlene had never heard of the El Rancho before, but evidently it had been located about two miles out of Cayley, near the intersection of the Island Highway and the old Cayley Road. Lightning had struck the restaurant, and it had instantly caught fire and burned to the ground. No one was hurt, according to the report in the newspaper, although the restaurant was a total loss and the staff, the cook, four waitresses, and a bartender, were left without work, and it would be some time, if ever, before the restaurant could be rebuilt. The storm had been the worst on the south coast of B. C. in something like thirty years, and the El Rancho hadn't been by any means the only casualty. A forest fire had started over on the Sunshine Coast, just north of Sechelt. A house had burned down north of Nanaimo. Power had been out, in some cases for days, throughout the Gulf Islands, sections of the Sunshine Coast, the east coast of Vancouver Island and even parts of Vancouver. A forest fire had started somewhere near Lake Cowichan, and was still burning, in spite of efforts to extinguish the blaze, Arlene read, without paying close attention. When she'd finished with the paper she folded it up and put it on the hall table beside the telephone, so that David could read it when he got home from work.

CHAPTER FIVE

Catherine's father left for his office at the sawmill in the morning, and then her mother made herself a cup of coffee and took it outside and sat with it at the patio table. Sometimes her mother smoked a cigarette. If it was cool she wore a sweater on top of her pink quilted housecoat. Catherine watched her from the kitchen. Her mother read and smoked and took little sips of coffee and looked up at the trees, and the sky; she watched the clouds scudding past, a gull coasting on the air currents. Catherine tried to play with Matt. He was still in his PJs and his diapers needed to be changed. He stank of pee and the stale apple juice that had dribbled down his front. He walked around the house trailing his favourite blanket behind him. He sucked his thumb. When Catherine tried to take his hand, he pulled away: No, no, no, he whined. The radio on the kitchen counter was on. *The mercury today is headed toward a pleasant high of seventy-six degrees*, a man's voice was saying. *Lots and lots of summer sunshine in store for us today.* Then he said, *And now let's hear from Debbie Reynolds and the Ames Brothers, singing their hit song, "Tammy."* Catherine danced around the kitchen floor in her socks. She slid and slipped, pretending to do the jitterbug. Pretending she was Debbie Reynolds with her freckles and pigtails and her blue jeans. Matt tried to dance with her, bending his knees and bobbing up and down in one spot like a beach ball. Catherine's mother came inside and walked past them on her way to the stove to pour herself more coffee. "You're a pair," she said to them. "Where did I get you two from, anyway?"

Later, Catherine's mother made peanut-butter and blackberry jam sandwiches on white bread wrapped in waxed paper and packed them in a straw basket along with three apples and a box of raisins, and then they walked down to the public beach. Arlene pushed Matt in his stroller. He had had his bath and he was dressed in his clean blue romper suit. Catherine walked beside the stroller, holding his hand. He stared at everything, the houses, the trees, the lawn sprinklers. Catherine's mother was wearing a blue dress with pearl buttons down the front. Her hair was in a ponytail that swung back and forth with every step she took. She wore sunglasses, and red lipstick. Catherine remembered her own tiny sample tubes of lipstick, pink, red, orange, and a strange purplish colour, like the skin of a plum, which she had hidden with the perfume samples in the back of her Sweet Sandra doll, in the cavity where the batteries were supposed to go. No one would ever find them, she told herself; no one would think to look inside Sweet Sandra, who used to talk, and now, even when she had new batteries, could only growl through her stiff plastic lips.

At the beach, Arlene parked the stroller and kicked the brake on with her foot. She took the striped beach blanket out of the wire basket on the back of the stroller and spread it on the ground. Then she got out two plastic sand pails and two plastic shovels for Catherine and Matt to play with, and a book for herself. She smoothed suntan oil on her bare arms, picked up her book and started to read. Catherine pushed her hands into the sand. Matt turned his pail upside down and said, "Gone, all gone." "What's all gone?" Catherine said. "There wasn't anything in your pail, Matt. It's empty." She could see some kids playing at the edge of the water. Their mothers were standing up to their ankles in the water, watching them. A black dog was bounding in and out of the water. Splashing and shouting, the kids ran out into the water, and the dog barked and wagged his tail, leaping up at them.

"I want to go swimming," Catherine said.

"We're not going in the water today," her mother said.

"Why?" Catherine said.

"Because. We just aren't."

"I want to," Catherine said. She unbuckled her sandals and slipped them off her feet. She took off her socks and stuffed them into her sandals. Then she got up and started walking across the sand toward the water. One of the mothers tossed a stick into the water, and Catherine saw the dog run into the water and then back out with the stick in his mouth. "Good boy," the mother shouted at the dog. The dog shook himself, showering everyone with water. The children screamed and splashed. A little girl in a red bathing suit came over and stared at Catherine.

"Hi," she said.

"Hi," Catherine said.

Catherine's mother walked up to her, with Matt in her arms, and took Catherine by the hand.

"She can stay and play," one of the mothers said. She put her hands on her hips. She was wearing a shiny blue bathing suit stretched tight across her tummy. She had a round freckled face, and her nose and her shoulders were red and peeling from sunburn. "I don't mind keeping an eye on her for you," she said. "The water gets deep awful fast here." She bent down and grinned at Catherine. "What's your name, dear?" she said. "Can't you talk? You can talk, can't you?"

Catherine's mother said, "That's very kind of you, but we aren't going in the water today. My daughter doesn't have her bathing suit."

"Gee whiz, you came to the beach without your bathing suit?" the woman said.

Catherine felt her face getting hot. Why had her mother made her come to the beach in a dress? A dress with straps and a frill around the skirt. The little girl in the red bathing suit crossed her eyes and pulled a face. Catherine smiled at her. When Catherine and her mother and Matt went back to their beach blanket, the little girl followed them, and knelt in the sand beside them. She watched as Catherine's mother brushed the sand off Catherine's feet.

"You'd better go and play with your friends," Catherine's mother said.

"I don't have to," the girl said. Her nose was running, and she wiped it on her arm. Catherine's mother said, sharply, "I beg your pardon, young lady?"

The little girl said to Catherine, "My name is Phoebe. I'm six. How old are you?"

"Five," Catherine said, holding up her hand. She told Phoebe her name. She saw that Phoebe's bathing suit strap was held in place with a safety pin. Her yellow hair stuck out in a bright fuzz around her head. One of her front teeth was missing. Catherine pushed her tongue against her own teeth to make sure they were still in place.

Catherine's mother stood up. "We have to go," she said. "We have to pack up our things. Excuse us, Phoebe. Catherine has to say good-bye. Maybe we'll see you here another day." She picked Matt up and stuffed him into his stroller. At once he began to drum his feet against the metal footrest. He arched his back as if he was trying to propel himself straight out again. No, no, no, he screamed, and the women down at the water turned and stared. Arlene shook the sand out of their blanket and folded it up and shoved it into the stroller. She jammed her book and the sand pails and shovels on top of the blanket and pushed the stroller along the beach. The wheels got stuck in the sand, and she had to push harder and harder.

"Where are we going?" Catherine said. She walked beside her mother along the beach until they came to a rocky place shaded by tall arbutus trees. When Catherine turned and looked back, she could see the women and the dog and the children, but they were all far away and she could no longer tell which one was Phoebe. Arlene unpacked the beach blanket and spread it out on a small patch of damp sand. "The beach isn't as nice here," she said. "But at least we'll be able to eat our sandwiches in peace." Her sunglasses slid down her nose, and she pushed them back into place and smoothed her hair, adjusting a bobby pin at the side of her head. "Keep your sandals on, Catherine," she said. "Watch out for the sharp barnacles on the rocks. And stay out of the water."

Then she said, "Catherine, that girl, what was her name, Phoebe? Phoebe had a bad cold. I didn't want you to catch it from her. She was sick and she shouldn't have been playing at the beach with other children. She could be coming down with the Asiatic flu, for all we know. You have to be careful these days."

Dry leaves were drifting down from the arbutus trees, landing on their blanket and on the surface of the water, where they floated slowly up and down like toy boats.

"The tide is coming in," Arlene said. She sat on the blanket beside Catherine and Matt, taking sandwiches out of their lunch bag. She unwrapped a sandwich and passed half to Catherine, half to Matt. "Did you know," she said, "that the tide goes out and comes in twice every day? The moon's gravity pulls and pulls at the water, and then it lets it go. Every day and every night, even when we're all fast asleep."

Behind them, half-hidden behind a fence and bushes, was a house. It was small and grey, with big windows and two chimneys and a garden like a jungle. Next to the house there was a narrow dirt road that came right down to the beach. Catherine ate her sandwich. She drank some of the lemonade her mother poured into a plastic cup from the thermos. Her mother brushed at the skirt of her dress and picked up her sandwich and nibbled at it. She gave Matt another half of a sandwich. "You're a hungry boy, aren't you, Mr. Matty-cakes?" she said. "You're ravenous."

Catherine put her crusts down on the blanket. Imitating her mother, she brushed at the skirt of her dress. Dampness from the sand was seeping through the blanket into her dress and her panties. She finished her lemonade and put the cup down beside her crusts. She crossed her legs at the ankles and stared at the little perforations in the toes of her sandals. Flowers and stars. Her sandals were red, with two straps. She watched the sea being pulled higher and higher up the beach by the force of the invisible moon. Her mother stood up and started picking up the crumpled pieces of waxed paper and the left-over sandwich crusts. "Are you finished?" she said to Catherine. "Are you ready to get moving?" She tossed the crusts down the beach and soon a gull landed and took the crust in his beak. Catherine watched as he strutted around, the crust wedged sideways in his beak, and then she got up and took a slow, careful step in his direction. Two more gulls appeared overhead, circling, mewling like kittens. She was watching them and didn't see the car as it came down the dirt road toward the beach. She didn't see it heading straight into the water. She heard it, though. Later, she thought she'd felt the warmth from the engine passing across her legs like the breath of a big animal. She certainly heard the rumble of the engine, and the scraping and rattling noise the car made as it jounced over the rocks. She heard her mother cry: *Oh! Oh, my God!*

Catherine whirled around and saw a car, what looked to her like a dark green car with a high, blunt, rounded nose, rolling forward into the water. It seemed to be propelled for some distance like some kind of strange ugly boat, and then it settled in the waves as if it belonged there, as if this was the one place in all the world it wished to be. The water rose quickly around it, lapping against its sides. The car remained like that for a long time, half floating, looking like a rock, like one of the black rocks that jut out of the sea. A face appeared at a window, hands pressed to the glass. Or so Catherine thought. A child's face, the eyes dark, the mouth open as if the child were calling: *Help! Help!* Or was it just the water, the dark water, rising and falling against the car? It was hard to tell. Catherine was almost sure she could hear the cries. She covered her ears with her hands. And then she saw the car sink lower, the water rising and rising, until finally all she could see was the roof.

At first, Catherine thought it was meant to happen, like a scene in one of the movies her Nana took her to see when Catherine visited her in Vancouver. She thought of a very large Alice up on the screen with the ends of her hair wet and tangled as she tried to swim through the salty lake of her own tears. She thought of all the cartoon characters she had seen, who ran right off the tops of mountains and kept going, until they made the mistake of looking down, and then they exclaimed, "What! Oh-oh!" And down they went, down and down.

Catherine's mother ran to the edge of the water. She stood there, then she ran back up to Catherine and said, "I have to get help. I have to find a telephone." She ran over to the fence in front of the little grey house. "Where's the damned gate?" she said, pulling at the fence. She went around to the

side of the house, running up the dirt road the car had travelled down. Then she ran back to the fence in front of the
house and climbed over it, bunching her dress up in her
hand to get it out of her way. "Goddamn," she was saying.
"Goddamn it to hell." Catherine watched her mother jump
down on the other side and run up to the house. She
pounded with her fists on the door. Catherine saw her lean
her head on the door; she heard her saying, "Open up. Come
on. Answer the bloody door." She went to one of the front
windows and rapped on the glass. Then she ran back to the
fence and climbed over it. Her dress got caught and she had
to stop and pull it free. Then she climbed over some driftwood logs and ran past Catherine, shouting at her to stay
where she was, to stay with Matt. Catherine watched her
run down the beach in the direction of Phoebe and her
mother. Catherine thought she was going to fall, she was
running so fast. She kept stumbling and slipping on the
rocks. She stopped and waved her arms in the air. It seemed
the other people on the beach were still the same distance
away from Catherine's mother; it seemed she couldn't get
closer to them no matter how hard she tried. At last she
turned and ran back to Catherine and Matt. She stared at
Catherine, her eyes dark and her mouth open, her breath
coming in gasps. Bending over slightly, she pressed her hand
to her side and said she had given herself a stitch, a stupid
stitch in the side. Then she said, "All right, all right now,"
and turned and stumbled down to the edge of the water
and held out her arms to the car, as if pleading with it to
come back, to come out of the water.

"Goddamn," she said finally. "Goddamn it to hell." She took off her shoes and threw them toward Catherine, and one landed in one place and one in another place, and then she ran straight into the water in her bare feet, and Catherine, watching, began to cry, and Matt, pulling himself upright, started crying as well, his mouth a great square, tears rolling down his face, and they both stood there on their rumpled gritty leaf-strewn blanket. Catherine held Matt's hand tight. Her mother's dress was wrapped in heavy wet folds around her legs, so that she lost her balance and slipped deeper into the water. A wave came up on the beach and washed over one of her shoes. Catherine kept her eyes fixed on her mother's head, which was all she could see. She thought: She will die, she will die. I must get someone to help.

At the other end of the beach everything looked exactly as it had looked before, the black and white dog bounding up and down, the children splashing and running in the waves. The mothers all stolid, unmoving, their hands resting on their hips, their round bare shoulders pink and ordinary. No one looked up, or shouted, or came any closer. No one, for a long time, saw what Catherine saw: the black, terrible water, the shadows of the trees falling across the beach, the empty windows of the little house, watching, watching. The slow, sullen lapping of the waves against the dull green roof of the car, which looked silly, really, like a joke, like part of a game, sitting in the middle of the sea, where, clearly, it did not belong, and should not be.

Catherine would say later to her father: I wasn't scared. I didn't cry. This didn't feel to her like a lie; it seemed absolutely true. She told her father that no one was in the car, she didn't see anyone in the car. It was just a dumb old car, she said. She couldn't remember a single person doing anything. There were grownups at the beach, and they acted as if nothing was wrong. No one cared about the car, she said, her voice shaking, her hands cold and jittery, so that, finally, she had to sit on them to keep them still.

Catherine and her father were in the living room, while her mother was in the kitchen washing the dinner dishes. This was a long time after the day at the beach; days and days later. Catherine yawned until her eyes watered. Every night she had a bad dream and woke up screaming. The minute she woke up, she forgot what the dream had been about. Her father had to come into her bedroom and turn on the light beside her bed. He had to take her in his arms and pat her back and say, There, there, it's all right. There's nothing to be scared of.

Read to me, she would say to him, and he would pick a book out from the pile on the floor beside her bed. *Winnie-the-Pooh*, and *Now We Are Six*, and *The Wind in the Willows*. In the middle of the long nights her father read her poems about Christopher Robin, and about bad Prince John, and *the King is in his counting house, counting out his money*, and pies baked with four-and-twenty blackbirds. These were poems she already knew by heart, and could recite in her head, faster than her father could read them. Except that before he got through the second poem, she would fall asleep, and when she woke her father would be gone, the night over, the sun shining in her window.

What did she dream about? her father wanted to know. Nothing, nothing, she said. She couldn't remember. A doll. There was a doll with rosy cheeks and long black curls in the dream, and the girl from the beach, Phoebe. Phoebe was following her up and down the beach. The safety pin in her bathing suit sparkled in the sunshine. Catherine was afraid of Phoebe. A little afraid. Only in the dream.

"I know a girl called Phoebe," Catherine told her father. "I might see her at school, when I go to school, and play with her. She had a cold."

"Yes, I'm sure you'll see her," her father said. "You'll make lots of nice friends once you start school."

"No one saw that car," Catherine told her father. "No one saw it but me and Mama and Matt. And Matt cried his head off." She wished she could explain to her father exactly what had happened. She wished she could tell him so that he could see everything just as she had seen it, but she was afraid. She was afraid that the truth would frighten him, and make him cry, too. "No one did anything," she said at last.

"Well, that's not true," her father said. "Your mother did something, didn't she? She tried to help the people who were in the car, didn't she? She was extremely brave, don't you think? And the police helped, too, didn't they? You must have been frightened, Catherine. You must have been frightened, and very worried about your mother."

Catherine shrugged. "No," she said.

Her father said, "I would have been scared, if I'd been there. I would have been scared, to see Mommy diving into the water like that."

"She got her dress all wet," Catherine said scornfully. "She wrecked her good white shoes."

Catherine remembered riding home in the police car. She sat in the back seat beside one of the policemen, who held Matt on his lap. The policeman's uniform, his pants and his jacket sleeves, were soaked from going in the water to help her mother. Dark brown pants turning black all the way up his legs. Come with me now, he had said to her mother. Give me your hand, he had said, leading her out of the water.

"My husband will come and get us," her mother had said, when he and the other police officer had tried to help her into the police car. "If I could just get someone to phone him. He'll come and get us. We'll be all right." Then the ambulance driver came over and said to her, "You get home right now, ma'am. You get home and have a nice hot cup of tea with lots of sugar in it. That's the ticket. Have a hot shower. Take it easy. You let this officer give you and the kiddies a ride home."

Someone had wrapped a blanket around Arlene, but she was still shivering, the skin around her mouth a bluish colour, her hair, no longer fastened in a ponytail, dripping wet. She looked small, huddled up in the police car, her face half hidden in the blanket. "I really tried," she had said to the policemen. "I even got hold of the door handle, but I couldn't open the door. And the window was down. I thought it was rolled down, just a little, and I could see, I could see—I don't know. It was really dark down there. The car had stirred up the sand. I kept trying, I really did. If I'd known what to do, maybe I could have—I don't know."

"At least we got a ride home in a police car," Catherine said, and her father smiled and patted her knee. "We can talk about this any time you like, Catherine," he said. "Whenever you remember anything about that, you know, that day, that *accident*, that unfortunate accident that happened at the beach, you come and tell me. Promise? Promise, Catherine?

Arlene was a hero. A man came from the newspaper and took her picture. He wanted her to go down to the beach with him, so he could photograph her at the actual scene of the accident, but Arlene refused. She said she didn't think it would be in very good taste, and the man from the newspaper said, "Well, Ma'am, you could be right." Instead, he took a picture of her sitting in a lawn chair on the patio, with Matt on her knee and Catherine standing beside her. Arlene had been to the hairdressers to have her hair shampooed and set. She already had the appointment, she said to Catherine's father; it wasn't that she went to the hairdresser to get ready for the newspaper reporter. She hoped no one thought she had. As soon as the reporter left with his camera and his notebook, she wished she'd never posed for him. She knew it was going to look like she was trying to be a celebrity, she said. The worst thing you could do when you were a newcomer in a small town was be a show off.

"I don't even want to look at it," she told David when he brought the newspaper in from the front porch. David said the picture was fine; it made him proud of her. "No one's going to think you were showing off, Arlene," he said. Arlene took a quick look at the newspaper and said, "There, that's just what I was afraid of. I look smug. It just invites comparison."

"Nonsense," he said. He showed the picture to Catherine. There she was with a bow in her hair. She was holding onto her mother's hand. Her mother had her chin raised to see over the top of Matt's head, and she had a small, tight smile on her face. Catherine's father read out the words beneath the picture: *Mother of two risks life in valiant rescue bid.* "There, now," he said. "It's the truth, isn't it? Isn't that exactly the way it happened?"

CHAPTER SIX

Catherine leaned her forehead on the glass display case at the bakery. She couldn't decide between oatmeal chocolate chip or coconut macaroons with candied cherries on top. A fat woman kept getting in the way of her seeing if the bakery had her favourite cookies, vanilla with a layer of strawberry icing. The woman's slip showed under the hem of her dress, and she was wearing black shoes laced up so tight the skin on her ankles looked pinched and red. She was talking to another woman, and when she stepped back she bumped into Catherine. She turned around in a hurry and glanced down at Catherine, then stared at Catherine's mother with her mouth open.

"Oh, my," she said. "Here's Mrs. Greenwood. How are you, dear? Are you feeling better? We were all so worried about you."

"I'm fine, thank you," Catherine's mother said firmly. She put Matt down on the floor, where he stood unsteadily, sucking on his fingers. She went over to a table by the window and picked out a loaf of bread, and came back to the counter and took her change purse out of her pocket. "Don't put your fingers all over the glass," she said to Catherine.

One of the women told Catherine's mother she was so pleased to meet her at last. "This is such a pleasure," she said, "I'm Mrs. Jantzen and this is Mrs. Bowles." Mrs. Jantzen put her hand on Catherine's head and said she had lovely hair. Was it permed, she wanted to know, and Catherine's mother said, "No, it's not. It's natural."

The woman called Mrs. Bowles adjusted her glasses and said, "Oh, it's a shame, isn't it? It's such a shame about that poor Myrtle Kriskin. Honestly, her life was so sad. And then to have it end so tragically. And her poor little boys. Poor little souls. Billy, and what was the other one's name? Eddy. Billy and Eddy Kriskin. They never had a chance between them, did they?"

"Mind you, that Myrtle had her mind set on a course of destruction," said the second woman, the one called Mrs. Jantzen. She wore glasses with pink rims, and had black hair in tense little curls all over her scalp. Her dress was patterned with huge flowers that looked to Catherine like curled-up dead-white sleeping babies, their arms folded over their heads. "That girl never had a serious thought in her head," Mrs. Jantzen said. "And she liked to drink. Drink runs in her family. Her father died of liver disease and I know for a fact Myrtle was scared the same thing would happen to her."

"It didn't help that her husband left her," said Mrs. Bowles. "It was a sin, the way Eugene Kriskin left Myrtle alone with those two little boys and ran off with that girl who worked in the shoe store in Ladysmith. You have to wonder where his mind was."

Catherine watched Mrs. Jantzen adjust her glasses before she said, "Well, you have to give Myrtle credit. She was trying her best to get her life sorted out. She was selling cosmetics door to door, and waitressing at the El Rancho Café. And then it burned down, and there she was, out of work again. Everything she tried seemed under a curse. No wonder she thought there wasn't another thing left she could do."

Suspended from the ceiling above Mrs. Bowles' head was a strip of fly paper stuck all over with dead flies. Catherine tried not to look at it. A wasp trapped behind the venetian blind was bumping in a demented fashion against the window.

Catherine's mother took a one dollar bill out of her purse and handed it to the woman behind the counter. "Oh, nonsense," she said suddenly. "It was an accident. She was just taking her kids to the beach for the day. She must have hit the gas when she meant to hit the brakes. She panicked. It's not fair to say that she did it on purpose. That's slander. It's worse, even. Speaking ill of the dead."

"Well, excuse me," Mrs. Jantzen said. "But I have lived in this town a whole lot longer than you, Mrs. Greenwood. You don't know half of what goes on."

"No, but I've got a pretty good idea," Arlene said. She put her change in her purse and picked Matt up and balanced him on her hip. She gave Catherine the loaf of bread to carry. It was still warm from the bakery oven, a big square loaf of brown bread. Catherine held it in front of her as if it were a beach ball, the kind you inflated with air, and she and her mother walked out of the bakery into the bright sun. "What about the cookies?" Catherine said. "You forgot the cookies. You said we could have some cookies."

Her mother put Matt in his stroller and took the bread from Catherine and put it in the wire basket on the back of the stroller. She pulled her sunglasses out of her pocket and put them on, then she took a tissue out of her pocket and wiped her nose. She kneeled beside Catherine and tidied Catherine's hair with her fingers. She stared into Catherine's face. "How you doing?" she said. "How's Catherine doing?"

"Fine," Catherine said. "I'm fine."

"Well, that's good," her mother said. "How would you like an ice-cream float?

"You forgot the cookies," Catherine said. "You promised," she said.

"Tomorrow," her mother said. The cookies could be for tomorrow and the ice-cream float could be for today.

As soon as they got settled in a booth at the café, her mother ordered a 7-Up float with chocolate ice cream for Catherine, a dish of Neapolitan ice cream for Matt, and a coffee for herself. She lit a cigarette and helped Matt to eat his ice cream, a tiny spoonful at a time. The float came in a tall glass with silvery beads of moisture running down it. Catherine scooped the frothy bubbles off the top of the float with a long thin silver spoon and let them dissolve with a little frizzle on her tongue. Her mother kept looking at her and asking how she liked her float, and Catherine nodded her head and waited until she'd swallowed a mouthful of freezing-cold ice cream before she said, "It's delicious." She smacked her lips to show how much she liked it. She smiled at her mother and her mother just kept smiling at her and smoking her cigarette and drinking her coffee.

"You know, that Myrtle person didn't want to drive her car into the sea," her mother said. "It was an accident. It couldn't be helped." She butted her cigarette out in the ashtray and got a dollar out of her purse and put it on the table. "Accidents are things that can't be avoided. They're fate. I believe in fate. I think I do, anyway." She picked up the dollar bill and folded it in half and put it down again.

"I'm not finished," Catherine said. She watched her mother rubbing her forehead with her fingers as if her head hurt. Catherine took her straw out of her float and licked the ice cream off it. She felt full of bubbles and pop, as if she might throw up. She looked sideways at the jukebox selector. There was no music in the café today; there was no smiling Mr. Dods to give her a dime and show her how to play "How Much Is That Doggie in the Window" on the jukebox. Where was Mr. Dods? Dead, floating in the water? Or just gone to some distant, sad place where Catherine couldn't ever see him again?

"There's no hurry," Catherine's mother said. She pulled a paper napkin out of the dispenser and spit on it and wiped it over the corners of Matt's mouth. "Finish your float," she said to Catherine. "We've got lots of time. I don't have anywhere else I want to be."

"This goddamned hellish town," Catherine's mother said. "What is it about this place? Honest to God, I swear it's under some kind of curse!"

She was sitting in front of her dressing table in a black lace dress with a scoop neckline and little cap sleeves. Her hair was pinned up in a French roll, and she was fastening little pearl and diamond earrings in her ears. She and Catherine's father were going out for Chinese food, not in Cayley, but in another town up the island, where there was a restaurant with a ceiling made out of stars, and candles on every table. So Catherine's mother had told her. Catherine was lying across her parents' bed, her head propped on her hands, watching her mother. Her father was putting gold cuff-links in his shirt cuffs. Matt was leaning on the side of the bed, singing away to himself and staring into space, which was what he did all the time. He was in his own little world, Catherine's mother said.

Catherine's father put on his suit jacket and brushed his hand vigorously across the shoulders. He took a look in the mirror and adjusted his tie. "This town isn't any different from any other town," he said. "Not as far as I know."

"You think so? Sometimes I think I'm living at the funny farm. It's getting so I'm afraid to get out of bed in the morning."

"Arlene, you're exaggerating."

"You don't know the half of it. Small towns. I hate them. Honest to God, I do. I'm fed up to the back teeth with small towns. I wish I lived in a city. I wish I lived in New York City. Or Vancouver. I could at least go to plays, and the symphony, and go shopping whenever I felt like it. I might even might some interesting people." She put her lipstick on, then blotted her lips with a tissue. She sprayed Evening in Paris perfume on her neck and her wrists.

Today was Catherine's mother's birthday. When Catherine asked her how old she was, she said, Don't ask. Then she said, "Well, if you must know, I'm twenty-five. Lord, I'm getting old, aren't I?"

Catherine's father had given her mother a present: a two-strand pearl necklace that came in a grey velvet box shaped like a clam shell, with *Symon's Quality Jewellers* in fancy gold letters on it. He lifted the necklace out of the box and fastened it around her neck, then he placed his hands on her shoulders and smiled at her reflection in the mirror.

"You do like it?" he said.

"I do. I think it's gorgeous. Have you got the catch done up properly?"

"I think so," he said.

Catherine's mother studied her reflection in the mirror and picked up her comb and fiddled some more with the front of her hair. The doorbell rang, and Catherine's father ran downstairs to answer it. It was the new baby-sitter, a girl called Rebecca. She was wearing red pedal pushers and saddle oxfords. She sat on the floor in Catherine's bedroom and Catherine watched her rearranging the furniture in the doll house. The doll house was a present from Catherine's Nana. It had tiny painted mother and father dolls and three children with rosy cheeks and a black and white dog. Rebecca moved the dog into the kitchen. She made the mother walk into the kitchen and say, "Now who let the dog in?" Then Rebecca saw the Sweet Sandra doll sitting on top of the toy box and went and got her and turned her over before Catherine could tell her not to. The cover for the little cavity where the batteries went fell off, and Catherine's gold lipstick tubes and perfume samples fell out and went all over the floor. Some of them rolled under the bed.

"What's that stuff?" said Rebecca, laughing.

"Oh, nothing," Catherine said, scrambling under the bed. For a moment, she lay perfectly still, her hand about to close on one of the sample lipsticks. There was a Nancy and Sluggo comic book lying open on the floor, and her rumpled nightie, which she had forgotten to pick up and put under her pillow. There was a dust bunny that floated off the floor when she blew at it. From here she could see, under the edge of the dust ruffle, through the open bedroom door and out into the hall. She could hear Matt chattering to her parents. She could hear her mother telling him that he was a good baby, he was her best baby boy. She saw her father's feet in his black shoes as he walked toward the bedroom door.

Catherine could see and hear quite a lot from under the bed. There was a sound in her ears like the sound the sea made. She imagined herself disappearing from sight, sinking deeper and deeper into something dark and unfathomable. There was a quick, urgent sense she had of memory sliding away from her. She felt as if she ought to grab onto something. But what? What was there solid enough and strong enough to hold on to? She removed the top from one of the miniature perfume bottles and sniffed. It stunk. What was that smell, anyway? Tea bags, and bathroom cleaner. *You just have the sweetest little face*, a small far-away voice whispered in her ear. *Cosmetics are the most fun.*

Catherine started to slide backwards out from under the bed, making what seemed to her like a long return journey to the ordinary world of her bedroom. For a moment, when she stood up, brushing dust from her shirt, she saw herself from a distance, as if she were someone else. She saw herself as Rebecca might see her: a five-year-old with tangled hair and a pink and blue bedroom on the top floor of the house, and a doll house where tiny people trotted happily from room to room and saw from their windows a sky full of stars and the sea at night. She saw a girl who had a beautiful mother who wore pearls and black lace dresses, and who was a hero, a genuine hero, going into the black water where nothing, nothing, was known or made the least sense.

CHAPTER SEVEN

The dining room at The Peking House had a false ceiling painted jet black to resemble the night sky. In the blackness fake stars, little pin-pricks of incandescent light, shone unwaveringly: the heavens on a starry night. Arlene was nibbling on tiny celery sticks, radish roses, carrot curls, all served ice-cold in a glass dish, and in between she was sipping her martini and trying to feel as if she was celebrating her birthday. She knew she was supposed to be having a good time. But she felt too tired, or too bored, she wasn't sure which it was, to eat, or even to talk to David. She kept tilting her head back and looking up at the ceiling. Imagine if God lived up there, she thought. A little scrunched-up facsimile of God, temporarily domiciled in a Chinese restaurant, reserving judgement, keeping an eye on all these dressed-up people with their chopsticks and their bottles of soy sauce. She wondered what this God would think of her. She wondered if he would like her new pearl necklace. She took another drink. She was beginning to feel a little—not unpleas-antly—drunk.

"You aren't eating a thing," David said to her, spooning thick red sweet-and-sour sauce over everything on his plate, and she sat up a little straighter and said, "I will, in a minute."

David began talking about the manager at the mill, a man called Howard Glass. Arlene had met Howard Glass once, when she had picked David up with the car after work. This was in June, just a month after they'd moved to Cayley, before all the weird things started happening. The tempera-ture that day had been about ninety degrees. She'd been sitting in the car, in the parking lot outside the mill office, where there wasn't a single bit of shade. Matt was in his car seat beside her, and Catherine was jumping up and down in the back seat, making a racket. And this tall lean man with a long, narrow face and a brush-cut had walked out of the office with David. He had come over to her car and had shaken her hand through the window. He had said, Pleased to meet you, ma'am, as if he had a starring role in a movie about the wild west. Pleased to meet you, too, I'm sure, Arlene had drawled, without thinking what she was doing. David had given her a funny look, as if trying to say, This is the mill manager; show a little respect, for goodness' sake. Howard Glass hadn't seemed to mind; he just ducked his head so that he could look in the car. He said, Hi there young lady, to Catherine, which was nice of him. Most men didn't bother with children, Arlene had noticed. And then he smiled at Matt, and asked Arlene how old her baby was, and when she said seventeen months, which was what he'd been at the time, he'd said, My, he's a big boy, isn't he? A fine-looking little guy. Thank you, she had said. We like him, too.

In any case, Howard's wife Julia had been away in Toronto visiting her family for the past six weeks, but now she was back, and Howard was putting on a party for her. David told Arlene all this while he was helping himself to more fried rice. He told her the party was going to be a cook-out in the Glasses' backyard, which overlooked the sea. They had a barbecue pit, and Howard was going to do the cooking. It would be very informal, David understood. People were just supposed to turn up and have a good time.

"I know you'll like Julia," David said. "The first time I saw her, I had a feeling you two would get along. Howard and Julia are two of the nicest people I've ever met. They're very sociable. And did I tell you their daughter is the same age as Catherine? It'll do Catherine all the good in the world to have someone to play with."

"Catherine doesn't need anyone to play with. She has all these imaginary people she's friends with. I can hear her in the backyard, chattering away to them." Sometimes David could be very bossy, Arlene thought. And he always got very earnest and enthusiastic about the people he worked with, especially when they were his superiors. He wanted to make himself indispensable. He wanted to be everybody's buddy. She didn't. She didn't care if Howard and Julia Glass liked or hated her. It was completely immaterial to her.

"I think she's probably lonely," David went on, still speaking of Catherine. "She's getting to an age where she needs to get away from us now and then. Here," he said, "have some fried rice. This is your birthday, you're supposed to be enjoying yourself. Look, I could get the waiter to bring you something else, if you like."

"Oh, I'll try the chow mein. And a little fried rice." She picked up her fork. "It's so dark in here you can't tell what you're eating. I could be eating the napkin for all I know," she said. She reached for the plate of sweet-and-sour pork. "I might as well try a little of this, too," she said.

When she and David had finished dinner, the waiter brought a birthday cake to their table. It had an inch of chocolate icing on top, and a lighted sparkler stuck in the centre. Everyone in the restaurant seemed to be watching. Arlene thought, Now what am I supposed to do? She sat there with her hands folded in her lap, smiling until she thought her face would crumple up like cellophane. A woman, a complete stranger, wearing a dress with a crino-line that rustled like dry grass, stopped on her way to the powder room and squeezed Arlene's arm and said, "Many, many happy returns, dear." Arlene said, "Why, thank you." As soon as the woman had gone, Arlene said to David, "How embarrassing." She leaned her head on her hand and looked sideways at David. He smiled and poured wine into their glasses. Arlene picked up her fork and poked around in her birthday cake and licked some icing off her fingers and said, "I don't want to go home, ever," and David laughed, but the truth was, she was serious. Well, partly serious. She'd like to live in a fancy hotel somewhere, in Los Angeles, or Hawaii, or New York City, and get waited on hand and foot and eat three times a day in a dining room and never wash another dish in her life.

She and David had coffee and she had a cigarette. Then she excused herself and went down a hall and up a flight of stairs to the women's powder room, where she used the toilet and then studied herself in the mirror over the vanity, smoothing her dress over her hips and turning sideways to make sure her stomach wasn't sticking out. She put on fresh lipstick. She undid her French roll because it was making her head ache, and combed her hair out around her shoulders. On an impulse she took off her new pearl necklace, which suddenly felt too heavy on her neck, and dropped it into her purse. Every birthday, she expected something completely unexpected and extraordinary to happen, and, honestly, here it was her twenty-fifth birthday, she was a quarter of a century old, and she was still waiting.

On the way home, just as David was turning off the highway onto the old Cayley Road, Arlene saw they were about to drive past the place where the El Rancho Café had burned down. She turned around to see if she could tell where the exact location had been. She wanted to stop and get out and walk around whatever remained—the foundations and maybe one tall brick chimney, a short flight of concrete steps that had once led to the entrance. She imagined the ground in all directions faintly warm, a lingering after-effect of the lightning strike, smouldering embers sparking beneath her feet like the sparkler on her birthday cake. She even started to ask David to pull over to the side of the road and turn around, then realised he'd think it was a dumb idea.

David turned to look at her, and said, "Did you say something, honey?"

"No," she said. "I forget what I was going to say." She subsided into her seat and closed her eyes and felt the car speeding through the darkness. She felt as if the vacant land where the El Rancho Café had been, including the tall cedar trees that had surrounded it, were following along after their car like a floating island. That girl, Myrtle Kriskin, had worked at the El Rancho. She had worn one of those frilly little caps on her head, Arlene supposed, and an apron, and she had taken orders for French fries and Salisbury steak and deep-fried oysters and Molson's beer. Arlene had never in her life seen Myrtle Kriskin, not really, but she could picture her perfectly: a tall, thin, gawky young woman, with sharp elbows and jutting knee bones, pale heavy-lidded eyes, translucent skin, a noticeable overbite, an unconsidered way of speaking. Myrtle had been awkward and brash at the same time, Arlene would bet. Endearing and annoying. The picture she got of Myrtle was so clear at times that she felt as if she had known her, as if in some way they'd known each other for a long time. But even though Arlene felt desperately sorry for her, she knew she and Myrtle would never in real life have been friends; they were entirely dissimilar, their lives were too far apart. Arlene had read in the newspaper that Myrtle Kriskin had been twenty-five years old, the same age as she was, and now Myrtle was dead and would never get a day older. But Arlene would. She knew she would. One day she'd be old; she'd be an old, old lady, bent and frail and no longer beautiful, and when she was very, very old, she'd die and cease to exist. Once you were gone, that was it, in her opinion.

What were the chances of being struck by lightning? What were the chances of death by drowning? Why did these risks exist in life? She should ask David. He was an accountant, he could probably work it out for her on paper. He loved coming up with a logical mathematical solution to any problem you could think of. She opened her eyes and sat up straight. She could see a thousand bugs flying at the headlights. She rolled the window all the way down and let the cool night wind blow on her face. The old Cayley Road was narrow and winding and seemed to go down and down further into a sort of midnight-black canyon.

"I wonder how the kids are doing?" she said.

"By now, they're fast asleep," he said. Arlene was suddenly in a hurry to get home to them. She pictured them not asleep, but floating in the summer night like creamy petals from a plum tree, fat rosy cherubs, their hands held out to her. She couldn't wait to tiptoe into their rooms and check on them, make sure they were covered up, their sheets tucked neatly under their chins, see that their windows had been left open sufficiently wide to let in fresh air without causing a draft.

Motherhood was paradoxical, Arlene had discovered. When she was with her kids all day she thought she'd go mad; then, when she was separated from them, even for a few hours, she was desperate to be with them again. She didn't know what she wanted. Not only as far as her kids went, either. In general she didn't know. She wished she did. On her eleventh birthday, her father had told her she had a choice: she could succeed at life, or she could fail to succeed. It was up to her. He had presented her with a notebook with a dark green cover like a June bug's back, and he'd told her to write down her objectives in it. She was to do this every week, and then, every month, she was to go back and read what she'd written. At the end of the year, he had said, she would be able to see what she'd achieved and what she still had left to work on.

Don't tell me what you write, he had said. I don't want to know what you write. It's your personal notebook. Just make writing in it a habit you never get out of. He had told her that Socrates, or was it Plato, had said that the unexamined life was not worth living, and that she should give that notion some thought. He had held the notebook in his hands, running his thumbnail down the binding, riffling through the pages, considering them seriously, as if he could read something wise and beautiful already written there. Each page had a thin gold line at the top, and the edges of the pages were gold. It was an expensive notebook, Arlene could see. Her father had always admired quality. He had been one of those people who said, very seriously: You get what you pay for. His hands and even his fingernails were dead white. He wore a gold wedding ring on his left hand, and a gold signet ring set with a small diamond on his right hand. When he gave her the notebook, it still felt warm from his touch.

She kept the notebook for years in a dresser drawer that was empty except for a cherry-wood box that held her baby jewellery: a tiny gold locket on a chain, a silver bracelet, a necklace of seed pearls. Every night, for a few months after her eleventh birthday, she got the notebook out of the drawer and sat on the edge of her bed with it open on her lap. She chewed on her pen and thought, what do I want to be? She couldn't imagine herself an adult. She didn't especially want to grow up. When she was a child she hadn't ever dreamt about being married and having children, the way her friends had. The most she'd wanted was a kitten, a puppy; she would have been happy with a goldfish in a glass bowl. Finally she'd wiped the end of her pen on her skirt and wrote, even though it wasn't true: *I hope some day to be married, and to be a mother. I would like to have four children, two boys and two girls. This year I want more than anything to get an A in geometry.* Her handwriting was atrocious, and she had got an ink smear right across the page and on the side of her hand. *I want to learn to speak French and to play tennis*, she wrote doggedly. She wrote things she thought her mother and father would approve of, even though her father had promised they wouldn't ever look at the notebook. She was too superstitious to write about what she really wanted, which was to be beautiful, to be absolutely gorgeous, to be a talented dancer or singer, to have her own car and a leopard-skin coat and a golden retriever that followed her around. She couldn't wish for anything that really mattered to her, in case she brought bad luck on herself. Luck was a vital force in her life, she was convinced; she had believed in a jealous, spiteful god, the kind that did, in fact, live in the ceiling and was able to see every single thing you did, every minute of the day, and knew all your thoughts from the inside out. Perhaps she still did

As they drove up the drive, Arlene thought the trees and shrubs in the backyard looked unfamiliar, especially by moonlight. They hadn't lived at 131 Alma Avenue in Cayley long enough to go through a change in seasons, to see the trees leafless, or the yard covered in drifts of snow, or crocuses coming up in the flower beds. They hadn't lived here long enough for homecoming to seem routine. The trees and shrubs in the backyard didn't look familiar by moonlight. Where are we? Arlene said, wandering around the back yard. Where in the hell are we? she said. She kicked off her high heels and looked up at the real stars that shone down on the town of Cayley from some unimaginable distance. Was this Cayley, or some unknown land? she asked. David took her by the hand. He put his arms around her and waltzed with her across the lawn. You're here, he said. You're here on the edge of the earth, in the town of Cayley. He waltzed with her between the pots of geraniums. The kitchen lights were on, illuminating the patio. I don't want the night to end, David said. He lifted her hair and kissed her ear. She told him she didn't want her birthday to end, either. But he had to take the baby-sitter home, and she had to get inside and check on the kids. She pulled her hand out of his and went into the house. The radio was playing in the kitchen. The baby-sitter was asleep on the sofa in the living room. She'd kicked off her shoes in the hall, and Arlene nearly tripped over them on her way to the stairs. She ran upstairs and went to Matt's bedroom to check on him. She leaned over his crib, just looking at him. She brushed her fingers across his cool, moist forehead, and in his sleep he frowned and threw an arm out. One bare foot stuck out from under his blanket, and she gave it a tickle before tucking it in and pulling the blanket straight. His teddy bear was on the floor, and she picked it up and brushed it off and put it at the bottom of his crib. He sighed, and then his breathing went back to normal. Nothing woke Matt up once he was asleep.

She could hear the car backing out of the driveway, and then there was just the sound of crickets outside in the grass. It seemed to her that the crickets in this town made a different sound from other crickets; they were rowdier, more insistent. She and David had moved so often, six times since they'd been married, she had formulated a philosophy for herself: the first three months in a new town were the hardest. Three more months after that, and the worst was over; you knew where you stood. You'd learned the hours the grocery store was open, and the library, and the doctors' offices, and the times of the church services. You'd found out if your garbage got collected, or if you had to take it to the dump in the trunk of your car. And six months later, you finally felt as if the house belonged to you, or at least you knew where everything was, and you were reasonably certain the furnace wasn't going to blow up when you turned it on. It took a year, at least, to unpack every last box, and to get the butcher to know who you were and that you wanted all the fat cut off your sirloin steaks, and then it was just about time to move again.

In Catherine's room, Arlene's foot sent something skittering across the floor. Damn, she thought. She was trying to be absolutely quiet because Catherine was the lightest sleeper in the world, and the last thing she wanted was to wake her up. She thought she had seen whatever it was she'd kicked glittering in the glow from the night light. She got down on

CAROL WINDLEY

her hands and knees and felt around on the floor until she found a small glass tube. What in the hell is this, she wondered, standing up and going to the door, where, in the hall light, she could see that it was a vial of perfume. She uncapped it and took a sniff. Violets and roses and something nasty, like cider vinegar that had gone off. Trust Catherine. Where on earth had she got this from? Not that Arlene really had to ask. She could just imagine Myrtle Kriskin pressing it into Catherine's hand, and saying, Now, don't tell your Mummy, she'll get mad.

Good old Myrtle, she knew everything, didn't she? Her strong hands with their perfectly manicured nails tight on the steering wheel of her car, her teeth biting into her lower lip, and then suddenly she made a decision, and pressed her foot down hard on the gas pedal. *Hasta la vista!* Happy holidays!

Maybe the sea had looked to her like a highway, a wide dark road she could travel forever, while her kids amused themselves in the back seat with comic books and crayons and sticks of Spearmint gum. She hadn't meant for things to go so damnably wrong, Arlene was sure. But it must have been there, at the back of her mind, the powerful possibility of pure madness, one chance in a million to go for something big and unambiguous and irrevocable.

Arlene curled her fingers lightly around the perfume vial and tiptoed to the side of Catherine's bed. The blankets were slipping off, and Catherine's PJ top was up under her arms, but Arlene didn't dare try to cover her up. She'd be awake in a flash, trying to tell Arlene her dreams, wanting a glass of water and a trip to the bathroom. Or she'd wake up crying from a nightmare and want the lights left on, and her father to read her a story. Her hair was spread out across her pillow, a dark mass of curls and tangles Arlene longed to touch, just to feel how springy and soft it was.

From this side of the house Arlene could hear the sawmill, a steady mechanical whirring and clanging. Every town she had lived in, since she got married, was built around a sawmill, or a pulp mill. The mills all sounded the same; they all smelled the same, or nearly the same, of sulphur and wood preservatives, a cocktail of chemicals, a witch's brew; they lit up the night sky with the same sick orange glow. The towns were all the same, too. Old towns, with rows of cheap company houses and small narrow stores with fake fronts, and the sea at the end of the street, always cold and fretful, and the big ships waiting to carry the lumber off to some foreign place no one in the town could even begin to imagine, and the men walking out of the mill, setting their feet down hard on the road, lunch buckets under their arms. They always walked with their heads down as if the most they wanted out of life was a view of the ground. They didn't talk to each other. They went home to their wives and children, to the lives they'd made for themselves, the lives they had got used to, and had learned to put up with.

Arlene lived in these towns because she hadn't written a single important goal in her notebook. She hadn't taken her father's advice—she hadn't bothered to plan out in advance what she wanted from life. Engaged to be married at seventeen. Married at eighteen. A long white satin dress with a train, a veil edged with scalloped lace. Red roses in her bouquet. *Married in white, you'll look a sight; married in blue, your love will be true.* Wasn't that what she and her friends had said, at school? *Happy the bride the sun shines on.*

Her grandfather led her up the aisle and gave her away. Her mother's father, Grandfather Myles. Grandfather Myles had silver hair he wore brushed forward and cut in a little fringe over his forehead. He kept joking with her in the limousine on the way to the church: He didn't know if he wanted to give her away, he said. He might keep her, instead. She was his sweetheart. His favourite granddaughter. Why would he want to give her away to some young man he didn't even know? Why would he do that?

It had been raining, and then it had cleared up. Grandfather Myles made the chauffeur stop the limousine and he and Arlene got out and stood in a city park, on the wet grass, and he lit a cigar and she smoked a cigarette. She and her Grandfather Myles stood under a leafy green tree next to a rose garden and Arlene held the end of her veil and the train of her dress over her arm and tried not to notice that her satin shoes were getting wet. She felt as if she were dressed up in some ridiculous out-of-date costume. She picked a shred of tobacco from her lips and her fingers came away stained red with lipstick. She felt as old and as sophisticated as she was going to get. A soon-to-be married woman. We should play hooky, she said to her Grandfather Myles. Good idea, he said. Let's fly the coop. He'd do anything she wanted, she knew that. Her hands were shaking; she was shivering as if it were cold. The limousine driver was standing on the sidewalk with his hands in his pockets, waiting for them.

The sun burned off the clouds, and it turned hot and muggy. When Arlene and her grandfather got back in the

limousine, the streets were steaming, a ghostly white va-
pour rising into the air of the city. *Happy the bride the sun
shines on.* Her grandfather had suddenly said to her, Do you
know what day this is? June the sixth, he said, the sixth
anniversary of D-Day. He was an expert on the war; he knew
every battle, all the important dates, the victories and de-
feats. Every day in the calendar had military significance to
him. If he'd been in charge, the war would have ended eighteen months earlier. That was what he claimed. You're getting married on D-Day, he had said; that's a good sign; you'll
weather all the battles. Full steam ahead! he said to the driver.

In her bedroom, Arlene switched on the light and opened
her hand and took a good look at the perfume vial. It looked
sinister, as if the amber liquid in it were some kind of poison. For some reason, instead of tossing it into the wastepa-
per basket beside her dressing table, she put it in a drawer
next to her scarves and gloves. Then she took off her black
lace dress and hung it up in the closet, inside a garment
bag. She took out her earrings and went into the bathroom
and washed off her makeup. She went back into the bedroom and put on her best nightgown, white silk with a blue
ribbon threaded through the lace inset in the bodice. She
heard David unlocking the front door, and then he was
bounding up the stairs, taking them two at a time. He came
into the room pulling at the knot in his tie. He undid his
cufflinks and put them in a glass tray on top of his chest of
drawers. He put his hands on her shoulders and whispered
Happy Birthday in her ear. "Where's your pearl necklace?"
he wanted to know. "Did you put it in a safe place?"

"Oh, God, yes," she said. "My pearls. I almost forgot." She found her purse and took out the necklace, the pearls nestling cool and heavy in the palm of her hand, as if they were alive. The clasp was made up of tiny diamond chips in platinum. Or was that silver? It was an expensive necklace. She shouldn't have taken it off and put it in her purse. She could be thoughtless; careless. She knew she could. The pearls were all exactly the same size, like marbles. She placed them against her face. They felt cool, soothing. Nacreous. Wasn't that how pearls were described? The word sounded to her as if it meant death, decay, entombment, but it didn't mean any of those things. It had something to do with pearls, the outer covering of pearls, she was pretty sure. Now, where was the case from the jewellery store? She remembered David opening it to take out the pearls when she was getting ready to go out. She opened all the drawers in her dressing table, rummaging through things. Her fingers brushed against the perfume vial and she drew her hand away quickly, as if it had scorched her fingers. It was so cheap, so insignificant, a terrible little object, just the kind of forbidden thing a five-year-old girl would treasure. Arlene had a sudden vision of Catherine walking into the house that day, her face plastered with makeup, all blue and pink, like a miniature harlot, with gobs of black stuff all around her eyes. She'd been so pleased with herself. Arlene shouldn't have gotten mad at her. She should have laughed, because, really, it had been funny. If only she could be more patient with Catherine. They were too much alike, that was the problem. They both had quick tempers; they both said and did things they regretted later.

She found the case for the pearls under a scarf on the floor beside her bed. She put the pearls inside and let the case fall shut with a snap, then put it away in a drawer. She straightened the lace doily her silver brush and comb were on. She looked at herself in the mirror. She wet her lips and pulled at the curls over her forehead. David came over and said, "Excuse me. The concierge told me I would find you here."

"And here I am."

"He said today was your birthday. He said I would find you in a particularly festive mood."

"The concierge is a beast. But he was right." She took David's hand and led him toward the bed. She slipped her nightgown over her shoulders and let if fall to the floor at her feet. She pulled the blankets back and got into bed. David lay down beside her. In the pale wash of moonlight it seemed to her their arms looked so similar, they had the same skin, the same eyes and hair, they were the same identical person, each empty and sorrowful and in need of this act of completion, this nourishment.

She woke briefly in the night and her first thought was of her notebook, her birthday notebook, with its shining cover, its blank pages. She'd lost it long ago, she didn't even know when, long before she and her mother had moved for the first time after Arlene's father died. If she had it now, she'd write in it. Starting tonight, the night of her twenty-fifth birthday. She'd examine her life and learn from her mistakes, just as her father had advised her to do. And this time she'd be honest with herself. She wouldn't be so afraid to say what she wanted. The idea pleased her, even though she knew by morning she would probably have forgotten about it, or, if she did manage to remember, it wouldn't seem as important to her anymore. Then, just as she was falling asleep again, she thought of Myrtle Kriskin. She saw her in the distance, on the far side of what seemed to be a grass-hockey field. She was just standing there in the sunlight, in a blue dress, with an Alice band holding her hair away from her face. Arlene didn't suppose that in real life Myrtle had ever worn an Alice band, but this was clearly a younger, plainer version of Myrtle. Arlene was calling to her, telling her to wait, but the words were getting lost in the wind. It was the most frustrating experience. She started to run, but before she got across the field she saw that she'd been mistaken. No one was there.

CHAPTER EIGHT

What Arlene remembered about her father was that he'd been very busy. He hadn't had the time to play softball or tennis with her, or take her to the circus, which was what she had imagined other fathers did. She couldn't even tell for certain, after all this time, if he had loved her, if he ever had. Her mother liked to tell her that her father had adored her. That he had thought the world of her. Arlene remembered that he gave her presents, quite expensive presents, and occasionally she overheard him bragging about her to his friends: My daughter did this, my daughter did that. He only ever admonished her through her mother. Eunice, he would say, get Arlene to put her bike away. She left the damned thing out in the drive again. Eunice, I think you should have a talk with Arlene's teacher, find out why she got a C in geometry. Why a C? What in the hell kind of grade is that? Eunice, Arlene's hair is hanging down her back in rat's tails. Why don't you take her to a hairdresser, for God's sake?

Did he do this because he was used to delegating responsibility, giving orders? Had it been impossible for him, for some reason, to talk directly to her? Arlene couldn't figure out what the correct answer to these questions was. Eunice had clicked around after Arlene's father on her high heels, fluttery, eager, her smile bright, two little circles of rouge high on her face, asking him did he want tea, did he want cocoa, would he like a martini? Did he want to invite those new people, the Gregorys, for dinner next week? Did he want to see a certain play, go to the movies? Did he want a quiet night at home? Cocktails? Dinner for twelve?

Arlene's father had silver hair he combed straight back from his forehead, a black moustache with silver flecks in it, clear grey eyes, large and wide-set, straight black eyebrows, firm unlined skin that looked tanned even in winter. It was true: her father had looked as if he spent his time sunbathing on the beach, when the truth was he never took a holiday, he never stopped working. When women talked to him, Arlene had noticed, they always carried on as if they were sixteen years old, giggling and blushing, or they gave him intense, wide-eyed looks and spoke to him in whispers, as if they were in awe of him, which they probably were. She'd been in awe of him herself.

Her father was old when she was born. He was twenty years older than her mother. He was used to living on his own and not having any responsibilities outside of his work. He was a successful lawyer. He was part of some kind of conglomerate that owned a parking lot in downtown Vancouver, a night club, and an apartment building in the West End. Nothing that happened to him after his forty-second birthday had caused him to make the slightest changes to his routine, Eunice said. He'd behaved as if a wife and a daughter were incidental items he'd jotted into his appointment calendar to compensate for a tendency he had to forget they existed. Eunice claimed this was the plain truth: he had written a reminder to himself about his wedding day; he had marked in red ink the week his first child was due to arrive. It was an anecdote Eunice told at parties, as if she were proud of it, as if it proved she had married a successful man with a complicated, exciting life. *See what I have done?* she seemed to be saying. *See this house, this furniture, the paintings on the walls, this man? Isn't this amazing? I can't get over it myself!* She went around damning everything she had with her enthusiasm. She brought down curses on her head, in Arlene's opinion, through her own immodesty and childishness. She would never change; she hadn't changed, not even when everything had been taken away from her.

In the mornings, Arlene's father had left for his office while Arlene and her mother were still in their dressing-gowns at the breakfast table. He had his breakfast, a glass of orange juice and a soft-boiled egg, at five-thirty in the morning, when Eunice and Arlene were still asleep. He wore a hat and a three-piece suit under a long overcoat, and carried a black leather briefcase. Arlene could remember him clearly. As he came into the kitchen to say good morning to her and her mother, he was buttoning his overcoat, brushing lint off his sleeves. He was jingling his car keys in his hand before he even got to the front door. When he was at home, in the evenings, those evenings when he didn't have a meeting or an appointment with a client or with his business associates, he propped his briefcase open on a chair, and took papers out of it and rustled them in his hands, as if they were a deck of playing cards, before he spread them out carefully on his desk. Arlene had glimpsed him through the half-open door of his study. She wasn't allowed to disturb him. She wasn't allowed to go in unless she was invited. At times he turned his chair toward the bay windows, and the evening light that bathed his handsome face, his half-closed eyes, seemed to emanate from some foreign, exclusive location half a world away.

He died when Arlene was eleven years old. He was gone practically before she had time to get to know him. She missed him almost every day, even after all this time. She still wondered what he would think of her, if he could see her now, and what he would think of his grandchildren. She'd like to know. But she never would; she had to imagine to herself what he would think, what he would say. Her father existed only in her imagination. Over the years he'd likely undergone so many changes in her mind that he wasn't even the same man anymore. And she was aware that she kept changing her mind, about how much she had loved him, about how much he had cared about her and Eunice, about how willing she was to forgive him for leaving her.

Chapter Nine

David and Arlene were second cousins twice removed, or third cousins once removed; Arlene could never remember which, even though Eunice had worked it out for her once, using her eyebrow pencil to draw a cactus-shaped family tree on a paper napkin in the lunch room at Eaton's, one Saturday afternoon in September, 1949. This, according to Eunice, was the story: Arlene's great-grandmother, Daphne Gamlin, and David's grandmother, Rose Gamlin, had been first cousins. Daphne Gamlin had married Norman Stott, who had a fruit orchard in the Okanagan. Three daughters were born to them; the middle daughter, Clare, had married Hector Myles and they had moved to Vancouver, where Hector had briefly owned a men's clothing store on Granville Street before going into the insurance business. Clare and Hector were Eunice's parents. Rose Gamlin had married a clergyman, Eunice believed, or a teacher, one or the other;

in any case, he was a Greenwood, and they'd had four or five children, one of whom was David Greenwood's father.

Eunice had an ancient photograph of Daphne and Rose Gamlin, taken when they were girls. Daphne, who was seated, had black hair and heavy dark brows and a thin un-smiling mouth. Rose was standing, her narrow hands resting on Daphne's round shoulders. Her head was lowered as if someone were about to throw something at her. She had a sheepish smile on her face and a flower of some kind, possibly a white gardenia, pinned loosely to her hair. Rose and Daphne didn't look in the least like cousins, whereas Arlene thought she and David did. They were both fine-boned and tall, with naturally-wavy auburn hair. At least, Arlene's hair had been auburn when she was a child; as she got older it had darkened, but it still had a definite reddish tinge. They had the same large eyes that turned down slightly at the corners; the same chin, with a tiny indentation in it.

They met at a tennis party in July, 1949. It wasn't really a party; it was just a few people Arlene knew batting a tennis ball back and forth one warm afternoon at Stanley Park. Arlene was seventeen. David was twenty-nine, although with his strawberry-blond hair, slightly freckled skin and long skinny legs, he had looked about twenty-three at the most. Even that had seemed old to Arlene. He had been wearing a black sweater with a white collar and white pants with a grass stain on one knee. He had just finished getting beaten at tennis by Gordon Shaw. Arlene's best friend, Iris Muir, had a crush on Gordon. She was afraid that he liked Arlene better than he liked her. "Leave Gordon for me, and you can have David," Iris had whispered to her. "You're welcome to both of them," Arlene said; men didn't interest her in the least; she thought Iris was crazy to follow Gordon Shaw around everywhere and write his initials all over her school books. But if Arlene had to pick between Gordon and David, it would, she decided, be David Greenwood, not Gordon Shaw. David was almost as shy as she was. When Iris introduced them to each other, he went red and looked away, which immediately made her feel sympathy for him: Neither one of them had an inkling of what to say or do. His hair was falling in his eyes, and Arlene noticed he kept trying to comb it into place surreptitiously. When they'd finished playing tennis, they went to a drug store for something cold to drink. Arlene remembered that she and David had sat quietly at the soda counter, sipping their drinks and ignoring each other, while Gordon and Iris and another couple, friends of Gordon's they'd met on the way to the drug store, laughed and talked and had a great time.

Arlene and David didn't discover they were related until Arlene finally got up the courage to introduce him to her mother. "And where are you from, Mr. Greenwood?" Eunice asked David once they were all seated in the living room. It was a hot afternoon and Eunice had pulled the drapes shut to keep out the sun. "What was your mother's maiden name?" Eunice asked David. "Where is your family from? And what did you say your father does for a living?"

Arlene signalled to her mother not to be so rude. "Don't ask so many questions, Mother," she had to say, finally. Her mother had flapped her hand in front of Arlene's face, setting up a storm of dust motes. "Hush, darling," she had said. "I'm just trying to get to know David. David, I was wondering, was your grandmother, by any chance, a Gamlin?" she asked. And when David looked surprised and said, "Yes, Ma'am, she was," Eunice gave him a broad smile. "Well," she said, "have I got news for you. You and I are kissing cousins, Mr. Greenwood."

At first, Arlene refused to believe it was true. She thought it was just some story her mother was making up. Eunice liked to be outrageous; she liked to tease people, Arlene especially. This time, however, she claimed she was simply being factual. She brought out the old photograph to show Arlene. Arlene had never known her great-grandmother; she was barely aware the Gamlin branch of the family existed. Eunice had a way of relating everything to herself, anyway. In her mind, if something didn't have direct relevance to her, it might as well not exist. The only people she cared about were people she considered her close family, her best friends, and then she was absolutely devoted to them, or claimed that she was. She told Arlene later that out of the whole Gamlin clan, her mother, Clare, had been the nicest, and certainly the best-looking. She told Arlene that Daphne Gamlin had gone ice-climbing with one of Queen Victoria's younger sons on a glacier in the Rocky Mountains and that he'd paid her the compliment of telling her she was courageous and fearless, for a woman; Rose, on the other hand, had never, as far as Eunice knew, done one single interesting thing in her whole life. Not that there was anything wrong with that, Eunice added; more of the Gamlins took after Rose than Daphne. David especially, Eunice said. He's very Rose-like, wouldn't you say? she said to Arlene.

David played the ukulele. He drove a green Morris Minor. The year before he met Arlene, he had started work as an accountant at the pulp mill in Powell River. He told her he was spending his summer vacation at a friend's house in Point Grey. He had been in the army during the war, but he hadn't got any further away than Ottawa, where he'd worked in an office that had something to do with British Lend-Lease. The first thing Arlene noticed was the power she had over him. If she was quiet, for any reason at all, he immediately thought she was annoyed with him. If she turned down an invitation to go out for dinner or to play tennis or to go to a movie, even for a perfectly legitimate reason, his feelings were hurt. He telephoned her several times a day. He took her out for ice cream, and to go swimming at Kits beach. He took her to the Pacific National Exhibition to see a miniature carnival constructed entirely out of ordinary toothpicks. Arlene had stood on tiptoe, trying to get a good look, and David had pushed a path through the crowd so that she could see it up close. She said, "Why, it looks like something in a fairy tale," and he had promised to buy a box of toothpicks and some glue, so that she could try making a toothpick Ferris wheel at home. She had a brief vision of the two of them working at the kitchen table at her house, their heads close, their hands stuck all over with glue and toothpicks, a steady rain falling outside the window.

He took her to see the World of Fashion show, and bought her a ticket on the P.N.E. prize home, which was said to have a dream kitchen supplied by the B. C. Electric Company. He walked ahead of her, taller than most of the people in the crowd. She fell behind, looking at the exhibits.

"Where did you get to?" he said, marching back to her and taking her by the arm. He kept asking her if she was warm enough, if she was hungry, or tired, or if she could think of somewhere else she wanted to go. Did she want to go to Happyland and ride the Shoot-the-Chutes? "No, thank you," she had said, laughing. Then she wished she had said yes: It was a beautiful evening, warm, thin crimson clouds drawn like threads through a mauve twilight. She'd never been on a real date before, and she felt like doing something different, exciting, wild. But she didn't have the faintest idea how to tell him she'd changed her mind. At times he seemed as adult and unapproachable as some of her mother's friends. He seemed like one of the teachers at her school, prim and respectable, wearing a tie and a sports jacket. Was it possible to ride the Shoot-the-Chutes, hollering and shrieking, with your hair blowing all over the place, with someone like that?

As soon as he was away from her, in Powell River, the letters started arriving, three a week, five a week. She wrote back. When she should have been studying Virgil and Homer, and learning off by heart a soliloquy from *Macbeth*, and studying her trigonometry, which she was hopeless at, she was writing long letters to David Greenwood. The letters began as polite little notes and gradually got to be five or six pages long. Practically nothing happened in her life that she didn't report to David in her letters. She just hoped that she sounded sensible and reasonably smart, and that she didn't make too many spelling mistakes. *Love from Arlene. Love from David.* She read and reread David's letters, which she kept in a shoe-box. She contemplated bundling them up with a pink ribbon, as if they were real love letters, but she was afraid Eunice would discover them and tease her, and start quoting lines from them in an exaggerated, mocking tone of voice, something Eunice was quite capable of doing.

David believed in abstract qualities such as truth, honour, fairness. He believed in romance and true love, but only, it seemed, as a preamble to marriage. In January, he came down from Powell River on a Saturday and told her that from the first moment he'd seen her standing beside her friend Iris in the shade of a weeping willow tree at Stanley Park, he had known he wanted to marry her. He couldn't get her out of his mind, he said. He stood with his face turned away, as if his attention was riveted on the dead geraniums in the flower box under the front window. Nothing ever got done around their house, Arlene thought. As soon as David left, she was going to clean up the garden, toss out the old geraniums, rake the leaves off the front lawn, do some weeding. Where had Eunice put the garden rake, she wondered. She and Eunice had to get themselves organised, or everything was going to fall apart around them.

Even at that age, at seventeen, it had seemed to Arlene that her life was made up of fragments. At times she had a frantic feeling that if she could only gather the fragments together, piece them together into a whole, she would immediately have a better understanding of who she was and what she was supposed to do with her life. As it was, she was haunted by a sense that she was incomplete, unfinished, and she didn't know how to rid herself of it. If she had grown up in a proper family, if her father hadn't died when she was so young, perhaps she wouldn't always have been fighting this sense of unease, of disquiet. Was it possible that being married and having children would quell these feelings? She didn't know; frankly, she was too frightened to find out. Even after she'd told David that, yes, she would marry him, and he had given her a diamond engagement ring, she told herself she could change her mind any time she wanted. Even on her wedding morning, when she and Grandfather Myles were standing in a park getting their feet soaked in the wet grass while the limousine sat at the side of the road, she had believed she could still get out of it. She had been ready to fly the coop. What if she had? She pictured herself and Grandfather Myles in one of those two-seater bi-planes. She'd be wearing a leather helmet and goggles over her wedding veil. They would buzz the church, flying low and fast, making one hell of a racket. They would drop some kind of bomb on the church roof. She pictured Eunice on the sidewalk, looking up in amazement, her mouth wide open in shock just seconds before the bomb hit.

Please keep in mind that this bomb is purely a figment of the imagination. Arlene saw those words as if they were a cautionary warning on the wall, similar to a glowing Exit sign at the front of a darkened theatre. She imagined she and Grandfather Myles landed the bi-plane on the lawn in front of the rectory, an impossible feat, but nevertheless they carried it off to perfection. They ran breathlessly to the church and staggered up the aisle, doing a sort of fox-trot in place of the wedding march. Grandfather Myles breathed like a steam engine. Arlene handed her bouquet over to Iris Muir,

her best friend in the world and her Maid of Honour. Iris's
eyes kept misting over with emotion; her cheeks were almost as red as the roses in Arlene's bouquet. In front of the
altar, Arlene bowed her head meekly like a figure in a Medieval painting. She was shaking with suppressed laughter.
Her left hand raised of its own accord, and a wide gold wedding band appeared on her finger. *For better or worse, in sickness and in health. Change the name but not the letter, change
for worse and not for better.* Only that didn't apply to her.
May to Greenwood. They were both kind of pretty names,
she didn't mind which one she had, to be honest. She didn't
care if she didn't have a name at all, if she evaporated and
dissolved in the morning air. People she was evidently related to but had never seen before in her life were wiping
tears of joy from their eyes as she and David walked arm in
arm down the aisle. They were the hitherto undiscovered
descendants of Rose Gamlin and of Daphne Gamlin, men
and women with dull black hair and thick eyebrows, wire-
rimmed eyeglasses and open, honest faces. Where, Arlene
wondered, were the auburn hair, the fine bones, the heart-
shaped faces? Perhaps the Gamlin story was a myth, something Eunice had made up on the spur of the moment. No,
it was real enough: David's father had a keen interest in genealogy; he'd tracked all these missing relatives down in his
spare time, and Eunice had mailed them invitations. Most
of the Gamlin clan, Arlene noticed, were wearing service-
able navy blue; they looked like a convention of friendly
morticians or hardworking selfless members of the Gideon
Bible Society.

June 6, 1950. Her married life began on the anniversary of a famous battle and then progressed as placidly as a pond filled with Bird's Custard left to set at room temperature. At the age of eighteen, it was what she wanted more than anything else. *I do, I do, I do.*

Arlene was in the living room, reading, when the phone rang. At first, she just let it ring. That morning, she had found her copy of *Anna Karenina*, which she'd been looking for all week, under the sofa, against the wall. She'd been retrieving Matt's red India-rubber ball for him when her hand had encountered the corner of the book. "This is what I get for never sweeping under the sofa," she had said to Matt. She had given him the ball, and he had, mercifully, stopped crying. Then she had pulled the book out, brushed the dust from the cover, opened it at random and started to read. She read two pages and became engrossed; she settled down on the sofa and put her feet up. She had already done a load of laundry and hung it out on the clothesline, and she was tired out. Housework exhausted her; sometimes when she was ironing, she felt so tired she thought she had a fatal illness of some kind. She thought she was going to sink to the floor in a heap beside the basket full of towels waiting to be folded up, and her children would find her like that and never get over the shock. All those little pleats and bows on children's clothing. All those pillow slips and tea towels. Not to mention David's shirts, one clean shirt for every single day of the week, like those packages of silk underwear with *Monday, Tuesday, Wednesday,* embroidered on them in red silk.

It was such a relief to read, Arlene thought, just to read and not think about anything else. She knew this whole book practically off by heart; she could read and daydream at the same time. She kept turning the pages and the morning sun poured into the room and she could hear birds singing outside. She began to relax; she was floating in a stage halfway between reading and sleeping. And then the phone rang and rang, and finally she had to put the book down and go into the kitchen to answer it. It was her mother, Eunice, phoning. She wanted Arlene to drive up to Nanaimo to get her.

"Do you know where I am? I'm at the ferry terminal," her mother said. "I wanted to surprise you."

"Oh, Mother," Arlene said. "I can't pick you up. I have a million things to do. And we're going out this evening. Can't you take the bus?"

"No," her mother said. "I can't take the bus." She would, she said, walk over to the Eaton's store and wait for Arlene there. "It won't take you that long to get here. I have your birthday present for you."

"It's going to take me at least two hours to get there," she said. "You don't want to wait around that long, do you? I still haven't washed my hair."

"Don't bother with your hair," she said. "I'll help you with it later. Just come and get me." She said she'd buy a magazine and read it while she had a cup of coffee at Lindsay's lunch counter, and then she'd go to Eaton's. It was a beautiful day; she'd just putter around. Don't be too long, she said; she was dying to see the babies. She always called Matt and Catherine the babies, as if they were newborn twins Arlene had found in a basket on the front steps. Catherine's not a baby anymore, Arlene always said, She's starting school in September; she's a great big girl.

But I can't pick you up, Arlene said silently after she had hung up the telephone. I have to get ready for a party. And the kids are still in their pyjamas. I haven't even washed the breakfast dishes. If I don't do another load of laundry, there won't be any clean diapers by this evening. She should have lied and told her mother David had taken the car to work. Arlene wished her mother would stay in Vancouver and look after her dress store, but it was the dress store, her mother claimed, that gave her the freedom to do whatever she pleased. Five years ago, Eunice and two other women who were friends of hers had bought a dress store. All three of the women were widows. Their store was called Natalie's Dress Shoppe, but among themselves they referred to it as The Widow's Weeds. There had never been a real Natalie; it was just a name they'd picked out one afternoon when they were all smashed on cocktails. Their names were Eunice, Olive and Rosemary. All three of them wore what they called basic black dresses to work, with pearls and measuring tapes, and the cords on their reading glasses twined together in a big mess on their bosoms. As far as Arlene could see, they spent more time gossiping among themselves and with their customers than they ever spent running the shop. And one of them was always off on a jaunt of some kind. Trips to Europe, holidays in Hawaii or Palm Springs, California, week-ends at the homes of their married children. *I just have to see those babies*, Eunice had undoubtedly said, removing her measuring tape and rolling it up neatly before she put it away in a drawer. Maybe she even took one of those little pincushion things off her wrist and plunged a straight pin into it before putting it away. *I just have to visit my married daughter and my two precious grandchildren.*

Arlene said to Catherine and Matt, "Guess who's coming to visit us? Nana. She just got off the ferry from Vancouver. We have to go pick her up. We have to be all dressed and ready to go in fifteen minutes. Do you think we can manage to do it? Catherine, do you want to go upstairs and pick out something to wear?" Arlene could tell she was talking to herself. Matt was drooling and cooing to his India rubber ball. Catherine was lying on the floor with her hands folded on her chest, staring up at the ceiling. Neither one of them said a word. Arlene didn't know where to start. "Well, you two look like a couple of prize dopes," she said. She should run a bath and plunk both of them in it. And she would, in a minute. First she had to lie down on the sofa and read two more pages. Just two more pages. And after that she'd definitely get herself and the kids ready to go. She loved this part of the book: Vronsky twirling the ends of his moustache. Being Vronsky, of course, he looked as if he'd just stepped out of a bath; his eyes "gleamed still more brightly." That made him sound devious and vain. Poor Vronsky; he wanted to be a demon-lover; he wanted to be irresistible, and yet he was simply the most ordinary man, absolutely fallible. That was his fate; his punishment. As far as she could tell, even the pleasure he felt in listening to music, waltzes and polkas and military choirs, had to be sort of appended to his soul, like a tail to a paper donkey. There were times when Arlene quite frankly preferred Karenin to Vronsky. The thing was: Could any woman, in real life, ever have fallen in love with either one of them? Arlene's secret fear was that David was another Karenin. She didn't think so; that was just nonsense. David was the kindest, warmest man alive; he was nothing like Karenin, who was cold as ice, and stern and proper. But honourable, like David.

Arlene put her book down on her chest and looked at her watch. What time had her mother phoned? She couldn't remember. She skipped ahead in the book; she arrived at a snow storm at a railway station. She pictured Eunice waiting not in front of the Eaton's store in Nanaimo, but at the St. Petersburg train station, wrapped in fur, her nose and eyelashes frozen white, a nineteenth-century carpet bag, stiff and brittle with cold, dumped at her feet. Anna and Vronsky were off in a corner turning their shining faces toward each other, each mistakenly thinking the other an extraordinary, unearthly vision of beauty, strength, individuality. Love, perfect love, Arlene thought, dropping the book to the floor and getting off the sofa. How could she lie here reading like this when her mother was relying on her to pick her up? How could she be so irresponsible?

She threw some clothes on, and bathed the kids, dressed them in clean clothes, laced up their shoes and found them each a toy to take along—a rubber cow that mooed when squeezed for Matt, a baby doll in a bunting suit for Catherine—and got them into the car. She backed out of the driveway and headed for the highway. Every now and then she glanced in the rearview mirror and observed the town of Cayley disappearing, slowly replaced by forests of maple, alder, fir. It was as if the quiet streets and the old-fashioned houses and the smattering of small shops hadn't yet come into existence, and this was all just forest, just beautiful wild land. She and the children were the only inhabitants; they were wild themselves, untamed, half-enchanted beings. She glanced over her shoulder at Matt and Catherine, both of them sitting in the back seat, good as gold. The wind was blowing in Arlene's open window and gently stirring their curly hair. A feeling of pure happiness took possession of her. She wanted to keep driving until she'd circumnavigated the globe, scrutinised every desert, every riverbank and meadow in existence. Matt and Catherine would learn to speak ten or twelve languages; they'd get to know Eskimos and Dahoumey warriors and Laplanders wearing those little needlework caps, and they would be the wisest and most silent children, utterly devoted to Arlene and their splendid unending voyage.

Then she saw Catherine kneeling on the back seat, trying to roll down the window, and she said, "Leave the window alone, Catherine." It didn't matter how hot it was, you couldn't have the car windows open with a baby roaming around in the back seat. Not when you were doing sixty miles an hour on a highway. Then she thought about how all the windows in Myrtle's car had been rolled nearly all the way up. It had been a hot day, just like today, and she'd been driving slowly through a small town. And her kids had been past the age where they were likely to climb out of a moving car. It didn't make any sense. If the windows had been down, perhaps the children wouldn't have drowned. She had to stop thinking about this. It made her feel light-headed. She was holding onto the steering wheel so tightly her knuckles were white. She had the feeling the car was going to fly off the highway and hit a tree or something. When she reached Nanaimo, she was relieved to be able to slow down. She pulled into a no-parking zone outside Eaton's and there was her mother, dressed for a garden party in a powder-blue duster over a polka-dotted dress, a suitcase in one gloved hand and a giant shopping bag in the other. Arlene was always surprised when she first saw her mother after an absence: she was younger than Arlene remembered, and smaller, and prettier. Eunice came over to the car and put everything down on the sidewalk and embraced Arlene, who had got out of the car. "Arlene, I was worried sick," she said. "I thought something awful must have happened to you." Arlene started to apologise, but Eunice straightened up and said, "Oh, it's all right, I kept myself amused. It wasn't so bad." They went around to the back of the car, and Arlene opened the trunk and put her mother's suitcase and bags inside. Her mother was waving at Catherine, who had climbed into the rear window and had smushed her face against the glass.

In the car, on the way home, Eunice kept turning around and telling Catherine and Matt that when they got home, she was going to make them cupcakes with blue icing and they could have a party. They could play musical chairs. Eunice had a television set at home in Vancouver, and she told Arlene they had to hurry up and get one, too. They were missing out on the June Taylor dancers and all kinds of things. Eunice told Catherine that the June Taylor dancers did their dance routines in unison, waving their arms and kicking their legs as high as they could all at the same time, so that from a distance they looked like huge flowers with their petals unfolding in the sun. Arlene glanced in the rearview mirror and saw Catherine listening with her mouth open, a bright fixed stare on her face, as if she were in some kind of a trance. Eunice never stopped talking; Arlene could feel her head starting to hurt already. She would have to take an Alka Seltzer before she could go to that damned party at the Glasses' house. She would rather keep quiet than talk any day; if she ever had to take a vow of silence, she would consider it a privilege. Where did Eunice get her energy from? More to the point, why did she think every little thought she had was important enough to broadcast to the world? As soon as Arlene pulled into the driveway and turned the engine off, she started. "Is that your garbage can smelling like that?" she said as she clicked up the walk to the back door in her high heeled shoes. "I guess it is," Arlene said, wearily. Her blouse was sticking to her back with perspiration. It was blazing hot at the back of the house; the petunias Arlene had planted along the back wall of the house, which she never remembered to water, were as bedraggled and limp as old used-up facial tissue, and of course Eunice had to stop and say she'd get the garden hose and water them as soon as she'd changed out of her good clothes.

When they got inside the house with all of Eunice's suitcases and shopping bags, it was so hot Arlene immediately started opening all the windows. Eunice, cool and calm in her duster and pearls, the pleats in her polka-dotted skirt still knife-sharp, sat at the table and rummaged through her shopping bag, bringing out presents for the kids: a wind-mill for Matt, a set of doll clothes for Catherine, a shirt for Matt, a set of barrettes for Catherine. Arlene made a pot of tea and put it on the table with milk and sugar and poured a cup for Eunice. She made peanut butter and blackberry jam sandwiches for Catherine and Matt. Eunice told Arlene to hurry up; she had to sit down and open her birthday present. And then when Arlene did sit down at last with a cup of tea, Eunice kept the present—obviously a dress box from Natalie's Dress Shoppe, wrapped in dark blue paper, tied up with pink ribbon—on her lap, and said to Arlene what did she think, she had a message for her from her old school chum, Iris Muir. It seemed that Iris and Gordon Shaw were engaged to be married—at last, after all this time. Arlene said, "Oh, that's nice." She licked peanut butter off her fin-ger and wondered why she felt such a sharp pang of envy.

Iris was a registered nurse, Eunice said, the head of an entire surgical ward, but she was going to quit work after the wedding. Gordon was some kind of engineer; he worked all over the world. Arlene got the message: Gordon and Iris would live in exotic hot places, in those low bungalows with shutters on all the windows and servants to chase the flies out and peel the potatoes for supper.

"Iris is going to send you a letter," Eunice said. "She told me to be sure to say hello, and to tell you that she'll write. I met her one morning outside St. Paul's Hospital. She was wearing her cloak and her nurse's cap. I told her being a nurse suited her. I don't know why you didn't go into nurs-ing, Arlene. You were always prettier than Iris Muir. You were in too much of a hurry to get married, I suppose, just like me."

"I suppose," Arlene said, counting to one hundred in her head. She left Matt and Catherine with her mother in the kitchen and went upstairs and filled the tub with lukewarm water and immersed herself, ducking her head, letting the water cover her face for a moment. Then she propped her head up on the edge of the bathtub and held her legs up one at a time as if she were one of the June Taylor dancers. For a long time she lay still, and stared up at the ceiling. Finally, she climbed out of the bath and dried herself off. She dressed as far as her underwear and put on her house-coat and sat in front of the mirror, combing her hair into sections and winding it into pin curls. She knew she was going to look a sight; her hair would never be dry by six o'clock, but she kept at it, methodically winding and pin-ning. In the mirror, her head was getting smaller and flatter. Iris Muir's round face with its wide calm mouth and round innocent hazel eyes floated up out of nowhere and displaced Arlene's image in the mirror. She was about ten years old again, wearing a plaid dress with a little white collar edged in lace.

I am the repository of your deepest secrets, Iris said softly, quoting herself from the past, from that day in September Arlene thought she had forgotten but obviously had not. *My lips are sealed*, Iris promised from inside the mirror, drawing her finger emphatically across her lips, zipping them shut.

Arlene put her elbows on her dressing table and leaned her chin on her hand. She felt terribly sad. She had told Iris all about Duff, Eunice's horrible boyfriend. Duff, with the little bristly pig-whiskery moustache and piggy eyes the colour of gravel. Not even Eunice knew that Duff had pestered Arlene in a perfectly disgusting fashion when she was just a schoolgirl, fifteen, sixteen years ago. Not even David knew, because Arlene had never told him and she never would. Iris Muir was the only one who knew because she and Arlene had held hands over a ditch full of rain water the year they were in fourth grade, and they had taken a solemn vow to tell each other all their secrets. Their secrets entered each other's souls like breath condensing on winter air; then the two of them went around, chilled and sober, doing their schoolwork and playing hopscotch and never, ever telling.

Arlene sat up straight and started to rub cold cream slowly into her face and neck. She was glad Iris was finally going to marry Gordon. Good for Iris. It was strange that every single life was completely different. No one knew what was going to happen between the time they were born and the day they died. No one had an inkling. Each fresh day had the promise in it of nothing but uncertainty, of some unexpected moment of joy or anguish that would have to be lived through. How was anyone supposed to draw comfort from that?

Catherine came into the bedroom. She ran to Arlene's side and then stopped dead, staring with interest at the pin curls on Arlene's head. Arlene could see this brief, assessing look cross Catherine's face. *I'll never in a million years do that to my hair*, the look seemed to say. Catherine told her that she and Matt and Nana were making blue icing for the cupcakes. Except that Catherine called them cakes; she had a habit of shortening words, as if it was her desire to refuse everything its true worth. Or, perhaps, thought Arlene, it was just evidence of that *differentness* that afflicted—or blessed?—everyone. A child had a harder time concealing it than adults did, that was all. She grabbed hold of Catherine and pulled her onto her lap and kissed the nape of her neck. Catherine was warm and solid and her skin smelled of cake batter and icing sugar; she was just packed with unspent energy, and secrets, her own little harmless secrets, Arlene supposed, her hoarded treasures, like that terrible little perfume vial. And she was real. She was absolutely real. Arlene tried to hang on to her, even though she was wriggling and squirming and demanding to be put down. Arlene just wanted to hold her, to hold on to the sweetness and *goodness* of her, the sanctity of her being. It seemed to Arlene that it ought to be possible to start your own life over again in your children, and in this way to make a better, stronger, truer life for yourself, and then go on from there, never missing a beat or taking a false step.

Chapter Ten

From the shelter of a hydrangea bush, at the side of the Glasses' house, Arlene had a clear view of the garden party, and of the garden itself: the flower beds and shrubs and the green lawn, which sloped gently down toward the cliff. Beyond was the pale, tranquil, silver-blue sea, the same colour, nearly, as the distant mountains on the coast. Twenty or more people were standing around the garden with drinks in their hands. They were dressed in summer pastels and crisp whites, and they were, all at once and without any hesitation, being social and convivial and *strange*. Which was to say, strange to Arlene, who had never seen any of them before. Except for Howard Glass, who was at the barbecue pit wearing a tall white chef's hat and a long white apron. It looked like the ideal summer party: sedate, urbane, admirable; perfectly put together.

Arlene felt as if she stood at the threshold of a great room. Everyone in the room was having a good time, and she was excluded. That was the feeling she had, and it was pure nonsense. She was standing next to the house, a big, handsome brown cedar shingle house, two-and-a-half stories, with massive stone chimneys and white trim around the doors and windows. A damp, earthy, ancient, not unpleasant smell came to her from the house's stone foundations, or possibly from the broad-leafed creeping plants that grew profusely in the soil around the house. Beside the hydrangea there was an immense fir tree, its trunk obscured by ivy, its heavy dark branches framing the scene below and casting one side of the garden into shadow. For a moment she felt as if she existed in the present and the scene before her was taking place in the past. The men and women were shadows moving slowly in the deeper shadows of the trees. If Arlene wanted, she could walk away right now and no one would know that she had been here. She could walk home and make herself a cheese sandwich and eat it in the living room, alone, while her mother read the children their bedtime story.

She moved onto the footpath, and at the same moment she heard a door opening somewhere overhead, and then a small dog erupted from the house and ran across the verandah, and leapt at the railing, barking furiously. A little girl with long fair hair ran up to the dog and crouched down beside it. In spite of the fact that she was a very small, thin child, she grabbed the dog's muzzle with uncompromising swiftness and screamed in the dog's ear, "Ethel, shut up."

The little girl then stared rather haughtily down at Arlene. A young woman was standing beside the little girl. She was wearing a shapeless rose-coloured cotton shift. Her hair, which looked to have been quickly sheared with no thought given to style, hung limply on either side of a pale, impassive face.

The dog's barking had alerted everyone to Arlene's presence. Like the little girl, the people in the garden stared openly, and some began walking up the path toward her. Arlene wanted to shrink back into the shadows of the tree, but she remained where she was, smiling tentatively, her handbag over her arm, hands clasped primly in front of her, her feet in her ridiculous white pumps neatly together. A perfect lady. She hadn't done a thing wrong, had she? She was an invited guest. She was supposed to be here, looking like an idiot, a specimen on display. David had dropped her off and had gone back home to get the bottle of wine Arlene had left on the kitchen table. Arlene wished she'd gone with him. She wished he were here now, to deflect this curiosity.

A woman came toward Arlene, at the same time calling to the girl in the pink dress, "Put Ethel in the laundry room, would you, Hazel, and shut the door. Give her a dog biscuit." As soon as the woman spoke, there was silence. There was instant order. Even the dog shut up. Arlene saw Hazel pick up the dog, then take the little girl by the hand and lead her into the house. A door slammed shut.

"Hazel is supposed to be keeping Abigail and Ethel occupied," the woman said. She placed her hand on Arlene's arm, and said. "To tell you the truth, I don't know which is worse, the dog or my little girl. Ethel is the dog. My daughter is Abigail. They should both be on a leash. You're Arlene, aren't you? I've been looking forward to meeting you. I'm Julia, Howard's wife. You and Howard have met, haven't you? Howard thinks the world of David. Where is David? I haven't seen him all evening. Let me get you a drink, Arlene, then I'll introduce you to everyone. Our guests are much more congenial than our dog and our child, I assure you." She touched Arlene's arm lightly for emphasis. "At least," she said, "I think I can safely promise that no one's likely to bite."

Julia Glass was tall, with a smooth brow and a prominent, nicely shaped jaw. In a way, although she was very elegant in appearance and seemed terribly efficient and organised, she reminded Arlene of those little jointed wooden puppets. Every gesture was deliberate, emphatic, and yet jerky, and seemed, Arlene thought, slightly overdone, or forced. After watching her for a while, Arlene found herself imitating her. She couldn't move her hand in a normal manner; she had to sort of inscribe the movement on the air, the way Julia did. It made her feel like a school teacher. But then, Julia was a school teacher. Wasn't that what David had told her? A teacher of home economics? She was wearing a green dress with a full skirt and a round neck. Julia's skin was brown, like pale wood. Her eyes were narrow, blue, intelligent. Her hair was smooth and blonde, upswept in a chignon. Her hands were large, firm, cool. She took hold of Arlene as if Arlene were a rag doll, which indeed was what she felt like, and manoeuvred her toward a crowd of women. "Everyone wants to meet you," she whispered in Arlene's ear. "But don't worry, they're all very nice. You're going to like them. Wait, you don't have a drink. What can I get you to drink? A cocktail?"

"Oh, that would be nice, please," Arlene said. She watched as Julia walked across the lawn, threading her way through little groups of people. Then Hazel appeared again on the verandah, this time minus Abigail and the dog. Hazel leaned over the railing, holding her mop of hair back with her hands, and said something to Julia, and Julia went halfway up the steps, and she and Hazel spoke together.

Arlene opened her purse and took out her cigarette case and lighter. A man broke off a conversation he was having with another man, and came over and said, "Allow me." He lit her cigarette and then lit one for himself. Arlene inhaled deeply and at once felt better. She smiled at the man, who introduced himself to her as George. He had freckles on his nose and fleshy protruding ear lobes and a prim-looking mouth. He began to say inconsequential things about the party, and how it wasn't often there was such a "social event"—he minced the words, trying, Arlene thought, to sound ironic, or cynical or something—in Cayley. Almost the entire population was here, he said, everyone who was anybody. "Don't let this shindig fool you," he went on. "Normally nothing happens here." He gave her a look, and said, "Well, I guess you might not agree with me." His wife had to get away every so often, he told Arlene. She was in Vancouver at the moment, staying in a hotel and shopping and going to the movies.

"Oh, I'm used to small towns," Arlene said. "This isn't the first small town I've lived in."

"Well, you don't look like a small-town girl," he said. "I mean that as a compliment, of course."

"My mother lives in Vancouver," Arlene said. "We get over to visit her fairly often." She stood with her cigarette in her hand, trying to balance herself on her high heels. In the warm yellow light of the evening sun George's freckles stood out like a swarm of fruit flies. And then Julia arrived and handed Arlene a drink.

"Sorry I took so long, Arlene," she said. "Now, have you two been introduced? Arlene Greenwood, meet George Wagner."

George said, "We've met, more or less." He smiled primly.

Arlene transferred her cigarette to her left hand without spilling her drink, and she and George shook hands, which seemed awkward, considering that they'd already been talking for ages. "Well, George," Julia said. "It never fails. Hazel just told me there's a call for you on the phone."

George Wagner dropped his cigarette on the grass and trod on it with the toe of his well-polished oxford and said to Arlene, "Please excuse me. Lovely party, Julia."

"Oh, but you'll be back, won't you?" Julia said.

"I hope so," he called over his shoulder.

"The hospital called," Julia said. "We have two doctors in Cayley, and George is one of them." She bent down and picked up the cigarette butt George Wagner had discarded and threw it beneath a tree at the edge of the lawn. "Now, Arlene," she said, "let me introduce you around."

Arlene then met a number of women. How many children did she have, they wanted to know. What were their ages? They volunteered information about their husbands and their children. The husbands worked at the mill, or ran a business of some kind; the children went to school, or were too young for school and stayed at home with their mothers. It was so nice, they said, to see a young family with children in the old Rutledge house. The Rutledge House,

Arlene wanted to ask, what was that? It was a name she had never heard before. Everyone smiled encouragingly. Arlene knew they were assessing her. Well, of course they would be. She looked around, wishing she knew what to do with her cigarette. One of the woman was named Betty, and one was Louise, another was Sharon, or was it Cheryl? And there was a Grace, somewhere in the crowd, and a Vera. There was a Dorothy, as well, who was expecting a baby practically any minute. How would she ever remember these people, or manage to put the correct name to the correct face. She saw the way Julia glanced at these same women, her friends, presumably. Even when she was smiling, her blue eyes remained cool. Did Julia like these women? Was she close friends with any of them? Arlene wished she was like Julia: self-assured, articulate, breezy. She kept looking at Julia, admiring everything about her, her assurance, her laugh, the way she stood, even those sudden emphatic gestures. Arlene tried to maintain a similar posture, especially when a couple of the women took her hands and asked her, in very compassionate tones, how she was, if she was fine, completely recovered, if she'd got over that unfortunate incident. Arlene knew at once they were referring to the accident at the beach, her failed moment as a heroine, and that they were dying to know the details, every little thing she'd seen. She wriggled her hands out of their grasp and smiled like mad and said, Oh, she was *fine*, just fine.

Arlene was also introduced to an odd little woman with big, bright blue eyes in a small, child-like face. She took Arlene's hand avidly in hers, which was as cold and tough as a claw, and hung on tight. Arlene, uncertain what to say, stared, without meaning to, at the woman's teeth, which were smeared with crimson lipstick. Julia introduced her to Arlene as Miss Caroline Bluett. She was an English teacher at the high school, and she had just got back from a summer in England.

"I've been teaching for so long I had God in my senior English class just a couple of years before the flood," she told Arlene. Then she squeezed her eyes shut in a sort of coy wink and opened them wide again. Arlene took a quick step back and her high heels sank into the grass. She said, "Oh, excuse me." In desperation she dropped her cigarette on the lawn before it burned her fingers.

"Oh, don't listen to Caroline," Julia said. "Your students are devoted to you, aren't they, Caroline?"

"They despise me," Caroline Bluett said. "They despise me. I don't care. I always tell them I'm not in a popularity contest." She fiddled with a chiffon scarf at her neck, and said, "Arlene, you must come and have tea with me one afternoon soon. You can both come. You and Julia." She leaned toward Arlene. "I'll tell you a secret, dear," she said.

"A secret?" said Arlene.

"Yes," said Caroline. She beamed. "I've moved the old occupants out of your house and I've moved you in," she said. "You and your family. I've got everything just the way it ought to be. Wait until you see!"

Howard Glass placed a steak on a flowered china plate and handed it to Arlene. Would she like barbecue sauce on the steak? he wanted to know. "Oh, no, thank you," she said. She looked at the steak, wondering how she was ever going to eat it. Howard got her to pick out a baked potato from the grill, and then transported it to her plate with a pair of tongs. He directed her toward a long table, constructed of sheets of plywood on trestles, with white linen tablecloths spread over them. On the table there were salads, jars of mustard and relish, more baked potatoes in foil, bowls of sour cream, butter, salt, pepper, oil-and-vinegar dressing, vases of summer flowers. Marigolds, roses, daisies, huge chrysanthemums, in little round glass vases. Paper napkins. A fat wasp droned in amongst everything. Julia waved it away. She made Arlene sit in a chair, with a napkin spread on her knee and her plate on the napkin.

"Aren't they a nuisance," said Mary. Mary was David's secretary. She sat down beside Arlene and began to eat her potato salad. "The wasps, I mean. I hate them more than anything. There was a wasp nest under the eaves outside the office window, and I was terrified one of them was going to get in and sting me. Mr. Greenwood got someone to come and spray it with poison."

Arlene said, "Mary, could you tell me the time?" and Mary transferred her plate to her right hand and looked at her wristwatch and said it was eight-thirty, nearly eight-thirty-five.

"Thank you," Arlene said. It was already beginning to get dark. A mosquito must have bitten her on her elbow; it was itching like mad and she had to keep putting her fork and knife down to scratch it. Where *was* David? Where in the hell was he? She was beginning to worry that he had fallen over the edge of the cliff, or had been run over by a car out on the street. But if there had been an accident, surely someone would have told her by now? She kept looking for him, thinking he had to be here, and for some reason she was unable to see him. Perhaps he had had to go back a second time, for something else, his camera, or a sweater. But even so, he should be here by now. Something awful must have happened; she couldn't think of any other explanation. Or maybe he had noticed that the car was almost out of gas and had driven to the B/A station for a fill up. Still, how long would it take to get gas? And was the gas station open at this time of night? Finally, at eight-forty-five, she excused herself to Mary and went over to Howard and asked him if she could possibly borrow their phone. He'd taken off his apron and was standing near the barbecue, drinking whiskey on the rocks.

"My mother's baby-sitting," she explained. "I told her I'd give her a call, to make sure the kids were asleep, and that everything was all right."

"Oh, Arlene, dear girl, you can borrow the phone as long as you promise to return it," Howard said. He smiled at her and took her plate from her and put it on the table. "That's a joke," he said. "An old joke." He called Julia, who broke off a discussion she was having with Miss Bluett, and came over and said, "Yes, of course you can use the phone. You can do anything you like. You're the guest of honour. Come with me," she said, taking Arlene's hand as if she were a child. "I'll show you where the phone is."

The interior of Julia's house was all gloom and stale mottled air. Dark massive furniture. Dark endless floors. Arlene felt as if she'd momentarily lost her sight. Behind a door the dog was yapping and whining, and when Julia opened the door the dog ran out and she bent and picked it up. "Naughty girl," she crooned to the dog, who twisted around in her arms in an effort to lick her face. "Isn't she naughty? What a pest. Do you have a dog?"

"No," Arlene said. "No, we don't have any pets. Tentatively she petted Ethel, a scrawny beige-coloured poodle with close-set black eyes and sharp little fangs.

"I've never had a dog," Arlene said. "Or a cat."

"Never? Not ever? Oh, you should have a pet. Last summer Ethel had a litter of five puppies; they were adorable, you should have seen them. We sold every one of them, which is too bad; you could have had one. They were lovely puppies, weren't they, Ethel? Hazel is upstairs getting Abigail ready for bed. I promised Abigail that once she was in her nightie, she could come downstairs and say goodnight to everyone. There's the telephone," Julia said, pointing at a table at the distant end of the hall. She switched on a dim amber light in a wall sconce beside them. "You go ahead, Arlene. I'll be right outside. Oh, and the powder room is there, if you want it, just past the stairs."

"Thank you," Arlene said. She walked down the hall, passing what seemed to her half a dozen closed doors. Her footsteps echoed alarmingly on the wood floor. Should she have removed her shoes? It was too late now to take them off, she thought. When she reached the telephone table she picked up the receiver, then realised she could see through a wide arched entrance into the living room, which was full of large sofas with flowered chintz slipcovers. There was a piano with a potted fern on top of it, and a coffee table with a stack of books and magazines on one side and a large glass ashtray on the other. The fireplace hearth was black marble. All her life Arlene had been homesick for rooms that looked exactly like this. And look: bookcases stuffed full of books. She would love to open one and sit down on a sofa and read, never mind the party. The operator came on the line and Arlene gave her the number, and then she was talking to her mother, who said, "Oh, Arlene, is that you? I was just making myself a cup of tea. Wait while I take the kettle off the stove." Arlene waited. Then Eunice said, "How's the party, dear? Are you having a good time?"

"Mother, have you seen David?"

"Well, yes, I have. He's on his way right now. He just went out the door."

"He just went out the door? Mother," Arlene said. She put her hand to her head. "What happened? What's wrong?"

"Arlene. Just enjoy the party," Eunice said. "Everything's fine. David will tell you all about it when he gets there. He was going to phone you, but I told him he'd be there in less time than it takes to tell."

"He's already hours late. Are Catherine and Matthew asleep?"

"Well, yes, they are. Fast asleep in their beds."

"Tell me what's wrong. Tell me right now."

"Arlene, I already told you, nothing is wrong. Listen, the stove is still on, I'm dying for a cup of tea. Honestly, I haven't had a moment to myself all evening."

"Is Matthew all right, Mother?"

"He's fast asleep, darling. Children are very resilient. I'm going to say good-bye now, Arlene. I'm going to make my tea. Have a good time. Good-bye."

"Oh, mother," Arlene said. But her mother had hung up.
"Damn," Arlene said. Very resilient. What in the hell did
that mean? She could walk home; it would take her only
about ten minutes, at the most. Whatever had happened, if
anything had happened, and she was sure something had,
it was her mother's fault, absolutely. Her mother wasn't a
responsible person, in Arlene's opinion. Well, she was responsible up to a point. She could manage a little dress store
with last year's fashions hanging on the racks, but that was
about it. Arlene started to walk into the living room, then
she stopped. She stopped at the point where the hardwood
floor ended and a rug began. It was a border, a magic line;
she couldn't go any further. She turned and walked out to
the hall, and there was Hazel with Abigail. Abigail was in a
long flowered nightie. She was such a pale, brittle-looking
child, Arlene thought. She looked as if she were made out of
Plaster of Paris, as if she were a cold marble model of herself. Catherine and Matt had dark hair and eyes, and good
colour in their cheeks; they were bursting with health, thank
heavens; they were handsome children and Abigail looked
as if she needed a tonic.

"Are you all right, Ma'am?" Hazel said.

"That's a good question," Arlene said. "I don't know if I
am or not." She smiled at Abigail. "All ready for bed?" she
said. Abigail gave her a stern look.

"Is there anything I can get for you?" Hazel said.

"No, thank you," Arlene said. She walked down the hall
with Abigail and Hazel. They went out onto the verandah.
Apart from the glow from the porch lights, it was almost
completely dark. There seemed to Arlene to be fewer people

in the garden. Paper napkins were lying around here and there on the grass. Arlene took a cigarette out of her handbag and lit it. She stood at the bottom of the stairs and David appeared at her side, saying, "Arlene, I've been looking everywhere for you," as if she were the one who'd been three hours late for the stupid party. It seemed a long, long time ago that he'd dropped her off on the street outside the Glasses' house. Behind her, on the verandah, Abigail's high thin voice was singing out, or, more exactly, screeching out, "Night-night. Night-night, ladies and gentlemen," and people were calling back, "Good-night, Abigail," and blowing kisses in her direction.

"Precocious little shit," Arlene said.

"Arlene," David said. He had a glass of beer in his hand. "Have you been drinking, sweetheart?"

"No. How are Matt and Catherine?"

"They're fine. They're asleep now."

"I'm going to wake them up to say good night as soon as I get home. I want to make sure they're okay."

"There was a little mishap, actually."

"I knew it. I knew it. What happened?"

"Matt fell and cut his head. It's fine, though. Nothing to worry about." He tipped his head back and took a drink. She could see his throat move as he swallowed, and for a moment she hated him, she hated the way he was teasing her and acting the big shot, the calm, rock-steady know-it-all. "Calm down, Arlene," he said. "It's not so bad. Eunice took the kids for a walk. You know how warm it was in the house, and Matt and Catherine were getting all fidgety and hot and they'd probably eaten too many of those gooey cupcakes Eunice made, and they didn't want to go to bed anyway. So Eunice decided she'd take them to the beach for a while, so they could cool down. But when they got to the hill on Third Street, she made a mistake. She let Matt get out of his stroller, and you know how that little varmint wants to run all the time, and then he fell and cut his head. It was one of those cuts that don't look like much, but it wouldn't stop bleeding. Luckily, I drove past just then on my way home for the wine. Remember the wine? I left it at home, after all. That's all right. No one's going to miss a bottle of wine. Anyway, it was a lucky thing I went back, because I was able to drive everyone home, and Eunice and I put cold compresses on Matt's head, and then we decided he needed to see a doctor, so we went to the hospital, and the doctor stitched up the cut. And that's all, really."

While she was drinking cocktails and being introduced to a bunch of crazy strangers, Arlene thought, her baby had been getting rushed to a hospital emergency room. "I'm going home," she said. She put her hand on the stair railing for a moment to steady herself. "How many stitches?" she said.

"Two. Nothing, really. He has a bit of bump, that's all. You even know the doctor. Dr. Wagner. He said he was talking to you when he got called to the hospital. Wasn't that a coincidence?

"Is he going to have a scar?"

"A scar? Dr. Wagner? I don't think so."

"David, that's not funny. What's wrong with you?"

"Arlene, don't go home. Matt is fine, I promise you. He's sleeping."

"He's probably concussed."

"He's not concussed."

Julia came over and then George Wagner, and Howard, and even funny little Caroline Bluett, who had, for some reason, tucked a russet-coloured marigold into her hair, and they all stood beside David and joined in, saying, "Oh, Arlene, don't go. We're going to have coffee in the house, in the kitchen. We're going to just sit around and talk. Please stay. After all, David just got here. The party's not over yet." Arlene felt furious with all of them. It occurred to her that she could make a scene, a small scene, by wringing her hands and throwing herself at David in anger and beating his chest with her fists. But all the scenes she'd ever staged in her life, she realised, had taken place only in her head. She didn't have the faintest idea how to go about doing something dramatic in front of a crowd of real people. Besides, David was probably right, and Matt was fine. Children did survive quite awful accidents, and this hadn't been an awful accident. Even George Wagner, who was a doctor, and who had seen Matt, was telling her Matt was fine. But could she trust all these people? She looked at them, at their kind, encouraging faces, and thought how impossible it was to know what was really going on in anyone's head. Did it work the other way around? Or did people look at her and immediately know that her mind was full of nothing but doubt and uncertainty, along with a sense of apprehension that never quite went away?

It was a beautiful night, the warm wind laced with the smell of the sea, the stars coming out one by one, the moon hanging over the sea like a party balloon. And she did want to stay and talk to Julia. Lovely Julia with her puppet hands and feet and her gleaming blonde hair, like sculpted wood. Arlene knew she should go home; indeed, she wanted to go home more than she wanted to stay. She didn't know what she wanted. After a while, the party moved indoors, into Julia's enormous kitchen, which had a highly polished black tiled floor and white cupboards with glass doors that showed everything inside—neat stacks of china plates and cups and glasses. Julia made coffee and Arlene helped by taking coffee cups out of a cupboard, and filling sugar bowls from a canister on the counter. But then some of the women she'd met earlier began talking about the feeding schedules they had their babies on, and how old their babies were when they started sleeping through the night, and at what age they'd spoken their first word, or taken a first step. Every word they uttered made Arlene feel more worried about Matt. Was he all right? He'd never been hurt before, except for the times he bumped himself when he was learning to walk, or when she took him for his immunization shots. She spilled a spoonful of sugar on the counter and said, "Oh, damn," and brushed it into her hand and dumped it into the sink, where it melted into a silvery pool. The telephone on the wall behind her rang, and she felt as if an electric shock had passed through her body. She heard Julia saying, "Hello, yes, hello. Who is this?" It was nearly eleven o'clock at night, and Arlene stood there with her hand at her throat, sure it was for her.

Julia was saying, "Well, in my opinion that's not such a good idea. I'd prefer not to have to wake her up. We'd already agreed—," she said, and then she stopped talking and hung up the receiver. Arlene heard her say to Howard, "That was Hazel's uncle. He's decided he wants Hazel to come home."

"Right now, tonight?" Howard said.

"Yes, right now, tonight. I'll have to go and wake her up." Julia excused herself and walked out. Arlene could hear her steps, quick, purposeful, going down the hall and up the stairs.

Howard took his car keys off a pegboard on the wall near the kitchen door. Julia came back into the kitchen and said, "Oh, Howard, you can't drive. You've had an awful lot to drink, haven't you?" Howard pocketed the keys and said he was fine, he could drive with his eyes shut.

Arlene, not knowing what else to do, began handing around cups of coffee. She took around a tray with the sugar and cream on it. Then Julia got her to do the same with slices of dark chocolate layer cake. Caroline Bluett took a plate from her and held it up to the light as if she expected to discover something remarkable about its chemical composition. Then she asked Julia if this was a Devil's Food cake, and Julia said, No, it was a basic never-fail chocolate cake recipe with two eggs, and she'd be pleased to write it out for Caroline if she wanted it. Caroline said, Oh, no, dear, I don't want you going to any extra trouble. Julia said, Oh, it's no trouble. Then she said, Oh, Caroline, can you believe that uncle of Hazel's? It was all arranged. Hazel was going to stay the night and help with the cleaning up in the morning. Hazel was the most reliable girl in the world, she was a sweetheart, Julia said. It was her wretched uncle who did every single thing he could to sabotage Julia's arrangements. Her voice trailed off. "That sounds selfish, doesn't it?" she said. "But you know what I mean. I hate to think of Hazel being ordered around all the time by that man."

That man. The wretched uncle. Arlene didn't know who Julia was talking about. She looked up and there was Hazel with a little battered grey overnight case dangling from her hand. She was a dismal looking girl, Arlene thought. As soon as she saw the crowd in the kitchen, she tried to step back into the shadows in the hall, but Howard had his hand on her elbow and she couldn't move. She had a sweater on over the pink shift she'd been wearing earlier, and her face was shiny and blank-looking, as if she'd rubbed in too much cold cream before getting into bed. Frankly, Arlene didn't know what all the fuss was about. Surely the world wasn't going to come to an end just because a silly girl had to leave the house; surely midnight wasn't all that late.

"All set?" Howard said. Hazel nodded without raising her eyes. As soon as they'd walked out, people began talking. Arlene, her plate of chocolate cake balanced in her hand, heard Julia say that Hazel's uncle seemed to believe they had some sort of corrupting influence on Hazel. Someone else said, "Oh, no, that's not the case. He's just a miserable old tyrant. No one likes him."

"He's an odious man," said one of the women Arlene had met earlier—Louise or Cheryl or possibly Grace. "No girl Hazel's age should be living alone with a man like that, it's not healthy." Grace evidently lived about a mile from Hazel's uncle's place, and Hazel had done some baby-sitting for her, as well. Grace knew her as well as Julia did, or, Arlene understood, perhaps even better. Grace lived out on River

Road, the same road Hazel's uncle lived on. Grace said that she remembered when Hazel first went to live with her uncle, when she was only about seven years old. What had happened to her parents? someone asked. The mother had passed away, hadn't she? Grace said. She had contracted some kind of illness and had passed away after being sick for only a few weeks. It was the saddest thing, and of course the consequences were obvious: poor Hazel, alone and unprovided for. And what had happened to her father? Illness? Accident? He was such a vague figure. No one could remember him; he was probably still around somewhere. Arlene imagined a sad ghostly figure, an amnesiac, wandering the streets of town: Hazel's father. Maybe he would meet up with Myrtle Kriskin and they could commiserate with each other. She had a sudden startling vision of the town of Cayley as being composed of layer upon layer of water and air, a number of isolated, incompatible dimensions co-existing in the same location.

Caroline Bluett, still on the subject of Hazel's uncle, piped up, "Well, the man is her uncle, for goodness sake. And she has to live somewhere."

Grace shook her head and said, "Well, it's not a healthy situation, that's all I'm saying."

"I'm afraid I agree with you, Grace," Julia said. "I'm afraid I completely agree."

"Innuendoes," Caroline Bluett said. "That's all I'm hearing."

Arlene gathered that this uncle, whose name, it seemed, was Clarence Travers, had made Hazel quit school to look after his son, Wayne. The son was—how old now?—ten, eleven? According to Grace, Wayne had inherited his mother's good looks, but he was evidently a hellion.

Arlene tried to assemble in her mind a picture of Clarence, who sounded like an ogre, and Wayne, the "hellion" and the mother who had vanished. What a melodrama! she thought. She thought of Hazel, with her big dull eyes and her hangdog expression, her awkward plodding gait. Well, it was sad, it was all very sad, but she didn't know why it was affecting her so much. She didn't know why it was making her feel depressed. She cut another slice of chocolate cake and put it on a glass plate and looked around for someone to give it to, but it seemed that everyone had been served.

When Howard got back from driving Hazel home, he got a beer out of the fridge and went into the living room and began pounding out popular songs on the piano. People drifted out of the kitchen, gravitating toward the sound of music. Howard played fast and carelessly, his elbows stuck out, and when he took a drink from his glass of beer, he kept one hand on the keyboard, picking out the melody with a finger. Arlene listened for a while and then impulsively sat down on the bench beside him and they played a duet. She tried to keep up with Howard Glass. She tried to count in her head, one, two, three, one, two, three. Their fingers kept brushing together. "Sorry," she said, and he laughed and said, "What are you sorry for?"

The last time Arlene had played a piano duet with anyone had been at school. She and Iris used to stay behind in the music room after class. They had the permission of the music teacher, Mr. Grenville. Arlene and Iris had played simple arrangements of old love songs. Iris, who had been taking private lessons as well as lessons at school, had been a more accomplished pianist than Arlene. She had pretended to be the teacher, telling Arlene to hold her hands poised above the keys as if she were clasping a bubble in the curve of each palm.

"Whatever you do, don't let that bubble pop," Iris had said, repeating for Arlene's benefit the instructions her piano teacher had given her. Iris could stretch an octave plus one note; she had the most flexible hands in the world. She could bend her thumb over the back of her hand. She had a dead-white wart on the index finger of her left hand, which she said she'd got from dissecting frogs in biology class. Arlene was afraid she'd catch the wart when Iris took her hands in hers and made her fingers bend this way and that, prescribing exercises to make them more agile for the piano. For a little while Arlene had practised these exercises faithfully at home, instead of getting down to work on her algebra homework. She had laced her fingers together in front of her face, so that she could peer through the tiny spaces and see a tiny remote Eunice curled in a corner of the sofa with her eyes closed, listening to music playing softly on the radio. Sometimes Eunice smiled little exclusive fleeting smiles, as if the music made her think of something amusing or pleasant; other times she simply let her head drop forward. She slept as soundly as a child, and Arlene would have to wake her up and tell her it was time to get ready for bed.

People were gathering around the piano. They wanted Howard and Arlene to play their favourite songs. David put his hand on Arlene's shoulder and turned the pages of sheet music for her and Howard. She smiled up at him, forgetting that she was still mad at him, and for his benefit she added a couple of little show-off grace notes to the music. Then she and Howard stopped playing the piano because Julia had put a record on the hi fi. A few couples began dancing. Arlene danced a slow dance first with David and then with Howard. She couldn't jitterbug because her dress was too tight. Howard held her close and brushed her neck with his fingertips and sang softly, his breath reeking of beer. *What ever will be, will be,* he sang thickly into her neck. *Que sera, sera. The future's not ours to see.* His hands were sweaty and hot, as if he were a teen-aged boy at a school dance. He wore a ring on his little finger that pressed against the side of her hand. He told her she was a beautiful girl, a lovely girl, his favourite. *Beautiful girl,* he sang, inventing words to the music, directing her around an armchair, leading her closer to the bookshelves, where the light was softer, the room less crowded. "David's a lucky guy," he said. "Having a pretty girl like you for a wife." Arlene waltzed with him in her stocking feet and her brand new pink and white sheath dress from her mother's dress store. For a time she completely forgot about Matt's accident, the injury to his head she hadn't even seen yet; she forgot she wanted to rush home and make sure he was all right. She was perfectly happy, perfectly oblivious, in the unfamiliar circle of Howard's arms. It didn't matter to her that Howard was plastered and probably didn't even remember her name. This was a grownup party and for once in her life she was acting like a grownup woman. Every now and then she and Howard passed in front of the door to the living room and Arlene caught sight of David and Julia. Their faces looked like blank ovals, with round Os where the mouths were supposed to be. They didn't know what to make of her and Howard. At one point, David came over to her and took her arm, saying they really ought to go, it was late and her mother would be getting worried. Eunice? Arlene laughed. Eunice didn't know how to worry, she said; she was constitutionally incapable of worry; she didn't have the brains to worry. Is that your mother you're talking about? Howard asked. You're a case, he said, laughing. Arlene turned her back on David. She felt determined to stay where she was, to stay with Howard, who was very kind and sort of romantic in a noble goofed-up way, and very, very smashed. Once she left Howard for a moment to get herself a glass of wine, and she saw herself reflected in the window, her pink dress clinging to her breasts and hips, her hair falling rather dramatically in her eyes. She thought she looked quite glamorous. She didn't look like herself, but she looked gorgeous. Then she found Howard again and draped one arm around his hot sweaty neck and drank her wine and they danced, standing there, swaying in time to the music.

CHAPTER ELEVEN

Arlene made a list in her head of the things she wasn't going to do today: wash the breakfast dishes, do the laundry, sweep the floor, wash out the empty milk bottles, make apple sauce for dessert with the big box of apples David had gathered up from under the tree. Half of them were bruised beyond redemption, anyway. She was going to sit and let everything fall apart around her. Or else her mother could take care of the laundry and the apples. It was her mother's fault that she was worn out; it was her mother's fault that Matt had a cut on his head that had needed stitches. Apart from the fact that he would have a scar for the rest of his life, he could have contracted some dreadful disease, like blood poisoning or lockjaw. The doctor had given him a booster shot just to be on the safe side. And then what had that same doctor said to Arlene at the party? It was when she and Howard had got up from playing duets on the piano. George Wagner had come over and leaned his elbow on the mantelpiece, his drink in his hand, and he had said, sounding quite sincere, "your mother is a fascinating person, Mrs. Greenwood." His fat ear lobes had positively gleamed. Arlene couldn't imagine what he was talking about. Her mother was a birdbrain. A doctor in the vicinity was an absolute essential when Eunice was around. She was like a walking danger-zone. When Arlene had got home from the party, at about two o'clock in the morning, she'd gone straight into Matt's room and turned on the lamp. When she had looked at him, she had felt faint. He had looked like a young soldier wounded in action, his arms thrown helplessly out, a big wad of gauze bandage taped to his head. She was afraid he was unconscious, in a coma, that when he woke, if he woke, he wouldn't be himself, he wouldn't be funny, sweet, adorable Matt. He was perfectly cool to the touch and his breathing seemed normal. After watching him for some time, her hands curled tight around the crib rail, she decided he really was sleeping comfortably, and she turned off his lamp and tip-toed along the hall to her bedroom. David was already asleep, the sheet neatly folded across his chest, his mouth open, his breath smelling of liquor. She got in beside him and almost at once fell asleep, but then she was woken up by the sound of Catherine crying. It turned out a moth was flying around her bedroom. Catherine thought the moth was a bird; she kept screaming and flailing her arms around. She was kneeling on her bed, her face red and imprinted on one side with a pattern from her pillowcase. "Don't be such a big baby, a moth can't hurt you," Arlene said. Finally, in exasperation, Arlene grabbed her by the arm and hauled her upright and smacked her as hard as she could on the rear end. "Enough," she said, shaking her. She could feel her fingers digging into Catherine's arm, and she let go, she made herself let go, and Catherine collapsed in a heap on the bed, staring up at her, her eyes brimming with tears.

"Honestly," Arlene said, "your little brother is braver than you are." She was too exhausted to be patient. She caught the moth and held it in her hand until she got the screen on the window open. Then she threw it outside and went back to bed without saying another word to Catherine.

Another thing Eunice was responsible for: When Arlene was fifteen years old, she'd almost died from a simple case of appendicitis, because Eunice had insisted on dosing her with Milk of Magnesia. It was the year she and Eunice had moved into a cottage up the coast from Vancouver, and Eunice had got engaged to her boyfriend, Duff. Duff, whose real name was Dougal, used to anchor his big, fancy sailboat in the bay outside their cottage and then spend the fine weather sitting in a wooden deck chair on the grass above the sea, drinking gin and vermouth and puffing on a cigar. Eunice would mix the drinks and get Arlene to take them to him on a little silver tray, as if she were a waiter in a hotel. It was as much Duff's fault as Eunice's that Arlene had nearly died of a ruptured appendix. In fact, it was more his fault.

When Arlene got sick, Duff told her he could cure her bellyache if she'd just co-operate with him by repeating certain words, which he assured her would work like a magic charm. For example, she was supposed to say: "I am stronger than the pain. I feel well. I am healthy and full of strength."

"Go on, say it," he told her, giving her a prod in the arm with his knuckles. He was always finding some reason to touch her. He patted her hands and smoothed her hair and kissed her goodnight, his lips cold on hers. "A pretty girl like you doesn't want to waste time being sick, does she?" he said.

She lay in her bed in the dark, while Eunice and Duff were asleep, supposedly in separate rooms, although Arlene knew better. She repeated to herself, *This is a lie, this is just me thinking the wrong way,* while she burned up with fever and the pain in her stomach got worse and worse. She was afraid to wake her mother up, in case she got into trouble. Her comfort, her only solace, was the pain itself, which took on the shape of another being, concerned, solicitous, eager to lean up close and speak to her in some strange babbling tongue she couldn't comprehend but had to listen to with all her will.

Then Arlene slept all day. In the evening Eunice made her get up. Eunice gave her another dose of Milk of Magnesia and got her to try to eat a bowl of cream of asparagus soup from a can, and outside it was raining and raining and the wind was blowing the trees around. Duff played Solitaire on the coffee table in the living room and smoked cigars and every now and then told Eunice to put some coffee on. Arlene couldn't eat the soup. She was so dizzy that every time she moved her head the room seemed to shimmer as if she were looking at it through a sheet of cellophane. And then, without even knowing she was going to be sick, she threw up on the kitchen table and Eunice stared at her in horror and Duff yelled at her, *Did she think she was living in a goddamned pigsty?*

By the time her mother decided to put her into the back seat of the old Chrysler coupe and drive her to St. Mary's Hospital, which wasn't very far away, Arlene gone off into a hot brightly-coloured dream world of her own. She saw herself lying inside a box, and a magician in a tuxedo was cutting her in half with a saw, sawing and sawing away. When they got to the hospital Eunice ran inside and two nurses came back to the car with her. They helped Arlene up the steps into the hospital, which seemed from the outside not much bigger than a house, but on the inside was all wide shining hallways and doors leading into quiet empty rooms. No one stirred; it was a house of the dead; it was the city morgue, Arlene said, or thought she said, and then she wondered why no one was laughing at her joke. It was the summer of 1947, a mere ten years ago. So much had happened since then. She was an entirely different person from that frightened lonely fifteen-year-old girl who knew she was going to die and disgrace herself and her mother. *There is no sickness, no pain; everything is hunky dory in a world made according to a blueprint, all the stars and all the flowers positioned in some kind of orderly relationship to one another. Concentrate on these facts, and this pain, which is a manifestation of your own negative thinking, will be gone, gone, gone.*

At the hospital the nurses had to tell Eunice that the doctor was on the mission boat, on his way back from a trip up the coast. Because of the storm he was delayed. No one knew when he'd arrive at the hospital; no one knew if it would be that night or three days in the future. So the nurses said. Arlene had a memory of Eunice standing in the door to the room where they had put Arlene to bed in a white hospital gown. Eunice was shouting at the nurse and stamping her foot on the floor, and the nurse raised her hands at one point as if she was about to strangle Eunice. For a moment Arlene had wondered if at long last someone was going to have the nerve to actually do it. Then she must have fallen into a sort of sleep. It was all bleakness and fever, anyway, and a velvety darkness filled with sparks of dull gold light, and the nurse taking her temperature every few minutes and making her keep ice packs on her stomach. At the last possible minute, the mission boat made it to St. Mary's Cove. Arlene was saved. After the operation, she got to stay in her hospital bed for two weeks, receiving a course of sulpha drugs to cure the infection she still had in her blood. Her meals, mostly scrambled eggs and mashed potatoes, were brought to her on a tray. The sun shone brilliantly on the water below her hospital window. The hospital occupied the loneliest, smallest plot of ground imaginable, on the shore of a cove with rocks and arbutus trees rising above the water. She watched a blue heron standing motionless as a statue for hours, waiting to catch a fish. At night she slept without dreaming. She would have liked to have stayed there; the nurses could have given her a job in the kitchen, peeling potatoes or something. But one day Eunice and Duff came for her. Eunice brought her some clothes to wear home. Duff brought her a present, quite a nice present, a Kodak Brownie camera of her own. He took the camera out of the box it came in, and snapped her picture standing in front of the hospital's main entrance, and then she got in the back of the car, and Duff drove her and her mother back to the cottage.

She'd been thinking about that time ever since last night, when she was in the Glasses' kitchen, passing around slices of chocolate cake. Everyone had been talking about poor Hazel and her awful uncle and Arlene had started to remember Duff. Didn't the mind make some strange connections? She had started to remember the summer she'd turned fifteen, and she and Eunice had lived at St. Mary's Cove.

What became of the photograph? She didn't know. She didn't care. Well, yes she did; she wished she could see it right now. She'd like to compare the fifteen-year-old she'd been to the person she was now. She had a vague idea of how she'd looked in the photograph: thin and pale, a convalescent squinting uncertainly in the sun, utterly compliant, not a negative thought anywhere in her head. For about a year afterwards, she'd dreamed of becoming a nurse, a starched white veil covering her hair, a round watch with a second hand pinned to her apron. And now it was Iris Muir who was the nurse, and Arlene was a married women with two children. And she was sitting on a chair on her patio, holding a hand over her eyes to shade them from the sun, because she had a headache, a hangover, and she was tired out. She was trying to drink a cup of coffee, but it tasted to her as if the cream was sour, and the coffee was too cold now, anyway. And here was her family descending on her, Matt with his poor little head covered in bandages, and Catherine with her hair in tangles around her face and blackberry jam on her chin, and David, who lowered himself gingerly into the chair beside her.

"How's the party girl?" he said. He had showered, and was dressed in slacks and a short-sleeved shirt, his damp hair neatly combed, his eyes shadowed and swollen-looking, skin thin and white as tissue paper.

"I'll survive," Arlene said, looking away. "And I'm not a party girl." They'd already been through this, earlier, in their bedroom. "It's true I wanted you to like Julia and Howard," David had said to her. "But I didn't expect you to throw yourself into Howard's arms." They'd been in bed, lying side by side, and Arlene had thrown the covers back and got out and turned to look at him. "I didn't throw myself at him," she had said. "How dare you? You were the one who made me stay when I wanted to come home. You know I didn't want to go to the stupid party. I hate parties. Go and make friends with Julia, you said, have fun for a change. Well, I didn't have fun, if you must know. I danced with your boss. I was polite to Julia. I did the best I could. You don't have to yell at me." Then, he'd apologized. He'd reached across and grabbed hold of the hem of her nightie, and he'd pulled her down beside him, and she'd pretended to lie there as unyielding as a china doll, until he'd said he was sorry, his lips close to her ear, the warmth of his breath on her skin. "Forgiven?" he'd said, pushing the neck of her nightdress down and kissing her bare shoulder, her neck. "Am I forgiven?"

"I was up with Catherine in the night," she said, now, accusingly. "I had no sooner fallen asleep than I had to get up again. She was having a fit over a moth flying around her room."

"I wasn't," Catherine said. She glared at Arlene and let her baby doll slip out of her grasp to the ground. It hit with enough impact to activate its voice box, which gave out a little mewling sound. Arlene said, more sharply than she had intended, "Pick up your doll, Catherine. You know better than to treat your toys like that."

"Don't be so critical of the child," Eunice said. "She's just a little girl, Arlene." She stood in the open doorway, wiping her hands on a tea towel.

"I'm her mother, aren't I?" Arlene said. Who was Eunice to criticize? The way Eunice worked, the very people she was supposed to look out for were the ones she let down, time and time again.

"How old is this house?" Eunice wanted to know.

"I haven't got the faintest idea," Arlene said. "David, how old is the house?"

"Oh, Lord," David said. He shut his eyes and leaned his head back. He brushed his fingers across his forehead.

"This house," said David, "was built in 1907. That would make it, what, fifty years old?"

"I would have thought it was older than that," Eunice said.

"The old Rutledge place," Arlene said.

"Who are the Rutledges?" Eunice said.

"I don't know," Arlene said. "Who are the Rutledges? That's the question of the hour, it seems. Last night at the party someone said to me, Oh, you're living in the old Rutledge place. It was Miss Bluett, I think. I met so many people last night, I can't remember who said what. Did you meet Miss Caroline Bluett, David?"

"Miss Caroline Bluett, whose father used to have high tea on a regular basis with the poet laureate of England, Alfred, Lord Tennyson?"

"Who told you that?"

"Miss Caroline Bluett did. She told me that her father used to go to the Isle of Wight during the summer so that he could be near Tennyson. She didn't actually say he had high tea at Tennyson's home, admittedly, but that was the impression I got."

"Oh, well, maybe it was true." Arlene said absently. She was trying to remember what it was Caroline Bluett had said to her last night. She had said that she'd got the old Rutledge house all ready for Arlene, then she'd moved her in. No. Someone else had mentioned the Rutledge house. Miss Caroline Bluett had simply said, I've moved the old occupants out of your house, and I've moved you in. But what was that supposed to mean? Arlene must have heard her wrong. Or else it was just Miss Bluett, just the way she went on, saying strange things for effect.

Eunice was interested in the age of the house because she thought David and Arlene should consider renovating. Or restoring. The original beauty of the house had been covered up, over the years, Eunice said. Had they examined the plaster around the fireplace? Eunice thought it might be hiding a more interesting surface, like ornate stonework, or even marble. And what if the ceiling in the living room was a false ceiling? It was worth a look, she said. She had a friend in Vancouver who'd bought a house in Shaughnessy that turned out to have been built for a railroad baron in the early 1890s by a famous architect. By the time this friend of Eunice's had finished restoring it, the house was worth thousands more than she'd paid for it. In Eunice's opinion, David and Arlene should bring in a builder to have a look at this house.

"Oh, I don't know," David said.

"It wouldn't hurt to look, surely," Eunice said.

Arlene got up and followed Matt across the lawn, then waited while he crouched down and began a slow examination of the grass. She raised her hand to shade her eyes. This town was hotter than any place else she'd ever lived in her life. The sky over Cayley seemed smaller than a normal sky; the sun got trapped in it like a hornet in a window. Ever since May, when she and the kids had arrived, it had been hot, except for the storm in July. She was looking at the apple tree, its branches weighed down with apples the colour of straw, the tall fence, the lilac shrubs, the gate with its sturdy iron latch, the very gate through which, a few weeks ago, Myrtle Kriskin had stepped with her sample cosmetics. Eunice knew almost nothing about that whole episode, and Arlene didn't intend to tell her. It made her so angry, sometimes, when she thought about that stupid accident. It had been such a waste of life, such a heart-wrenching waste. Ever since then, she had been waiting for another disaster. A shout, a quick movement, the sound of someone running, and she thought immediately that some catastrophe had occurred. She would tense, her jaw clamped tight. Her hands would begin to shake, her heart would pound. What now? she would think. She had the sense that people were counting on her; she had to respond at once to some emergency taking place outside her line of vision, where she couldn't make out what was going on. Or, even worse, she felt as if she didn't have any business being here. Why was she alive, when others died young, tragically young? What was she supposed to do to prove her worth? Or was it all absolutely random? *The wicked shall flourish as the green bay tree*, her Grandfather Myles used to say to her, quoting from the bible. She wasn't wicked, and she wasn't good. She was like a bath of lukewarm water; she was nothing in particular. She kept a low profile, it seemed to her, trying to avoid the unspeakable, the unbearable. She wasn't unusual in this, was she? It hurt her to think that she was some kind of moral coward, but she didn't know how to undo the banality of her existence, she really didn't.

Impatiently, Arlene pulled off her sweater and held it over her arm. She looked at her son, who was crouched down, pulling at a dandelion.

"What's that, Matty-cakes? Is that a dandelion?" she said, bending over to see what he was doing. He looked up at her, with the sweetest look of confusion on his face, and then he frowned and put his hand to the bandage on his head. "Does it hurt, darling?" she said, bending down beside him. "Oh, look at this nice yellow flower, Matt," she said. She picked the flower and gave it to him, then picked one for herself. He stood up, the flower in his fist; then he toddled back toward the patio, to show his father and his grandmother what he had, his beautiful dandelion. He called it a dandy-lee, which Arlene thought was a very inventive word for a child as young as Matt was. Catherine came running toward him and started shepherding him forward, her hands on his shoulders. "Don't be bossy, Catherine," Arlene said. "Let him get where he's going under his own steam."

"'Break, break, break, / On thy cold gray stones, O Sea!'" Eunice suddenly said.

"Pardon me, Mother?" Arlene said. "What on earth are you talking about?"

"Tennyson. It just came back to me. David was just talking about Tennyson. Isn't it odd the things you have rattling around in your head? Your Grandfather Myles loves Tennyson. He's forever quoting him. Or is that Longfellow?"

"Tennyson," Arlene said. "Everyone knows that poem. Everyone does it at school. I used to know the whole thing off by heart."

"You know, Arlene, you and Miss Bluett have a lot in common," David said.

"She invited me to tea," Arlene said. "Me and Julia Glass."

"Julia Glass and I," said David.

"No, just me and Julia," Arlene said. "She didn't mention you." She sat down beside David, and handed him the dandelion she'd picked. Matt gave his to his grandmother. Eunice held the dandelion and went on talking to Catherine about school. "It's so different nowadays, isn't it?" she was saying. "When I started school, I had a teacher who made us cry. She was a terror. She used to throw chalk at us."

"Oh, Mother," Arlene said. But Eunice couldn't frighten Catherine; she was leaning against her grandmother's knee, staring up at her with a rapt expression on her face, asking, "Did she throw chalk at *you* Nana? Was she mean to you?" It occurred to Arlene, as she watched, that Catherine was very much like her grandmother; it was no wonder they got along together so well, they were two of a kind, sturdy and oblivious; durable.

Eunice said, "Oh, I was a very naughty girl at school. I used to put my hands over my ears so that I couldn't learn a single thing. I didn't want to know how to read or write. It was just an idea I had at the time, that I didn't want other people's thoughts cluttering up my mind. I wanted to be at home with my mother and my Aunt Sarah Stott, who never got married and lived with us. She was my mother's sister. She had a pointed nose and buck teeth, but she had the most beautiful auburn hair, so long she could sit on it. She taught me how to make finger-crochet pot-holders, and she taught me how to read."

Arlene stood in the open door and looked at her mother, her children, her husband in something like disbelief. Who were these people? David had wandered out into the yard. He was pacing up and down, his hands behind his back, a gentleman surveying his estate. He came to the apple tree and pressed his hand to the trunk and looked up into the branches, as if spellbound. Arlene felt as if a certain violence had been done to her spirit. She had been moved too abruptly from the previous night's party, all those strange faces, all that booze, the subterranean atmosphere of the Glasses' vast dark house, and then she'd been plunked down here in this bright Beatrix Potter landscape. Little children lisping at their mother's knee. Butterflies in the flowers, birds singing in the trees. Would summer never end? She felt in the pocket of her housecoat for a cigarette and walked through the kitchen as she lit up, and then she went upstairs and ran a bath and stood watching the water pouring from the tap as she smoked and with her free hand massaged the back of her neck. Then she turned off the taps and went to her closet and stared for an age at her clothes, trying to focus her mind on what she was going to wear.

That weekend they drove over the Malahat to Victoria, Eunice sitting in the back seat with Matt and Catherine. They went to the Poodle Dog Café on Government Street, which was celebrating its eighty-first anniversary with a special Labour Day Dinner: fresh shrimp cocktails to start, followed by roasted Vancouver Island turkey with stuffing, green peas and carrot sticks, and cranberry sauce. Eunice was the only one who didn't care for turkey; instead, she had a grilled dinner steak with champagne sauce and fresh sautéed mushrooms on the side. For dessert David and Eunice had blackberry pie, and Arlene and Catherine had a pineapple sundae, and Matt had a dish of ice cream. Arlene had thought she couldn't eat a bite after the amount she'd had to drink the night before, but she was ravenous. She ate more than anyone, and then she had to undo the top button of her waistband so that she could breathe. After dinner, David and Eunice had a brief argument about who was going to pay the bill. Eunice opened her handbag and started rifling through it, putting her lipstick and comb and hankie in her lap and then replacing them. In the meantime, David had removed a ten- and a two-dollar bill from his wallet, and summoned the waitress. "Well, thank you very much, dear," Eunice said. "This was meant to be my treat, you know. You'll have to let me pay for the gas." Arlene snorted. "What was that supposed to mean?" Eunice said, and Arlene said, "Oh, it's just you, Mother, it's just you."

The waitress, who had bright red kiss curls like inked-in commas all around her face, waggled her fingers at Matt, and said, "What happened to you, little guy?" Eunice jumped up and grabbed Matt out of his highchair before Arlene could get to him. "He just had a little accident," Eunice told the waitress. "He thought he could run before he could walk."

Later, they went to Beacon Hill Park and strolled around the flower beds. This was Eunice's idea: She thought they could exercise off their dinner. David had brought his camera, and Arlene got him to take a picture of her and Eunice and the children standing next to the sundial in the rose garden. He said he wasn't sure if there was enough light left for the picture to turn out, but he took it anyway. He also took a picture of Eunice by herself, sitting in a wooden swing, her ankles neatly crossed and her handbag in her lap. She was wearing a crinoline under her dress, and its ruffled hem showed beneath her full skirt. David took a picture of Arlene standing in front of the duck pond. She smiled for the camera, and tilted her chin up. It was a beautiful evening, a mild breeze ruffling the leaves, the evening sun intensifying the green of the trees, the red and yellow of the roses. Matt and Catherine were running around in little circles on the lawn, and David was running after them, his camera in his hand, pretending he couldn't keep up to them. Then, when he caught them, he put the camera in his sweater pocket and held Matt under one arm and Catherine under the other and turned them around in a circle—Arlene trying to shout at him to put them both down before they got sick—and then they got back in the car. David drove along the Uplands, and they picked out the houses they wanted to move into if they ever became fabulously wealthy. Arlene's choice was a big butter-coloured house that had its own gate house near the road, behind a high fence of stone and black wrought iron. David and the kids could live in the big house, she said, and she'd live by herself in the little house. They could communicate by telephone, or by sending each other letters and cards at Christmas and on birthdays.

"You'd get lonely," Eunice said. "I know you. You'd just wither away from loneliness if you lived on your own."

"I would not," Arlene said. "I like being alone." Matt was asleep in her arms and she tried to adjust his weight without waking him up. His shoe was digging into her leg, and she pulled it off and let it fall to the floor at her feet. To her dismay, she saw that the bandage on his head was slightly stained with blood. What if the bandage got stuck to his stitches? What if they couldn't get it off? If they'd had any sense, they would have kept him quietly at home, instead of taking him on a sightseeing trip to Victoria. She bent and kissed his head. Eunice's voice went on and on, climbing with them into the mountains and then down into twilight and the first star hanging over the mountains and the village of Mill Bay.

Chapter Twelve

After Catherine left for school in the morning, Arlene pushed Matt in his stroller to the library, the post office, the bakery, the grocery store. If necessary, she invented errands for herself: a letter to mail, a book that had to be returned, a few incidental items to be picked up: bread, baking powder, oranges. Sometimes she fell into a sort of a daydream and forgot where she was going, what she was doing, and she kept walking, down Yew Street with its small, neat houses in their tiny fenced yards, around the corner and past the mill, where David was at work, past Sam Wong's Grocery Store, past the side of the hospital, steam billowing out of what must be the laundry room. If it wasn't raining, she stopped at the park and sat on a bench while Matt tried to push his stroller over the grass by himself, his favourite occupation lately. "Oh, you're a strong boy," she told him. "How strong are you?" And he laughed and puffed out his cheeks and wrestled the stroller over the grass, his head swivelled around to make sure she was watching..

When the weather was clear, she could sit on the park bench and see, to the north-east, the snow-covered mountain peaks on the mainland of British Columbia. She had been to Hawaii once, to Ontario as a child, and every summer she and David drove up to the Okanagan to visit his family, and they were planning a trip to Disneyland in the near future. But the truth was, the scene in front of her constituted the geographic extent of her life thus far: Vancouver, the Sunshine Coast up as far as Powell River, the Strait of Georgia, which she'd crossed about a hundred times. *Terra cognito*, so to speak. Her own husband was her putative second cousin once removed: she looked at him and saw a reassuring blend of the known and unknown, the alien territory of the opposite sex made familiar through the medium of a similar bone structure, almost identically shaped ears, nose, eyes and chin. David was the described and named world, operating according to a plan laid down God knows how many generations ago by those dependable Presbyterian Gamlin genes.

And here was Matt, two years, one month old, his stroller abandoned, toddling over to her with an old dead maple leaf crunched in his hand, his dreamy eyes so dark and lustrous they were more brown than blue, more the eyes of George Francis May than of any Gamlin ancestor. She wiped his cold dirty hands on her hankie, then opened the bag from the bakery and gave him an oatmeal cookie, which he began to chew on with complete concentration, examining the cookie minutely before each bite. Little silvery beads of moisture sparkled on his thick auburn hair. She couldn't see the mountains on the coast today. It was a damp, foggy February morning. The sea was reduced to a mere lake, a cold silver-grey, quiescent, like a sheet of hammered-out metal. A gull on a red-and- white buoy some distance from the shore was waiting patiently, just waiting, as if for a horizon line to magically reappear. Anything that had happened here in the past, along this stretch of shoreline, was erased, undone, obliterated. All that was left was peace and a tired-out middle-of-the-winter feel. The damp air seeped into her clothes, her flesh; her wrists and elbows ached from the chill; even so, she'd rather be here than at home.

Once, David came home for lunch and there she was, at twelve-fifteen in the afternoon, her hair uncombed and a pair of his thick socks on her feet to keep them warm while she read and read and read. She had forgotten the time. She had forgotten to look at a clock. The breakfast dishes were still sitting on the table, greasy toast and cereal glued to the sides of the bowl. Catherine was sitting on the floor playing with Arlene's pink rubber hair curlers, getting them hopelessly tangled in her hair. Matt was nibbling the tips off the leaves of a spider plant, which at least was not supposed to be poisonous, or so she assured David. As an excuse, she had quickly invented a sore throat, a slight headache, a stuffy nose, and David had immediately felt sorry for her. He had made himself a cheese sandwich, clearing a space on the table for his plate. He had poured her a cup of hot, sweet tea. Before he went back to work, he had found the thermometer, and had taken her temperature.

"Well, Arlene," he'd said, "at least you don't have a fever."

"No, I'm fine," she'd said. "Whatever it was seems to be passing."

Eunice used to say to her: Why can't you be more vivacious? Why can't you make more of yourself? No man's going to look twice at an old bookworm like you. You're going to ruin your eyesight with all that reading. You'll have to wear spectacles, and you know what they say about girls who wear glasses. "What am I going to do with this girl?" Eunice used to say to David, before Arlene and David were married. It was no one's business what kind of girl she was. She'd never been the kind of girl they thought she was, anyway. No one knew her. She was a young woman sitting on a damp park bench looking out at a fogged-in sea. She had a freezing cold toddler pulling at her knee. Ninety per cent of the time she was happy and ten per cent of the time she was holding herself together to the best of her ability.

Watch the woman pick the child up and wipe cookie crumbs from around his mouth. Watch the woman cover the child's cold face with her warm kisses. Watch her pack him into his stroller, tuck his favourite woolly blue blanket, without which he refused to engage in any normal activities, around him. Watch as she pulls his warm wool mittens onto his hands. Watch her being a good mother, because she is. Watch her being an almost-perfectly-happy and very fortunate young woman, because that, she tells herself, that is what she is.

After she left the park, she walked past the road that led down to Miss Caroline Bluett's house. This time Arlene kept walking, but last week she had turned down the road that led to Miss Bluett's house and had walked as far as the beach. It had been a fine day, but cold, with a light frost lingering wherever the ground was shaded from the sun. There had been frost on the beach, too; a white fur of frost on the driftwood logs above the high tide line. The tide had appeared to be coming in, and near the shore the water had been a dark, opaque green. Arlene had turned the stroller around and had started back up the road, when the door of Miss Bluett's house had opened and Miss Bluett had appeared.

"Is that you, Mrs. Greenwood?" she'd called. "Aha, I thought I recognised you. Come in, won't you? Please, come in, dear, and warm up by the fire. Bring the little boy inside, where it's warm. Come in."

There was a gate that opened into Miss Bluett's side yard. It had opened at a touch, surprisingly, as if it were a completely different gate from the one she'd wrestled with that day in August—that fateful day, she'd almost felt like saying—last year, and she had walked through, pulling the stroller after her. She closed the gate and pushed the stroller up to the steps and lifted Matt out and carried him inside the house, trying at the same time to pay attention as Miss Bluett told her she'd taken the day off school because she'd woken up with a migraine headache. Actually, it had kept her awake during the night, she said. She'd had an absolutely dreadful night. At three o'clock, she told Arlene, she'd been up making herself tea and toast to settle her stomach. The headache seemed to have gone, she said, but she still felt weak, drained, no good for anything, really.

162

"Here, sit by the fireplace," she had said. "I'll put the kettle on for tea. Little boy, would you like a glass of milk?" Matt stared at her. Miss Bluett had electric blue eyes in a little wizened face. She had a mischievous grin that flickered on and off like a neon sign. She disappeared into her kitchen and reappeared moments later with a glass of milk, which she handed to Arlene. She vanished again, and returned with a tea tray and a plate of mince tarts, her leftover Christmas baking, she explained. She was wearing an extraordinary iridescent mauve taffeta housecoat that looked to Arlene like a Balenciaga ball gown, with a nipped-in waist and a full skirt. Miss Bluett's white hair was carefully arranged in a pageboy. She was wearing mauve lipstick. She was an exotic butterfly. She put the tray down on the coffee table and poured out the tea. She kept fidgeting, wiping her fingers across the surfaces of her furniture, adjusting books and magazines and ornaments, apologising for the dust on the coffee table, for the stack of newspapers on the floor in front of the sofa, saying that Hazel Byers usually came to clean for her, but this week she had telephoned to say she had a cold.

"Everything looks lovely to me," said Arlene. This was the first time she'd been in Miss Bluett's house. She did think it was lovely; she liked the confusion, to be honest, the Westminster clock on the mantelpiece that had stopped with its hands at four-ten, the plants creeping up the walls as if they were making a futile attempt at escape.

Arlene held the glass of milk while Matt held onto her arm with both hands and tipped his head back, drinking greedily like an infant chimpanzee. He didn't mind in the least that the milk came from a stranger's unseen kitchen, that it had been served to him by a butterfly-woman with mauve lipstick he'd never in his life seen up until that morning. He had his blue blanket clamped securely under his arm. Arlene had brushed her finger across the tip of his nose and he had blinked and stared at her sombrely. A fire was burning in the grate, sparks flying up with a crackle. A sofa beneath the big front window, Arlene had noticed, was piled high with knitted afghans in a variety of colours, and all kinds of cushions, quilted, flocked, embroidered, tufted. Miss Bluett's handiwork, Arlene imagined. The windows behind the sofa took up almost the entire wall and looked directly out onto the beach. Heavy drapes were pulled to the side, out of the way, and crushed against the wall. There seemed to be an abundance of everything, a scattered richness. Next to Arlene there was a wall of bookshelves. She craned her neck to the side to read the titles: *A Glorious Wind: A Study of William Wordsworth*. And *Gentians in Spring: Coleridge, Keats and a Fabulous Mysticism*. Was she reading correctly? She leaned forward and took a closer look. Yes, those were the titles. The books, many of which had torn or folded paper stuck between the pages, looked ancient. They gave off a musty odour that was not in the least unpleasant and made Arlene think of old silk gowns, drifts of fallen leaves. She thought of how Catherine went around the house with her school books pressed to her face, infatuated with the way they smelled. And yet, it was true, wasn't it, that each book possessed its own odour, unique as a fingerprint. These ancient, strange books were identifiable by smell—mould, dust, mildew, ink, leather, paper, glue, gold leaf, pressed flowers, food stains—as much as by subject, author, title. Arlene believed so.

Miss Bluett had at last settled in a rustle of taffeta on the sofa. She rearranged a few cushions around her. "I see you're admiring my father's library, Mrs. Greenwood," she had said. "He was a great bibliophile. An ardent reader and scholar. His name was Percy Bluett. Books and literature were all he ever seriously cared for, all he valued. Until his eyesight began to weaken, and then he had his other great interest to fall back on, fortunately."

Miss Bluett was the only member of her family left alive in Canada, she had told Arlene. The only one. It was a lonely position to be in, but she'd learned to rely on her own company and her own resources. She'd known from the time she was very young that she would never marry and never have children. No one in her family was prolific, she had added; family was something that simply didn't seem to accrue, in her case. Her mother had passed away when Miss Bluett was still in her teens. Her father had passed away eight years ago, at the age of ninety. Imagine! Miss Bluett said. He'd been in good health right up to the end, she said, with the exception of his eyes; he'd had cataracts, and he'd waited too long for surgery to be of any use. Right up until the last months of his life, however, he'd made dinner every single night, so that she wouldn't have to start cooking the minute she got home from school. "He always said that if Milton had managed to finish *Paradise Lost* while blind, then he himself could certainly put a roast in the oven and set the table. He was like that, very good-tempered, very kind. I really miss him." Miss Bluett smiled and stirred her teaspoon in her tea. Then she said that Arlene must call her Caroline. She hoped that Arlene would visit her often and that they would become friends. Perhaps Arlene would like to join the Cayley Historical Society. It happened that Caroline was president this year. It was, she had said, a strictly amateur group and met once a month from September to May in people's houses. One day, they hoped to raise enough to start a little museum, a museum of local history with its own collection of artefacts and its own archives. The village of Cayley, and the outlying areas, Sunrise Beach, South Cayley, the Valenzuela Farm area, out near the Valenzuela mud flats, those places were all rich in history. There were a lot of old photographs, old letters, indeed old stories, that desperately needed organising and recording before they were lost.

"Perhaps when my children are a little older," Arlene had said, trying to hold her teacup steady in her hand while Matt clambered into her lap. She could see he was getting fed up. He stuck his thumb in his mouth and bugged his eyes out at Miss Bluett, who said, "My, you're a big boy to be sitting in your mummy's lap."

Speaking of history, Caroline said, Arlene might be interested to know that this house had started out as an isolation ward for tuberculosis patients. "This was in the 1920s. When the hospital was built, it didn't have the room for an isolation ward, which meant that TB patients had no choice but to be sent away to the Tranquille Sanatorium, in Kamloops. They were separated from their families for months, even years. One of the first doctors at the hospital," Caroline said, "had the idea of separating the isolation ward from the hospital entirely, and since there wasn't any space available on the hospital property, it got built here. In 1920, when it was built, this house was just one big room, wide open to the sea winds, with screens to keep out the mosquitoes. In the winter, the screens were taken down and the house was glassed in, just as it was now. A fire was kept burning day and night. The nurses had to run down the hill from the hospital as a regular feature of their duties, to check on whichever patient happened to be living here at the time. Temperature, pulse, sputum specimen. Then back up the hill to the hospital, in rain, snow, ice, in the dead of night. Can you imagine?" Caroline had said. "People wouldn't put up with such conditions now, would they?"

Arlene had been reaching for Matt's coat and mittens, and thanking Caroline for her hospitality, when Caroline had stood up, cushions tumbling to the floor all around her. "Wait," she had said. "Before you leave, there's something I would like to show you."

"Oh, Caroline, thank you so much for everything, but I have to go," Arlene said. "I have to get Matt his lunch. And I don't like to be away for too long, in case Catherine's school phones, or someone needs me." She had in mind an emergency, an injury on the playground. Now that the thought had come into her head, something was sure to go wrong. She really had to get home. How long had she been here? She had tried to look at her watch while she was in the process of grabbing hold of Matt's arm and working it into his coat sleeve.

"Oh, this won't take long," Caroline had said, very determined. "I don't show this to many people, but I want you to see it. I think you'll like it." She herded Arlene down a short dark hall, past the kitchen, to a room that seemed to have been added onto the house, a room with a low ceiling and a floor that sloped noticeably. Caroline went to the window and pulled back the curtains. In the centre of the room there was a big square table. Against one wall there was a storage cupboard with chrome handles and one straight-back chair. On the table, Catherine saw, there was a model town, like one of those old-fashioned English villages people displayed on their mantelpiece at Christmas time. Houses, streets, stores, trees, a village scene, the air around it hushed and still.

"Your house is right here," Caroline had said, placing her finger on a red roof with a dormer window at the front. "This is where you live."

"Yes," Arlene had said. She recognised the house, the garage behind the house, the trees, the walkway. It was very accurate. She put Matt down and held onto his hand.

"Your house used to be called the Rutledge place. The Rutledges lived there for years. But now it's your house. You live there now. It's the Greenwood place."

"This is amazing," Arlene had said at last. Cayley Minor, as Caroline had called it, seemed to float just above the table, a labyrinth of streets that began at the edge of a painted sea and rose up a wooded hill. There were buildings, trees, rivers winding through miniature green forests, farms with rolling pastures, cornfields, sunflowers glowing like a row of electric lights against a tall fence. A miniature tractor was in the process of ploughing a field. A scarecrow stood in a plot of garden at the back of a house. Here were the churches, hotels, beer parlours, the garage with miniature gas pumps, the Royal Canadian Legion with a couple of toy cars parked outside the door and the Red Ensign flying from a flagpole. Arlene had walked slowly around the table, trying to take it all in. Matt had trailed along at her side, too overwhelmed, it seemed, to even try to reach up and touch something. She had bent over, reading the street signs, the little hand-lettered signs on tiny green poles. Ashlar Street, Yew, Pine, Esplanade, Maple, Third Street. Here were the post office and the library, all the places she walked to, all the streets she'd walked along. Here was Miss Bluett's—Caroline's—house, and inside it, presumably, Cayley Minor, an even smaller version of a walled village, medieval, unassailable. No one could get in; no one could get out. Here was Arlene's house, shrunk down to the size of a child's plaything, a curio. Arlene saw that the doors of the houses actually opened. Or at least some of them did. The door of her house did. And the windows opened outward on tiny brass hinges that made a creaking sound, audible if you bent close. In some of the houses were miniature people, carved, it seemed, from wood. Arlene saw herself inside 131 Alma Avenue: a skinny little doll that surely was meant to be her. She was standing at the window. She had black pinprick eyes and a woolly wig stuck on her head. And there was a skinny little man doll, as well. David. Arlene shivered; she couldn't help it. All she could think of was black magic, a kind of voodoo. The David figure was near the open front door, its arms slightly extended in welcome. Or to fend someone off?

Why? she had wanted to ask. She had looked up and seen Caroline watching her avidly, her eyes bright and cheeks flushed. "This is amazing. It's incredible," Arlene had said. "It's everything, isn't it? The whole town."

"My father started building Cayley Minor in 1917. I will tell you the story. He had been out of work. The war was on, and younger men were going over to Europe to fight, and dying there, or else coming back home on crutches, or with their heads in bandages, and there was my father, doing nothing but growing strawberries and green runner beans. It drove him crazy. He got a part-time job washing floors at the high school, where I was a student. Can you imagine how it pained me, to see my father, who was a scholar and a teacher, swishing a mop around in a pail of dirty water in front of my friends? My mother said to him, Percy, this is foolishness, you don't have to work at all. Finally, he listened to her. He quit his job at the school and got the idea of constructing a model of the town. Once he'd begun, he kept at it for the rest of his life, because of course a town is never finished. It continues to grow, to change, doesn't it? Just like a little boy does." Caroline had dusted a roof top with a finger. "Now I am the caretaker," she had said. "Well, what do you think?"

Arlene stood up and pushed her hair back. It felt like wool, thick, unmanageable, glued to the top of her head. What did she think? Cayley Minor appalled her and made her want to laugh at the same time. It was captivating and ludicrous and gave her the creeps. "I think it's extraordinary," she had said at last, and Caroline had smiled at her radiantly and had said, "I know. It is, isn't it?"

*

Arlene pushed the stroller up the hill. She'd hadn't been to see Caroline since that day. Frankly, she wasn't sure if she had the courage to visit her again. In any case, Caroline wouldn't be at home today; she'd be in the classroom, teaching teenagers how to read the poems of William Wordsworth and how to write grammatical sentences. Arlene had the strange notion that Caroline was in control of the real town of Cayley as well as her classroom and her miniature city. All the streets were sentences, precise grammatical units. Subjects and verbs, places and actions, irrevocable actions being worked out in two places at the same time. And then the sentences strung together to make up paragraphs, the paragraphs recounting the history of the town, the life of the town, perhaps even in some supernatural and terrible sense the future of the town. An image came to her, of Caroline's father Percy hunched over that table, putting together a scale model of Cayley—one-sixteenth of an inch to the mile, Caroline had told her. Day after day spent working, hunched over a worktable with pots of paint and little hammers and nails. And then those little wood figures. It made her think of the carnival she'd seen with David at the Pacific National Exhibition, years ago, the summer they'd met. A carnival made out of toothpicks, with a delicate, airy toothpick Ferris wheel that looked as if it could transport you to another planet. Although he'd never got around to it, David had intended to build a toothpick carnival of his own. Arlene remembered how he'd saved boxes of toothpicks in a kitchen cupboard, until they'd moved and she'd thrown them out. She understood—she thought she understood—that it all had something to do with a desperate hunger for perfection. Constructing miniature replicas of the real thing. That was how it seemed to her. It was like the artificial night sky at the Peking Restaurant, a velvet, moonless sky full of glorious fake stars. She could easily imagine the kind of mind that wanted to make things over again, better than the original, more manageable, easier by far to keep under control. She was like that herself, she sometimes thought, but she had absolutely no idea what medium she should work with, what substance she was supposed to plunge her hands into and shape and mould and impress with her own ideas and images. Besides, she was too lazy. She was. She'd rather create things with her mind. She'd rather sit on a park bench, or on the sofa in her living room, and read and dream up places and people she'd never seen, and plan how she'd change her life if she had supernatural powers and could do it all with a couple of magical phrases, without having to lift a hand.

CHAPTER THIRTEEN

In the Christmas concert Catherine and Phoebe were angels. They stood on bales of hay piled up behind the manger and covered with a tarpaulin. The manger was made out of cedar and fir boughs arranged over a wood frame. Catherine and Phoebe wore long white gowns made of old bed sheets. They had wings strapped to them with gold cords that went under their arms and crossed over their stomachs and tied in the back. Their arms were wrapped in strips of aluminium foil and gold net fabric. Abigail was the Virgin Mary. She sat under the cedar and fir boughs in a blue dressing gown with a lace runner from her mother's dining-room table on her head. In her arms she held a giant dimpled baby boy doll in a knitted sailor suit. The doll belonged to Miss Shelby, and before that it had belonged to Miss Shelby's mother. When Miss Shelby walked past Abigail, she bent and patted the doll on its plastic curls as if she believed it was a real baby.

Phoebe and Catherine had lines to speak from memory. Phoebe went first. She drew in her breath, then hesitated as a silence filled the auditorium, everyone lost in it, waiting, waiting, clearing their throats and rustling their programmes, until, finally, Phoebe let out her breath and recited: *For behold, I bring you good tidings of great joy, which shall be to all people.*

Then Catherine said, *For unto you is born this day in the city of David a saviour, which is Christ the Lord.* A song from the school choir followed: "O Little Town of Bethlehem." The Three Wise Men clumped onto the stage and knelt before the manager. The aluminium foil on Catherine's sleeves crackled in the slight breeze from the fan above the stage, a sound loud enough to wake the Baby Jesus if he were a real baby and not Miss Shelby's old boy doll. From where Catherine was standing, miles above the surface of the earth, it didn't seem that she and Phoebe were part of this performance, this *tableau*, as Miss Shelby called it, at all. She and Phoebe were friends, no matter what anyone said, including Abigail. Who would ever dare say Catherine couldn't be friends with Phoebe Sceats? Who would say anything mean about lovely, golden, giggly Phoebe? This was the season of goodwill, which meant you had to be friends with Phoebe Sceats, even if she didn't have a proper bathroom at her house, even if she wore second-hand penny loafers that were too big for her feet. *God rest ye merry gentlemen, let nothing you dismay*, Catherine sang with the choir. She filled her lungs with air and floated in a sudden uncertainty of space. Her palms were tingling. For a moment she was afraid she was going to fall off the bale of hay through the roof of the manger. Phoebe grinned at her, her bright frizzy hair like gold tinsel around her head, and Catherine raised her arms higher, or not her arms, but her angel wings, and, singing, looked out at the auditorium, at her parents with their pale oval faces, their outdoor coats and scarves bundled around them. *Joy to the World!* she joyfully sang.

Catherine and Phoebe were the king of the castle and everyone else was a dirty rascal. She imagined herself and Phoebe holding tight to each other's hands, floating far above the school, the town, above the distant lights of the town, above the sea, the dark islands. Even in the darkness they could see every single thing; they could see the dark mysterious sea with its cargo of secrets rushing eagerly up to the shore. They were angels. With their gauzy wings and glittering gowns. Angels floating forever in the endless starry sky.

In school, Phoebe sat on the other side of the room from Catherine, dropping her books, her pencil case, her ruler, thud, thud, crash, on the floor and asking permission a hundred times a day to get up to sharpen her pencils and go to the washroom. Please, Phoebe, please do try to remember you're in Grade One, Miss Shelby kept saying.

Catherine thought of Phoebe as that girl from the beach, that girl from that day at the beach. She wanted to be friends with Phoebe, but how could she be friends with fat, cheerful Phoebe with her bathing suit held together with a shiny safety pin, her black and white dog galloping in and out of the waves? Phoebe belonged in a dream, a distant dream getting smaller and farther away. The day Catherine's mother had walked into the sea in her dress, and Phoebe had been there. Phoebe had seen the police pulling Catherine's mother out of the water, all wet and soaking and blue from the cold. *Phoebe knew everything.*

On the first day of school, Phoebe had been waiting for her. She had been leaning against the stucco wall in the girls' patio, at the back of the school. "Hi," she had said. "Want to play on the swings?" Catherine had tried to run away, but Phoebe was persistent. "Let's play hopscotch," she had said. "Let's run around the school, let's look in the windows and see if we can see Miss Shelby." Phoebe stood on one leg and crossed her eyes. She flapped her arms, pretending she was a bird. Then she took a black jawbreaker from the pocket of her dress and brushed bits of dirt off it and offered it to Catherine, who said, "No, thank you. I'm not allowed to eat candy."

"This isn't candy," Phoebe said. "It's gum. Here, you have it."

Phoebe took Catherine's hand and pried it open, depositing the jawbreaker on Catherine's palm. Catherine popped the jawbreaker into her mouth. It tasted like black liquorice. It tasted like Phoebe's sweaty hands. Catherine sucked on the jawbreaker and Phoebe grinned at her. Phoebe was wearing a yellow dress. She was all yellow, her bright frizzy curls the colour of sunlight, her dress a buttery yellow, her skin tanned golden from being outdoors all summer. On her feet she had scuffed old penny loafers, no socks. She had a big soft-looking bruise on her leg, below her knee, and a dirty Band-Aid stuck on her arm. Phoebe was round, soft, shaped like a ball, a floppy stuffed doll. In class she breathed through her mouth, and muttered audibly to herself, and when Miss Shelby sat with her, going over her work, Phoebe would start to cry. She would bend over her exercise book with her nose almost touching the page, tears running down her round smudged cheeks, and she would draw in her breath as if she were strangling to death. Miss Shelby would sigh and hand her a tissue and tell her to dry her eyes, that she was a big girl. Obediently, Phoebe would mop at her eyes, and then have another go at her reading, slowly, slowly tracing the words on the page with a finger that turned white from the pressure.

"Let's not play with Phoebe Sceats," Abigail said. That was Phoebe's last name: Sceats. Abigail claimed to know all about Phoebe. "She lives in a shack," Abigail said. "It's filthy dirty. They have an outhouse instead of a bathroom. Phoebe Sceats stinks, doesn't she? Phew!" "Run," Abigail would say to Catherine, when they saw Phoebe heading towards them. "Quick, before she sees us!"

Catherine ran. But she liked Phoebe, persistent, buttery Phoebe with her scrunched-up lunch bag and her sloppy penny loafers. There were times when she liked Phoebe better than she liked Abigail, who always seemed to have a runny nose, green snot sitting on her upper lip like a blob of glue, and who didn't, to be perfectly honest, smell so good herself. Catherine wanted to be friends with Phoebe, but she was only allowed to be friends with Abigail Glass because her mother and Abigail's mother were friends. For a while, Catherine and Abigail had to wear identical outfits, pleated skirts that flared out around their legs when they ran or skipped rope, cotton blouses with long sleeves and cuffs, soft fuzzy angora sweaters, blue, yellow, pink, selected for them by their mothers, who went shopping together. They played with the same toys: nurse kits that came with cinnamon-flavoured candy medicine; cut-out dolls; colouring books. Every single thing one of them got, the other had to have. They were sisters, Abigail insisted. And most of the time Catherine did like Abigail, with her long braids, her surprisingly heavy, straight eyebrows and pale eyes that tilted up slightly at the corners.

The things Abigail knew: how babies were made and how they were born, popping right out of the mother's belly-button, and how girls were different from boys, and how to see ghosts in a dark room, and what vampires did, and what dead people looked like, and how to play gin rummy, and how to play "Chopsticks" on the piano. She knew all the swear words: fart, shit, fuck, dink, asshole, hell, penis, Goddamn, fink. Was fink a swear word? Catherine asked. Abigail shrugged. Sex, she said. Vagina. What else? She drummed her fingers on her knee, very business-like. Her pale narrow eyes stared straight at Catherine, as if—as if what? As if Catherine disappointed her, sitting there nursing that big stupid pink doll she'd got out of Abigail's bedroom.

Abigail showed Catherine how to lie down on the floor in the upstairs hall and put her ear on the hot air grill so that she could hear everything her mother and Abigail's mother were talking about in the kitchen downstairs. Also, if she looked through the grill at the right angle, it was possible to see them sitting there at the table having coffee and talking, miniature ladies with their elbows on the table, confiding in each other, consoling, completely unaware that they were being spied on. They passed from one subject to another seamlessly, their voices like bells chiming, birds chirping: hem-lines, they discussed, and whether or not to add garlic to roast beef, and how many teeth Matt had, and how to get rid of two extra pounds before Christmas. "Don't laugh," Abigail said, pressing her hand against Catherine's mouth. Abigail listened all the time; she knew everything. "My mother can't have any more babies," she told Catherine. They were back in Abigail's bedroom. "She had a big operation and now she can't have babies. She has a scar on her stomach." Catherine wanted to put her hands over her ears to keep from hearing any more. "Some people get a divorce," Abigail said. "If they hate each other, they do. And then they can't ever get married again to anyone else." Who was Abigail talking about, Catherine wanted to know. "People you don't know," Abigail said, winding the end of her braid around her wrist. "My Aunt Doris, if you must know. She got a divorce from my Uncle George. I'm never getting divorced."

"I'm never getting married," Catherine said. She was still thinking about the scar on Abigail's mother's stomach. She was still repeating in her head all the swear words she'd learned from Abigail.

There was a strange smell at Abigail Glass's house, Catherine had noticed. It came up through the hot air grill along with the sound of their mothers' voices. The smell reminded Catherine of boiled ham and wet dog hair, and something else, the same kind of floor wax her mother used on the living-room floor. Dog poop wax, turtle bowl wax.

Abigail had a green turtle in a plastic bowl. The turtle's name was Angus. It ate raw meat and ground-up worms from the garden, and pooped a lot of thin little brown poops it kept stirring up with its green clawed feet. The turtle bowl water smelled atrocious—a word Miss Shelby used all the time, as in, "Phoebe Sceats, your printing is atrocious." As well as Angus the turtle, Abigail had Ethel, the poodle, who tried to bite Catherine on the leg once, when she ran up the stairs. Behave yourself at the Glasses' house, Catherine's mother told her. Try to remember your manners. Say please, and thank you. And don't run around and act silly, or that damned dog, pardon my French, will bite you on the ankle.

The Glass house. It was nothing like glass, as far as Catherine could see. Once, Catherine had actually been inside a glass castle. It was on the road to Victoria, a castle made out of old glass bottles, the walls smooth and cold, a pale blue light shining in. Her father had paid fifty cents each for her and Matt to walk through it. *Visit the Glass Castle!* a sign on the side of the highway said. Adults $2, Children 50¢. Catherine's mother talked about how beautiful the Glasses' house was, how old and finely built, how historically important it was to the town of Cayley, having been built for the owner of the original sawmill, and how she would give anything to live in a house like the Glasses' house. But whenever Catherine was there she felt as if she were changing shape, or losing her normal shape. Was that what she meant? It was hard to describe. Her nose tickled. She wanted to cough, or sneeze. More than that, she felt herself becoming smaller and smaller beneath those high, dark echoing wood ceilings. Her hair slipped out from its elastics and barrettes. The sash of her dress came undone and trailed on the floor. She had to go pee. She was thirsty, hot, itchy, her hands were sticky. She stubbed her toes on the hall runner and almost fell down. Abigail led her through the rooms of her house. "Come on," she said. "Come on!" She led Catherine upstairs to her bedroom, which was painted pink and white, with a four-poster bed with a frilly pink valance and a pink satin bedspread, matching pink boudoir lamps on white night tables, white scatter rugs, starched net Priscilla curtains tied back at the windows. Catherine sat in a white rocking chair with one of Abigail's plump baby dolls on her lap. Abigail told her a man had once died in this house, died or was murdered, and his ghost came into her bedroom at night and glowed white as the moon. He was all white except for his eyes which were like green light bulbs. Catherine said, "You're making that up," and Abigail crossed her heart and said she wasn't making it up, honest, it was true. Abigail invented a game, which consisted of shutting herself and Catherine up in one of the unused rooms up on the third floor, and pretending they could hear a ghost, the same ghost who came into her bedroom, the ghost of the owner of the original sawmill, who had built this house and lived here, when he was alive. Now his ghost came walking down the hall, its steps getting slower and slower as it got closer to their hiding place. Were they pretending, or could they really hear a ghost? Catherine crouched behind the door, holding tight to Abigail's cold hands. She sometimes thought she would die of fright, or wet her pants, but she didn't. She didn't dare. Abigail would call her a chicken, a cry-baby. The truth was, she would do anything Abigail asked her to do. She would shut herself up in a dark closet with the ghost, if necessary. She would, and in fact, did, follow Abigail down a trail through the trees behind Abigail's house until they came out on a rise of ground above the old Cayley Road. They ducked down behind the bushes, the blackberry vines and Scotch broom, and then, when Abigail said *Run!* they ran out to the edge of the hill and threw rocks at the passing cars. Not big rocks. Pebbles. A handful of pebbles. No one saw them. No one ever looked in their direction, as far as Catherine could tell. The cars and trucks came into sight, travelled along the road, then disappeared around a corner. Abigail dug her elbow into Catherine's arm and said, "There, did you see that man? He waved at us. He waved and stuck out his tongue. He was mad. He was yelling at us. Did you see that mean old man?"

Catherine and Abigail, throwing rocks at cars on the old Cayley Road, and shouting, "Hey there, Mr. Driver, hey there, Mr. Car Driver!" and then running back to their hiding place. Squatting behind the Scotch broom, with its dry crackly pods that smelled of black liquorice and made Catherine think of Phoebe's jawbreaker melting in her hand on the first day of school. Then, once Catherine and Abigail had rested, once they'd caught their breath, they ran back out to throw another rock, another handful of pebbles. The rocks either rolled down the hill or landed in the ditch at the side of the road. Catherine thought: we aren't hurting anyone. What if her mother found out? Her mother would spank her, and send her to her room. But her mother would never find out. No one ever came here. That was what Abigail said. It was her secret hiding place; she was going to build a fort here one day, in the trees. Except she didn't get the chance. One day Hazel caught them. She was at Abigail's house, doing the housecleaning, and Abigail's mother must have said, It's so quiet here, where are those girls? Where did those naughty girls get to? And she sent Hazel out to search for them. And look what she found!

"You bad girls," she said. She grabbed hold of Abigail's wrist before she could throw the rock in her hand. She took the rock from her and chucked it in the bushes. "What kind of stupid game are you getting up to?" she said. "Don't you know any better?"

Catherine stepped away from Hazel. She walked backward, letting the pebbles fall from her hand.

"Are you throwing rocks at the cars? Are you?" Hazel said. She held onto Abigail's arm. "You little devils. You naughty girls. What will your mother say?" she said. "What will your mother think? Don't ever do it again. Do you understand?"

Hazel told them a secret: There was a dog in the sky, a real dog. It was in orbit. "Look up there," she ordered, pointing toward the sky, which was a cold November blue, a few high, thin clouds passing like smoke in front of the sun. The crazy Russians had shut a little dog up in a rocket and sent it into space, and now it was going to orbit the earth until it died, Hazel told them. She hated the Russians. She would save the dog and kill the Russians, if she could. She liked animals better than people, anyway. If she saw anyone hurting an animal, she said, it made her so mad she could scream. You're lucky I didn't catch you throwing rocks at a dog, she said.

She turned and made her way through the trail in front of Catherine and Abigail. She took hold of branches that were in their way and snapped them in half. She threw the broken twigs into the bushes, where they landed with a rustle, as if birds or small animals were scurrying around in there. "I should tell your mother on you," she said, wiping her hands on the back of her jeans and turning to glare at Abigail, who stopped and said, "It was Catherine's idea."

"It was not," Catherine said. "You're lying."

"Be quiet, both of you," Hazel said. "It was a dumb idea. The two of you get some dumb ideas in your heads, don't you? Don't do it again, or I'll tell on you, and that's a promise. You're a couple of little brats, aren't you? You'd better behave, or I'll tell your mother and then what do you think will happen?"

Chapter Fourteen

The night before the Christmas concert at Catherine's school Arlene had a dream. It was the kind of dream that remained in the mind, the mood of the dream, its intensity and emanations and colour, all impossible to erase. That evening, she had sat in the auditorium at the school watching the concert, watching her six-year-old daughter dressed as an angel, her head wreathed in light, her feathery wings white as snow, and all she could think of was the dream. It began in this way: She had been in a park with Catherine and Matt. The trees were a wonderful fresh, dewy, new spring green, and the grass was like velvet. Flowers were blooming everywhere, all along the footpaths, little bunches of sweet alyssum and blue and pink petunias, and other flowers that she had never before seen. The air was fragrant, and golden, and full of promise. She had been very happy, and she had told herself she would have to try to bring the children to the park again. They came to a pond, and Matt and Catherine stood as close to the edge of the water as they could get, and Arlene stood behind them, her hands ready to reach out and save them if they slipped. They were all entranced by the pond, the light shining on the water, the water lilies and duck weed, the ducks floating silently past. A dozen ducklings were trailing along after their mother, single-file, looking so happy to have hatched into such a pleasant world. And there were handsome white swans on the far side of the water, swimming in pairs, and Arlene told the children that they must have made nests in the long grass on the opposite shore. One day very soon, she said, their eggs would hatch, too, and the babies would swim along behind the parent swans just as the ducklings did. A baby swan, she told them, suddenly remembering the word, was called a cygnet.

There was a stone bridge spanning the pond, very picturesque, the water slipping beneath its graceful arch, ducks swimming under it, from light into darkness into light. Arlene was aware without paying any special attention that people were strolling across the bridge, and then she looked up and there was her father. He was wearing a grey tweed overcoat and a grey fedora, and his hands, which were resting on the side of the bridge, were gloved, so that only his face was truly visible, naked, the pure handsome lines of his face clear to her, and as familiar as if she'd last seen him earlier that very day. He still had a pencil-thin moustache, she noticed, and his eyes were as dark and lustrous as ever, as keenly intelligent, and observant. He missed nothing. He saw Arlene right off, and knew immediately who she was. He saw the children with her. With the most tremendous sense of relief and satisfaction she thought, Oh, I am so glad he is alive and not dead! Because now he can see his grandchildren. The terrible regret she'd always felt because her own father had never seen Matt and Catherine was removed. She saw that she had no cause for regret.

Furthermore, she saw clearly that the distance between her and her father was nothing, nothing. The time it would take her to reach him on the bridge was negligible; two minutes and she could be there, at his side. The distance between life and death was apparently quite deceiving. There was a permeable wall through which everyone was quite free to pass, in the same way that the water birds, the ducks and swans, were able to swim freely from light to darkness, from shadow into brightness. In her dream it was all splendidly clear, it was all sensible and true; it was a new science of existence, and Arlene was its discoverer. Her heart was beating so quickly; she was so happy. She waved to him. She indicated with a few simple gestures that he must stay where he was. She would get to him, she said. She would be there at once.

Chapter Fifteen

In July of 1960, Arlene and David packed up the Oldsmobile and drove to Summerland, in the Okanagan, to visit David's parents, who were holding a family reunion. David was paying Hazel Byers and her cousin Wayne Travers five dollars a week each to water the garden while they were away, and to mow the grass and put the newspapers inside on the kitchen table. Hazel was going to water the house plants. David had entrusted her with a key to the house, which Arlene thought was pure madness; David, however, said people like Hazel and Wayne had to learn responsibility somehow. People like Hazel and Wayne? Arlene had said, and David had said he meant young people, teenagers, young adults. Arlene said they'd better keep their hands off her possessions, and David said what she had to do was relax and put Hazel and Wayne and the house out of her head so that she could enjoy their vacation. Is this a vacation? she had then said. Is visiting your family a vacation? It is what you make of it, he had said. And she had laughed at him, and for about a hundred miles, every time someone said anything, she responded by saying, It is what you make of it.

It was raining in Vancouver, and foggy and cold on the Hope-Princeton Highway, and they had to put on their coats and turn the car heater to high. Then they swooped down out of the mountains and the sun was shining, the sky was clear and bright. They rolled down the windows and let the hot, dry interior wind blow through the car. The hills were a lovely brown colour, sorrel, Arlene called it, and the pine trees were dark green, without shadow, stark against the earth and sky.

At noon, they stopped and got out of the station wagon and spread a blanket on the ground and ate a picnic lunch beside a river. There wasn't another person in sight, and except for the traffic on the highway the only sounds were crickets in the grass. Arlene unwrapped the sandwiches and passed them out. The cheese in the sandwiches was starting to melt and turn slimy. Catherine took a bite and spat it out on the ground. Arlene pretended she hadn't seen a thing. She wrapped her own sandwich up and put it back in the picnic hamper. David went around taking pictures with his new 35 millimetre camera. He cupped his hand over the lens to keep out the glare from the sun and tried to get the children to stop hopping around long enough to have their pictures taken. Then he sat down beside Arlene and told her he couldn't believe how well he felt as soon as he got east of Princeton. This, he said, was the climate and the country-side that suited him best. It was probably where he should have stayed, where he should be spending his life. What they should do, he said, was move here, buy a place where they could have land, room to move, green fields. A paddock. A pony for the children to ride. Real snow in the winter. Cross-country skiing.

Arlene moved off the blanket and lay on her back in the dry rough grass. She shaded her face in the crook of her arm. "A pony," she said. "A horse. Cross-country skiing. What brought all this on?" She sat up and got her cigarettes out of her purse.

"Homecoming," David said. "Familiar terrain. I told you."

"What would you do about your job if we moved?" she said.

"I'd quit," David said. "That's what I'd do. I'd quit and start over fresh." He was sitting on the ground, his arms resting on his knees. He was looking at the river, at the green water running clear as glass over the rocks. "I could set up my own business," he said. "We could live on a ranch and have a horse and a dog and a truck for carting loads of hay."

Arlene was keeping an eye on Matt and Catherine, who were now tossing pebbles into the river. Matt was five years old; in September he would be starting kindergarten. He was beautiful. He had a faint scar on his forehead, a scar shaped like a silkworm that grew along with him, not getting smaller, not changing. Catherine was nearly nine. They were both tall for their ages, or at least Matt was, he was a good-sized boy, and they both had curly auburn hair, brown with auburn mixed in. Matt had a tendency to be introverted, like Arlene. Eunice said he was a carbon copy of his grandfather, George May. The other grandmother, Margaret, said he was the image of David's father Phil. Catherine was the exact opposite of Matt; she was excitable, volatile. You had to sit on her every now and then.

"If we're going to move, I want to move to a city," Arlene said. "I'd like to be able to walk down the street without feeling that people were looking at me, thinking, Oh, there goes Arlene Greenwood. She's never at home. Her poor husband, does he ever have a clean shirt or a decent cooked meal?"

"That's your guilty conscience speaking," David said. "Not the neighbours."

"You'll never quit your job," she said.

"I might."

"You wouldn't. You're too conservative."

"I'll surprise you one day," David said. "And be careful what you do with that cigarette. The grass is dry as straw."

Arlene went down to the river and threw her cigarette butt in the water and Catherine said, "Mummy, don't do that." "I'm sorry," Arlene said. She put her arm around Matt's shoulders. "What river is this?" she asked David when he came and stood beside her. He put his arm around her and kneaded his fingers in the hollow above her collarbone and said it was the Similkameen. Arlene was thinking she'd do it, she'd move to a farm in the interior and keep a dog, a horse, cows, goats, if that was what David wanted. She tried to picture herself baking bread and nursing a sick calf, walking out at night barefoot on a light skin of snow, a winter moon shining down on her. But she knew that David had no real intention of moving to the interior of the province, or of giving up his job and along with it his pension plan and his stock options, or whatever they were called. They would have moved by now, except for a hundred reasons, a hundred interventions, such as recessions in '58 and '59, labour unrest, strikes, lockouts, threatened take-overs. The lumber and paper markets had been in a slump, David said, but a recovery was underway. Still, it paid to be cautious, he said; they were better off in Cayley than out in the sticks somewhere, which was where they could easily end up, if he started agitating for a transfer. The company didn't like pushiness, he said. It was wiser to stay in the background.

She shook the dried grass and bread crumbs from the blanket and folded it up and put it in the back of the car. She picked up a toy car Matt had dropped in the grass and stood with it in her hands, the rubber tires resting on her palm. Where did this river go? she wondered. Where did it end up? She imagined it making its way towards the sea. She imagined molecules of water from this river washing up at last on the shore at Cayley, in front of Caroline Bluett's little house with its musty old books and overstuffed sofas and its small lost hidden town, miniature streets and houses with their glossy painted roofs and empty rooms inhabited by nothing but ghosts and half-remembered history.

They got back into the car and drove the rest of the way to Summerland without stopping. It was six-thirty in the evening by the time they arrived at David's parents' house. As soon as David stopped the car, his mother and father came out of their house. Arlene got out of the car and held the door open for Matt and Catherine. They had just finished fighting over who had the biggest share of the back seat, who had eaten most of the gummy bears. Arlene wanted to shake them both. She told them to get out and say hello to their grandmother. Margaret ran up to them, wiping her hands on her apron, and knelt down on the ground and gathered the children to her and kissed them and hugged them. Margaret had thick white hair she wore cut sensibly short. Under her apron she had a print house-dress, and she was wearing sensible shoes that laced up. She was famous not only in her own family, Arlene understood, but throughout the area, for never sitting down and taking a break from work.

"Oh, you've grown," Margaret was saying to Matt and Catherine. "Do you have a kiss for your Granny?" David's father, Phil, bent over and kissed Arlene on the cheek, and slapped his son hard on the shoulder and said, "Good for you, you got here in time for dinner. We've been keeping everything hot for you."

Arlene could smell turkey roasting from where she stood: Christmas in July. An overheated kitchen, with flies buzzing at the screens. She felt dispirited, just thinking about it. "Oh, we've been feeding our faces all day," she said. Then a dog came careening around the side of the house, barking frantically, its long ears flying and its stumpy little tail wagging, and Catherine immediately ran to Arlene's side.

"It's all right," Margaret said. "Star won't hurt you. She's just saying hello. You remember Star, don't you, Catherine? You can pet her, if you want."

Catherine went over to the dog. She and Matt petted the dog on the head, rubbed her behind the ears.

This was where David had grown up, Arlene thought, in this gracious two-storey lakefront house in the middle of green fields and apple orchards. He'd told Arlene he'd learned to swim before he was four years old. Later, when he was in his teens, he'd water-skied while his parents sat on the verandah watching him. He'd taken a bus to school along with his sister Brenda and his brother Robert and his brother John, who had died in the war. David's father owned a building supply store in town. His mother had taught Sunday School at the United Church for forty years. Well, it had been the Methodist Church to start with, then it had become the United Church. David liked to get the details straight when he told her anything, as if it mattered to her which church Margaret was teaching Sunday School at. When he was growing up, David had had a dog called Laddie, possibly even a whole series of dogs called Laddie, and now his parents had a cocker spaniel called Star. In addition, they had three cats and a painted turtle that lived outside in the summer in a pen with its own pond. They had a swing set, a wading pool, a picnic table, a rowboat tied up at their own little wharf. They had five grandchildren, including Brenda's new-born baby daughter Jessica. Brenda and her husband Gilbert and the baby and their two older children were arriving later, Margaret said. A lot of people were arriving in the next few days, and a lot were here now, coming out of the house singly and in pairs, the fruit of the genealogy research, evidently, people from all over the country, dressed in their summer gear, sprigged dresses, sports shirts, tennis shoes, Bermuda shorts, sleeveless dresses exposing fat arms, pocked skin. Everyone smiling. Arlene felt like crawling back in the car and driving away, but they had her. They had her in their grasp. They kissed her, hugged her, told her how well she looked, how pleased they were to see her. She'd promised David she'd enjoy herself, for the children's sakes. But they tired her out. She wasn't used to so many people at once, so much talking and laughing and getting acquainted.

Whenever Arlene was here, she snuck into the living room alone, and opened the enormous family Bible, which had a heavy leather embossed cover, and turned to the entries for Births, Deaths, Marriages. She traced her finger over the long list of names and dates, the different colours of ink, the fine, silky paper, the different styles of handwriting. She found her wedding day: David Philip and Arlene Clare, June 6th, 1950. Their wedding picture was on a table, in a gold frame: Arlene in her wedding gown, a bouquet of red roses in her hands, David at her side in his black wedding suit. And there were what looked like a hundred other framed photographs, of weddings, babies, Christmas, Thanksgiving and birthday dinners and parties. The whole damned family. Enough of a crowd to get lost in, easily. Catherine in a red velvet dress with a white lace collar, a huge white satin bow in her hair, little black patent leather shoes on her feet. And there was Matthew as an infant, propped up on a cushion, smiling happily at the camera while he tried to stuff a fat bare foot in his mouth. These were photographs Arlene remembered packaging up and mailing to Mr. and Mrs. P. Greenwood, R.R. #3, Cottonwood Road, Summerland, B.C.

The Bible seemed to be the only book in the Greenwoods' house, except for some church publications, Sunday school material, sheet music for the piano, a few copies of *Popular Mechanics* and *Ladies' Home Journal*. Margaret and Phil weren't readers. They didn't have time, they said. Phil was kept busy running his building supply store. He had a staff of ten, including the men who drove his delivery trucks, and every Dominion Day he put on a big cookout for them, followed by a fireworks display. Then there were his church and political interests. And Margaret had her Sunday School lessons to prepare, and gardening and endless housework, baking bread every morning, and putting up preserves, canning the vegetables and fruit she grew. Whenever Margaret did get around to sitting down, she had her knitting in her hands, or a piece of needlepoint, or some quilting, or mending. Stitch, stitch, the needle flying in and out of the cloth. Margaret made Arlene feel more redundant than usual by constantly telling her to sit down, to rest, for goodness' sake, to take some time for herself while she had the chance. Obligingly, Arlene relinquished her children to Margaret, knowing that at least with this grandmother they were unlikely to come to harm, they were unlikely to end up in a hospital emergency ward getting stitched back together. She went outside and sat on the wharf, in the sun, dangling her legs in the lake. Slowly she rubbed suntan lotion all over her arms and shoulders and face, enjoying the feeling of the hot sun on her skin. She was the odd one out, it seemed to her, at any gathering of David's family. She was the one they didn't quite know what to do with. Or else it was her, being difficult, as Eunice always used to tell her. Arlene put on sunglasses and a straw hat.

It was four o'clock in the afternoon, three days after they'd arrived. David was running around the house playing tag with the kids and his brother-in-law, Gilbert, who owned a

Chevrolet dealership in Penticton. In the evenings, David and Gilbert and Phil kicked a soccer ball around on the lawn. They played volleyball and badminton. They shadow-boxed, as if unable to contain their energy and exuberant sense of camaraderie. Earlier in the day, Arlene had overheard David's father telling him he should re-locate to the interior. She'd come out onto the deck with her baby niece, Jessica, asleep in her arms. At first, Brenda had been a little reluctant to trust her with Jessica. She had taken her right out of Arlene's arms once, saying she was going to put her down in her cot, but Jessica started to fuss. She sucked her breath in and started to scream. Brenda was helping Margaret bake about a thousand loaves of bread, the usual twice weekly offering, and at last she had relented. "Take her," she had said. "Drop her in the lake if you want."

"You don't have to worry," Arlene had said. "I do know how to hold a baby. I have had a little practice." "Oh, I know," Brenda had said, trying to smile. "They don't trust me," Arlene had said to Jessica. Jessica had given her a suspicious Greenwood look before going back to sleep. The baby had pale ginger-coloured eyebrows that met over her nose, and white-blond hair that stuck out around her scalp like the frayed end of a nylon rope.

Arlene had walked up and down the hall between the front door and the back door with the baby, patting her on the back and singing to her softly, then she had gone out onto the deck. She could see a fruit orchard on the far side of the lake, rows of trees that from this distance were only a design, a pattern placed daintily on the face of nature. Her father-in-law and David were standing at the far end of the deck, discussing the likelihood of the Soviets launching rockets into the Pacific Ocean. It was Phil's favourite subject, it seemed to Arlene. From the way he spoke, she wondered if he thought the Pacific was no wider across than Okanagan Lake. She wanted to tell him he reminded her of a certain door-to-door juice machine salesman she'd met the week before, a man whose sales pitch was constructed around horror stories of poisoned air and poisoned food. She had opened the door one fine morning last month, and there he was. He had handed her his card: *Nature's Own Juice Extractor. Since 1946. All of Nature's Goodness in a Glass!* And there was his name: Eugene Kriskin. She had looked at him in shock and in return he had given her the blandest smile: She was just another prospective customer.

"As you know," he had said, his foot planted on the door sill, "Strontium 90 is a substance that gets into teeth and bones, especially in the case of children. That's a depressing fact, but it's a scientific one. And the good news is, there is something you can do to protect your family. If I could just take a few minutes of your time? There's no obligation whatsoever."

He wore a grey suit and carried a bulky black leather case. His hair was pressed into tight little waves above a narrow forehead. He had a dark mole, like an old-fashioned beauty spot, near his mouth. It made him look as if he were disputing his own words. His tie was patterned with some kind of abstract design, like the symbol for atomic radiation. It was true that the world was a more dangerous place now than at any time before. David told her so all the time. His greatest fear was that there would be another war, a nuclear war. He had made her read a pamphlet called *Evacuation and Survival Plan for Greater Vancouver Target Area.* The pamphlet became his bible for a while, his guidebook to better living. Their basement was stocked with canned peas and Argentinean corned beef and boxes of Nabisco Shredded Wheat. David's brother had died in the war; the man his sister had been engaged to had died in the war. If another war came along, David swore he would be a pacifist. He would rather go to jail than fight, and it wasn't that he was a communist, either. No one could say that. Wasn't Canada a peacekeeping nation, a Middle Power, a bridge-builder? David had nightmares about nuclear war. Arlene didn't. She had other, more immediate things to have bad dreams about. Her mind couldn't take in the possibility of any disaster beyond the ones she fought daily: accidents, serious illnesses, house fires, lost children.

She adjusted Jessica in her arms and stood there listening to David and his father and at the same time remembering the morning Eugene Kriskin had called at her house with his juice machine.

Thank you very much, Mr. Kriskin, she should have said right away. Thank you, but I'm not interested. If it had been anyone else, that was what she would have said. Instead, she heard herself saying, "Well, if it won't take too long, I guess."

That morning Matt had been in the kitchen, kneeling on a chair at the table drawing on a sheet of white paper David had brought home from the office. "That's a very nice picture, young fellow," Eugene Kriskin had said. Matt had given him an indifferent look, and had gone back to his drawing of spaceships and little space creatures with bug eyes and antenna. He had scribbled some blue and red lines across the background. "What are those?" Eugene Kriskin had said. "Are those comets?" Matt kept on scribbling. Arlene said, "You should answer when people speak to you, Matt."

"Do you mind?" Eugene Kriskin had said, indicating the sink. He took off his jacket and pushed his sleeves up and began scrubbing his hands. He whistled through his teeth. He began assembling the machine on the counter, a piece at a time. She watched him, scarcely breathing. She wanted him to go on assembling *Nature's Own Juicer* forever, breathing through his mouth, making an adjustment here or there to the machine. He took a plastic bag out of his black leather case and opened it and spread out on the counter carrots, celery, potatoes, a sprig of parsley, a tomato. He took out a paring knife and began slicing up the vegetables. His hands were quick and sure. All the while, he was talking about vitamins A and C, and how superior the natural sources were to the artificial. Arlene listened and watched, thinking: How clean are those vegetables? He asked her for a glass, and she handed him one from the drainboard. After turning on the juicer and letting it operate at top speed—he showed her how easy it was to set the dial for any of three speed settings, low, medium, and high—for a few minutes, he turned it off and poured a thick bright orange liquid from the spout of *Nature's Own Juicer* into the glass. Then he gravely handed it to her. She took a sip. "Take your time," he said. "Savour the bouquet." He took a second glass from the drainboard and poured some juice for Matt.

"Kids go for this," he said. "They have a natural instinct for pure foods." He waited in silence while she drank a little more. "Well, what do you think?" he asked. "What's the verdict? Isn't that the most flavourful drink you've ever tasted?"

What he liked to do, he had told her, was to use vegetables and fruit from his own garden; then he could be absolutely sure of the purity of the finished product. "You have a garden, Ma'am?" he said. She nodded. "My husband grows vegetables," she said. The taste of carrot juice coated her tongue, the roof of her mouth. It was fibrous, neither sweet nor salt. What she wanted to say was, Would you like to step outside and see the garden? Would you like to see the place where your ex-wife, your late ex-wife, Myrtle, painted my daughter's face with lipstick and rouge and mascara? Is that why you're here? Why are you here?

"Come on there, young fellow," Eugene Kriskin said to Matt. "Drink up. Don't you know when something's good for you?"

"He's never been very fond of vegetables," Arlene said. The human body was composed mainly of water. She'd learned that at school. Every living thing was composed mainly of water. The surface of the earth was covered in more water than land. Some people found that difficult to believe. She could buy this juice machine. David wouldn't mind; he might even think it was a good idea. It wouldn't kill her to buy *Nature's Own Juicer*, even though she'd probably never use it. How many juice machines had Eugene Kriskin sold that morning? she wondered. How many was he likely to sell in a week? She thanked him, and told him she'd have to think it over. She'd have to speak to her husband.

"Why, that's no problem," Eugene Kriskin said. There was, she saw, a fine film of sweat on his forehead. Just for allowing him to do a free demonstration, he said, he had a gift for her. A potato peeler. He told her a convenient instalment plan was available for payment. There was a three-year guarantee on the electric motor. Frankly, he thought that anything that would counteract the radiation and chemicals in the air and water was a darned good investment. He gave her such a weary, patient smile that she almost changed her mind, but didn't, because she was afraid he'd think she pitied him. Eugene Kriskin. She thought he did know who she was. It was such a small town, he had to know. He knew who she was, and he had forgiven her for letting his two little boys drown. Or hadn't forgiven her, and wished to curse her secretly while he stood at her kitchen sink diligently scraping the skin from vegetables. But it hadn't been her fault. It hadn't. She had stood on the front steps watching him walk down the street to his car. She had waited for him to look back, so that she could wave good-bye, but he put his black leather case in the trunk of his car, walked around and got into the driver's seat and drove away.

Now Phil was saying he had his hopes pinned on presidential candidate Richard Milhaus Nixon to put the brakes, as he put it, on Krushchev. Arlene had been standing there, saying nothing, thinking about Eugene Kriskin, wondering idly how he managed to support himself, not that it was any of her concern. But it was, in a way. It was her concern.

Then she heard herself telling Phil that if she were a citizen of the United States, she'd vote for John F. Kennedy. It was a strange thing, but she felt as if she were arguing on behalf of Eugene Kriskin. She was arguing for an end to the arms race on behalf of the purveyor of *Nature's Own Juicer*.

"Oh, why is that?" Phil said. He gave her a cold smile. "I suppose it's because you think Kennedy's good-looking. A lot of women are going to vote for him for that reason. It's a hell of a way to use your vote, I'd say."

"No," Arlene said, "it isn't that. It's just the way I'd vote. In the States, I'd vote for the Democratic Party. Here, I vote Liberal." This wasn't quite true; she had forgotten to vote in the last election.

"Well, you're one of the very few," Phil said. "You're a member of a real minority."

"Arlene," David said. "Don't argue with Dad."

She gave David a cool smile. Go to hell, she nearly said. She could see she was making Phil mad, but she couldn't stop. Politics wasn't an interest of hers, but she was enjoying herself. "Lester Pearson won the Nobel Peace Prize, didn't he?" she said, pleased to have suddenly remembered this fact. "If he won the Nobel Peace Prize, he's good enough for me. I don't even mind Krushchev all that much," she added defiantly. Phil gave her a stiff little smile.

"You don't know what you're saying, young lady," he said. "That's your problem. You just don't know what you're saying. You should think of that little baby you're holding. You should think of the future."

"I do," she said, deliberately sounding meek. She didn't feel like discussing the subject any further with Phil. The baby she was holding smelled of vomit and talcum powder and heat rash medication, and her tiny face was collapsing into a furious grimace, as if she was about to howl in rage. "I do think of the future," she said, patting the baby's back, jouncing her up and down to keep her quiet. "Doesn't everyone?"

Eunice had been invited to the family reunion, but she had sent her regrets, saying she was going to be too busy at the store. She told Arlene one of her business partners, Olive, had gone to Calgary to visit her sister, which left Rosemary and Eunice to look after their annual summer coat and suit sale. And Eunice had reserved a seat to see Cole Porter's *Can-Can*, which was in its fifth week at the Strand Theatre. Eunice had already seen it once, and she had loved it; she wanted to buy tickets for Arlene and David. She knew David, being a big Frank Sinatra fan, would love it. Arlene would have preferred seeing *Can-Can* to driving all the way to Summerland, to be honest, but she didn't have any choice in the matter. She wished Eunice were here, walking around in her spike heels and one of the latest dress styles from Natalie's Dress Shoppe, giving Margaret fashion advice, telling her what she could use on her hands to get rid of her freckles, elbowing Margaret aside to use her spotless kitchen to bake blue cupcakes for Matt and Catherine.

The same representatives of the Gamlin clan who were at Arlene's wedding were at the reunion. Every room in the Greenwoods' big house filled up with men and women in summer-weight navy blue, their eyes grave and intelligent behind wire-rimmed glasses. They paid special attention to Arlene, asking her about her life in Cayley, if she had good friends, if she was able to find interesting things to do, if she had hobbies, if she managed to get any time to herself, apart from the children. Time to herself, time to recharge the batteries, was very important, they said, for a mother of young children. The Gamlin women, who were of course married and had children, and in one case, grandchildren, bore different, although at the same time strangely homogenous-sounding one-syllable last names—Ford, Good, Best, White. They liked to take Arlene for walks with them around the Greenwoods' splendid garden. They plucked peas from the vine and ate them raw; they bent down and rapped their knuckles against barely-formed cucumbers and discussed the merits of blanching apple slices against putting them straight into the freezer with just a sprinkling of sugar. They wore their hair, which was neither completely grey nor brown nor black, in precise finger waves. They were in their forties and fifties; one of them was a Public Health Nurse and one was the constituency secretary to an elected Conservative Member of Parliament. They placed their hands on Arlene's elbows and steered her around hazards only they perceived, a pothole on the driveway, a clump of what might be poison oak, a squelchy place in the lawn where the sprinkler had been dripping water. They picked cherries from overhanging branches and filled her cupped hands with them, urging her to eat them quickly, before Margaret discovered what they were up to. They stood out on the road and had a spirited discussion about its name: Cottonwood Road? Where were the cottonwood trees? What did a cottonwood

tree look like, anyway? one of them asked. Another said the
name must surely refer to the poplar trees along one side of
the road. Poplars and cottonwoods belonged to the same
family, didn't they? Did anyone know anything about tree
species? Perhaps the original cottonwood tree had blown
down in a storm, or been removed, someone said. Or perhaps the cottonwoods were here, and they couldn't see them,
one of them suggested, and they all laughed merrily, as if
she'd made a joke.

There were really only four Gamlin women. Harriet, Joan,
Diane and Edna. Arlene adored them all. In their company
she felt calm, serene, cared-for, capable of accomplishing
anything she wanted. She studied them, the way they smiled
and joked companionably at each other, the forthright way
they walked, their arms swinging at their sides. They kept
telling her they were having a wonderful time, they were so
glad they'd come, if only to see Arlene again, after all this
time since Arlene's wedding. Ten years! They exchanged
addresses and telephone numbers with her, and told her
she must come and stay with them. And Arlene said she
and David would love to have them for a visit, they really
would, they simply must keep in touch in future. The cocker
spaniel, Star, kept pace with them, wagging her tail, a different sort of dog altogether when she was with them.

One morning toward the end of the week, Arlene woke David
at dawn and made him put on his shorts and a T-shirt and
follow her outside. When they'd first arrived, they'd been
sleeping upstairs in David's old bedroom, with high-school
pennants tacked to the wall and an ancient teddy bear sit-

ting on a toy chest, and his old geometry set in a metal case on his desk, but then more Gamlin relatives had arrived, and they'd been moved downstairs to a smaller bedroom. In order to leave the house, they had to tiptoe down the hall and through the sunroom, where David's brother Robert was asleep on a cot. On the porch steps, Arlene held out her hand and showed David what she had: the keys to his father's truck. She'd removed them from a hook on the kitchen wall before she went to bed the night before. She had noticed that while their car was hemmed in on all sides by other vehicles, Phil kept his truck at the top of the drive, with its nose pointed expediently toward the road.

"Arlene, what in the hell are you doing now?" David said. She told him to shush. She held onto his hand, pulling him along until they were around the side of the house and out on the drive. "What in the hell are you up to?" he asked her again. She turned and looked at him. He was smiling faintly, limping along in a good-humoured way with his shoes and socks in his hands. The sun was just coming up behind the hills on the other side of the lake. All those brown hills with their small spiky trees, and then the lake, blue and calm as an open eye. The birds were starting to sing. One of Margaret's calico cats was stalking something in the petunia bed. It was a beautiful morning. Arlene walked up the drive until she got to the pickup truck. She opened the driver's side door and got in. David stood beside the truck and said, "This is my father's truck, Arlene."

"Just get in," she said. "Hurry up, would you." As soon as he had climbed into the cab and shut the door, she started the engine and drove out onto the road. She had never driven a truck before, but she liked this, the clunky gear shift and the metal clutch pedal that banged down hard against the metal floor when she stepped on it. She liked the way the rear tires chewed at the gravel and the back end slid to the side then straightened out when she speeded up. She liked the cloud of dust she was leaving in her wake. She had no clear idea of what she was doing. But once, walking down this road with the Gamlin women, she had seen a dirt road that led down to the lake, and it was to this road she was headed. David had his arm resting in the open window and he was looking out at the morning landscape. He tried telling her that his father would have a heart attack if he found out she had taken his truck, and then he had given up. David was thirty-nine years old and he looked about ten years younger. Young and reasonably handsome, responsible, a decent citizen. A man who voted for the right political party, which was to say the one his father told him to vote for. A man who saved up canned peas in the basement of his house in an effort to keep his family alive through a holocaust. She shifted into third gear and stepped on the gas and David said, "Arlene," just her name, as if attempting to call her gently back to the real world. Tough luck, she thought; she wasn't ready to return yet. Here they were, two criminals in a stolen truck. It was too good to be true.

She turned down the dirt road and parked facing the lake, beside someone's property line, which was marked by a wire fence and an irrigation pipe that led uphill through an orchard of cherry trees. The lake was gold, pure gold, the sun's light spreading out across the water like a flame. Arlene turned off the engine. There was no wind, only the extraordinary stillness of dawn, leaves hanging motionless, moist with dew, on the trees.

"Let's go swimming," she said.

"We can't go swimming, Arlene," David said. "We don't have our swimsuits, for one thing."

"I meant let's go swimming in our birthday suits," said Arlene.

He put his hand flat to his forehead. He kept repeating her name, "Arlene, Arlene. Arlene, what has got into you?"

"I've never gone swimming in my birthday suit," she said. "What about you?"

"Not for one hell of a long time," he said.

She opened the truck door and slid out. She started to unbutton her shirt. She kept her eyes on David, who was sitting in the cab. She noticed that he couldn't help smiling at her. She took off her shirt and folded it up and put it on the hood of the truck. She unzipped her shorts. David jumped out of the truck and said, "Arlene, stop that." There was a house barely visible through the cherry orchard, and he was looking toward it. "Someone might see you, for Pete's sake." he said.

"It's five o'clock in the morning. Everyone is asleep, and anyway, they don't know who I am. They can't even see us down here. I can't believe you, David. You old fuddy-duddy. Come on, get out of your clothes. I'm going into the water."

What she wanted to say to him was this: If they could just step outside of their ordinary selves, even for the briefest time. She wanted to be some other kind of person, not just a mother and wife, not just Arlene Greenwood, but someone completely different, someone with a more spacious, less predictable life, a wider perspective on life, and she wanted David to be the same. He was standing there beside the truck, scratching at the back of his neck, looking pained. He didn't understand in the least what it was she was trying to do, she could tell. Just this once, before they went back home, she wanted to imitate the reckless exuberance she'd observed in David and Gilbert and even in her father-in-law. Running around the house hollering like ten-year-olds, playing badminton, tossing footballs at each other. Animal high spirits. It wasn't fair that all she got to do was hold onto Jessica and hear the details of how long Brenda had been in labour. All she got to do was walk sedately around the Greenwoods' property with the Gamlin women, all of whom she earnestly wished to emulate, in every respect, but not just yet. Arlene reached around to unhook her bra and then she stopped. The morning air felt chillier suddenly. There was a bird singing nearby, a sad repetitive song. She felt tired, all the energy she'd woken with drained out of her. She reached for her shirt and shook it out and slipped it on. "All right. You win," she said.

"Oh, Arlene, honey, this isn't a contest, is it?" David said. He came over and started doing up the buttons on her shirt. He smoothed her hair off her face and then kissed her on the mouth. "You chicken shit," Arlene said. "I know," he said.

"It's such a small request, to go skinny-dipping. What if I asked you to do something really wild, David. What would you do then? Head for the hills?"

"It's just that everyone around here knows my parents. Everyone knows me. If anyone saw us swimming in the nude, they'd be sure to tell my parents. Think how upset they'd be." Arlene looked at him without saying a word. When she got back into the truck, she said, "And you were the one talking about quitting your job and starting over fresh with ponies and green pastures. That'll be the day."

He started the engine without looking at her. He put the truck into gear and backed out onto the road, then he drove back to the house, obeying the speed limit and taking care to park the truck in the right direction, just as they had found it. Arlene jumped out and they walked between the parked vehicles, the Dodge and Ford cars and station wagons that belonged to the Greenwood and Gamlin clan, and the wonderful red Studebaker Hawk that David's brother Robert drove. She should have stolen the Studebaker instead of the truck.

"Arlene," David said. "Are you all right? Are you sulking?"

"Well, yes, I guess I am," she said. "Sulking is what I do best. It's the only thing I'm allowed to do."

"Oh, come on, Arlene," he said, trying to take her hand.

Someone had opened the front door; the dog had her nose pressed up against the screen. Any minute she would start barking at them, Arlene thought. She could hear Margaret in the kitchen already, moving things around, putting the coffee pot on. David was pulling Arlene along, around the house to the safety of the sunroom. She thought: The great truck robber and her accomplice seek shelter at the hideout, just in the nick of time. Robert was already up, his cot neatly made up with a Hudson's Bay blanket folded at the foot. The windows in the sunroom were open, and a light cool breeze was coming in. In Arlene and David's room, Catherine and Matt were just waking up, sliding out of their rollaway cots, rubbing the sleep from their eyes. "Where's Granny?" they wanted to know. Arlene told them Granny was in the kitchen waiting to give them breakfast. "Go find her," she said. Matt started to climb back into his cot and David fished him out and gave him a pat on the rear end of his pyjamas. "Go see Granny," he said. "Both of you go help Granny with breakfast. She'll like that. Take your brother with you, Catherine," he said. "There we go."

Arlene felt ice-cold, as if she really had gone swimming in the nude in Okanagan Lake. She got into bed and pulled the covers around her, and David got in beside her and pulled the covers off. He said she didn't need a blanket; he'd warm her up. "I locked the door," he told her and she told him the door didn't lock, it was broken, and he was going to get found out, and it was a small town and everyone was going to know what he was doing. His parents were going to be too ashamed to be seen in town. She laughed, and he said, "To hell with the door. Be quiet, sweetheart." He put his mouth on hers and pulled the pillow out from under her head and threw it on the floor. He put his arm under her waist and lifted her towards him and she put her arms around his neck and then she remembered that she didn't have her diaphragm in, and she told him to wait, or rather, she was going to tell him, but it was a golden morning, the birds singing like mad outside the window, the house smelling of coffee and bread baking, distant voices murmuring, children's laughter, all of it far off and no concern of hers, and she didn't have the least desire to interrupt what was going on. Instead, she made a mental effort to invoke some kind of magic spell to protect her, and then she must have just put it out of her mind.

That morning, while Arlene and David were still in bed, David's mother slipped and fell on her shiny freshly waxed kitchen floor and broke her wrist. Arlene couldn't help thinking it was something she'd done to teach them a lesson for being irresponsible. She could hear the dog barking frantically. Doors were slamming. When she and David got to the kitchen, Margaret was sitting on a chair, her face drained of colour, saying, "This is ridiculous, this is just ridiculous. I can't think how I could be so careless." Someone was trying to get her to drink a cup of hot, sweet tea, to help her get over the shock. She waved it away. Then Phil and Brenda took her to the hospital. Arlene and the other women had to take over, quietly baking and making salads and looking after the children. They all felt a little guilty, Arlene thought, because up until now Margaret had been doing almost all of the work herself. That was the way she wanted it, but still, they all felt partly responsible. Margaret came back from the hospital unusually subdued, a snow-white plaster cast on her wrist and her arm in a sling. She sat outside in the shade in a lawn chair because it was so hot in the house, and her children and grandchildren came to her and sat on the grass beside her. She had a mild apologetic expression on her face, as if her spirit and not merely her wrist had been broken.

That was how she appeared in the photograph she mailed to Arlene and David three months later, at the beginning of

October. It was a glossy eight-by-ten black-and-white group photograph taken on the second-to-last day of the family reunion, by a professional photographer Margaret had hired.

Here were the Greenwoods, then, and their near kin, the Gamlins, along with their assorted descendants, family members, children, nieces and nephews, on a bright cloudless Friday morning in July, 1960. Everyone was smiling. Lovely healthy smiles, good strong teeth, decisive jaws, crinkly little laugh lines around the eyes. The smiles of individuals pleased to be related to one other by the virtually indissoluble bonds of blood and marriage. The children clustered in the first row like flowers. They looked strangely formal, for children. The girls were wearing those stiff little hats adorned with artificial flowers that were popular a decade earlier, Arlene remembered, in the fifties. They held their hands primly clasped in front of them. The boys had their arms at their sides, as if about to sing the national anthem. The baby girls, in their parents' arms, were dressed in frilled nylon lace, the baby boys in those miniature white nylon shirts with the attached plaid vests and fake bow-ties. At the centre of the picture stood Margaret and Philip Greenwood, Margaret's arm cradled in a sling that looked like a huge triangular baby's diaper. Edna, Harriet, Diane and Joan, the Gamlin girls, descendants of the original Rose and Daphne, stood solicitously on either side of Margaret. David and Arlene were at the end of the second row, just behind the children. Arlene was wearing a light-coloured cotton shirt, and her hair was long, hanging over her thin shoulders. She was leaning slightly toward her husband, but her face was turned away, as if her attention was on some distant view.

Arlene thought: These people will always look like this; they will always smile like this. For them, it will always be morning; it will always be summer. Their hands will touch just so, the kindliest, most gentle gestures. A slight shadow will fall, for no particular reason, across a face. Someone else's face, Harriet's in this case, will turn out slightly blurred, although no one can ascertain why this should be so. Someone will look younger than he or she, in fact, is, or prettier, or taller, or thinner, or older.

Photographs are mysterious; they are and they are not the truth, at the same time. Only Arlene, for example, can look at this image from the past and see the future concealed within it. She believes she can, at any rate. Isn't there a slight variation in the light, just where she's standing? A presence made of light. It's beautiful and astonishing and just a little frightening. She hasn't told anyone, including David, of her suspicions, even though nearly three months have already gone by. There doesn't seem to be any point. For some reason, she has the feeling there's plenty of time. She doesn't seem to have many of the usual symptoms, in any case. Perhaps it's all in her head, like her case of appendicitis when she was fifteen years old. She hands the photograph to David when he gets home from work and waits for his reaction. She thinks of it as a test. Does he see it? Is he capable of detecting the luminous future, in form half firefly, half angel, trailing its gauzy insubstantial dream presence through the photographic emulsion? Perhaps not, perhaps he sees nothing of the kind, perhaps it is all in her mind. He is, however, clearly delighted with the photograph, and immediately telephones his mother to tell her how pleased they are with it, and to thank her for sending it to them.

CHAPTER SIXTEEN

It was all very well to pretend nothing was happening, but even she couldn't do it for much longer. It was November. Then it would be December, and five months would have gone by. She walked along the street beside the hospital, carrying grocery bags and loaves of bread from the bakery, a scarf covering her hair. Matt had started kindergarten. Arlene missed him. Every now and then she missed him. In the store she'd started to look for him, she'd held out her hand to him, but of course he wasn't there.

Without thinking she walked down the side road to Caroline's house. No one was at home. The windows glared blankly in the sun. November and it felt more like June. She took off her scarf and stuffed it in her coat pocket. She put her bags down on the ground, undid her coat and rested against the fence. She felt weak, and ravenous. She should have had breakfast, but she'd been too busy getting Catherine and Matt ready for school. It was very quiet. No one about, the tide in, water like silk lapping at the sand, the rocks. The salt smell of the sea intoxicating. She went down to the beach and stood there, looking at the sea, the islands, the distant mountains. She went right to the edge and kneeled down and put her hand in the water. It was almost unbearably cold, but she kept her hand there. Sea water healed wounds. Her mother believed that. When Arlene had cut her foot on a barnacle, Eunice had told her to go swimming and the sea water would kill the germs. She believed that salt water stitched the wound together like catgut. A little way out from shore there was a rock rising from the water. Arlene couldn't remember having seen it before, although it must always have been there. Brown rock folded and pleated. In places the light of the sun drew a golden incandescent warmth up from the surface of the rock. The sea was green near the shore, and clear as glass. Farther out it was a pale, coruscant blue, a brilliance that hurt the eyes.

She splashed her hand in the water, and a ribbon of seaweed wound itself around her fingers. She took her hand out of the water and peeled the seaweed away and held it up, then wiped it off on the hem of her coat. A ribbon of gold on emerald cloth. When she looked up she saw them. Two little boys were sitting on the rock. They were facing away from her, looking out at the sea. They were wearing shorts and T-shirts. She could see the curls in the delicate nape of the neck. The delicate curve of the spine under the thin cloth. They were fragile as birds huddling together, taking what comfort they could from each other's presence. A gull flew over, but the children did not look up. They were fixated on something far off. Without thinking, Arlene stepped into the water. She had the sense she could walk to them, walk across the water to them. What were their names? What if she called to them? Billy, Eddy. Would they turn and look at her, and what would such a look mean? Would they beckon to her, make her, at last, obey, follow them into a world of light and silence?

She took a step. The water came to her ankles. It sloshed against her legs. The boys remained motionless, their arms bare and thin as sticks beneath the sleeves of the T-shirts. She thought: I'll die if I stay in this freezing water. I'll catch cold. She stepped out and took her shoes off and emptied the sea water out of them. What if someone came along and saw her? They would think she was out of her mind, and perhaps she was.

When she looked up the rock was vacant. It was just a golden brown rock covered with barnacles and stained from the sea. Had they ever been there? It was the state of her mind. She was in a panic. She had trapped herself in silence, in a little whirlpool of negation, denying what was obvious to her and soon would be to others. It was a game she'd started and couldn't seem to get out of. With her numb cold hands she put her wet shoes back on her cold wet feet, and she walked back up the road. She had to stop and go back for her groceries, the yeasty bread and the bag of apples and a few carrots and a tomato. Then she walked slowly up the hill toward home.

Chapter Seventeen

On certain days a column of thick black smoke rose from the smokestacks at the sawmill and covered the sun, and everything became dark and strange. Behind the smoke the sun floated like a dull red, mean-looking eye. If you stared at it, Catherine's mother had warned her, it could burn the eyes right out of your head. But knowing this made Catherine want to look even more; she wanted desperately to stare at the dead floating star the sun had become. But just here— and just temporarily, as if a witch with a weird sense of humour was learning some new magic spells.

Catherine was walking with Abigail Glass down Ashlar Street. They were dressed in Julia's old clothes, which they had removed from a cardboard box in Abigail's front hall. Mrs. Glass had gone through her closet selecting all the clothes she didn't wear anymore, or had started to hate, and had folded them up in the box. The clothes were for Hazel Byers. Hazel was too poor to buy her own clothes, Abigail had told Catherine, kicking at the box on the hall floor. "Why should Hazel get all this stuff? It's not fair," Abigail said. "Hazel is a cross-eyed old whore."

Abigail pried the box open and started hauling out silk blouses and rayon dresses. She held them up to herself in front of the mirror in the hall. "How do I look?" she asked Catherine. She tied headscarves under her chin and wobbled around in her mother's high-heeled shoes. She walking into the living room hunched over, her head shaking. "Oh, I'm so old," she said, her face wizened. "My hemorrhoids are killing me." Then she said, "Let's both pretend we're old." She said they should dress up as very old women and walk through town, fooling everyone who saw them. Catherine could see that they weren't fooling a single person. They were walking through this smoky dim town in dresses that trailed on the ground, their hands gloved, their hats ornamented with feathers and little wisps of net veil, and people were smiling indulgently at them and saying, "Why, hello Catherine, Hello Abigail."

Catherine was carrying her marble collection in a purple Seagram's Whiskey bag with a gold drawstring as if it was an evening bag. Her other arm was supported by a folded pink chiffon scarf tied around her neck, like the sling Granny Greenwood had had to wear last summer with her broken wrist. Catherine wished she did have a broken wrist, then she could have her plaster cast autographed. Nothing ever happened to her. She started to limp. Abigail started to limp, too. She was carrying an umbrella from her mother's hall closet and she began to use it as a cane. "Take my arm," she said to Catherine. "Lead me, for I am quite blind and troubled with the rheumatism." They were wearing Julia Glass's makeup, her orange-red lipstick, powdered pink rouge, and black mascara they'd applied with a little stiff-bristled brush. Mad clowns. That was what Catherine thought they looked like. They walked down the hill toward the mill. What if their fathers looked out of their office windows and saw them? Abigail said she hoped they did. Her father wouldn't know who she was. He was a kook, she said. He wouldn't notice shit if he stepped in it.

Catherine tripped on her hem and Abigail said, "Oh, did you almost fall on your buttocks, my dear?" Then they sang a jingle from a radio commercial for a dress store in Nanaimo where Julia liked to shop: *There she goes, there she goes, all dressed up in her Jean Burns' Clothes.* Except they substituted "All dressed up in Julia's old clothes."

"Stop it, you're killing me," Catherine said, sitting down on the curb. Now she had the hiccups, which was also funny and made them laugh even harder.

Was Abigail Glass a good influence on Catherine, or not? Catherine's mother wished someone would answer this question for her. Because she had a suspicion that Catherine was goaded by Abigail Glass into behaving like an orangutan. I am not, Catherine said at once. And yet it was true that after playing with Abigail she wanted to be less like herself and more like Abigail. She felt a pressure inside her head, behind her eyes, that made her want to move through her life at a faster rate. She wanted to be a smaller person than she was, with bones like pipe-cleaners and eyes as pale and purely clear as water, and braids so long she could wind them around the delicate circumference of her wrists. She wanted to be an only child who slept in a pink canopy bed. More than anything, she wished she could do something impossible: she wished she could enter Abigail's dreams, go directly into the strangely populated rooms of Abigail's sleeping, reckless brain, and abide there for a time. She imagined herself filled with power as a result. She would have what Abigail had, or at least what it seemed she had: the concentrated, erratic adult attention directed at an only child. She would be allowed to stay up until eleven o'clock watching television; she would get to sip wine in a crystal wine glass with her meals, she would know how to use swear words as fluently as Abigail did, and she would, just possibly, get the almost flawless scores Abigail managed to pull off on Friday morning math drills.

Abigail and Catherine walked as far as the park and sat on the swings. They slumped over and stared at the grass, their arms hooked through the chains and their gloved hands hanging free like appendages they'd never seen before. The wind made the hems of their dresses flutter around their ankles.

Abigail said, "I know a secret about your mother."

"You do not," Catherine said. "What secret?"

"Well. If you don't know, I'm not going to tell you."

"You have to tell me," Catherine said. "You have to tell me now." She kicked at the dirt under the swing, where the grass was worn away. She was wearing running shoes under Mrs. Glass's old pink silk dress. There were dark patches on the skirt from a puddle Catherine had accidentally stepped in. The sun was shining, but palely, and low in the sky. Her shadow lay like a bundle of old clothes at her feet. "You're lying," she said quietly. "You don't know any secret about my mother. You're a liar."

"I'm not. I know something about your Mom you don't know. I heard her telling my Mom. *I have to tell someone*, she said. She started to cry and my mother held her hand. *There, there, you can tell me, dearie.* That's what she said. I saw her through the hot-air grill."

"Abigail, you're such a liar. Your mother doesn't ever talk like that."

"She does when you're not around." Abigail got off the swing. She started to walk toward the road. "Well, if you don't want to know," she said. "It's no skin off my nose." The scarf she had wound around her neck came off and floated to the ground. Catherine ran up behind her and stamped on the scarf. "Get off that," Abigail said. "You little shit."

"Don't swear at me," Catherine said. "Anyway, I know a secret about your Daddy."

"My Daddy," Abigail sneered. "You don't know piss-all about my Daddy."

"I do." Catherine bent down and picked up the scarf. "This is the ugliest scarf I ever saw," she said.

"I know," Abigail said. "My mother has bad taste."

Catherine started to laugh. They both laughed. They started to stagger around, clutching onto each other. Then they separated. "What do you know about my Daddy?" Abigail said. She pushed her mother's black velvet hat back on her head.

"I'll tell you if you tell me what you know about my mother."

"Want to shake on it?" Abigail said.

"Abigail. Just tell me."

"You first."

"All right. Your Daddy drinks too much. He gets drunk all the time."

"I know that, stupid," Abigail said. "Everyone knows that. Poor old Howard. But here's what you don't know. Your mother is pregnant."

"What?" Catherine took a step back.

"It's true. Your mother is going to have a baby. She told my mother."

"Liar."

"It's the truth, Catherine."

"I'm never playing with you again," Catherine said.

"You'd better get out of my mother's stuff, then," Abigail said. "You'd better give all that stuff back to me right now."

Catherine refused to see her best friend Abigail Glass. They'd had had a fight, and now they weren't talking. Instead, Catherine went with Matt to their father's office, to meet his new secretary, Miss Mullis. Miss Mullis was tiny, not much taller than Catherine, with light brown absolutely straight hair to her shoulders. She had green eyes. She spoke with an English accent that entranced Catherine. Miss Mullis let Catherine and Matt take turns sitting at her desk. She had a chair that swivelled, and an Underwood typewriter and two African violets in pots on her desk. Catherine placed her fingers lightly on the keys of the Underwood. Over the top of the typewriter, she could see her father standing beside his desk on the other side of the room, showing Matt a huge book with a dark green cover. "See how the number in this column is exactly the same as this number over here in the last column on this page," he was saying. As if, Catherine thought, as if Matt, who was not quite six years old, found this information of interest. Matt nodded his head and swung his legs, trying to make his father's black leather chair go around in circles, the way Miss Mullis's did.

What Catherine especially liked at her father's office were the muted sounds of office machinery, murmured conversations from adjacent offices, the smell of duplicating fluid, hot coffee, perfume and cigarette smoke all mixed together. Imagine I work here, she wanted to say to her father. Imagine I'm sitting at a desk stapling pages together, and stamping each page and signing my initials neatly in the bottom corner. She could see her hands, tanned and neat, fingernails coated with clear nail polish, like Miss Mullis's hands, expertly rifling through sheets of clean white paper.

One day, their father promised, he was going to take Catherine and Matt on a tour of the sawmill. He was going to show them the green chain. He had worked on the green chain, he said, at another mill, a long time ago, in Prince George, long before he got married to their mother. Working on the green chain was the hardest job he had ever had in his life. It had forced him to grow up, he believed. It had made a man out of him. He had paid his way through university by working on the green chain, he said. He had developed muscles in his arms that he wished he still had.

On the way home, Catherine and Matt sat in the back seat. Matt kneeled on the seat so that he could see out the window. He said he didn't want to work at a sawmill when he got older. It was too noisy. It smelled funny. He was going to be a cartoonist.

"Well, I think you'll be an excellent cartoonist," their father said. He turned a corner, one hand on the steering wheel, the other fiddling with the defogger controls on the dash. It was a cold day and the inside of the car was misting up.

"Who would want to be a stupid old cartoonist?" Catherine said. "What a dumb idea," she said. The truth was, she could easily imagine Matt drawing cartoons and walking around with black smears of ink on his face. She pictured a grownup Matt in jeans and a black sweater: a beatnik artist. She knew about beatniks, about artists; she knew about starving in attics. She'd read a few books on the subject. It pleased her to think that she probably knew more than her father did, certainly more than Matt. Her father told Matt all the time that in his opinion he had the makings of a talented artist. His teachers told him the same thing. On his birthdays he always got art supplies. All Matt ever wanted to do was sit at the kitchen table and draw. It wasn't possible to sit down anymore without getting India ink or water colour paint all over your hands or clothes. Matt drew men in space suits riding on comets. He was crazy about Buck Rogers and Superman and Lois Lane. And anything else that had to do with rockets and satellites in orbit, and creatures that arrived on the earth infested with dangerous alien microbes or man-eating mould spores. He drew the mould spores with keen, malicious expressions and long grasping tentacles. When Catherine told him none of this weird stuff was real, it was crazy stuff, it was pure baloney, he punched her on the arm and told her to mind her own business. He made sure that no one was looking before he landed the punch. And then, when Catherine yelled, he looked at their mother with the biggest, most innocent-looking eyes, those dark eyes that were in fact neither truly brown nor dark blue. *Who, me?* He was in love with a robot from an old movie, called *Tobor*, which was robot spelled backwards. That was something else he loved, backwards writing. He hadn't even learned to write in the right direction, and he was always getting Catherine to help him print words like ROCKET and BOMB on pieces of paper that he then held up to the bathroom mirror. TEKCOR BMOB. Tupidsay Attmay, Catherine said in pig Latin. Figure that one out, Mr. Genius, she said. She told him she liked one of his pictures, and he gave it to her. She thumbtacked it to the back of her bedroom door. She did like it. Smiling bug faces inside a flying saucer. People the size of carpenter ants on the ground, running screaming in every direction. It made her think of Cayley, the sky over Cayley, when the smoke from the mill covered the sun in midnight black.

Catherine and Abigail sat in the car while Abigail's mother delivered the box of clothes to Hazel Byers's house. Julia Glass told them they had to sit quietly and behave themselves. Then she got out of the car and walked toward the front door, right past a big brown dog tied to a tree. The dog leapt at her, barking. Catherine was afraid Julia's mother was going to get ripped to pieces while they watched. Abigail rolled down the window and shouted, "Kick him in the teeth, Mom." Julia Glass turned around and said, "I warned you, Abigail." She went back to the dog and bent down and talked to it, and the dog stopped barking. It let Julia Glass pat it on the head. It sat down in the mud and watched her as she went right up to the door.

The yard was all churned up with tire tracks, but there was no vehicle in sight. It was starting to rain, and Abigail's mother put the box down on the front steps and pulled her raincoat hood over her head before she knocked at the front door. The house looked cold and vacant. Whoever was in there wanted to stay hidden, Catherine thought. Why come out and get stared at? People would like to get a good look at Hazel and cranky old Clarence Travers, Catherine imagined. Last month, Hazel's cousin, Wayne Travers, had been sent to jail for six months for trying to rob the grocery store on the old Cayley Road with one of his father's souvenir World War I guns. The story was that the gun wasn't even loaded, but Catherine's father said that would hardly make a difference if the victim of the robbery was under the impression that it was. It was still a serious crime, Catherine's father said, and Wayne got away with six months at a juvenile detention centre because he was just fifteen years old and this was his first crime.

What was going on out there? Catherine wiped her hand over the fog on the window. There was Hazel, standing in the open door with her arms folded across her chest. She was wearing a baggy pink sweater and blue jeans with the cuffs rolled up and old saddle shoes. Catherine had an impulse to get out of the car and walk through the rain and mud and past Hazel, into her house, where she would assume a new identity, immerse herself in the reality of another life. Once, Catherine's mother had said she considered it unfair that everyone was stuck with a single chance at life. But it seemed to Catherine that there had to be a process by which you could radically change everything: your name, your face, your fate. For a while she'd wanted to be Abigail Glass. Now she imagined herself living in Hazel's house, making do, learning to cope with a mean old uncle and a cousin who was in jail. Catherine, alias someone else, taking a glass from a shelf and pouring herself a glass of clouded tap water while she peered out a window at Mrs. Glass and Abigail.

Then Abigail pushed her aside and rolled the window down, letting the rain blow in. "Hi, Hazel," Abigail shouted, and Hazel glanced once in their direction and waved. The dog was sitting on its haunches in the mud, staring at Hazel.

"Well, I don't know if that went over very well," Abigail's mother said when she got back into the car. She watched as Hazel went into the house with the box in her arms, then she started the car and backed down the driveway. "Maybe I should have kept the damned clothes and given her the new stuff I just bought, the coat off my back, for God's sake. I might have felt better about it. I hate giving people my cast-offs. And you know, Hazel is so gracious. She just smiles and says thank you as if in a secret life she's Emily Post. I guess she's grateful for anything. Not that that makes it any better." She turned onto the old Cayley Road and shifted gears and accelerated. The windshield wipers were slapping across the windscreen. Abigail's mother drove in silence to Catherine's house, and kept the engine running while Catherine got out. It was already getting dark; the lights were on in the windows of Catherine's house. "Say hello to your mother," Abigail's mother said, more cheerfully. "Tell her I'll give her a phone call. Tell her I hope she's feeling well."

"I will," Catherine said, slamming the car door shut. She knew she wouldn't, though. She never referred to her mother's state of health. Or whatever it was. Her mother was walking around with a stomach like a basketball. She still had her skinny arms and legs. She held her arms slightly away from the sides of her body, as if her stomach was leading her around against her will. Her hair was long, nearly to her waist, and she didn't bother to curl it anymore. She wore Catherine's father's shirts over her skirts to accommodate the basketball. When Catherine got home from school in the afternoon, her mother was usually sitting at the piano, playing classical music from Catherine's easy piano books, hitting as many wrong notes as right ones, it seemed to Catherine. Playing chords, one after the other, slow and solemn, and at the same time trying to drink a glass of milk, which she hated, for her health. Drinking milk and trying to smoke a cigarette, even though she complained that smoking made her feel sick. When she lay down on the sofa to read a book, she fell asleep with the book open on her chest. She slept a lot. No one else Catherine's age had a mother in this condition. Catherine hadn't told anyone at school. She didn't talk about it to Abigail. Her mother didn't talk about it much, either. There was a baby sweater she'd started knitting in pale yellow wool on miniature needles and had then given up on. Catherine had no idea where it was now. The last time she'd seen it, it had been balled up on top of the bookcase, beside one of her mother's figurines—an old-fashioned woman holding onto her enormous flower-trimmed hat while an imaginary wind tugged like mad at her china petticoats.

Chapter Eighteen

When Wayne Travers was an inmate at the juvenile detention centre for attempting to rob a corner grocery store with an antique gun, Caroline Bluett wrote him a letter in which she gave him what she considered good advice. That was, she told him to use his incarceration as an opportunity to concentrate on his schooling and to develop a pragmatic attitude towards life. She didn't use those exact words, of course, but she did attempt to be encouraging, brisk, matter-of-fact.

While you might be tempted to think your life is fixed on a certain path, she had written, it is in fact still very malleable and can be put to whatever use you choose. This is true at least while you are young; as you grow older, you will find the opportunities for rehabilitation and conversion diminishing. I mean this as a warning, of sorts, although you are certainly free to take it as you please. You may not consider me an ally or one of your prime advocates; however, the fact is that I do, to a certain extent, take an interest in your future. Please do not hesitate to contact me, she wrote, if, when you return home and go back to your studies, you need any assistance in those subjects with which I have some expertise, including English Literature, Grammar, and History. I would be glad to be of help.

She spent a fair amount of time on the letter, sitting at the desk in her living room looking out at the sea, doodling on a scratch pad and questioning her motivation. She hadn't known she was going to write a letter to Wayne Travers, and certainly not one kindly offering him assistance, until she actually sat down to do it. She thought she was doing it out of genuine concern. If she had any sense, she would have written an entirely different letter to the young man, pointing out to him that she knew perfectly well he had been stealing from her. She didn't have a witness to his misdeeds; she didn't have the kind of corroborative evidence that would be needed to get the police involved. Or she didn't think she did. Anyway, she knew what he'd been up to. Whenever Wayne Travers had been at her house, ostensibly waiting for Hazel to finish her cleaning, Caroline would later find that items had gone missing. These included, over a period of nearly four years, a silver card tray that had belonged to her mother, two silver napkin rings, an exquisite fountain pen with a gold nib that she'd treated herself to for no particular reason, a miniature chess set that had belonged to her father, more than seventy-six dollars from her purse, a crystal bud rose with a gold stem, which had been a thank you gift from an English relative who had stayed with her years ago. There were probably other things, as well, that she hadn't missed yet. She supposed that, in total, he had stolen three or four hundred dollars worth of her possessions. More than that, probably. Enough to go to the police about, certainly.

So why hadn't she? It wasn't that the things he took were worthless or that they meant nothing to her; they did. She was very fond of the silver card tray, even though it was outmoded and had no use in this day and age. No one came calling and left a card politely behind to announce their intention, which was a shame, she thought. And the lovely little chess board with the ivory pieces that fit in a tiny drawer in the base had been one of her father's most treasured possessions. Perhaps she missed the chess game more than anything else. No use, however, in mourning what was gone. And besides, there was the alternative possibility: she really didn't care. This was a bold and liberating thought. None of her possessions was of any real importance to her, with the exception of the books, of course, and also the little miniature town in her back bedroom.

Now, on a February evening, when she entered the closed room and turned on the lamp in the corner, long shadows fell across the streets of Cayley Minor. Shadows of trees and house chimneys, shadows of fences and gates and street signs. It was as if a full moon had risen and was shining down on the earth with great energy and compassion. And it was hers, as well, this energy, this compassion. She believed so. She loved the little town, and everyone who lived in it, all the wooden stick people with their wide-awake eyes and their restless, lively minds. She placed her hand gently on the house at 131 Alma Avenue. She felt energy flowing from her into the house. The husband and the children were at home, no doubt. The children were asleep, the husband was reading, watching television, making himself a sandwich in the kitchen. Arlene Greenwood wasn't at home; she was in the hospital. She was in the maternity ward, having given birth prematurely to a daughter. Julia Glass had given Caroline the news Thursday morning at school, in the staff room. Julia had rushed in, uncharacteristically late, to say that David Greenwood had phoned her just as she was getting ready to leave. He had sounded excited but worried, Julia said. Evidently the baby weighed only four pounds. Let's pray it all turns out for the best, Julia had said. Caroline told her that she, too, had been premature. When she was born, she had weighed four pounds, eight ounces. She had survived, of course she had; she didn't give up easily. And Arlene's baby would survive as well, she knew she would, and she told Julia Glass so.

Caroline turned off the lamp and went back to her desk and wrote a brief message in a card congratulating Arlene Greenwood on the birth of her daughter. *I was so very pleased to hear of the safe arrival of a daughter. I hope that you and your new baby are both well. Please give my congratulations and best wishes to Mr. Greenwood and your other children.* Did that sound all right? She had a little gift for the baby, as well. A pink silk dress with blue smocking around the bodice, and little puffed sleeves. She wrapped it in pink tissue paper. Then she sat at her desk quietly for a while, listening to the sea and the wind in the arbutus trees in front of her house. After awhile she began to feel drowsy, and she made herself get up and get ready for bed. Then, once she was in her

flannelette nightie and was going around the house turning out lights, she began to feel wide awake again. She made
a mug of Ovaltine and drank it in her kitchen. Then she put
on her coat and a pair of warm socks and went outside and
walked on the beach. It was cold. There was a new moon, a
scimitar of light. She picked out some of the winter constel-
lations, the ones her father had taught her when she was a
child: Orion, Pegasus, Taurus, the Pleiades in their brilliant
cold fearful isolation. The sea was fretting against the shore.
She felt for a moment lonelier than she'd ever felt in her
life; then she remembered that the hospital was on the other
side of the hill and Arlene Greenwood was there, and her
new baby, and the truth was, probably half the people in
this town were still awake, on a night as cold and clear and
as beautiful as this, keeping watch with her.

CHAPTER NINETEEN

Catherine's father kept walking around the kitchen in circles, talking about the baby, what a darling little thing she was, how she cried like a tiny kitten, how the palms of her hands were creased up like onion-skin paper. Joan Mullis, who had stayed with Catherine and Matt while their father was at the hospital, made him a fresh pot of coffee and poured him a cup, and he drank it standing in the middle of the kitchen. Joan gave him some telephone messages she'd written down, and he looked at them blankly and then said, "Oh, Eunice. Where the heck is she? I've been trying to get hold of her. She's the only one who doesn't know. Well, children," he said. Under his sweater he was wearing his blue-striped pyjama top, the collar sticking up under his ear. He ran his hand through his hair and told them they had this tiny baby sister. He put his coffee cup down on the counter and measured a space between his hands. That was how big the baby was. They were thinking of calling her Elfkin or Thumbelina. How did they like that? The thing was, she was so small she lived inside a buttercup. She slept in a sparrow's nest. She had these little wings and flew around the hospital nursery, singing to the other babies.

"Daddy, tell the truth," Catherine said.

"I am. Wait until you see for yourself."

The next day, after school, Catherine's father took her and Matt to the hospital. They weren't allowed to see their mother; no one under the age of twelve was allowed into the maternity ward, but they were allowed to stand in the hall and look through a window into the nursery. There were two new babies in there. One was a boy baby wrapped in a blue blanket. He slept in a cot, facing the window. The other baby swam in a glass tank filled with light. This was their new sister. All she wore was a diaper. To Catherine, she looked like a wrinkled brown nut lying on a white cotton sheet. There was a tube taped to her skinny little arm. Catherine's father was right: the baby was small enough to sleep in a sparrow's nest. Her chest was moving up and down like a piece of cloth caught in a breeze. "Is she asleep?" Catherine asked. The baby's eyes were shut, but her thin little arms and legs were twitching as if she were lost in some kind of bad dream.

"Yes," he said. "She sleeps a lot. She's trying to pretend she hasn't been born yet." He took hold of Catherine's hand, and Matt's hand, and knelt down. "They took her wings away," he said. "They told her she wasn't a real angel. She's a baby. A real baby. She has to lie still and gain weight."

"What's wrong with her?" Matt said. He stood on his tiptoes and tried to look into the window. He pressed the tips of his fingers against the edge of the glass.

"There is nothing wrong with her," their father said. He swung Matt up in his arms and held him so that he had a good view into the nursery. "She's just small. She was born six weeks early. She's a premature baby. That's all."

"What's her name?" Matt said.

"Diane," their father said. "Diane Cecilia Greenwood. She's going to be gorgeous. You can see it already, can't you? A gorgeous little girl."

Joan Mullis invited them to dinner. The previous night, they had eaten at the Glasses' house, and Julia Glass had given Catherine's father three frozen casseroles to take home. He had put them in the freezer. Tonight, he said, it was Joan's turn to feed them. Joan Mullis lived out of town, on a narrow country road that led off the old Cayley Road. Her house was set back in a field, with tall dark trees at the end of the field, and split rail fences that went around the fields and the gardens. There was frost on the walk, and on the front steps. The air smelled of woodsmoke. Catherine's father knocked at the door, and when Joan opened it the smell of roast beef dinner rushed out into the night and surrounded them like fog. Joan said, "Please, come in," and took their coats and hung them on a coat rack in the hall, then led them to the back of her house, to the kitchen, where there was a small round table, plates and knives and forks squeezed together, the backs of the chairs touching. There were white candles in the centre of the table, and a sprig of holly, just as if it were Christmas Day, when in fact it was nearly the end of February. Catherine and Matt stood in the middle of the room, and then Joan told them to have a seat at the table, or they could go into the living room if they wished. Do whatever you like, she said, smiling, and Catherine pulled out a chair and sat down, and Matt sat beside her. Catherine knew perfectly well that her mother was in the hospital, but she had a vague and terrifying sense that she was in fact very far away, in an unreachable, unknown foreign country. An image came into her mind of a building beside a tropical sea, white sand, palm trees, strange music, wind chimes hanging in a tree, her mother sitting on a verandah reading a book. She did want to see her mother. She did miss her. She wanted to see her at their piano at home, carelessly picking out a line of melody with one finger. She thought: What if I start to cry in front of Joan Mullis, in her little hot kitchen?

Catherine's father sat on a wooden stool in the kitchen and talked to Joan as she shredded lettuce leaves for a salad. He asked Joan what she thought about her new typewriter, at the office, an IBM Selectric that corrected typing mistakes. "Soon machines will do all our thinking for us," Catherine's father said. "We'll get lazy and fat," Joan said. "And we'll forget how to spell."

"I never could spell," Catherine's father said. Then Joan said, "Dinner is almost ready, it really is. I just have to finish this salad."

"Please, don't hurry," Catherine's father said. He said they weren't hungry, which wasn't true, Catherine thought. Her stomach was rumbling. Joan put out a dish of chocolate-covered raisins and nuts on a corner of the table and told Catherine and Matt to help themselves. She showed them a bowl full of ornamental gourds she had grown in her garden, and had picked and dried and painted with shellac. They were like small brittle pumpkins, and they rattled when Catherine picked them up. She held them to her ear and shook them gently, one at a time, and then put them back in the bowl in the centre of the table, beside the sprig of holly and the candles.

Then Catherine's father said, "Come outside, kids. I want to show you something." And Catherine and Matt had to put their coats and boots on and their father took them out through the back door onto the porch. And there, in the middle of a field was a miniature city, rows of white houses with flat roofs and narrow slits for windows, an African village, huts with thatched roofs set around an empty space. This was a city of bees. It was a great metropolis composed of hives. So Catherine's father said. He knelt beside her and Matt and spoke quietly to them. The bees were inside their houses, he said. All they had until spring was eat and sleep. Winter lifted a wand made of wind and ice over the bees and they had no choice but to close their downy eyes and fold their wings and sleep. Like the baby, Catherine said, and her father and said, Yes, in a way. Like the baby.

Joan came outside with a coat thrown over her shoulders. She said, "Here is my family, all tucked in for the season." This was her third year of keeping bees, she said. Last winter it had been cold and some of her bees had died, and she had been furious with herself. She hadn't fed them enough; she hadn't kept them warm enough. There was a skill in keeping a colony of bees alive through a winter, she said. No one would believe how much honey they ate, just to keep their body temperature up in the cold.

"Do they sting you?" Matt asked.

"They do. Sometimes, when I'm just walking in my garden one of my bees comes along and stings me for no reason. But when I'm taking the honeycombs from the frames, I wear a special hat with a thick veil. And a pair of special overalls, and gloves. I'm very careful. You have to be careful, or else you can get yourself into trouble. And I have something called a smoker, which is absolutely essential. One day, in the summer, you must come and watch as I take the honey from the hives."

Matt held onto Catherine's hand. His breath was visible on the night air. He looked like a very intense little dragon spitting smoke. Catherine thought: The hives are all the houses in Cayley. And inside the houses the people are asleep and dreaming. They are disguised as bees, and they are dreaming about what will happen when morning comes. And then in the morning, the dreams the bee-people have will come true. They know this will happen, it is the way they live, half in their dreams and half in their city of hives. She thought that the new baby, Diane Cecilia, who was no bigger than a bee, had been in one of these dreams, and then at dawn she had managed to escape through one of the narrow windows and she had flown straight to Catherine's mother; she had flown into her eyes like fine grains of sand. And then she had been born.

CHAPTER TWENTY

Arlene got the box room over the stairs ready for the baby to move into. She painted the walls eggshell white. She painted the window and door trim a rose-petal pink. She set up the old portable Singer sewing machine on the dining-room table, and, at night, after the children and David had gone to bed, she made pink polka-dotted curtains and a matching quilted crib coverlet. The house got cold at night, and she had to wear a thick sweater and wool socks. She made herself cups of hot sweet tea. She sat alone in a pale circle of light, the machine whirring in her ears like the wings of a heat-crazed damselfly. Arlene knew she was trying to make amends for pretending that the baby hadn't existed. She hadn't done a thing to get ready; all Diane had was leftover stuff from Catherine and Matt: nighties with old mashed-banana stains on them, and sweaters that had shrunk in the wash. Now at least, when she was a little older, the baby would have her own bedroom, with Catherine's old Raggedy Ann doll on top of the chest of drawers, and a clown lamp Arlene had ordered from the Simpson Sears new spring and summer catalogue. At the moment, the baby was sleeping in a bassinet in Arlene and David's room, and Arlene was still getting out of bed every two hours so that she could make sure the baby was breathing. She was nearly three months old and she weighed ten pounds, six ounces, a tiny baby, still, with wrists like match sticks, but she was catching up. She had big blue eyes, silky hair in a fringe over her forehead. She seemed to have the reasonable, trusting, Gamlin personality, which was just as well; she would be able to bring herself up with a minimal amount of help from Arlene. Arlene felt too old to be raising another baby. She was only twenty-nine, but she felt older. The year she'd got married, 1950, seemed to belong to the distant past. It was nineteen sixty-one now, the beginning of a new decade. John F. Kennedy was the President of the United States, and Jacqueline Kennedy was the first lady. She was almost exactly the same age as Arlene, and some people said Arlene bore a resemblance to her, her eyes and the way she walked, her smile. Arlene liked to believe this was so; she was crazy about Jacqueline Kennedy and bought every magazine that had an article in it about her. Last month the Soviets had put a man in space in a rocket ship, and Arlene had read in a news magazine that scientists had come up with a new theory that the universe was in a constant state of flux, galaxies spinning apart like clouds of pollen on the wind, nothing stable or certain anywhere. Needless to say, the truth of this theory wasn't apparent in the town of Cayley, where the exact opposite was the case and nothing ever changed from year to year.

The new curtains, once Arlene had them up, framed a view of the town, the branches of a weeping willow tree that grew at the side of the house, and the shimmering blue of the ocean. There was a freighter anchored in the harbour, a sailboat passing in front of one of the islands. When Arlene was in the hospital with the baby, David had come to tell her he'd just been offered a promotion to the company's head office in Vancouver. She'd been standing in the hall in front of the nursery window, staring fixedly at her six-day-old star-fish baby in the incubator. She had been concentrating on passing her strength to the baby, giving her the will to live.

"Well, what do you think?" David had said, after he'd told her. "Aren't you pleased?" She had turned and looked at him as if she hadn't understood a word he was saying, and indeed she hadn't. "I can't think about it now," she said.

"I have to give them an answer," he said. "By tomorrow morning."

"Tell them to wait."

"I can't," he had said.

The next day, when he came to visit her, he told her he had turned down the promotion. The deadline for a decision had come and gone. He'd turned down the transfer to Vancouver. "Fine," was all she could say.

"I thought it was what you wanted more than anything else," he said. "I thought you'd be pleased. Well, just don't forget you had the chance."

"I won't." She knew even then she'd made a mistake. But how could she think about moving when she had a premature baby to worry about? If he'd asked her at any other time. If he'd waited until she could concentrate on what he was saying, she might have been getting ready to move to Vancouver. She might have been there already, putting these curtains up at an entirely different window, in a new house, looking out at a different street. What an idiot she'd been. Now she was going to have to stay here, in this town, with its hard blue borders and its abrupt terminations, by which she meant, she thought she meant, the sea and the dark forests, the mountains that gave the illusion of a barrier high and impenetrable enough to keep out of the rest of the world.

The truth was, whatever was wrong with this town, it was still a lot nicer than most of the towns she and David had lived in since they'd got married. She could console herself with this, at least. Cayley wasn't as raw, as unfinished-looking as most. It had some charm. It had old-fashioned houses and flower gardens and big gracious-looking trees and labyrinthine streets with old narrow sidewalks. And the mill whistle was melodious; it was like a tiny concert four times a day, a subtle and yet sombre reminder alerting everyone to the inexorable passage of time.

When she'd been in the hospital, Arlene found out later, Eunice had been on a plane flying to California to be with Grandfather Myles, who had suffered a mild stroke the day before. She'd flown to Los Angeles and then she'd taken a bus to San Clemente. Eunice hadn't told anyone because she hadn't wanted to upset Arlene. She'd had no idea the baby was going to arrive early, of course. When she got to her parents' house, her eighty-three-year-old mother had come out onto the front steps to give her the news. Eunice had said, For God's sake, let me catch my breath! Everything happened at once, Eunice said. She seemed to live her life in the vortex of a whirlwind. When she'd arrived at the hospital in San Clemente, she told Arlene, Grandfather Myles had been sitting up in bed complaining about the food they were serving him, which wasn't like him at all. He never complained. And the food was quite good; she'd eaten what he left untasted on his tray. Another thing, he adored Eunice, but he scarcely seemed to know who she was. He treated her as if she were another attendant, someone responsible for the quality of care he was receiving, or not receiving. He kept sending her to the hospital gift shop for a newspaper or a chocolate bar. Then he became silent, morose, almost. There was an IV drip going into a swollen blue vein on his hand. A pulse was beating frantically in his temple. Eunice described all this to Arlene. She started to cry. She told Arlene Grandfather Myles had passed away two days later, in his sleep.

"I know," Arlene said. It was the simple truth. She had, in fact, known the exact hour that Grandfather Myles had died. She didn't know whether or not to tell Eunice, in case it upset her. The thing was, she had dreamt that Grandfather Myles came to visit her in the hospital, two days after the baby had been born. He'd pulled a chair over beside her, and folded his overcoat and put it on the foot of her bed. He had a newspaper with him, and he sat down and opened it and began to read. If she didn't mind, he said, he would just sit quietly and catch up on what was going on in the world. Arlene said that was fine with her. She lay back on her pillows and thought that now Grandfather Myles was here, she could relax. The baby would survive. She would be forgiven for not taking better care of herself, and not eating properly, and for not telling anyone, including Dr. Wagner, about her condition for such a long time. Everything would be fine. In her dream, she'd smoothed the blankets over her legs and reached for a cigarette and lit it. She was supposed to be trying to quit, but there seemed to be two levels of consciousness operating in her head, and in at least one of them she knew this was a dream and she could do anything she wanted, including having a cigarette, and no one would be any the wiser.

Grandfather Myles folded his newspaper up and put it on the foot of her bed. The lamp over her bed was on—everything in this dream was very exact, very realistic—and Grandfather Myles's silver hair glinted in the light. He had such beautiful hair, such fine skin, such lovely, kind eyes. He had a mischievous smile. Everyone who knew him loved him. Nearly eleven years ago he'd driven with her to her wedding. You want to run away from your wedding, he'd said. Fine, let's run away. Let's go while the going's good.

"Well, there's not much going on in the world at the moment," he said. "February is always a slow month, with a few notable exceptions. The Battle of Verdun began forty-five years ago today, February 21, 1916. No one expected the French would be able to hold off the Germans with such tenacity. But they did. I was thirty years old at the time. Captain Myles to the rescue. I wasn't at Verdun. I had a strange war, Arlene. Did I ever tell you the story? The Prime Minister at the time, Robert Borden, sent a bunch of us off to Siberia to try to get the White Russians on our side. Have you ever heard such an idea? We were going to help them overthrow the Bolsheviks, then persuade them to fight on our side against the Hun. But shall I tell you what it was like in Siberia? It was as peaceful as a Christmas picture post-card. I don't know if we ever did make contact with a White Russian. Borden's mistake."

Grandfather Myles paused and smiled at her. She couldn't believe how lucky she was that he was there, that he had managed to get to the hospital to see her.

"Fifteen years," he said. "Fifteen years in San Clemente, California, living on a good pension. Golfing and swimming and fishing off the San Clemente Pier. I've been very satis-fied with my life, but now that I have a chance to reflect, I do believe I would pick Siberia over California. Frost and austerity. Black bread and pickled herring. A stove with the oven door open for warmth. Someone reading Russian po-etry. Companionship. It's those very small moments that count, that make up a life. You must remember that, Arlene."

In her dream, Arlene had been able to see through the door of the ward to the hall, the half-shut door to the nurses' lounge, where the nurses were making themselves cups of tea. Soon one of them would come into the ward to wake Arlene and take her temperature and pulse. They would ask her how she'd slept. They'd bring her breakfast, a poached egg on toast on a thick china plate under a stainless steel cover. And tea, always too strong. And canned milk, which she detested. And then they would help her to get out of bed and put on her robe and slippers, and she would walk slowly down the hall to see the baby. She thought: One soul arrives and another departs, as if obeying a train schedule, or a principle in chemistry, where only so many atoms were allowed to take up residence inside any one molecule.

1967-1968

Chapter Twenty-one

Lisa McCann let the screen door of her house bang shut behind her. She stood at the top of the porch stairs and said, "It took you a long enough time to get here."

"It's a long way," Abby said, kicking at her bike stand. She pushed her hair off her forehead and wiped her face with the back of her hand. "And it's hotter than hell." Catherine leaned her bike against the porch. Lisa came down the stairs. She was wearing shorts and a white shirt, what looked like a man's shirt, too big for her, the sleeves rolled up past her elbows. She took Catherine and Abby down to the river, where, she said, they could cool down if they were so overheated. They sat in a row at the edge of the water, and Abby and Catherine took off their socks and shoes and stuck their feet in the water. The air was green, hot, damp, full of small white butterflies and bugs, like motes of dust.

Abby said, "Could you get me a glass of water, Lisa, or do I have to drink out of the river?" "Oh, sorry," Lisa said. She got up and ran into the house and came back with a pitcher of lemonade for them to drink, and three plastic glasses. She poured out the lemonade and handed the glasses around. Then Lisa picked a blade of glass and put it to her lips and whistled. Catherine put her glass of lemonade on the ground and picked a blade of grass and tried the same thing, but no sound came out. She ended up spitting, and had to wipe her mouth with her hand. Abby laughed at her.

"It's easy," Lisa said. She lay down on her back in the grass with her straw-coloured hair spread out around her and whistled up at the trees. Lisa had moved to Cayley in May, a few weeks before the end of the school term. In the beginning, Abby had been in charge of a group of girls at school who didn't want to be friends with Lisa. Then Abby decided that she and Catherine should make Lisa into a sort of project. She showed Catherine a magazine article she'd been reading that recommended *inviting a brand new friend into your circle*. Take the initiative, the article advised. Catherine wasn't sure if she wanted to be friends with Lisa McCann—tall, pale, gawky Lisa—who lisped like a baby, and was always dropping her books in the hall between classes so that some boy would pick them up for her. Abby said there was nothing else to do; it was the deadest summer ever; there was no one around, nothing to do. She phoned Lisa and told her they were coming to see her. "You remember us don't you?" she said. "Abby Glass and Catherine Greenwood? We sat in front of you in home room, you haven't forgotten us already, have you?" She smiled at Catherine. "We'll be there soon," she was telling Lisa. "Wait for us, okay?" She hung up the phone. Abby had cut off her long braids; her hair was short, smooth as a helmet, but she still had the same intense pointed little face and pale narrow mean-looking eyes. The little girl who had thought throwing rocks at cars was a good idea was still alive inside Abby's head. She could still make Catherine do whatever she wanted.

Lisa was skinnier than anyone Catherine knew. Skinnier than Abby. She was like an exaggerated version of Abby, it occurred to Catherine. She had very pale skin, milk-white, perfect skin, large, knobbly knees, long legs like a water-spider. Her eyes were pale blue, her front teeth stuck out; she had a delicate pointed chin that seemed to wobble when she talked. Or when she puckered up her mouth to whistle through a blade of grass. She could also weave several blades of grass into a bracelet, which she did, and then she tied it around Catherine's wrist, as if she were picking Catherine to be her friend. Abby looked at the bracelet and said, "Grass makes me break out in hives. I have the most sensitive skin in the world." "My skin is tough as leather," Lisa said. She told them her father was away. He was in the Canadian Army, stationed in Cyprus. Her mother was German, and didn't know how to speak English very well, yet, Lisa said. Lisa had been born in Germany, in a place called Lahr, she said, where there was this big army base. Lisa could speak English, German and French. A little. She had forgotten some of her French. So far, she said, she had lived in Germany and France and Canada.

"Which subject do you like best?" Abby said. "At school."

Lisa shrugged. "I like them all," she said. "What's your favourite subject?" she asked.

"I don't know," Abby said. "I hate them all."

Catherine tossed a pebble into the river. "Do you ever go swimming here?"

"Every day," Lisa said. She bent over and picked at a scab on her knee. "We can go swimming now, if you want."

"We didn't bring our bathing suits," Catherine said.

"I could lend you a bathing suit," Lisa said, and Catherine looked at Abby and they quickly said, "No," together. Then Lisa said that if they wanted to come back later, after dinner, she'd take them to a place further down the river where these guys she knew went swimming buck-naked and then lay on the river bank and gave themselves boners.

"What?" Catherine said. She laughed and glanced at Abby, who rolled her eyes as if to say, What can you expect from a girl like Lisa?

"Well, it's true," Lisa said. "I've seen them. They don't care who watches. They practically prefer to have an audience. It's a wonder they don't sell tickets."

"They sound disgusting," Abby said.

"They don't know I'm there," Lisa said. "I run away before they see me."

"Gross," Abby said. Catherine could see Abby was enjoying this; this was even better than she had expected. She could hear Abby saying, I don't think Lisa is what that magazine had in mind. I don't think she'd fit into anyone's *circle* too well.

"Do you guys want to see our barn?" Lisa said.

"And what do you keep in your barn?" Catherine said, and Abby laughed and said, "Maybe we shouldn't ask." Then she said, "Okay, Lisa, let's see your barn."

"I have to get home to help my mother get dinner," Catherine said. She was lying. Or was she? She couldn't remember what time her mother had said to be home. She splashed her toes in the river. The grass bracelet was making her skin itch, and she ripped it off and threw it in the river, and she and Abby stared at it bobbing around on the water.

"We've got enough time," Abby said.

The barn was at the edge of a field. It was on their property, Lisa said, but she and her mother didn't ever come here. They didn't use it for anything. When her father got back from Cyprus, he was going to get out of the army and start keeping a cow and he was going to get a horse for Lisa to ride. Catherine and Abby stood looking at the barn, which had a steep roof and planks missing here and there in the walls. The whole thing leaned to one side as if the wind could blow it over. One of the big doors was half-hanging off its hinges. Catherine walked into the barn. Sunlight lay in stripes across the dirt floor, and then there were these shadowy areas where anything could be hiding. There was a loft up high, and things hanging from the walls, old ropes, lengths of chain, rusty rakes, a garden hoe with a splintered handle. Lisa and Abby had followed her into the barn, and Lisa went over to a pile of old hay or straw and kicked her feet at it, so that a cloud of yellow dust rose up, and Catherine started kicking at it too. And then Abby picked up a handful and threw it in Lisa's face and Lisa picked up a handful and they were throwing it at each other as hard as they could. Catherine said, "Come on, cut it out," because it seemed to her they were on the edge of having a real fight. They had straw in their hair and all over their clothes, and they were laughing and swearing and sliding in the dirt, and once Abby got hold of Lisa's sleeve and pulled her to her knees. Lisa said, "I give, I give," laughing and nearly crying at the same time, and she crawled away from Abby on her hands and knees. Then she stood up and walked outside, and Catherine and Abby followed her and watched as she climbed into an apple tree and began picking apples. "We have way more of these apples than we can eat," she said.

"We have to get going," Catherine said. "It takes a long time to get home from here." She watched Lisa slowly picking apples. Slowly, slowly, examining each apple, carefully tugging each one from the branch. She folded up the front of her shirt, making a pocket to hold the apples. "Hurry, up, Lisa," Catherine said.

"They aren't ripe yet," Abby said. "They're green."

"They're supposed to be green," Lisa said. She dropped out of the tree. She landed on her feet and unloaded the apples one at a time from her shirt, putting them on the ground, then she brushed off her shirt. She told Catherine to wait while she went back to the house to get a bag. "We can't," Catherine said, but Lisa was already gone, flying across the grass, ducking her head to avoid the branch of a cedar tree. When she got back, she put the bag on the ground, picked up two of the apples and shoved them down the front of her shirt. She stuck her chest out.

"How do you like these apples?" she said. She waggled her hips and strutted up and down with the apples jutting out from her skinny chest, one slightly higher than the other. Abby laughed, snorting through her nose, and Catherine told her to get a hold of herself, to calm down before she had a fit. But she was laughing, too. Lisa was funny, Catherine had to admit; she was a clown; she was putting on quite a performance. Quiet, shy Lisa, swivelling her pelvis and sticking out her chest with its two little round apple breasts.

"Va-voom," Lisa said, strutting in a circle around the apple tree. She paused and shook a dry leaf out of her hair. She pouted and looked at them from under her pale eyelashes. She told them she was going to go to New York City and get a job as a fashion model. She was tall enough already, she said, and she had no hips, which was a good thing, because if you had hips you could never be a model. She tossed her head, and her fine straw-coloured hair flew out like strands of embroidery silk. Rapunzel, Rapunzel, Catherine thought; let down your hair. She was fascinated by Lisa, who she thought actually was beautiful in a weird kind of way, as if she had come from a different planet, or at least a completely different part of this planet. And she had. She had been born in Germany; she spoke German, and French, or so she said. She and her mother conversed in a foreign language alone together beside the silent gold river, and the river listened to them and made an answering sound, on and on in the moonlight, Catherine imagined. She imagined the sound of the river at night, a star-lit night, the sky that absolute velvet blackness, the stars sparkling like small cold fires.

Lisa told them she weighed one hundred and four pounds and she was five feet eight inches tall. Abby said, "You're not five-foot-eight, Lisa. You're nowhere near five-foot-eight." She was five-six, she said, and Lisa wasn't any taller than she was. They stood back to back and Catherine walked around them, taking measurements with her eye. She said they looked about the same, but the top of Lisa's head was definitely a little bit taller. "I am too five-eight," Lisa said. She took the apples out of her shirt and held them out, one in the palm of each hand. She resembled, Catherine thought, a slightly wacky Greek statue, a teenage goddess. She had sharp cheekbones, and her blue eyes tilted up at the corners.

Abby said, "Oh, Lisa, you'll never be a model. Everyone wants to be a model. You'll just get disappointed if you set your mind on something like that."

Catherine didn't say anything, because she didn't want to offend Abby, who was, after all, her best friend, but the truth was she had no trouble at all imagining Lisa as a model, even though her front teeth stuck out. She could always get her teeth fixed, later on. That's what Catherine would do, if she were Lisa.

When Catherine got home, her father was standing on the patio with a beer in his hand. Her mother was sitting on the edge of the concrete planter Catherine's father had made, with the help of Howard Glass, the summer before. Blue and white petunias were straggling over the edge of the planter, and Catherine's mother was picking off the shrivelled dead flowers and letting them drop to the ground. She looked at Catherine and said, "What in God's name happened to you?"

"Nothing," Catherine said. Her mother told her to go upstairs and take a shower, and change into some clean clothes. "And hurry up," she said. Catherine looked her.

"Can't you do what you're told?" her mother said. "For once."

"What's wrong with you?" Catherine said, and her mother said, "Oh, just leave me alone for a few minutes."

Later, when they were all having dinner, Catherine found out that her father was being sent up the coast to a sawmill where a fire had destroyed part of the office. He had to set up a new payroll and personnel office and get everything up and running, he said. The job would, he estimated, take about three weeks. Catherine's mother was upset because she'd be left alone at home. The whole summer, she said, cooped up in the house with the kids. Catherine's father said it wasn't the whole summer. And, anyway, there wasn't a thing he could do about it. Catherine's mother didn't see it like that. She thought someone else could go in his place. I don't know why you're making such a fuss, Catherine's father said, and her mother got up and walked out of the kitchen. Catherine's father poked at a lettuce leaf with his fork and cleared his throat and said that Catherine and Matt would have to help their mother out. They'd all have to pull together and behave themselves while he was away.

"I don't see why we can't come with you," Matt said.

"It's just a small town," Catherine's father said. "There wouldn't be anywhere for you to stay. There wouldn't be anything to do. I'll be home on the weekends. And it's only three weeks."

Two days later he left on a seaplane that took off from the dock in front of the sawmill, and two days after that Diane became ill with a fever that turned out to be the start of chicken pox. At the same time the weather changed and it rained every day. Diane refused to stay in bed; she spent most of the day sitting on the living-room floor in front of the TV with a blanket over her head, eating red Jell-O and drinking apple juice. Matt and Catherine took turns reading to Diane, and they reported to each other on the stages of her illness. Matt told Diane the blisters were called pustules. He told her if she scratched them she'd be scarred for life. Their mother said, "Shut up, Matt. You know," she said, "I could have predicted this. I knew what it would be like without your father around." She went through all the drawers in her desk until she found the record of their illnesses, and said that, Yes, Matt and Catherine had had chicken pox already. Thank God for that, she said. She stayed in her housecoat all day. She lay on the sofa reading, her feet propped up on a cushion. Catherine made canned cream of mushroom soup and toast for dinner three nights in a row, and they ate in the living room. They all kept yawning and falling asleep and not getting dressed until the afternoon. They watched TV and did jigsaw puzzles and drank ginger ale. Catherine thought about Lisa McCann. She imagined that out near the river, where Lisa lived, it was still hot, the sun was still shining. She wondered if Abby and Lisa were friends now. She thought of phoning Lisa, but she had nothing to say. She thought about going out, even for a walk, but she didn't feel like it. Her mother kept slamming the windows shut because every half hour the Centennial Caravan, which was parked outside the elementary school, played a recording of *Ca-na-da!* Canada was one hundred years old, and Catherine was trapped in her house, not taking part in the celebrations, not driving across the country to Expo '67 as some of her friends were doing with their families.

Then one afternoon Abby phoned Catherine and said she was going on a date. "Promise not to tell my parents," she said, then she said, "Well, don't you want to know who I'm going out with? You'll never guess." "I don't want to guess," Catherine said. Finally Abby told her that Cal Dimitriou had invited her to go to a movie in Duncan.

Catherine knew who Cal Dimitriou was. He was at least twenty; he was nice looking, not especially tall. A lot of girls liked him. He had quit school after grade eleven to go fishing and to work in his parents' seafood restaurant. He came from a big Greek family, and his sisters and brothers, even the ones who were married and had their own children, worked at the restaurant. Why was someone like Cal Dimitriou taking Abby on a date? Catherine knew he'd already had lots of girlfriends and they were all older than Abby, prettier than Abby. Well, more mature than Abby. More experienced than Abby. More experienced with dating, with going out with men. It was summer and Catherine was imprisoned in her house, and here was Abby telling her she was going on a date, her first date, and it was with Cal Dimitriou.

Catherine hung up the phone and went back to sitting on the floor in front of the TV with Diane. She patted Calamine lotion on Diane's chicken pox and thought about Abby getting ready for this secret date. Phone me, tell me what it was like, Catherine had told Abby. Abby didn't phone; she came to Catherine's house. When Catherine opened the door, Abby fell inside, saying, "I have to talk to you."

Catherine's mother appeared and said, "Oh, it's you Abby. Aren't you afraid you'll catch chicken pox?"

"It's all right, Diane isn't contagious anymore," Catherine said. She and Matt were experts on diseases. They'd been reading a medical book they'd found in the bookcase. It was an old book with black-and-white illustrations, but it was full of interesting information, and not just about chicken pox, either. Catherine and Matt got it out of the bookcase whenever they had a chance and thumbed through it quickly, passing the book back and forth when they came across the sections on human sexuality, pregnancy and childbirth. They had to bury their heads in the sofa cushions to keep from laughing out loud. They knew everything now; they knew everything there was to know.

"I had chicken pox when I was three years old," Abby said. "I almost died. I got a rare complication called encephalitis of chicken pox. It's fatal in one per cent of the cases. I was in the hospital for weeks."

Catherine's mother looked at Abby. "Please," she said. "I don't need to hear anymore."

Upstairs, in Catherine's bedroom, Abby described how she and Cal had had dinner at his parents' restaurant, some kind of fish in a tomato sauce, and how his sisters had made such a big fuss over her it was almost embarrassing. Then they had gone to a James Bond movie in Duncan. They shared popcorn and a Coke with two straws. "We sat this close together," Abby said, sitting on the bed beside Catherine, her arm touching Catherine's arm. "Then," she said, "after the movie we drove home the long way, down all these little back roads. And—and then he kissed me."

She laughed, they both laughed. What was the kiss like? Catherine asked, and Abby told her it was impossible to describe. She would have to find out for herself, when she had a boyfriend. After Abby left, Catherine found herself standing in the hall, in front of the door, with her eyes half-closed, as if she was trying to see beyond the walls of the house. What was out there? Romance, with a Greek boy with lovely tight black curls all over his head, lips that were always moist from drinking Greek wine. She knew the name for Greek wine: retsina. She had come across it in one of her mother's library books, a novel set in Greece. Retsina and seasoned rice wrapped in grape leaves, black olives, goat's cheese. She knew more than Abby did about what Greeks ate. There had also been a lot of kissing in the novel. Perhaps she would never be kissed by anyone. It seemed a possibility at this moment. Perhaps she'd never have a boyfriend. Instead, she would live like Miss Bluett, in a small house by the sea. Like Miss Bluett she would be an English teacher. She would spend her time reading, except that she wouldn't have any children to interrupt and drive her out of her mind. She would remain unmarried, a spinster. She said the word slowly, *spinster*, and imagined herself dressed in black, wearing sensible, although not unattractive, shoes, taking a chequebook out of a large black handbag, fiddling with the catch on a rhinestone necklace. She imagined a certain competency and clarity of mind accompanied the state, or condition, of being a spinster. A lack of sentimentality. A hardness, even ruthlessness, unmistakably discernible at times behind the soft, rouged complexion and modest gaze.

Hazel came into the kitchen at Abby's house just as Abby was starting to tell Catherine about Cal, about something Cal had said or done the previous evening that had made her furious, that, now that she thought about it, was still making her absolutely furious. They were sitting at the table drinking Cokes. It was eleven o'clock on a Saturday morning early in September. Abby was annoyed that she'd been interrupted by Hazel, who was emptying a bucket of dirty water down the sink. "God, Hazel," Abby said. "If my mother saw you do that, she'd have a fit."

"What she doesn't see won't hurt her," Hazel said, rinsing the bucket and putting it on the floor. She peeled off her rubber gloves and came over to the table and showed Catherine her engagement ring. Catherine held the tips of Hazel's warm moist fingers and told her it was a gorgeous ring. Hazel was engaged to marry someone called Norm. He was a mechanic at the Gulf station and a volunteer with the Cayley Fire Department. If he was who Catherine thought he was, he was short, with a long, extremely thin face, and fine brown hair. He looked cheerful, friendly, she thought. Hazel was getting married in December. She was going to continue housecleaning for Abby's mother and all her other customers, because she and Norm were saving up to buy a house, she told Catherine. She was going to have everything just the way she wanted it. And she wasn't taking any nonsense from Abby, either, she said.

"I'm doing this floor next," she said. "Go on, go outside, it's a nice day."

"Don't talk to me like I'm six years old, Hazel," Abby said.

"Well, don't act like it, then," Hazel said.

Catherine said, "I do like your ring, Hazel. I think it's beautiful."

"Oh, God, that ring doesn't mean anything. I'll be married before Hazel," Abby said.

"Want to bet?" Hazel said.

Abby went down the hall to get her jacket and Catherine's from the hall closet, then came back, and she and Catherine went out onto the verandah. They leaned on the railing, looking out at the trees and the sea. Abby glanced behind her at the open kitchen window, and said, "Why don't we go down to the beach, where we can at least have some privacy?" "All right," Catherine said, and she and Abby ran down the stairs, across the lawn, past the blood-red leaves of the Japanese maple Abby's father had planted to mark the grave of Abby's beige poodle, Ethel Mertz, who had died last summer at the age of fifteen years. Then they climbed down a narrow flight of wood steps that led to the beach, where Abby sat on a log and pulled a crumpled cigarette packet out of her jacket pocket. She offered one to Catherine. "No, thanks," Catherine said, then she changed her mind and sat down beside Abby and took a cigarette, and Abby lit it for her. The sun didn't reach down here during the day. The rocks were covered with a green slime and everything was damp, including the log they were sitting on, and the air was chilly, but the sea was dancing with light. Catherine did up the buttons on her jacket with one hand while holding the cigarette in the other as if it were a live bomb that could go off. Abby picked up where she'd left off when Hazel had interrupted her, telling Catherine that last night that damned Cal had hardly spoken a word to her, and she had no idea what she'd done wrong. He'd driven around with the car radio blasting, completely ignoring her. She might have liked to go somewhere for a Coke, or a milkshake, but he didn't ask what she wanted to do. That was Cal: he was temperamental. He was used to having his own way. And he had the nerve to call her a spoiled child.

"Oh, well," Catherine said. "He probably didn't mean it." What was she supposed to say? Abby drew her fingers roughly through her hair. Her eyes were outlined in black makeup. She kept chewing her silver fingernails, taking a drag on her cigarette, telling Catherine that Cal had the nerve to tell her he wanted to marry a Greek girl, a girl who would understand his culture, a girl who knew how to cook properly. He wanted to have a large family, six or seven kids. He wanted to marry someone who was Greek Orthodox. She hated him when he talked like that. If she wanted to, she could make him marry her like that, she said, snapping her fingers.

Catherine dropped the cigarette on a rock and extinguished it with the toe of her shoe. She thought Abby was crazy to talk about marrying Cal. She was only sixteen years old. Catherine remembered her own mother telling her that she'd known, when she was seventeen years old, that her destiny in life was to marry Catherine's father. Catherine usually detected a small question mark left hanging in the air, however: Was her mother satisfied with her destiny? Now it seemed she couldn't wait to get away from all of them. As soon as Catherine's father had got back from the sawmill up the coast, and Diane had got over the chicken pox, Catherine's mother had left for a week on her own in Vancouver. She had stayed at their grandmother's apartment. The day she came back, Catherine's father drove them all to the ferry terminal in Nanaimo to meet her. They waited and waited for her to appear in the crowd of disembarking foot passengers. And then, when they finally saw her, they hardly knew her. She came toward them in this quick, careless way, a traveller with a few rushed minutes to spare. She was wearing jeans and an Icelandic sweater, her hair in a single braid down her back. Catherine's father had said, "Arlene, you look like a hippie," which had made Catherine's mother laugh with delight, as if he'd paid her a compliment.

Catherine stared at the ice-blue sea and the mysterious treed islands floating beneath the September sky, taking it all in, the beauty, the quiet. She'd like to live on an island, she thought, and be a recluse as well as a spinster. She could grow string beans and potatoes in a little garden and light her cabin with kerosene lamps. Cayley was a small, small town, and hardly anyone ever left for good. Most people never left at all. Every year two or three of the kids who graduated from Cayley Secondary School went away to become lawyers, teachers, doctors, ministers, although not many even made it through university. It was too hard to stay away from home. If they did make it, they came back to Cayley and married someone local and set up an office here, or they took over the family business. She'd seen it happen, just in the ten years her family had lived here. There was nowhere else like this, people said. The trees, the sea, the fresh air, they said, not caring to mention those occasions when the smoke from the sawmill turned a clear summer day into the dead of night. In her view, there was a serious dichotomy—a word she had just learned—between what people imagined they saw in Cayley and what really existed.

Abby got up and walked to the water's edge. She picked up a rock and threw it into the waves. Catherine, watching her, thought that Abby was one of the kids who would leave Cayley as soon as she finished school. Abby would have an important career of some kind; she'd have an extraordinary life, and she'd never come back to this town.

Catherine got up and went and stood beside Abby. She picked up the flattest rock she could find and skipped it across the water. Then they had a rock-skipping contest, which Catherine won, or they both won, it was hard to see whose rock skipped farthest, then they climbed back up the steps—forty-two, Catherine and Abby counted together, forty-two rickety steps that swayed under their weight—and Catherine went home.

For weeks after that Abby found some way to sneak off with Cal on Friday nights, while her parents assumed she was at Catherine's house, or out with some of her girl friends. She told Catherine on the phone that Cal had parked on the side of a logging road out near Mt. Prevost and the police had arrived and asked Cal for his driver's licence and his registration. One of the police officers kept shining a flashlight in Abby's face, asking her what her name was, where she lived, if her parents knew where she was. She said, Yes, they know, and get that light out of my eyes, but the fact was her parents didn't know where she was. She'd been afraid the police would drive her home, wake her parents up, say, Here is your sixteen-year-old daughter, who we found in a parked car on a deserted logging road at one o'clock in the morning with her blouse undone. Was it? Was it undone? Catherine asked, and Abby said, Oh, Catherine, for God's sake. Catherine was on the phone in the front hall, and Matt ran past her, his feet thumping as he took the stairs two at a time, and at the same time she could hear the television in the living room. Her father was watching The Ed Sullivan Show. Topo Gigio, the little Italian mouse, was saying, *If I go to sleep, kiss-a-me goodnight, kiss-a-me goodnight*, followed by loud audience laughter. Matt ran back down the stairs. He went into the living room and began talking to their father. Diane was upstairs being put to bed by Catherine's mother. This was what Sunday evenings were like, always, every Sunday. As soon as she got off the phone, Catherine was going upstairs to wash her hair. On Abby's end of the phone line there was silence. Catherine imagined her alone in her pink and white bedroom, the door closed, her parents reading in the living room downstairs. "Are you there, Catherine?" Abby was saying. "What's going on? You have to promise me right now that you won't tell anyone what I told you. About the police and Cal." Catherine said, "I won't. I won't tell anyone."

After she talked to Abby, Catherine wondered if what she felt was jealousy. Wasn't she a little envious that Abby was going out with Cal? Abby was leaving Catherine behind. There were girls at school—girls like Abby—who spoke of boys, marriage, dates, kissing, of "going all the way," who spoke in secrets and a sort of shorthand that referred always to the future. The future they intended to fully occupy, participate in. There was something very physical and substantial and practical about these girls, Catherine thought, even though they were what could be called dainty, even exquisite, ethereal, with their tiny manicured hands and lacquered hairdos. They drew attention to themselves. They wore nylons that made an audible shivering sound when they crossed their legs in class. The heels of their shoes clicked nervously, persistently, on the classroom floors. They cleared their throats in a very feminine way, as if about to profess something startling and also reassuring. Their boyfriends were already causing them trouble, forgetting to pick them up after school, flirting with the carhops at the A & W, spending their money on their cars instead of saving it up. Between classes, these girls hashed out their problems in the washroom while fixing their hairdos and sneaking a cigarette. Catherine felt as if they were learning a secret language—had in fact already acquired a secret language—a means of growing out of childhood toward some kind of new and better condition. She looked like them, or at least she did when she took the time; she knew how to imitate them, a little. No one would ever guess, she didn't think, that mostly she felt excluded and vaguely retarded. Perhaps she did have some kind of mental block. She couldn't even think of any boys she especially wanted to impress. Even Lisa McCann knew how to flirt. She flirted with the other girls' boyfriends and with the teachers. She flirted shamelessly with the new Social Studies teacher, Mr. Schram. Catherine didn't know how she had the nerve. If Catherine were going to have a crush on anyone it would be Mr.

Schram. He might even cause her to change her mind about being a spinster. In her dreams she placed herself and Mr. Schram in vivid juxtaposition against some unknown backdrop, painted skies, exotic trees, tropical breezes, *Blue Hawaii,* Elvis serenading them from a flower-decked stage, herself in a trailing white garment with a flower lei around her neck.

CHAPTER TWENTY-TWO

A wedding. Snow falling. Late morning, the sky black as night, streetlights shedding a damp pink light on the wedding guests as they stood outside the church watching Hazel and Norm being handed into a car by Abby's father. Catherine heard Julia Glass, who was standing beside her, say, "Oh, doesn't she make a lovely bride?" It was the truth, Catherine thought: Hazel did look lovely, her eyes brilliant, her skin luminous, her entire self gloriously made over for this one day. Or, who knows, for more than one day, the wedding ceremony possibly containing elements of magic hidden beneath the familiar words and capable of changing the participants forever, changing their personalities, their luck, their fate. If that were true, getting married would be almost worthwhile, Catherine thought, depending, of course, on the outcome of the magic invoked.

Hazel was settling herself beside Norm in the back of the car, fussing with her veil, smiling prettily at everyone. Julia had made Hazel's wedding dress by hand; she had laboured over it for weeks; the inside of the dress as beautifully finished as the outside. So Catherine had heard. She had also heard, from Abby, that Julia had taken Hazel to the hairdresser's at eight o'clock this morning to have her hair styled, her veil pinned in place. Julia had paid for the flowers in the church and for Hazel's bouquet of red roses and stephanotis. There was nothing she wouldn't do for Hazel, for Hazel's wedding, it seemed. Abby said it was revolting, all that money, all that effort. Abby was supposed to be Hazel's bridesmaid, but at the last minute she'd said she couldn't do it, she didn't want to get dressed up and have everyone looking at her. Instead, a friend of Hazel's called Georgia was the bridesmaid. Georgia was, Catherine had heard, related in some way to Eugene Kriskin, who couldn't be at the wedding because he was living in Bellingham, Washington, with his second wife and her three children.

Now the wedding car, which was driven by Howard Glass, which was in fact Howard Glass's car, a long, very black Lincoln Continental, festively speckled with confetti and snowflakes and swathed in crepe paper streamers and rosettes, was pulling away from the curb, on its way to the photographer's studio. Catherine waved at the departing car, and then her mother took her arm and they began to walk down the street to their own car, their heads bent against the blowing snow. Before they had gone very far, however, there was the sound of someone running up behind them. It was Julia.

"Wait, Arlene," Julia said, "don't run away. There's someone I want you to meet." Catherine was shivering. Her new winter coat, a sort of fake astrakhan, brown and nubby, flared out around her. Her shoes were wet. Snow was settling like a cap on her bare head. Her mother stalled, and Julia started pulling her back toward the people in front of the church. "I know it's cold," she said. "But there's someone I want you to meet." Why was she in such a hurry to leave, anyway, Julia wanted to know. It was true that, in spite of the cold and the snow, the wedding guests didn't seem eager to go anywhere. There was Hazel's uncle Clarence in his ill-fitting dark suit, navy-blue trousers rippling over the tops of his shoes, head back, cheeks flushed, accepting all the good will and congratulations. There was Wayne Travers, skulking, hands in pockets, wearing a shirt and sweater and jeans. Catherine smiled at him. She knew he'd seen her, but he looked away.

Julia Glass was introducing Catherine's mother to Mr. Schram, Catherine's Social Studies teacher. What was he doing at Hazel's wedding? Catherine wondered. A car came around the corner, and the sound of conversation was lost in the noise of the engine and the drawn-out swoosh of wheels slipping on the wet road. "Treacherous," a voice said. Catherine heard Julia saying, "Arlene, I'd like you to meet Brian. He started teaching here in September. Brian, I'd like you to meet my good friend, Arlene."

Abby was standing beside her mother, her eyes downcast, lips painted silver-white, knees trembling in the cold wet blasts of air. Abby and her mother hadn't spoken to each other for three days, Abby had told Catherine. This was partly because Abby had absolutely refused to be a bridesmaid for Hazel's wedding. It also had to do with Abby's boyfriend, the infamous Cal Dimitriou, who Julia had discovered in his car snuggling—her word, uttered in an outraged, scandalised tone, according to Abby—with her daughter, parked on a side road near the sea, out near Sunrise Beach. How had she known where to find them? Abby kept saying. She's such a witch, she knows everything, you can't get away from her, she had said to Catherine.

Mr. Schram was wearing a dark raincoat, a tan scarf around his neck. Catherine noticed that the tip of his nose was red from the cold. Miss Bluett, who was bundled up in fake furs and Christmas corsages, took his arm. She was telling Catherine's mother that she'd insisted Brian accompany her to the wedding. She hated attending weddings on her own, she said. Catherine's mother smiled politely. Snow kept falling, falling, transforming the main street of town, altering the way sound travelled, changing the perspective, so that nothing looked or sounded familiar. The church bells were ringing. Abby walked down the sidewalk, placing one foot in front of the other as if she were on a tightrope. Then she turned and walked back.

"It's a pleasure to meet you," Mr. Schram said.

Catherine's mother smiled. "How do you do?" she said. Catherine saw that, in this spectral winter light, her eyes had taken on that lovely strange luminous colour they sometimes had: blue floating like ink on the dark brown iris.

"Are you going on to the reception?" Miss Bluett asked.

"No," Catherine's mother said. "No, I don't think so. Catherine and I are just on our way home."

"Oh, but you have to come to the reception," Julia Glass said.

"We'd like to, but we really can't," Catherine's mother said. She put her hand on Catherine's arm. Look how the snow is sticking to the road, Catherine's mother said to Miss Bluett. Already! Already getting icy and dangerous. She wanted to get safely home before it began to accumulate, she said.

Halfway home and her mother hit the side of her hand lightly on the steering wheel and slowed down. She said, "You know, we should go to the reception. Why did I say we weren't going? What's wrong with me? You'd like to go, wouldn't you Catherine? We have to get a piece of wedding cake to take home for good luck. Julia will think I'm being mean, not going to the reception. She put so much work into this wedding."

"You said you didn't want to go," Catherine said. Her mother had told her before they got to the church that she didn't like receptions, that they went on and on and the food was always terrible and the music was terrible, and no one ever spoke to you. Catherine didn't particularly care if she went to the reception or not. The car did a sideways, slow-motion slide in the snow, and Catherine's mother took her foot off the gas pedal and removed her hands from the steering wheel and let the car straighten itself out.

"Oh, no one will even notice if we change our minds," she said. "Will they?"

Arlene regretted her decision to go to the reception as soon as she walked into the Legion Hall, which was redolent of wet wool, wet rubber boots, spilled beer. Snow was melting in dirty puddles near the entrance. Cold air flooded in every time the doors opened, bringing up visible goose pimples under the chiffon and tulle of the assembled female guests. Hazel and Norm were sitting at the head table—well, the only table, really, apart from a long table the food was set out on. The food seemed to be mostly sandwiches cut into triangles and dyed pink and green and blue. Arlene kept her coat on and found a chair against the wall. Catherine had disappeared with Abby; Arlene couldn't see either of them. Hazel was blowing kisses—a highly uncharacteristic gesture, it seemed to Arlene, but one that suited her, oddly enough, and made her seem for once careless and (here was an old-fashioned word) winsome—to people on the other side of the room, possibly even to Arlene. She smiled vaguely in return. A memory came to her of Hazel standing beside Abigail on the verandah at the Glasses' house, all those years ago, when Arlene had just moved to Cayley. Hazel had been pale, unsmiling, shy, a stodgy looking unattractive girl. Everyone had felt sorry for her—poor Hazel, living with her cruel uncle and being made to do all the work and look after her little cousin, Wayne. There had been suggestions of deliberately inflicted insults, deprivations, a hint of scandal. Through it all Hazel had plodded steadfastly forward. Whatever had happened to her in her life she had kept quiet about. And now look at her: as happy and as self-important as any bride, her eyes sparkling, her cheeks nearly as pink as the roses in her bouquet. Arlene wasn't sentimental; she never cried at weddings. But she was truly pleased to see Hazel so happy.

Julia came over to Arlene with a green-hued sandwich on a paper plate. "What are you doing here by yourself?" she said. "Here, have a sandwich, have two. Would you like something to drink? A glass of wine?"

"Oh, no, I'm fine," Arlene said. She refused to move. She didn't want any wine, she said. As soon as Julia had gone she picked up the sandwich between her thumb and forefinger and tried to figure out what was in it. If that was salmon paste, she wasn't touching it. The sandwich was warm and soggy; it was probably highly poisonous by now. She put it back on the plate and allowed herself an inward sigh. How was she going to get through winter? The short days, the rain, the long dark evenings, everyone sitting in front of the television. And Christmas. The shopping, gift wrapping, crystal bowls of fruit and mixed nuts set out on the coffee table, sprigs of holly Scotch-taped to the mantelpiece. Baking Christmas cake and sugar cookies and shortbread, none of which she liked very much. Inviting people over for drinks: Howard and Julia, among others.

The bride's uncle was stammering his way through a speech. The bride and groom were smiling and occasionally pecking at each other's cheeks. Arlene could smell snow, a scent that transported her to a field of white, a clean scoured distant landscape, memory eradicated. She could see Mr. Schram on the other side of the room, his tan scarf draped over his jacket; immaculate white cuffs. He was being careful not to look in her direction, or so it seemed to her. Was he afraid of her? In his hand he held a glass of beer, from which he occasionally drank. In spite of his long hair, in spite of the fact that he was young, he had a nicety, a pre-

ciseness, about him that she found a little irritating. Who
did he think he was? she found herself thinking. The handsome new teacher, obviously, entertaining the ladies. Julia
and Miss Bluett. Even so, she found herself trying to hold
on to the sense of irritation. It warmed her; it brightened
the dull room; it gave her something real to contemplate.
Now she tried to will him to glance in her direction, but he
kept talking earnestly to Caroline Bluett. He was, Arlene had
to admit, a nice-looking man. He had a lively intelligent
aspect, a nicely-shaped head, which was one of the things
she tended to notice. Why was he avoiding her? Wouldn't it
be common good manners to come and say hello to her,
after they'd just been introduced?

Arlene gave up. She stopped staring at Mr. Brian Schram
and got up and found a garbage can near the kitchen door
in which to deposit her sandwich and paper plate. Then she
went in search of Catherine and Abby. They were in the
washroom, looking at themselves in the mirror, and talking, or at least Abby was, and when Arlene opened the door
Abby jumped nervously, and hit the back of her hand hard
on the faucet. "Ouch," she said. "That hurt."

"Oh, I'm sorry," Arlene said, not that it was her fault,
except that she had walked in on them. Abby had cut herself. There was a sharp metal edge on the faucet, she discovered. It had left a gash on Abby's hand, and blood was welling
up quickly in the wound. She got Abby to hold her hand
over the sink while she ran cold water on it. "It stings,"
Abby said, trying to pull away. "I know. I'm sorry," Arlene
said, holding tight to Abby's hand, forcing her to keep it
under the cold water, the only first-aid measure she knew

of. Abby's hand was thin and cold, strangely resistant, as if the skin and bones were capable of denying themselves to Arlene, capable of refusing her care and comfort. All right, fine, Arlene thought, turning off the tap. There was a chill, damp wind coming in an open window high in the wall behind Arlene. Blood was running into the sink and down the drain. Arlene wanted Catherine to find Abby's mother, but Abby said she didn't need her mother, she was fine. "Are you sure?" Arlene kept asking. "It's just a cut," Abby said, staring fixedly at the blood. Arlene asked Catherine to see if she could find the packet of Kleenex she kept in her purse, and, when Catherine handed it to her, she took out a wad of tissues and got Abby to press it against the cut. Abby said she'd find her father, and get him to take her home. "Or we could take you home," Arlene said. "Catherine and I are leaving now, anyway."

"No, thanks," Abby said. "I'll be all right." She sounded odd, her voice small and distant, and Arlene began to wonder if she was going to faint. She herself felt faint, and no wonder, the washroom was such a grimy unpleasant place, and there had been the sight of all that blood swirling down the dirty drain. Why were they staying here? She opened the door and let Abby walk out ahead of her. Howard Glass was standing in a corner, talking to another man. He had a glass of beer in his hand. Arlene saw him turn and look at Abby, then bend his head as if to hear her better, and Arlene thought, well, that's all right, then. "Get your coat," she said to Catherine. "And then we can get out of here."

*

It snowed for three days; then the weather changed, the snow melted, the sun shone. Arlene forced herself to do some Christmas shopping and she made shortbread and a light fruit Christmas cake. She finished sewing Diane's angel costume for the Christmas concert at school. She sat near a window, in sunlight; the surprising warmth, the clarity of the light reminded her of other Decembers, other Christmas seasons, and then she remembered that her father had died three weeks before Christmas, in 1943. He had dropped dead on a street corner in downtown Vancouver, outside the building where his office was, the office where he kept that wonderful representation of the solar system. He had suffered a heart attack, very sudden, no warning signs, as far as anyone knew. The doctors had assured Eunice her husband wouldn't have had time to suffer, and yet the effect of his death on Eunice, and on Arlene, had been violent enough. In the days that followed, Eunice, distraught, had tried to injure herself, or worse, by throwing herself down the stairs. She had lain sobbing like a child in a sprawl on the floor, her negligée in a tangle around her thin, bare thighs. She had tried to drown herself in the claw-footed bathtub in the second floor bathroom, her face like a lily beneath the scented water, eyes wide open and blank. Arlene had been the one to find her, on both occasions. She had remained calm; she had phoned her grandparents. She had phoned the family doctor. Cars had started pulling up outside the house, people were running in, running past Arlene on their way to Eunice. It was all Eunice's terror, Eunice's sorrow, her suffering. Eunice had never thought to offer Arlene the least comfort, and when Arlene remembered this, now, she felt taken aback at the undiluted strength of her anger, her hurt.

Eunice and Arlene had stayed in their house for another two years, but it hadn't been the same without George Francis May walking briskly through the halls, or working in his study on his law cases, or marching into the kitchen demanding hot coffee from the housekeeper. So Eunice sold the house and she and Arlene moved out. By then, the war had ended. They moved to a smaller house near Stanley Park, in the West End, with a huge monkey puzzle tree in the front yard. Arlene would have been happy there, except that her mother met Duff, who talked Eunice into buying the cottage at St. Mary's Cove. Arlene was nearly fourteen; Duff used to call her sweetheart and princess. He used to say she reminded him of his own daughter. He used to brush his hand, the fingers of his hand, over the side of her face. He told her blue was her best colour and next to blue, red. He bought her Jockey Club perfume. He did these things to make Eunice jealous, Arlene thought. Eunice certainly took note. She was struggling, trying to figure out how to live in a damp, dark old cottage in a community with one store and one gas station and no hairdresser. She worked all day, chopping firewood, baking bread, heating water on the stove, scrubbing the wood floors, washing salt spray off the windows, and then at night she collapsed at the kitchen table. She cradled her head in her arms. She shut herself in her bedroom, slamming the door so that the cottage shook on its flimsy foundations. Duff padded around the room, silent at first, then humming under his breath, circling Arlene where she stood. Closer and closer. His face inches from hers, his breath on her face. His hand stroking her arm. She doesn't love us, he would say, of Eunice. We're adrift in the same boat, aren't we? She'd be okay, your mother, if she wasn't so temperamental. She thinks she's the Vitagraph Girl. Tragedy queen. He moved his thumb back and forth slowly on her arm, his eyes staring into hers, and he kissed her, a self-conscious, practised kiss, as if he was trying to impress her, he was such an accomplished seducer, irresistible, but why hadn't she pulled away, slapped his face? Instead she stood there while he forced her mouth open with his tongue, placed his hand heavily on her breast, and then a sound from Eunice's bedroom, Eunice getting up off the bed, opening a drawer, and Duff moved away. He stared out the window at the sea, morose, his shoulders defensively squared.

Oppressive, the memory of the young girl she had been, the silent obedient girl who had followed Eunice around and had dreamt of independence, of some day achieving independence. What was it Eunice had done? What had she done to both of them? She had tried to salvage what remained of her life after Arlene's father's death; she had tried her best to ignore the fact that the damage was irreparable, there wasn't anything she could do to restore what she'd lost. She had bulldozed ahead, not paying the least attention to where she was going, or what she was doing.

One day Duff had taken her and Eunice sailing, and they'd arrived at a small uninhabited island. Duff had anchored the *Dawn Louisa*, and they'd rowed ashore, and Duff had tied the rowboat to a rock, and they'd gone exploring. It had been a beautiful island, utterly silent except for the sound of the wind in the fir trees. The trees grew right to the shore; the interior of the island was impenetrable and dark. White sand beaches, bleached driftwood. The heat of the sun. They'd fooled around at the edge of the forest, picking wild strawberries, and they'd collected shells, and watched red-billed oyster-catchers, and a blue heron standing at the water's edge. They'd walked as far as they could around the island before encountering a rocky point of land that prevented them from going further, and they had turned back. At one point, Duff had taken off by himself into the trees, crashing around, making more noise, Eunice had said, than a bull elephant on a rampage. Don't pay him any attention, Eunice had said. He's probably just gone to take a pee. After a while, she and Arlene had kicked off their shoes and started paddling in the waves. The water was a deep, clear blue and so warm they had felt as if they were in the tropics. Finally, when a long time had gone by—neither one of them had a watch—and Duff still hadn't returned, when he hadn't emerged from the trail he'd hacked into the trees, they'd walked back to the beach where they'd landed, and there was Duff, knee-deep in the waves, pushing the rowboat away from shore. When he saw them he said, Hurry up, girls, time to get going, and he was all bluster and noise, wading back to shore, pulling the boat along with him, then heaving it back up on shore, making a big fuss about helping them in. It had been clear to Arlene that he'd intended to abandon them on the island without food or water. She still believed that this was true. Perhaps he had meant it as a joke, and he would have come back for them in an hour or so, the big hero, wiping tears of laughter from his eyes:

Look what a trick I've played, look at Robinson Crusoe and his boy Friday, lost souls. On the other hand, he might have been trying to get rid of them permanently. Imagine that, imagine having been the intended victims of a murder plot that hadn't worked out.

Eunice hadn't seemed to understand what had been happening. She'd got back in the rowboat and had insisted on rowing, and there had been a wind, choppy waves slapping against the side of the boat, and the *Dawn Louisa* white and pristine and distant, always distant, the likelihood of boarding her becoming remote, improbable, as Eunice pulled strenuously on the oars, putting her whole heart into the effort, attempting to bridge the gap between where she was and where she wanted to be.

David told Arlene the best thing to do was to forget the past. If it makes you unhappy, he said, then don't think about it. Eunice had done her best, he told her. There was no point in blaming Eunice. No point in harbouring anger and resentment. Far better to be thankful for all that they had in the present, their children, each other, good health, a sufficient amount of money. More than sufficient, really, he said. What they should do, he thought, was go for a holiday, all five of them. They could drive across the country, or fly as far as Nova Scotia or New Brunswick, and then buy a car and drive home. They could camp out some nights and stay in motels other nights. Why, it would be great fun! Think how good it would be for the children, to see the entire country, from one coast to the other, from sea to sea. He got up and went to the calendar on the kitchen wall. He turned it to the month of July and ran his finger along the page. Howard, he said, was planning a vacation to Europe in July, or was it August? He and Julia figured it was going to be the last summer Abby would go on a trip with them. It was the same with their family, he said. Before long, Catherine would be leaving home to go to university. And then Matt would leave. They'd spent so much of their lives being parents, he said. It would be quite amazing to have some time to themselves. Diane's only eight years old, for God's sake, Arlene said. David came over to her, to where she stood in front of the glass doors. Time goes by, he said. Oh, a philosopher, she said. He laughed, and put his arms around her and kneaded her shoulder and neck, his fingers pressing into the tender, sore muscles until she couldn't help wincing. He told her to take a deep breath, and for goodness' sake, try to relax. He said she was all knotted up. Of course she was. He was driving her crazy.

In another ten years, he said, even Diane will be ready to leave home. Before you know it, he said, we'll be on our own. That's something to look forward to, isn't it? he said.

Abby wanted to give Catherine the rose-coloured silk bridesmaid's dress her mother had made for her to wear at Hazel's wedding.

"Stupid bloody thing," Abby said, dragging it off its hanger in the closet in Julia's sewing room. "Here, try it on."

Catherine took off her sweatshirt and jeans and stepped into the dress and Abby did up the zipper in the back. Catherine turned around in front of the mirror. The skirt was gathered, a sort of ballerina length, the same length as the rayon print dresses Miss Bluett wore to school. The hem was unfinished, and raw silk threads floated around Catherine's ankles.

"It looks a lot better on you than on me," Abby said.

Catherine thought the colour suited her, but she wasn't sure. She wasn't sure what her mother would say if she allowed Abby to give her the dress.

"I told you it was a stupid dress," Abby said.

"No, it's not," Catherine said. "I like it. I think it's really neat. But my Nana might want me to have a dress from her store." Catherine needed a new dress for the spring prom, which was in June. She had agreed to go with a boy she was friends with, not a boyfriend, just a friend.

In front of the window there was a dressmaker's headless dummy, a birdcage torso with a sweet-looking, nipped-in waist. It made Catherine think of a sailor's wife waiting for her husband to come home from the sea, even though she knew he had drowned and would never come home. Outside, in the Glasses' back yard, there were three headless fir trees. There seemed to be a silent reproachful communication going on between the dressmaker's dummy and the trees: How did we come to be in such a plight? they seemed to be asking one another. The trees had been topped last fall, because Abby's father was afraid that they'd fall on the house in a storm. Without the trees, the cliff would erode and crumble into the sea, which was all that had prevented her father, Abby said, from having the trees cut right down, the stumps blasted out of the ground. Then he could have complained about not having a windbreak, not having shade on a hot day. It was a difficult decision for him to make,

Abby said, deciding what he most wanted to destroy, the trees or the cliff, or both together.

Catherine got back into her jeans and h'er sweatshirt. Abby folded the dress up and wrapped it carefully in a piece of tissue paper she got from a drawer, as if Catherine were making a purchase. Julia's sewing room had everything, boxes of patterns, bolts of fabric, sewing baskets, different kinds of scissors. It was the sewing room of a home economics teacher, orderly, neat, everything where it was meant to be, charts on the wall, old pattern books piled in a corner. Catherine had taken sewing three years in a row from Abby's mother and she still didn't know how to sew very well, but it had been one of her favourite subjects. This year she went to the sewing room straight from her English class, and she sat there trying to sew a straight seam with Miss Bluett's voice still ringing in her ears. Miss Bluett as Lady Macbeth. *Stop up the access and passage to remorse, That no compunctious visitings of nature Shake my fell purpose.* And, best of all: *Come to my woman's breasts and take my milk for gall, you murdering ministers.* Everyone in the class was calling Miss Bluett Lady Macbeth by mistake, except it didn't seem like a mistake, it seemed perfectly natural.

Catherine went to the window and looked down at the ant people, her parents and her brother and sister and Abby's parents. Howard was cooking salmon steaks and potatoes in aluminium foil. Everyone was bundled up in sweaters or light jackets, because, although it was May, it was cool. A Japanese plum tree at the edge of the yard was in a froth of soft pink blooms, petals littering the lawn beneath its outflung branches. And the rhododendrons were blooming, pink and scarlet and white, fragile and yet exuberant splashes of colour beneath the disfigured fir trees. This was, in fact, the first Sunday afternoon salmon barbecue of the year. It was what they always did, Catherine's parents and Abby's parents, every spring, year after year. Howard and Catherine's father went fishing, and then they cooked the fish outdoors. They were such good friends. They were so close. They moved in silence; they opened their mouths and no sounds came out. Or so it seemed to Catherine from her vantage point beside the dressmaker's dummy. The adults were all holding drinks in their hands. Matt and Diane were sitting on wooden lawn chairs. Howard went over to Catherine's mother and started talking to her. He put his head back and laughed. Then he leaned in a little closer. He couldn't keep himself from touching Catherine's mother, on the arm, on the shoulder. Howard, whose dark-framed glasses and buzz-cut were so aggressively out of date they'd almost come back into style, brushed something carelessly away from the collar of Catherine's mother's coat. She took a step back. He leaned closer and inspected her glass. Catherine's beautiful mother. Catherine couldn't compete with her mother's beauty, even if she wanted to. No one would ever notice her when Arlene was around. It was the truth. Arlene had this strange quality, as if she were awake and yet still caught in a dream, the remnants of a dream world floating around her, powerful and green and resurgent, and sometimes Catherine almost despised her for it, as if in her mother this was a sign of weakness, or, even worse, of a strength that excluded everyone else, even her own children. Why couldn't her mother be like a normal mother, soft and sort of drooping with motherliness, her face flushed and damp from preparing meals and baking cookies, or laundering bedsheets, or whatever it was other mothers did? Or she could be the kind of mother who was brisk and managing, who volunteered as a Brown Owl, and knew how to start fires with twigs, and how to change a car tire, how to give life-saving mouth-to-mouth resuscitation at the scene of the accident.

Run away with me, Howard Glass had, on occasion, said to Catherine's mother. He didn't care who heard. He thought he was funny, obviously. Darling, he called her. Arlene, darling. Abby said her father was disgusting; he thought he was a lady killer, secret agent 007; he flirted with everyone, and to his face she had said, "Dad smarten up. You're embarrassing me."

"Don't you talk to me like that, young lady," he had said. "Remember who I am," he had said. "If you don't mind." He had glared at her. It didn't take much, lately, for Abby to make him angry; Catherine had seen the way his face darkened when Abby annoyed him. When he was really angry he pulled a handkerchief out of his pocket and wiped his face, to give himself time to recover. He blew his nose vigorously, as if anger were extruding from him, a sort of plasma. And wasn't it true—this suddenly occurred to Catherine— that an angry person used to be called phlegmatic, long ago, in the Middle Ages? So Mr. Schram had told them, Catherine recalled. He had told the class a Medieval physician would divide them into groups according to whether they were phlegmatic, melancholic—and there were two others, what were they?—sanguine and choleric. It was all based on personality and temperament; the humours. Catherine thought she would be classified as sanguine; Abby was melancholic, or maybe choleric. In any case, Abby's father shouted at her for chewing gum, for wearing too much makeup, for wearing her skirts too short—why she was scarcely decent! he said. He grounded her for not getting home on time, or for hanging out at the Turf Café after school, or else he threatened to cut off her allowance. He expected her to get As on her report card, and just to spite him she started writing in the wrong answers on her exams, and her marks began to drop. Catherine was shocked, and awed, by the obvious pleasure Abby took in this. Howard threatened to send her to an all-girls' school in Duncan, where she would have to work, or else, and she said, "Well, isn't that just too bad, it's too late. I've just about finished school." She said there wasn't any reason for her to get perfect report cards; she wasn't going to university; she wasn't going anywhere.

That was what she had been telling Catherine in the washroom, during Hazel's wedding reception. "One more year to go," she had been saying. "And then I'm leaving home and getting my own place. I can't wait. I'm going to get a job and make my own money, pay for my own rent, do whatever I please." She had wet her finger and expertly smoothed an eyebrow. Oh, she was so good at this, all the little touches. How Catherine envied her. In the mirror Abby had looked almost bruised, pallid, as if she'd already suffered immensely. She and Cal could be friends and lovers, she said; there was nothing wrong with that. She didn't want to go steady with him anymore, or get engaged, or anything like that. People put all these expectations on you. The last thing she wanted was to be like her mother and father. Stuck in a little marriage like that, with the house, and the car and the kids. Kid. Just one, her. She was supposed to be everything, a beauty queen and brain surgeon combined, so that they'd feel justified at last, their miserable little lives would be justified.

What if she'd got pregnant? she then said, pausing to give Catherine a cold stare, her silver eyelids and silver mouth shimmering. Wouldn't that have been the worst disaster? She would have had to marry Cal. Yes, Catherine had agreed; that would have been awful—unthinkable. What would Abby have done? And then the door had opened and suddenly her mother had crowded into the washroom with them, and Abby had been startled, her hand flying out involuntarily and hitting the tap. Catherine had moved back until she was pressed against the paper towel dispenser. I'm sorry, her mother kept saying; I'm so sorry. As if she were responsible for Abby's clumsiness. Catherine had felt like saying, Oh, for God's sake, shut up.

Later, Catherine thought about how Abby had always had a dark side to her nature that was useful, in a sense, because it counterbalanced Catherine's own personality, which she knew was far too unformed, childlike. Abby was stronger than Catherine, and yet she was also vulnerable. All her energy went into covering up the vulnerable part of her personality, Catherine believed. Abby wrote stories about young women who were abducted by pirates and taken out to sea, where they became pirates themselves and learned to fire cannons and take other ships captive and loot and burn and murder. She had a beautiful singing voice, although she refused to join the school choir because she didn't want anyone to think she was a square—a total suck-hole, was the term Abby used. In Abby's bedroom at the top of her parents' empty vast old house she had a Ouija board, which she kept wrapped in a length of blue velvet in her closet, and which she used to contact the spirits of the dead. She had spoken with the spirit of Myrtle Kriskin. Communed with her. She swore to Catherine that this was true. She had asked Myrtle what the future held, if she should take a hair-dressing course after graduation, or open a flower shop, or hitchhike across the country. According to Abby, Myrtle had first identified herself by spelling out her name on the Ouija board, and then her actual voice had whispered directly in Abby's ear: hairdressing is darned hard work, you're on your feet all day. Flower shops make your skin smell of nothing but bug spray and carnations. And she sure as heck didn't recommend hitchhiking, it wasn't a safe mode of travel for a young girl. Myrtle's breath had been so cold it had nearly made her ear go numb, Abby said. She'd asked Myrtle if she'd ever heard, where she was now, on the other side, of Janis Joplin, or the Beatles. In Abby's bedroom, Catherine closed her eyes and rested the tips of her fingers on the planchette. But she couldn't bear it; a faint memory came to her of a woman laughing, her hair bright in the sun, her eyes shining. And then someone weeping, and darkness, and Catherine's mother's voice saying, Get up off the floor, Catherine, and eat your dinner, which didn't make any sense, which made Catherine feel disoriented, frightened in a pe-culiarly urgent way. She thought: The place where Myrtle died is just down the beach, it's no distance at all. She felt as if someone were standing behind her, a ghostly form. She abandoned the Ouija board and went and sat on Abby's bed with her hands over her eyes, and Abby called her a big baby, a chicken, but she didn't care.

Abby was the first person Catherine knew who started dressing like a hippie, in bellbottoms and white muslin blouses with Nehru collars. She was the first person to start cooking brown rice and following a macrobiotic diet, keeping her dishes separate from those of her parents, as if to avoid contamination. She burnt joss sticks in her bedroom, and wore patchouli oil. She was one of the first in the town to smoke grass, to smoke it expertly, with panache, and she had learned to roll a joint. She owned a roach clip and a hash pipe, which she kept hidden in what she called a secret drawer in her desk. She could say things like, Wow, I'm stoned out of my head, and coming from her, it didn't sound totally retarded. She got these things from Cal and his friends, who were older, who had lived elsewhere, in Vancouver, Victoria, Seattle. Everything that was new and strange and exciting entered the town of Cayley, at least as far as Catherine and her friends, Lisa and the others, were concerned, via the agitated, spirited, slender form of sixteen-year-old Abigail Glass.

CHAPTER TWENTY-THREE

Caroline Bluett had a wicked secret: She was a cannibal ogress; or, to be more precise, she suspected she had in her something of a cannibal ogress. On certain nights she left her house and found her way by the light of the moon to the forest, where she got down on all fours and smeared dirt on her face and hands and ate wild berries and the thick fleshy fungus that grew on trees, and chewed vigorously on bark stripped from young alders in groves along the banks of a free-flowing stream. This makeshift fare could not, however, in any way satisfy the hunger of an ogress, which Caroline suspected was huge, elemental, desperate, burdensome.

This was the story: A long time ago her father had become close friends with an ethnographer who was travelling up the coast of British Columbia. The ethnographer's name was Jackson Sprague. His secretary and assistant was a Coast Salish man in his forties, who went by the name of

Edgar Jones. Dr. Sprague was an old man with thin white hair and arthritis in his hands and knees. He walked with a cane. He smelled most pungently of pipe tobacco. He wore a khaki jacket and a pith helmet, as if he were on safari in Africa, and carried around a portable writing desk outfitted with sterling silver inkpots and fountain pens. He pried up the lid of the writing desk and there were his notebooks, twenty or thirty of them, some of which he passed to Caroline, for her perusal. Page after page of beautifully formed upward-slanted script, strangely unintelligible, at least to Caroline, who turned the pages and murmured politely, before passing them back. For most of his life, Dr. Sprague had been studying the indigenous peoples of southwest British Columbia. He was particularly interested in early myths, in legends, in what he referred to as tall tales. Nothing alarmed Dr. Sprague. He was eager to uncover any legend or folk story, no matter how gruesome or unsettling, no matter how unlikely. In fact, he liked the grotesque best of all, Edgar Jones told Caroline. Caroline was in her early twenties; most of the time she was away at normal school, in Victoria, learning to be a teacher, but when Dr. Sprague and Edgar Jones arrived that particular summer she was at home. On the last night of their visit—they stayed at least three or four days, she couldn't remember exactly how long—Caroline had served a dinner of baked salmon, a nice large coho her father had caught that morning, out in his boat with Edgar Jones. With the salmon there were boiled new potatoes and green peas and white sauce. For dessert there was cake with strawberries and clotted cream. Oh, that wonderful long-ago meal; she could nearly taste it, nearly see the fragrant tender pink flesh of the salmon, the tissue-thin skin clinging to the opalescent whiteness of the steaming boiled potatoes. After dinner they sat around the fireplace, which was lit, because it was a cool evening, and foggy. The tide was high; the sea was washing up against the shore. They were drinking port and sherry. A spark flew out of the fireplace onto the carpet and Caroline got up and put her sherry on a side table and kicked the glowing ember toward the hearth, then stepped on it, holding her skirt out of the way and giving her foot, in its small, narrow pump, a decisive turn to be sure the ember was extinguished. She remembered the evening in minute detail. Her efficiency, her social graces, her sense of herself as a pretty young woman in a room full of men. She remembered Edgar Jones and Dr. Jackson Sprague watching her as if in a trance as she picked up her sherry from a side table and returned to her place on the sofa. Dr. Sprague cleared his throat preparatorily, then began the story of the cannibal ogress, who was not a real woman, but a malevolent spirit. A short, fat little spirit, with glittering dark eyes and strong hands. This was long ago, Dr. Sprague said, before Europeans came to the coast, when everything was more or less as it had been since the beginning of time, the land peaceful and secretive, the rain forests dark and silent. The cannibal ogress crept out of the forest at night, usually when there was no moon, and came to a village where everyone was asleep, and ran her hands over the faces of the sleeping children, trying to determine which ones she would take away with her. She was extremely strong physically, Dr. Sprague said, and as a result she had no difficulty carrying two or even three semiconscious children in her arms or slung over her shoulders until she came to the cave where she lived.

The cannibal ogress kept the children she'd stolen with her for some time. She fattened them up with bear meat and venison, and fed them the hearts of ravens and painted their foreheads and chins with animal blood and with dye made from plants. Her cave was full of lizards and snakes, which she kept for pets. You are mine, all mine, she would sing to them, to the lizards and snakes, and to her captives, the children. Or so the story went, Dr. Sprague added. The children couldn't see her; they couldn't see anything, because the cannibal ogress had sealed their eyes shut with an ointment made from the pitch of trees.

According to some versions of the story, Dr. Sprague said, the cannibal ogress was said to be the daughter of a sea creature. Other versions suggested that the last remaining cannibal ogress—they were never more than few in number, sightings were extremely rare—had fallen into the sea and drowned. In any case, near the entrance to her cave the cannibal ogress always had a big fire pit, and this was where she built huge roaring fires and roasted the children. She roasted them and ate them down to the bones and licked her fingers and belched. For a little while after this extraordinary meal, she appeared younger, more human. She went into the villages and was frequently mistaken for a relative, someone who had been ill and had recovered, or had gone on a long journey, and had been given up as dead or lost, and had miraculously returned. She lived among the people and they thought nothing of it; they even gave her small gifts and let her look after the infants. And then one day she would be gone, she would be glimpsed running away into the woods, smaller, older, stooped; even, it seemed, less human in aspect.

How could Caroline forget such a tale? After Dr. Sprague and Edgar Jones had left, she dreamed about the cannibal ogress. The figure that appeared in her dreams was not quite as wicked as the one Dr. Sprague had described. At twilight, Caroline sat on a log on the beach in front of her house, and a cannibal ogress came lumbering along and sat beside her and began weaving a garment out of the coarse sea-grass that grew above the high tide mark. The garment was for Caroline. If she wore it, the ogress said, it would protect her from bad luck, it would ensure robust health, long life. As she spoke, a wind agitated the surface of the sea, and Caroline imagined that it was responding in a playful, teasing, comradely way to the ogress, as if to remind her how puny she was compared to the sea's great power and resourcefulness. Even this small sea, beside this small town.

Are you going to stay with me forever? Caroline had asked the cannibal ogress, and the ogress had replied, Oh, we are so much of a kind, we are inseparable. Awake, Caroline considered this very unlikely. She was a rational person; she did not believe in ghosts, or in witches, or demons, and even less in ogresses. But she was lonely. And her dreams were always full of unlikely characters, not only the cannibal ogress, but also explorers from the high arctic, like Sir John Franklin, and Prime Ministers, like William Lyon Mackenzie King, newly elected, and quite jubilant, winking and toasting her with a glass of wine; and there was also her poor sweet dead mother, Cassandra, waving to her from the deck of a passing boat. The thing was, Caroline was frightened much of the time. She had to begin so many new things. While she was away at school she was living in a rooming house she didn't like. She was learning to become a teacher, and she wasn't sure if that was what she wanted. The cannibal ogress sat there weaving together the blades of sea grass and saying, Don't you have any faith in yourself? Take what you need. Just take it and keep going. No one will harm you, I guarantee. In these dreams, the cannibal ogress became a kindly figure. She wore a scarf tied around her head, like a Russian *babushka*. She wore three or four skirts, one on top of the other, and soft leather boots. Her eyes were the colour of dark moist cedar roots, and were perpetually squinting against the brightness of the sky. Her cheeks were broad and weathered, her skin a bronzed web of lines. She could, in this guise, have been a Mongol, a peasant woman from some far-off antique land, savage and wise. Then the cannibal ogress ceased to appear in Caroline's dreams; the cannibal ogress had become part of her. This was an idea Caroline got. She knew that it bordered on plain craziness, but she couldn't shake it off. The cannibal ogress looked out of Caroline's eyes and spoke with Caroline's voice. The whole procedure, the transformation, or internalisation, was unremarkable, on the surface, and certainly erratic, and forgotten for the most part, until Caroline stood at the front of her first classroom, and there were these rows of stolid unforgiving critical faces looking straight at her, or choosing not to look at her, but evading her altogether, gazing at the ceiling or out the window, pretending she wasn't even there. That was what upset her. That and the fact that most of the pupils in her classes didn't want to learn. They didn't want to read *Tintern Abbey*, or *Locksley Hall*, or even Archibald Lampman. They didn't want to memorise a soliloquy from Shakespeare. She honest to God tried her best to interest them, but they slipped lower and lower into their seats and stuck their legs out in front of them and got these ferocious bored stupid scowls on their faces and she wanted to shake them to death to get their attention—sometimes she told them she'd like to light a fire under them, get them fired up for a change, and that made her think of the cannibal ogress, and she had to smile, thinking how she could drag a few of her worst, slowest, most obdurate students out of their desks into the forest and burn them alive. She'd have their attention then, she thought. She might not be able to make a meal of their brains in the expectation of getting any wiser, and she couldn't eat their hearts and expect to get any braver, but she could roast them alive and eat their sweet young flesh, and surely, after such a decadent licentious feast, she wouldn't feel so inept, so threatened, she wouldn't feel like such a dismal failure.

It was because she wasn't much older than her students; it was because she was a woman, a young girl; it was because she had a quiet voice and she was shy and blushed all the time; she was used to being alone with her father at the edge of the sea, living in a small, isolated village. That was why she had so much trouble when she started teaching. In order to survive—and what choice did she have, there was no one to support her but herself—she had had to give up being young; she had consumed her vulnerable, innocent self and had acquired a carapace, shiny and hard and new:

the flinty impenetrable aspect of an ogress. She made sure she handed out lots of homework: memory work, essays, sheets of exercises in English grammar. She gave Friday-afternoon quizzes and twice-monthly examinations. She was a demon marker. She handed out detentions as if they were after-dinner mints. When necessary, she took the black leather school-board-issue strap out of her desk drawer and made the boys, some, at eighteen years of age, towering over her, stand still while she raised her arm high in the air and brought the strap down *thwack!* on the palms of their hands. She never smiled, except occasionally, in triumph. She was a terror. Now she was getting old; she didn't have to be as strict; her students had a natural fear of anything old; to them, she no doubt looked like a relic from the distant geological past. Now she could give out sympathy and advice to neophytes like Brian Schram, who had told her that he was afraid teaching was giving him an ulcer. Before entering the classroom, he told her, he actually trembled as if he'd been stricken with some rare form of tropical disease. His hands shook so that he could hardly hold the chalk. He stuck out his hands for her to see, his fingers splayed, and, to be honest, she noticed nothing unusual, although she made a little sympathetic clucking sound. He had to adopt a role, he said. The only way he could teach was to pretend he was someone else.

"Yes," she had said, "you have to be a bit of an ogre. You have to be a cannibal."

"Good advice," he had said, nodding seriously.

She and Brian became friends. She knew that his family lived in Ontario, and she had the impression he didn't have many friends in Cayley, and so she began to invite him to her house in the evenings. One Sunday evening, she invited him to dinner and cooked a pot roast, using her father's recipe, adding small white onions and celery and a bay leaf. They had wine with dinner, coffee and something sweet after dinner, and she put a recording of classical music—it seemed they both liked the Romantic composers: Brahms, Schubert, Schumann, most especially Schumann—on the old record player her father had bought her years ago.

In December, she talked him into accompanying her to Hazel's wedding. He had met Hazel several times before, when he had come to Caroline's house and Hazel was there, cleaning out the fridge or washing the walls. Brian, it seemed, liked Hazel. He admired her willingness to work hard, her pleasant demeanour, not that he'd ever discussed her with Caroline, as far as she could recall. And obviously Hazel had thought quite well of him. But should he go? he had asked Caroline. Would her family want him there, a stranger? Of course he should go, Caroline told him. If he didn't, she'd have to go alone, and she'd love to have an escort, if he'd be willing to accompany her. Then it's settled, he had said. He asked Caroline to help him select a wedding present. He browsed the shelves of the hardware store, deliberately pouncing on the worst specimens he could find: a vile green cat clock with a crooked tail for a pendulum, an orange glass serving bowl on a wrought iron stand, steak knifes with long curved fake-ivory plastic handles. Did people buy these things? he wanted to know. Did they use them? Were they proud of them, did they clean them, and look after them, and show them off to their friends? He could bet they did, Caroline said.

It occurred to her, as they crossed the street from the hardware store to the jewellery store, that Brian Schram could have been her son. She was certainly old enough to be his mother, if not his grandmother; she would, to anyone watching her walk at his side in this casual fashion, almost certainly look like a close relative of some kind. It was a cold day, the clouds so low and dark the sea and the forested mountains were obliterated. The town looked lost, small, drab. Her mood, however, was effervescent; here she was, a woman with a grown son, a favourite son, from whom she had been separated for some time, and who had surprised her by coming home early for Christmas.

In the jewellery store, Brian settled on a gift: a white bone china cream-and-sugar set, more costly than he'd intended, more than Caroline thought he should spend, although all she said was, "You hardly know Hazel. You don't need to give such an expensive gift."

"I know, but I want to," he said.

Caroline, in her new role as indulgent mother, almost offered to pay half, then caught herself and merely stood watching as he held the creamer up to the light and exclaimed over its translucency, which seemed to Caroline no less admirable or fine than the translucency of Brian's fingertips, which were unusually thin and delicately formed, the nails flat and rosy, trimmed nearly to the quick. Or was he, as a result of his nerves, in the habit of biting his nails? If so, she felt even more maternal toward him, and more determined to give him assistance, support, succour, whatever was needed. He took his chequebook from his pocket, and she gave him a warm, approving smile, and then they waited in silence in front of the display cases full of glittering gemstones, of gleaming ropes of pearl, of gold and silver, while his purchase was wrapped in tissue paper and put in a box, and a receipt was written out. Then they walked back to his car, and he drove her home, a quick trip down the frozen empty streets of town to the edge of the cold grey sea. He walked her to the door of her house and waited while she turned the key in the lock. There was a bitter wind blowing in off the sea. She paused and wiped at her eyes with a gloved hand. Brian kept talking, telling her how much he'd enjoyed the day, how much he appreciated her help. Then he began to make arrangements to pick her up the morning of Hazel's wedding, which was two weeks away, to sit with her in the church, to go to the reception with her. Yes, that would be lovely, she said. How good he was, she thought, her erstwhile son. She paused with her hand on the door handle and asked him if he'd like to come in and have lunch with her.

"Oh, thank you, that's very kind, but I mustn't keep taking up your time," he said.

"I've plenty of time," she said. "It's no trouble."

"You'd tell me if it was? A trouble, I mean."

"Oh, yes," she said. "I'd tell you."

"Well, then, lunch would be lovely," he said. "But you must let me help you."

"Oh, for heaven's sake," she said. She opened the door and they went inside. She took Brian's coat from him and hung it up, then removed her own coat—her wonderful new fur coat that wasn't really fur, but nevertheless made her feel like a rich, pampered matron, the proper mother of Brian Schram. In the kitchen she put the kettle on and took a loaf of bread out of the breadbox. And there were the two of them, at one-thirty in the afternoon, slicing bread and spreading butter and talking about school, about getting the end-of-term report cards written, and about the upcoming staff meeting at eight on Monday morning, which neither one of them wanted to attend, and when they'd run out of things to say about school, Caroline found herself telling him a little of the history of her house, which he had, more than once, told her he admired. She told him the same story she told everyone, about the TB hospital, or isolation ward, rather, and the nurses running up and down the hill in their long black capes.

Brian put the lid back on the mayonnaise jar, and went to the small kitchen window, where he stood looking out onto the backyard, a mostly unkempt area where blackberry vines were growing in under the fence and threatening to choke out the old boxwood hedge. What little light there was shone in on his face, giving his features an extraordinary clarity. Caroline, pretending to be rinsing the lettuce, couldn't help admiring the shape of his nose, the small bump on the bridge, the finely flared nostrils, the small cleft in his chin, the locks of hair pressed close against the pale cartilage of his ears, the somewhat severe, unadorned, even ascetic, all-of-a-piece construction of cheekbone, jaw, throat. Clay, the life breathed in to it. And young, so very young.

"What a wonderful picture," he said, unaware of her scrutiny. "I wish it were possible to present my students with images like that, from the past. Nurses in their long, dark capes hurrying up a moonlit street. A patient alone in an empty house, sitting up in bed with a cup of hot chocolate. You can never introduce that fineness of perception into a history lesson, can you? You ought to be able to, but you can't. History's all dates and names, outbreaks of violence, treaties, alliances. Big events; big names, lots of conflict. At least, that's how it seems sometimes, when you're trying to teach it. One girl in my grade twelve history class said her textbook depressed her so much she had to go for a walk to clear her head every time she studied it. I have to admit I sympathised with her." The very worst thing about this large, this *gigantically crude*, view of history, he went on to say, was that it made a person wonder: Was there any hope for the individual? Would those small brilliantly acute moments like the one Caroline had described even be possible, would they even be remembered, in a world that held the omnipresent threat of all-out nuclear warfare, biological weapons, mind-control, God knows what all? It was all such a mess, wasn't it? The only possibility for hope, as he saw it, was indeed on a very individual scale, one moment taken at a time. *Be here now*, as the new gurus of the human condition were saying. Didn't Caroline think that was true? She said she did think it was absolutely true.

And speaking of the future, Brian was saying, returning to the construction of his sandwich and sprinkling salt on a sliced tomato, he didn't have any clear idea what it held for him personally; he had no real plans, no idea of where he wanted to be five years from now. Life surprised him, he said. Look, for example, at where he was now, in a town he hadn't known existed until he'd actually arrived.

"No one ever leaves here, you know," she said. "It's the truth. I arrived with my parents when I was ten years old. My parents never meant to stay here, but they did. Everyone does. It's hard to describe. You'll find out. You'll try to leave and you'll be like a fly on a strip of flypaper."

He laughed. He must have thought she was trying to be funny.

After they'd eaten their lunch at the kitchen table, and she had poured them each a cup of tea, they went into her living room, and he sat on the floor pulling books out of her bookcase. He loved her books, he told her, even though they were old and dusty and made him sneeze. He read to her from them. She listened, sipping her tea, trying to pay attention, but soon her mind began to wander and she started thinking about other things. Outside it was getting dark. Soon the winter solstice would arrive; the year would close in upon itself, a tightly sealed bud containing what one sincerely hoped was a promise of regeneration. And then the year would end, and, Caroline realised, she would find herself removed an additional increment from the past, from her past, which she loved. She thought of the past as a series of vivid pictures exactly like images on a reel of film, sometimes static, sometimes flickering past so quickly they gave the illusion of movement. Herself at the age of ten or eleven, after having crawled through a broken place in the picket fence around the hospital grounds, getting her long hair caught in some blackberry vines. She'd been surrounded by wild shrubs, song birds, the light of the sun on the grass;

she'd been breathing in the smell of the sea and of the saw-mill, the invigorating odour of freshly cut lumber. In the distance she could hear the machinery at the mill. She had thought the thorns would never release her; she was a bird trapped in a snare, or—what was that lovely archaic word?—*springes*, trapped by *springes*, a helpless flutter and then death, although of course she hadn't died, she'd worked her hair free a strand at a time, her hands and arms scratched all over and bleeding. Her hair had been beautiful when she was a girl, the colour of wheat and fine as silk, although now it was grey and against her own better sense she wore it, year in, year out, in a pageboy, the fringe curled smoothly in front so that she suspected she looked as outmoded and frumpy as Mamie Eisenhower. At this moment she could see her reflection in the glass chimney of the antique coal oil lamp on the sideboard, her dark eyes and little pointed cat's chin. The lamp had been on the sideboard for ages; she used it occasionally, when the power failed in a storm. It gave enough light to read by. It had stood in the same place when her father was alive. She remembered her father tell-ing her that the invention of spectacles in the thirteenth century and the invention of the lamp in the seventeenth had at last made reading an occupation that could be seri-ously pursued. Before that, people had crawled into bed soon after dusk, bored nearly to tears, doors bolted against the beasts of the night. He had told her that when gas lamps were first installed in homes, the ladies had turned away from the brightness in fear; they had shielded their faces to protect their delicate complexions; they had opened para-sols inside their drawing rooms. For the briefest moment

Caroline imagined she could see her father sitting in his chair near the fire. His expression was animated; he looked as he had always looked when he was enjoying the company of his friends, the travelling ethnographer and his assistant, who had come by to talk and share an evening meal and then had, without knowing it, left behind a wicked troubled mischievous spirit.

The tide was high and the sea was sloshing against the driftwood on the other side of Caroline's fence. If she turned out all the house lights, moonlight would stream in the window. At least, it would when the moon had risen. In a corner of her sofa she curled up small as a child and for a moment closed her eyes. She covered her mouth and yawned. She wondered if Brian would ever, ever leave. She enjoyed his company, but only for a little while, and then she wanted to be alone—her natural state. More than anything she liked to listen to music on the radio and read and sometimes before she went to bed she went outside and walked on the beach in the dark. Brian had begun on "Little Gidding," not one of her favourite Eliot poems, although certainly apt, at midwinter's spring. "'In the dark time of the year,'" he intoned, "'Between melting and freezing / The soul's sap quivers.'" Was her soul's sap—unlovely term— quivering? The room was cold; she shivered. Brian stopped reading and sat silently turning pages. Then he gathered up and put away the poetry books. He got up and sat in an armchair—her father's chair. He propped one foot on his knee, placed a hand on his ankle. He began to tell her that once, a few years ago, he'd been engaged to a woman called Evelyn. She was an art teacher who liked to paint huge canvases of horses galloping across the prairie, clouds of dust rising beneath their metal-shod hooves. They'd planned out their future lives, the children they were going to have, where they'd live, where they'd take vacations, what kind of house they wanted. Then he'd lost his job at the high school where they both taught on the lower mainland, and he'd had to take a job miles away, in Prince George, and while he was there Evelyn had met someone else, and had got married. So she had one-half of the life they'd intended to share, and he had nothing.

"It was my fault, though," Brian said. "I expect I didn't make enough of an effort."

"Oh, you did the best you could, I'm sure" Caroline said, stifling a yawn. "You'll find someone else, someone much nicer. You'll see." She smiled at him. Those big dark eyes, like a puppy's eyes. Mournful, romantic, enigmatic, seemingly capable of genuine feeling. She thought: He's getting to be a little afraid; he saw what was ahead; he knew that thirty, forty years was not such an immense length of time: it was no protection at all. When he spoke of this Evelyn, Caroline got a distinct picture of a tall girl with jet black hair and a sulky mouth painted purple, the kind of person who wore pointy-toed boots to school and dominated the conversation in the staff room. The thing was, Brian was like a mirror in which Caroline was somehow able to glimpse her own life and see it as devoid of anything meaningful, which caused her a certain amount of anguish. Soon she would begin to fret once again over the absence of handsome young sons, beautiful graceful daughters. Another generation, had it existed, would have served as a bulwark, a citadel, a living city like a garrison, holding that great enemy, time, momentarily at bay. Perhaps all those years ago she should have persisted, and married Edwin Roy, that sweet-tempered lighthouse keeper. She could have married Edwin, if she'd wanted. Edwin had been a kind man, tall, with sloping shoulders and an accumulation of flesh on his hips that gave him an oddly soft, womanish appearance. He'd had a wide mouth and brown hair that hung over his forehead. She remembered him with affection. They could have produced a phalanx of apple-dumpling babies, rosy-cheeked, plump, fragrant. And besides Edwin, there had been a science teacher at the school, when Caroline was in her late thirties. He'd wanted to marry her, or so he had said, but then it had turned out he already had a wife living elsewhere. The wife refused to give him a divorce. The friendship between Caroline and this man, which she had briefly treasured, had ended like a bad farce, and not long afterwards, he had left the teaching profession to start up an insurance agency on Salt Spring Island. Semi-retirement; flight; abandonment, Caroline left on the shore, gazing tearfully after him. Well, not quite. She'd soon recovered. These were the things that happened to an ogress, unavoidably, and turned her inward, and made her an outcast. In a small town like this the unwritten social contract was, as Caroline well knew, based scrupulously on the assumption that everyone was alike. Those who diverged were viewed with distrust, if not active dislike. On the other hand, people like Caroline, spinsters who lived alone and walked around at night in gumboots, muttering to themselves under the stars, were a necessary adjunct to the social order. They confirmed everyone else's sense of impeccable normality. She didn't mind, but obviously Brian did. He did not, she couldn't help seeing, have her courage. And because he was here, sitting in her living room on a winter's afternoon, she felt responsible for him. She felt as if she had to take it upon herself to think of a remedy. But what? That night she couldn't think at all.

After Brian had left, she got out her knitting. She was making a sweater for herself, out of maroon-coloured wool. She knitted row after row of stocking stitch and watched the fire she'd lit in the grate. The floorboards of the house creaked and snapped as they usually did, as if beneath the silence one of the nurses was walking to and fro, tending to her patient.

One Saturday afternoon in May, Brian took Caroline out for lunch at the Dimitriou's seafood restaurant out on the old Cayley Road. In the car, she fiddled with her scarf, retying the knot a couple of times and then smoothing down her blouse collar while she looked at the passing scenery. On either side of the road new green leaves filtered the spring sunlight to a tender, dappled luminescence. Overhead, above the tangle of branches, clouds the shape and size of newborn lambs raced across a lavender-blue sky. It was a glorious day, a magnificent day, and she felt unable to speak. She felt slightly giddy, as if they were travelling through the landscape at the speed of light. They were both tired, she thought. It was nearly the end of the school year and she, at least, was worn out.

As soon as they were at the restaurant, and settled at a table, she made herself relax a little. She slipped her arms out of her coat and draped it over the back of her chair. In order to start up a conversation, she started to tell him that the Dimitrious' restaurant was built on the exact site of an earlier restaurant that had burned down nearly eleven years ago, in 1957. She'd been out of the country at the time, she told him, and as a result she'd missed all the dramatic events of that summer. She'd been in England, on the second real holiday she'd ever had in her life. She had enjoyed herself in England and had actually considered staying there. Her cousins had wanted her to. She had two cousins, both older than she was—or at least she'd had two cousins. Mildred had passed away since, of complications following influenza. The other cousin, Rupert, was an uncommunicative hermit who lived in a minuscule cottage in Sussex and slept outdoors and ate nothing but fruit and porridge. She was allowing herself to digress, however.

"There was a terrible electrical storm, that summer, and lightning struck what I believe was called the El Rancho Restaurant, which was located right where we're sitting. It burned to the ground. Evidently, flames could be seen for miles around. Anyway, nobody did a thing to this land for years afterwards, until the Dimitriou family came along. They've worked—well," she said, leaning forward a little, dropping her voice to a whisper, "I was going to say they've worked like Trojans. Maybe they're not from Greece at all; maybe they're really Trojans, descendants of Paris, or Hector, or whoever he was, or would have been, if Troy still existed." And here, as she spoke, was one of the Dimitriou girls. Helen of Troy, also known as Tina. Her teased and lacquered hair stood out around her head like ornate headgear. Her earrings were orange balls that bounced wildly against her neck when she moved her head. She gave Caroline and Brian each a menu and poured out two glasses of ice-water, and said, "It's nice to see you, Miss Bluett," and asked her how she was, and how school was going. To Caroline's amusement, she stood there with the water pitcher in her hand apologising for not working hard enough at school, for talking in class. It didn't matter how many years they'd been out of school, Caroline's former students always said the same things to her. We're sorry, they always said. We're so sorry. What they were after, Caroline believed, although they didn't quite know it, was absolution, forgiveness for multiple sins of commission and omission. Caroline told Tina she had been a good student. *You* were never any trouble, she assured her, although as far as she could remember this hadn't been entirely true. She seemed to remember sitting at her desk after classes on more than one stiflingly hot June afternoon while Tina Dimitriou served a detention, writing out hundreds of lines promising not to talk or pass notes or chew gum.

Caroline studied the menu, and then decided on baked salmon with a tossed green salad, and Brian ordered a steak sandwich and a beer. They ate and looked out at the narrow passage of water between the shore and the point of land opposite. They watched a log boom being pulled by a tug. The watched the gulls settling on the beach and the water and then taking to the air again. A bald eagle was circling at some great height.

Brian asked her about the Greenwood family. The daughter, Catherine, was in his Socials 11 class, he told Caroline. Such a good student, always polite, hard-working, co-operative. You couldn't wish for a nicer presence in the classroom, he said. Did Caroline know the family? Did she by any chance know Catherine's mother? He'd met her at Hazel's wedding, briefly. He'd hardly spoken to her. And since then he's actually seen her a few times.

"Well, how interesting that you should mention Arlene Greenwood," said Caroline. "I was just going to tell you a story about her. It was something that happened the very same summer the old El Rancho restaurant burned down. Which was, in fact, the summer that I met Arlene. For awhile I thought Arlene and I might become friends, but we haven't seen much of each other for years." She tore a piece off her dinner roll and spread it with butter. "My impression," she said, "is that no one really knows Arlene very well. I suppose her best friend is Julia. Their husbands work together, you know, and of course their daughters are friends." She paused and took a drink of water. It had always seemed to her, she said, that Arlene and Julia were pretty much opposites. Julia was a practical, sensible person, perhaps a little brusque, but extremely kind and generous. Not that Arlene wasn't equally kind, in her own way, but she always seemed distracted with her family, with those three children, and no wonder. Three children were a handful, and Arlene was a rather dreamy person—oh, very nice, quite interesting, but dreamy. A little stand-offish. Julia, of course, had been wonderful to Hazel, organising her wedding, putting as much thought into the preparations as she would for her own daughter. Mind you, she'd got more gratitude from Hazel than she'd be likely to get from Abigail, Caroline said to Brian. But that was an entirely different subject. Julia was a marvel, really she was. She sewed, prepared beautiful gourmet meals, kept an immaculate house; her students adored her, and she was an artist, as well. Had Brian seen any of her paintings yet? Well, he'd have to, sometime. They were quite good.

"Yes, Julia is amazing," Brian said. He picked up his fork and stabbed at a chip. "And what was it you were saying about Mrs. Greenwood?" He took a drink from his water glass and set it carefully down on the tablecloth. "Arlene, that is. I guess it's all right if I call her Arlene."

"I don't see why not," Caroline said. "What was I saying? Oh, I know. I was going to tell you what happened that summer, in 1957. It involved Arlene, and that's why I said it was a coincidence that you mentioned her name."

She watched Brian picking up the salt shaker and putting it down, all the while keeping his eye on her. He wanted to hear what she had to say, and at the same time he didn't want to appear too eager. This confused her for a moment. She thought: Is that why he brought me here? To learn what he can about Arlene Greenwood? Then she felt ashamed of herself, for suspecting his motives. He was simply trying to make conversation. She was in a strange mood today, for no apparent reason. Then she remembered she did have a reason. Last night Hazel's brother Wayne had called at her house and had talked her into lending him ten dollars. Well, lending wasn't quite the correct word, since she'd never see the money again. He'd thanked her, his blue eyes as clear and guileless as an infant's, his lower lip rosy as the skin of an apple. It wasn't the first time he'd come to her for money, either. If she had any sense, she would have said no and shut the door in his face, but she couldn't do that. He seemed to have rehabilitated himself, for which he certainly ought to be commended. Ten dollars wasn't going to bankrupt her. And this time, in exchange, he was going to do some yard work for her. He was going to rip out those blackberry vines outside her kitchen window, and then trim the boxwood hedge so that it looked like a proper hedge again.

Caroline sat up a little straighter in her chair. She tried to see where Tina had got to. She wanted a cup of coffee. Before she knew what she was doing, she was telling Brian how Arlene used to walk endlessly through the streets of town with her children, one of them holding her hand while she pushed the other in a stroller. She walked and walked, the children getting tired and impatient, so that she would have to pick the little girl up and carry her. This was Catherine, when Catherine was little. Then, when the children were older and at school, she walked by herself. She would sit on the bench in the park and look at the sea, and goodness knows what she saw there, what ghosts, what memories came in on the tide to haunt her. Because of what had happened when Caroline was in England, in 1957, the same summer the old restaurant had burned down. Caroline paused, and extracted a needle-fine fish bone from between her teeth. "Oh, dear, I almost swallowed it," she said. "That's the problem with fish, isn't it?"

"Yes, you must be careful," Brian said. "Are you all right?"

"Oh, yes," she said.

"Well, don't leave me in suspense," he said after a moment. "What else happened that summer?"

"There was an accident on the beach outside my house," she said. "I was away when it happened. It was a dreadful tragedy, the whole town was shaken. Now, of course, it's been forgotten. By most people. Although I've never forgotten it, and I'm quite sure Arlene hasn't, either." Caroline described to Brian how a young woman called Myrtle Kriskin had driven her car into the sea with her two young sons in the back seat, and how they'd all ended up drowning, in spite of the fact there'd been a crowd of people at the other end of the beach. "A hot summer day. There must have been lots of people at the beach. Arlene Greenwood was the only one who tried to help. She could have drowned, too. It was a genuinely courageous act. I've always admired her for it."

She looked at Brian, and saw a look on his face of disbelief. Was that what it was? Between his eyes appeared a multifoliate pucker of cynicism and amusement. His mouth was twisted at one corner. He had believed the story of the TB ward, the uniformed nurses rustling like dry leaves along the deserted midnight street. Why not venture out a little further, and believe that Arlene had attempted the rescue of a drowning family? Caroline certainly believed it was true. Well, in fact, both were true stories. They were as real as the intricate cross-hatching of fish bones on the side of her plate.

"You know how deep the water is in front of my house," she said defensively. "Anyway, it's always bothered me. Arlene came to my house for help, and I wasn't there. She wanted to use my telephone to call the police. Think how differently events might have turned out if I'd been at home."

Caroline balled her napkin up tight in her fist before tossing it down on her plate. She wanted to make the story more
compelling, more real, for his benefit, for the benefit of his
five senses, all of them twitching at her from across the table. He wanted to know everything. Such curiosity, in one
so young! It wasn't disbelief or cynicism knotting his brow,
she saw; not at all. It was an intensity of emotion, a desire
to immerse himself up to the neck in the whole story. He
made her think of her father unwrapping his books when
they arrived in the mail, the way his fingers snagged desperately at the string, the way he tried not to decimate the
paper wrapper in his eagerness. She found herself straining
at the edges of imagination and memory, trying her best to
come up with some corroborative evidence, some salient
detail that would bring the past to life. The whole story,
which was to say the story of Arlene and the drowning,
seemed to have taken place in silence, at some great remove
from the ordinary world, and all she could do was try desperately to pick up on a whisper, a murmur, and then attempt to convey the nuances to Brian. But there was too
much background noise. The restaurant had been quiet, it
had been almost empty, only a few people having lunch
besides Caroline and Brian. And now, from the kitchen, there
came the sound of cutlery and plates crashing together, and
what was surely the sound of glass breaking, perhaps one of
the water pitchers hitting the floor, and then bursts of laughter, shrill, slightly hysterical laughter, and in the midst of
all this what sounded like a baby babbling. Then the kitchen
door swung open and several girls Caroline knew came into
the dining room: Catherine Greenwood, Abby Glass, with a

baby in her arms, and Lisa McCann, along with Tina, the waitress, and one of her sisters.

"Oh, Miss Bluett, how do you like my baby?" Abby said, bouncing over to stand beside Caroline. The baby—an enormous boy baby in a blue romper suit—laughed and waved its chubby arms and legs around and shouted exuberantly at them all. Caroline took hold of a well-padded surprisingly cool bare foot. "He's a very nice baby, isn't he?" Caroline said. "Who does he belong to?"

"He's mine," Abby said. "Don't you believe me?"

"Well, no, I don't," Caroline said. "I think that's very unlikely." She saw that Abby's eyes were not smiling. They were cold and grey. Only her mouth was smiling, showing her small teeth, white and sharp as an infant's teeth, and the tip of her pink tongue. Always joking, Abby. Or at least always telling jokes, ambushing Caroline in the hall between classes: Why do elephants have red eyes, Miss Bluett? So they can hide in a cherry tree. Miss Bluett, what did the grape say when the elephant stepped on it? Nothing, it just let out a little wine. Giggling, spluttering, more amused, it seemed, by her jokes than anyone else was, raising her hand with its long nails like talons to cover her open mouth. And all the time her eyes, cold as ice, watching to see what kind of effect she had. As now: jouncing the big boy baby on her hip, her grip on it confident, one arm casually around its middle. She looked as if she could be the baby's mother, ripe and finished; replete. No wonder Julia said her daughter was making her crazy.

Catherine, Caroline saw, hung back from the others. Had she heard her talking about her mother? She was a pretty girl, like her mother, with dark hair curling wistfully around her face. She was wearing a red sleeveless shift and white shoes with thin straps. Caroline could see that outside the window the breeze had gathered strength; it was whipping the tree tops around like corn tassels. For no apparent reason Caroline remembered clearly how the wind used to blow across the ditches, which had since been filled in, but long ago had been open, at the edge of the school yard. The stagnant water had ruffled up, momentarily as blue and pure-looking as the open surface of a lake, and the wind had carried microbes from the water into the mild blue air, to be inhaled by innocent passers-by who then came down with an epidemic of gastro-enteritis. Spring was a dangerous season, hot one minute, cold the next, the wind carrying contagion and the spent petals of cherry blossoms indiscriminately.

Tina's sister, Maria, removed the fat baby from Abby and told Tina to bring Caroline and Brian a free dessert to make up for the noise, the disruption to the dinner. "Oh, I don't think I can eat another mouthful," Caroline exclaimed, and Maria had laughed and said, "You wait. You'll be surprised." Tina went to the kitchen and came back with two servings of baklava. The baklava was sticky and sweet and syrupy, tasting of walnuts and rose-water. And also, Caroline thought, closing her eyes for a moment, of the sparse dusty shade beneath a pine tree in a foreign landscape. The girls had dispersed. The fat baby had been carried away by his mother. Catherine and Abby and Lisa had, according to Tina, gone looking for Cal Dimitriou, who was supposedly in a garage somewhere on the property, working on his car.

Caroline opened her eyes and saw with amusement that a thin trail of syrup was clinging to Brian's lower lip and chin. He looked tired, as if this lunch had turned into a hurdle, an obstacle course. Caroline hadn't finished telling him about Arlene and the accident. And now she was too tired to make another attempt. She drank her coffee and watched the scene outside the window.

Was it, she wondered, a vestige of the cannibal ogress in her that gave her the idea of carving a doll to represent Brian Schram? He turned out well. He had a youthful, handsome face, a nice wide forehead, intelligent pomegranate-pip eyes. She had to find a way to make eyeglasses for him, or he would stumble around and get himself into trouble.

By the time she'd finished the doll it was nearly dusk. Outside, the air was warm, with a glossy enamelled look, raisin-coloured. The sea was perfectly calm. Caroline picked up a handful of pebbles and started tossing them into the water. She loved the sound they made: plunk, plunk. There was a speedboat roaring around out near the islands. A cool, nearly dank current of air rose from the surface of the water. Everything seemed to her to be connected by a network of invisible threads. Not only the objects that filled the night, the first stars, the dry leaves cascading from the arbutus trees; not only the visible, but also the unseen, which was to say the souls and hearts of the people who lived in Cayley, their raw uninterpreted emotional lives. This was later, some months after Hazel's wedding. It was later spring. Brian Schram was in the habit of coming to her house once or twice a week. He would bring a book with him. It would be some novel or book of poetry he'd been reading. Inside the book there would be a folded slip of paper, or even a sealed envelope. He left the book with her to be picked up later by a friend of his. Caroline knew who the friend was, of course. She didn't approve or disapprove of this arrangement. It didn't seem likely to cause anyone harm. In a way, she appreciated being at the centre of a conspiracy. It made her feel like a spy smuggling a dossier across a border, or like a conductor striking forcefully at the air with a baton and having an entire orchestra respond in respect and fear and love. She felt ferocious. It made her half believe there was someone beside her in the gloom. Someone walking toward her and then stopping, taking hold of her arm. She could almost hear a familiar wicked old voice in her ear. *Oh, we are so much of a kind*, the cannibal ogress said. Caroline didn't dispute this. She hugged herself against a sudden chill in the summer air, night cascading down out of the heavens. A wind stirring in the trees. She hugged herself and laughed, and there was no one to hear.

CHAPTER TWENTY-FOUR

Arlene paid twenty-five cents at the Hospital Thrift Store for a book on marine biology. It was an old book with a torn cover that showed the sea crashing against a rock outcropping on a sand beach. It was written in a lively humorous intimate style and went into the sex lives of clams and shrimp and octopuses in great detail. All her life she'd lived near the sea without knowing anything about the creatures that inhabited the tidal and intertidal zones, as the book referred to them. Now she was learning, among other things, about these little snails, periwinkles, properly called *Littorina*, a scientific word that meant shore-dweller. *Littorina* was a marine animal that didn't care for the sea. At least, this was true of this one variety of periwinkle, which situated itself as far from the incoming tide as it could get, in the uppermost regions of a rocky beach. If you dropped one of these periwinkles into the sea and kept it there, the book said, it would eventually give up and drown.

Marine animals, barnacles, snails, sea cucumbers, anemones, animals scarcely more sentient than vegetables, motionless, rooted, blind, were capable of acquiring, in the interests of survival, their own peculiar arts of offence and defence. The acorn barnacle, for example, kept its eggs and larvae concealed inside itself until it was ready to discharge them into the sea as little swimming animals called *nauplii*. There was an illustration in the book, a "greatly enlarged" photograph of a *nauplius*. Arlene got up and found a magnifying glass in the kitchen drawer where everything got put, and sat down again at the table and took a closer look. The *nauplius* was, the caption read, a microscopic animal with a single eye and three pairs of legs. It looked transparent, like a jellyfish. She showed the picture to Matt, who took a quick look, said, "Neat," and went back to reading the *Mad* magazine he'd propped against his glass of chocolate milk. Arlene thought: That glass is going to fall over. But she didn't say anything. In a family of readers, Matt was the most dedicated; his concentration and stamina, Arlene and David always said, were unrivalled. He was also an artist. He was also clumsy. Arlene knew the milk was going to end up on the floor. She watched him for a moment, her adorable gifted clumsy unspeaking son, then went back to her book. When the little infant *nauplii* got tired of swimming around in the sea, she read, they found a rock or something equally solid to fasten themselves to. Then they began the serious task of building themselves a cement-like protective shell. By the time they'd finished, they were adults, impervious, sightless, fixed in place, the little hinged door called an operculum firmly shut against the possibility of undesirable intruders. She partly closed the book, using her finger as a bookmark. She had to think about this. The similarity between an adult acorn barnacle's habitual mode of being and that of the adult human was too close to ignore. Was it merely the way of all flesh, if an acorn barnacle could be called flesh?

"Did you know hermit crabs steal their shells from other creatures?" Arlene said to Matt. After a moment he looked up at her.

"Yes, I did know," he said at last. He put his magazine down and took a drink of chocolate milk. "What is that?" he said, pointing at her book.

She opened the book. "It's all about sea creatures," she said.

"Let me see," he said, and she slid the open book across the table to him.

"Don't get chocolate milk on it," she said.

"I won't," he said.

"We could go to the beach and see if we can find some of these things," Arlene said.

"The pill bug? The flatworm? You want to find a flatworm?"

"Sure. Why not. We'll have fun."

"When do you want to do this?" Matt asked.

"Today, if you want. This afternoon."

Matt finished his chocolate milk and put the glass down on the table. He had a chocolate milk moustache he seemed unaware of on his upper lip. His glass was empty and, for a change, he hadn't spilled a drop. "All right," he said. "Fine with me. There's nothing else to do."

While she was getting changed to go to the beach, Arlene began to think about the muddy, unlovely beach at St. Mary's Cove, in front of the cottage where she and Eunice had lived. Arlene remembered how, at low tide, when you walked on the beach, you got squirted every few steps by a jet of ice-cold water, aimed with amazing accuracy by clams that had burrowed beneath the sand. Oh, there's that damned nuisance Arlene again, she imagined them saying to each other. One day, Arlene remembered, Eunice had decided that she and Arlene were going to dig up enough clams to make a nice big pot of clam chowder. The day before, she'd gone through their grocery receipts and balanced her cheque book, and then announced they were going to have to economise. They had to learn to get by on their own initiative, she said. Had they indeed been short of money? A short time later, when they left St. Mary's Cove and went back to Vancouver, Eunice had immediately paid cash for her house on Nelson Street, and for the Austin car. She must have had some reserves stashed away somewhere, Arlene thought. Eunice did worry about money. She made herself miserable worrying about it. She couldn't eat, she lost sleep. My husband used to look after my finances, she would explain to her friends, never mind that her husband had passed away twenty years ago. Even now Eunice would phone Arlene to say that she simply had to find a more reliable source of income than the dress store. And then a few days later, after Arlene had been lying awake nights worrying about her, Eunice would phone with the news that she was planning a weekend trip to San Francisco—a nice hotel, shopping, the theatre, the whole works, she would say brightly. Arlene had learned to think, well, that's just Eunice; she dramatises every single thing. But in 1948, Arlene, at the age of sixteen, had certainly believed her: They had no choice but to feed themselves by digging for clams. She could remember Eunice on the beach at low tide, in navy blue shorts that flared out like a tennis skirt, a red blouse tied around her midriff, a scarf worn gypsy-style over her hair, a pair of Arlene's old gym shoes on her feet. She had borrowed a bucket and shovels from a neighbour. The neighbour had gone into his work shed to find an old shovel he said he hardly ever used. You can't hurt this, he had said to Eunice. Later, Arlene had caught him watching them from his window. He was watching Eunice bend over to dig in the sand. Arlene had pulled a face at him, and had then turned away. It had been a fine clear day with a slight wind. The wet, muddy sand had been gleaming in the sun; tide pools had reflected the sky, the dazzle of light. It was not a beautiful beach, but that day it had looked beautiful. Or that was how Arlene remembered it.

They had collected a bucket full of butter clams, or what Eunice said were butter clams. They carried the bucket up to the house and dumped the clams into a washtub full of fresh water in the middle of the kitchen floor. Then Eunice sat down with a cookbook and began to read about clams. She kept getting up and looking in the washtub. Are these small clams, do you think, or medium-sized? she asked Arlene. Do you think they need to be soaked overnight in salt water? It says in the book to soak them in several waters. Several waters: What does that mean exactly? Well, we don't have time for all that business. I want to make chowder tonight, not next week. Do you think they're dead? she had asked Arlene, poking at them with her fingertips. Does fresh water kill clams?

I don't know a thing about clams, Arlene had told her. She had thought the dirty discoloured clams in the wash-tub looked disgusting. Were they, she had wondered, going through some sort of painful silent death agony? She couldn't imagine being hungry enough to eat them, even if they were disguised in chowder. Eunice had persevered how-ever, as she usually did when she set her mind on some-thing. She had cooked the clams, boiling them for hours in a Dutch oven on top of the stove, until the cottage smelled like a fish cannery. And then she'd added diced potatoes, carrots, celery, a pint of heavy cream, which she said was essential in spite of the cost, and finally she added pepper, salt, a dash of paprika. When the chowder was ready, Eunice brought two steaming bowls to the table, along with a plate of Saltine crackers. The chowder was thick and slightly gritty with sand, but Eunice had, Arlene had to admit, flavoured it nicely, and it was hot and filling. They were both hungry, and ate two large bowls each.

Then, hours later, Duff had returned from wherever he'd been, one of his unexplained, and as far as Arlene was con-cerned, too infrequent, absences, and he'd immediately started complaining about the smell in the cottage. Did a sewer pipe burst? he demanded, although he knew it was the clams simmering on the stove. Then he'd stirred a spoon around in the chowder and said it was a miracle they hadn't killed themselves, eating shellfish contaminated with red tide. Eunice had said, what do you mean? What red tide? Duff had said she should tell him immediately if either one of them developed any of the symptoms of paralytic shellfish poisoning and he'd see they got to a doctor. He had sounded absolutely earnest. He went to the telephone to see if he could get in touch with the poison control centre at some big hospital in Vancouver. Then he walked away from the phone, saying, no, he'd wait and see how they did. Eunice had wrung her hands; her face had become white, even the sunburn on her nose had faded. She had put her hand unsteadily to her head. She didn't feel very well, she said. Duff told her to lie down on the couch before she fainted. He said, "Do you have double vision? Is your mouth tingling? Can you repeat 'she sells seashells by the seashore' five times in a row?" Then he had looked at Arlene and winked, and Arlene had realised that this was his sick crazy idea of a joke. If there was a red tide warning, wouldn't their neighbour have warned them when he'd lent them his bucket and shovel? There would have been a sign posted on the beach. If they really were in danger, if they really were going to get sick, wouldn't Duff be telling them to get a grip on themselves, to ditch their negative thoughts and will themselves into a state of good health?

"It's all right, Mother," Arlene had said. "You're not going to die. Tell her the truth, Duff," Arlene had said, glaring at him. Finally he had sat down beside Eunice and had taken her hand in his, and told her he'd really got her going that time, hadn't he? "You should see the look on your face," he had said. "Oh, sweet Jesus, I haven't laughed so hard for years. You'd better shut your mouth, Eunice, sweetheart, before you swallow a fly."

Eunice had thrown the rest of the clam chowder out. That was the end of a life of self-sufficiency, as far as she was concerned. That was the end of harvesting the resources of the sea. She forgave Duff; she called him a character, a card, a kidder. She repeated the story to everyone she knew, even embellishing the details to make it more amusing. Then she went back to shopping for normal food at the grocery store in the nearest village. She filled her shopping basket with whatever she fancied, whatever she could get her hands on in those days of rationing: pork roasts, lamp chops, sweet potatoes, canned hams, stuffed olives, little stone crockery jars of Dijon mustard, French bread, artichoke hearts, pickled walnuts, whatever caught her eye, she said to Arlene. Whatever she and Duff, that card, might enjoy, or get a big kick out of.

The microscopic one-eyed *nauplii* must have spun their houses only in Arlene's imagination. In real life, the acorn barnacles glued to the black rocks beside the sea didn't appear to have experienced any kind of volatile free-swimming nursery stage before adulthood set in. They looked as if they'd been stuck in the same place forever and were, after all, only barnacles. And it was very hot on the beach, and other than the small crabs that scuttled out from under overturned rocks there seemed to be only a few large dead red crabs and some tube worm casings and that was it. She had brought Diane and Matt to the beach each equipped with a notebook and two plastic buckets and a garden trowel. They were going to collect specimens from the beach and identify them and write the names down in the notebook. She wanted to give her children the gifts of awareness and knowledge and reverence for the ephemeral odd-looking inhabitants of the sand and tides. And now she couldn't find anything to show them. Or was it the way she was looking at things? Her vision was adjusted to life on a human scale. She was looking at the shoreline and the sea, the sky, the islands and the clouds. What she needed to do was to concentrate on a very small area, the section of beach she was standing on. But even a very small area yielded nothing that specifically resembled a creature illustrated in her book.

"So where are the flatworms?" Matt said. He peeled the wrapper off some Double Bubble gum and popped the gum in his mouth.

"I'm not sure," Arlene said. "Look around and tell me if you see anything interesting." She took hold of Diane's hand and told her to stay close beside her. "And don't fall. You can cut yourself on these barnacles," she said. The shoreline didn't look as friendly and exuberant as it had seemed in the book she'd been reading. Farther up the beach a rotting fish head was covered in bluebottles. Arlene bent down and picked up a rock, and a little family of crabs scuttled out in a panic. Diane, who was kneeling beside Arlene, screamed and tried to back up and caught her heel in the skirt of her sun dress. She sat down hard on the rocks, and Arlene had to pick her up and comfort her. "I told you to be careful, honey," she said. "I told you to watch out."

Arlene put her down on a flat sandy part of the beach and held onto her hand. She imagined how they would look to someone walking along the beach. How they would appear against the hard glittering background of sea and sky. They were all tanned, from spending most of the summer outdoors. They were all agile, quick, eager, happy, most of the time, in each other's company. No one observing them would guess, Arlene was sure, that she had anything on her mind besides having a pleasant time at the beach with her children. She certainly didn't look like a woman in conflict with herself, one minute trying to be a respectable pretty carefree mother and wife and the next minute looking down the beach in the hope that he was walking toward her. It wouldn't surprise her in the least if she did see him. They had a kind of extra-sensory perception when it came to locating each other. She would be walking down Ashlar Street, and he would drive past in his car and stop and offer her a lift, which she would accept. They would meet at the library, where they whispered together about the books they were choosing while the librarian sat at her desk sneaking looks at them. On other occasions, she would be pushing a grocery cart along an aisle at the supermarket, and he would be standing in front of the breakfast cereals. It was a small town and there was only one supermarket, and yet it still seemed miraculous when they saw each other. They would stand there bemused, saying hello and then falling silent, and then they would both begin to talk at the same time. She supposed people must notice them. She certainly felt conspicuous and reckless. They stood close together, conferring over the different cereal brands, laughing at the prizes that were offered inside some of the boxes. Their hands would touch accidentally. They would get a little giggly and high-spirited, like school children on a field trip.

She had first met him at Hazel's wedding. Then she saw him again at Caroline Bluett's house. He had been sitting on the floor in front of Caroline's bookshelves. He had several books open around him, and a book open in his hands, and he was in the process of turning the pages when he turned to look at her and Caroline. He was wearing jeans and a black T-shirt.

Caroline went into the kitchen and came back with a cup of coffee for her. Arlene took it, and held it without drinking. She and Caroline sat side by side on the sofa in front of the window, and Caroline said, "Brian is going to take over my English classes."

"Most of your classes," Brian Schram said. "Luckily for me."

"I've retired this year, did you know?" Caroline said to Arlene.

"No, I didn't know," she said. "No one told me. I'm surprised, Caroline."

"Well, I wasn't planning to retire, not for another two or three years, but one morning I got up and started to get ready for school, and all I wanted to do was sit down and have another cup of tea. It was the first time in my life that I didn't feel eager to get into the classroom. When I got to school, I went straight to the principal's office and told him I'd had enough. I felt exactly like an animal that knows instinctively when it's time to die."

"Oh, Caroline," said Arlene. Then she said, "Catherine will miss you. Everyone will miss you."

"That's kind of you, but they'll forget me in a minute. They'll have Brian to keep them going. You be sure to read them Browning, Brian."

"Who?"

"Oh, Brian. You're a fiend," said Caroline. She smiled at him indulgently, and Arlene thought, she's flirting with him. She adores him.

After a moment's silence, Arlene said, "I think my daughter must have been in your Social Studies class. Her name is Catherine."

"Oh, yes, yes, I do remember Catherine," Brian Schram said. "You and your daughter look very much alike."

"Oh, do you think so? My younger daughter, Diane, looks like me, I think."

"Arlene has these lovely children," Caroline said. "How many do you have, Arlene? Is it seven, or eight?"

"Three," Arlene said. "Only three."

Then Caroline said, "Brian is going to have all my books. Aren't you Brian?"

"Caroline, I can't take all your books. These are wonderful books. First editions, rare books. I'm not an expert, but I'll bet there are some valuable books here. And they belonged to your father, didn't they? They must have sentimental value, as well."

"I'm not interested in what they're worth. They're probably not as valuable as you think, anyway. They've got mouldy-smelling over the years. The damp comes up through this old floor. Part of the cure for TB, I suppose. Kill or cure. I was going to give all of my books to a university library, but they'd probably just throw them away. They're too old, I expect, for scholarship. My father used to write to a bookstore in London, and they sent him whatever he asked for. If you want them, Brian, they're yours. I'm going to give away lots of things. My plan is to make my life very simple. From now on, I'll work in my garden and walk on the beach and take some trips. And get up in the morning whenever I please."

"Well, you'll have to keep the books for me until I can make some shelves in my apartment. I haven't had time to buy proper furniture."

Caroline asked Arlene if she would like more coffee. "No, thank you," Arlene said. She stared at the cold untasted coffee in her cup. "I'd better go home. I wasn't going to be long."

Brian Schram insisted on giving her a ride. "I'll give you a lift," he said. He used English expressions; he had a slight English accent. She thought he was probably younger than she was. A year or two younger. He was living in an apartment on the second floor of a two-storey wood frame building on the corner of Oak and Ashlar Streets. It was an ugly old building painted green, with two old fir trees at the side and no garden, just gravel and weeds and a narrow paved sidewalk to the front door. Everyone said the building should be pulled down. Brian said he didn't mind it; he had a nice view from his apartment, and every Friday his landlady brought him two loaves of bread she'd baked. He drove past the building on the way to Arlene's house and slowed down to point out which windows belonged to his apartment. He told her that he'd come to Vancouver Island on a friend's advice, to see Long Beach on the west coast of the island,

and then he'd heard from some other friends about a job here, at the high school. When he went to see the Superintendent, he was given the job. That suited him, in a way, he said, letting his life take its own course without too much interference from him.

He parked outside her house and she got out. She hesitated, then said "Well, good-bye. Thank you for the ride." "It was a pleasure," he said. The car windows were open and he leaned over and stuck his hand out the window and said, "It was really nice meeting you," and took her hand, or rather, she put her hand in his and he held on to it for a moment. It felt very awkward. She was breathing exhaust fumes from the car, and she had to bend her knees in order look in the window. She wondered if David was watching this scene from the window, but when she finally got herself free and was in the house, she discovered that he and the children were in the back garden. They were assembling a green kite with a gold dragon's face on it. They told her that they planned on trying to fly it at the beach if, or rather when, there was a good strong wind. There is no wind today, she had said. It's hot and muggy and it feels like rain.

It was just that he was lonely, Arlene told herself. He was living in that awful apartment on Oak Street. Once he got settled into his own life, he wouldn't need Arlene for a friend. At present, she was all he could see against the indistinct background of the town. It was like her futile search for interesting specimens of marine life. She wasn't able yet to discern what was there and what wasn't. She didn't have the correct names and images fixed in her mind. If she wanted to become more discriminating, she'd have to devote hours of her time to reading about marine biology. Circumstances changed, or were changed, over time. She kept reminding herself of this, as she and the children walked along the beach. She was staring at the nameless little islands across the water and telling herself that she had better watch out. This was a flirtation, the kind of thing she should have grown out of when she was eighteen years old, except that when she was eighteen she hadn't been interested in flirting.

She could see that Diane was getting too much sun. Her skin was fair, like David's, and tended to burn in no time at all. And she was saying that she had to go to the bathroom. Matt was complaining that he was getting hungry. He spit his bubble gum out on the beach. "Pick it up, Matt," she said. "I can't," he said. "It's all sticky. It's all dirty." "Well, you can't leave it there for someone else to step on." "What am I supposed to do with it?" he said. "I don't know. Bury it in the sand, I guess." She told him that the marine biology book she'd been reading began with a warning: *Leave the beach as you find it. Don't disturb anything.* "That's pretty unequivocal, isn't it?" she said. "What does that mean?" Matt said. "Unequiv—whatever."

"You know what it means," Arlene said. "And if you don't, look it up in the dictionary when we get home." Then she said, "It means there's only one way of interpreting something," although to be honest she wasn't sure if that was the right meaning or not. It was too hot to think. Matt picked up the gum and held it at arm's length, between thumb and forefinger. "Now my hand's all gooey," he said. He gave her a look, then walked past her.

"All right," Arlene said to Diane, "let's go home." They released the crabs Diane had collected in her pail, and then they walked back along the beach to the car. Arlene had left the windows down, but the interior was hot, the seats scorching, and Matt got in and jumped back out and said he'd rather walk home. "Oh, don't worry, it'll cool down once we start moving," Arlene said. She felt tired and dispirited. They should have stayed at home where it was cool. It was her fault for thinking they could all become amateur marine biologists in a single afternoon. She felt as Eunice must have felt after she had spent all day digging for clams, only to be told she might have poisoned herself and her daughter. What a cruel trick! Still, after all this time, Arlene was capable of suddenly feeling coldly furious with Duff. She wished she'd had a chance to poison him with a simple meal of clam chowder. She got Diane settled in the car; then she walked around to her side and got in. David had this thing about leather seats. He always drove an Oldsmobile and he always wanted leather seats, and Arlene couldn't see why. They were hot in the summer and cold in the winter. In the rearview mirror she caught sight of a car as it turned the corner and came down the road toward them.

"Hurry up, Mom," Diane said, kicking her feet at the dashboard. "Yeah, let's get moving," Matt said. Arlene didn't start the car. She sat there, thinking, I knew it, I knew he would come here. She waited until he got out of his car and came to her window. It was another coincidental meeting, and yet it wasn't; it was meant to happen; she believed it was fated to happen. And today her children were watching; they were listening to every word. "Hi," she said. "We're just on our way home." She told him that they had been identifying shells and crabs and looking for starfish, which they hadn't been able to find, probably because the tide was too high, and now they were going home. She tried to make it sound as if they'd had a much better time at the beach than they'd actually had.

He told her it wasn't a very good beach for marine life. The beach shelved away too quickly from the land. It got deep too quickly. The same thing that made it an excellent deep-sea port for ocean-going freighters made it an unsuitable area for finding a variety of marine specimens.

"Well, we'll have to try another beach some other time," she said.

"Perhaps you'd like company next time," he said.

"That would be nice," Arlene said.

"Mom," Matt said. "We have to go."

"I have to go pee," Diane said.

Arlene turned the key in the ignition. "Well, good-bye," she said.

"Yes. You, too," he said. He let his hand remain for a moment on the edge of her door, then moved back and put his hands in his pockets.

She backed the car carefully up the road. She thought: Now, wasn't that ridiculous? Everything I said sounded stupid. I couldn't say one sensible thing. She glanced toward the beach and saw him standing there, undecided, it seemed, about what he wanted to do next, and she gave a short beep on the horn and waved before driving off.

"Who was that?" Matt said.

"Just a friend, someone I met at Miss Bluett's house."

"What's his name? Does he have a name?"

"Matt. You know who he is. His name is Mr. Schram."

"Mr. Schram. Mr. Scram. Catherine's teacher, Mr. Schram-scram?"

"Yes, I think he was. Her Social Studies teacher."

"Oh, him. Catherine's in love with him," Matt said. "She writes his name all over everything. Mr. Schram, Mr. Scrambled Eggs. Mr. Shimmy Sham."

"Matt, I'm getting tired of you. How would you like to walk home?"

"Sure," Matt said.

"Well, you can't," Arlene said. "You can't walk home. So be quiet."

She stopped in the middle of preparing a meal of cold leftover roast beef and potato salad and thought: What am I doing? She was thinking of him, of Brian, her mind full of images: his face, his smile, the back of his head, his hands on the steering wheel of his car. She could clearly hear the tone of his voice, the inflection of his voice. She went back in her mind to the day they met, at Caroline's house. She tried to remember exactly how he had looked to her then. He had been sitting on the floor, looking completely at ease, in his element. A young man with dark hair, dark eyes behind glasses. He had been going through those dusty old books, turning each page as if he believed it was a delicate living thing. They were the same books she had looked at years earlier, long before he came here to live. She had been married, a married woman with two small children. She had been self-contained, remote, conscientious—oh, that above all else. She had chosen a certain kind of life and she was expending all her energy in making a success of it.

Arlene set the table. She turned on the radio and listened to the six o'clock CBC news. She chopped green onion for the salad, peeled the hard-boiled eggs, took a jar of mayonnaise out of the fridge. She poured a pitcher of water and added ice cubes. Her skin smelled to her of the sun and salt air at the beach. Her shoulders were a little sunburned, and she had pinned up her hair to keep it out of the way. Images of a beach filled her mind. Exotic, unidentifiable flowers, red against black, black against red, blue sky and sea. She pictured volcanic rock, although the rocks at the beach weren't volcanic. Were they? First the world began in fire and then, when everything was burned clean and pure, it cooled, solidified into a concave shape, waiting to be filled with the rich broth of life. And after a few centuries had passed, a few millennia of nothing but the sound of the wind, microscopic creatures began swimming eagerly through the oceans towards the rocks, where they took up residence. First the creatures of the sea arrived, and then aeons passed and finally Arlene herself arrived, assuming as she surfaced from the water an adult finished form. Well, not quite. She was thirty-six years old, she was married, she had three children, and she still didn't think of herself as adult. The Russians had sent a woman into space to study the effect of weightlessness on women, and Arlene had thought, don't bother. Just look at me. She refused to have any weight. In place of substance, she had a pure white light that flowed over the places where her body ought to be, where it would be, in fact, if she hadn't learned the art of resistance, if she hadn't become adept at absence.

She had to stop this. She had to come back down to earth. The more she considered the matter, the more clear it became that the last thing she needed was to start flirting with an unmarried man who was lonely and bored and addicted to poetry. He had asked her what she liked to read, and the first thing that came to her mind was *Anna Karenina*, of course, her favourite novel. But how could she mention to Brian Schram the name of a character from fiction who ruined her life by leaving her husband and child in favour of her lover? Karenin was, Arlene recalled, one of the last to become aware of his wife's infidelity. He refused to see what he couldn't bear to see. To begin with, he mistrusted everyone else's perception of events. He blamed others before he blamed Anna. At the same time, he couldn't help becoming a little remote toward Anna. And to his son. He was like the barnacle with its operculum shut fast, just in case. Poor Karenin. *How could they let it come to that?* he said, of other men, in other situations, the husbands of other women like Anna, not that Anna was in any sense comparable to other women. Arlene considered Anna unique. She was brave, volatile, shameless, ruthless, passionate. She was the opposite of Arlene, who knew that when it came right down to it, she wouldn't take the kinds of risks Anna took. Or, for that matter, make the stupid decisions Anna made. In any case, that was so long ago; it was in the nineteenth century. It was different now. This was Canada, not Russia; there were no grand parties in the palaces of grand-duchesses, no carriage rides through nights of sparkling frost and ice, no men in high leather boots and illustrious uniforms that showed off their handsome military posture; it was a different world, more prosaic, less romantic.

The thing was, Arlene had to teach herself all over again to see and to love certain known, reliable things: the way the late afternoon summer sun shone in through the open French doors onto the black and white tiled floor. The tall fir trees that grew at the end of the back yard and cast their lambent shadows along the newly mown grass. The solitary apple tree, with its twisted leafy branches, its unstinting seasonal offering of slightly tart, white-fleshed fruit. Diane's red tricycle parked beside the clay pot full of pink geraniums. Could anything in all the world be more beautiful?

He brought her his own books to read, one or two at a time: novels by Iris Murdoch, Patrick White, Lawrence Durrell, Saul Bellow, William Faulkner, V.S. Naipaul, J.D. Salinger. He called it an eclectic mix. She pretended she knew what he meant. She had vowed never to meet him "accidentally" again. She had promised herself. But here she was, talking to him in the lane between the back of the library and the tall fence at the side of the Anglican church's parking lot. She had been coming out of the library just as he was walking out of the post office—a chance meeting. Well, what a surprise, they said to each other, grinning like idiots. He had a letter in his hand, which he put into his shirt pocket. He had some books under his arm. He had said, Here, I have something I want to give you. They stepped off the sidewalk into the lane. They were standing beneath a maple tree that grew on the church side of the fence. The tree extended its branches in an enthusiastic, sheltering embrace, as if it wished to shield them from the hot eye of the sun and the casual, interested glances of passers-by. Arlene thought she and Brian swam in the green shadows like fish, like the shadows of fish, like *nauplii*. Nothing held them to the earth. He had with him a volume of John Donne's poetry. He opened the book, he read to her in a barely audible voice, only a few feet away from the street, where people Arlene knew were going about their ordinary business. *I wonder, by my troth, what thou and I / Did, till we loved?* The words entered her heart, her soul, her brain, her body. *And now good morrow to our waking souls, / Which watch not one another out of fear. . . .* "Take it," he said. "Go on. Borrow it. Keep it. It's yours."

She took the book from him and held it in her hands, feeling its shape and weight, the texture of its thin paper cover. He had another book for her, two books in fact, which he continued to keep under his arm in the unconcerned, confident way that young men, students, always held their books. He wore a white shirt, open at the neck; faded jeans; white sneakers. He was tanned. He wore a watch with a heavy gold band on his right wrist. Who had given him such an expensive-looking watch? His mother? A girlfriend? His hair had grown longer; it curled in the collar of his shirt. In her head she said, please no more of this. Don't lend me your books, I don't want to read your books, touch the pages you've touched, burn my fingers on the words you've read at night, lying on your bed at night, reading by the light of a lamp. *And now good morrow to our waking souls. . . .*

What was this about? she asked herself. Was this about literature, beautiful poems, beautiful novels? Was he anxious to transform her from an uneducated housewife into a brilliant little scholar? Down this secret lane the sunlight shone more brightly; the shadows were duskier and more secretive than anywhere else in town. The wind came around the corner of the library in playful gusts. Brian combed his hair away from his eyes with his hand. He smiled at her, at a leaf twirling like a top on its frail stem; at a pale brown spider descending in space before their eyes on its silvery filament. Arlene could hear traffic, occasional disembodied voices from the street. The mill was quiet because it had shut down for two weeks, partly because of an oversupply in the lumber market, and partly so that the unionised workers could take an unpaid holiday. Management was on holiday with pay. David was on holiday with pay, spending his time working in his garden. This afternoon, he had taken Diane and Matt to Joan Mullis's house to get some honey from her bees and to take a look at her beefsteak tomato crop, which, David had told Arlene, Joan fertilised with seaweed she gathered by the truckload from the beach after winter storms. Arlene could have gone with them, but she had said she wanted to walk to the library. She used to walk everywhere because it was what she liked doing; now she walked through the town as if she were under a compulsion to do so, because she thought she might see Brian, because she thought he might be looking for her.

He was telling her that he'd found the most beautiful place out near the river. He said that he was thinking of moving out there. By the most amazing good luck he'd found a small house for rent, a house suitable for a single person, and he wondered if she'd come with him to look around. He wanted her opinion. Before school started, he was flying to Toronto to visit his family. He indicated the letter in his shirt pocket. It was from his mother, he said. His mother's sister, his Aunt June, was going to be in Toronto, on holiday from Sussex, England. He'd be gone for ten days, and he'd like to know before he went if she thought he should move out there or not. The rent was a little high, but it was a nice place, he didn't want to miss out on it.

"I can't," she said. She turned the book of John Donne's poetry around in her hands. She looked down and saw that her feet, in sandals, were covered with dust from the road. "You don't need me to see the house."

"But I do," he said. "I have no one else."

"I don't see how I can," she said.

"You'll think of a way," he said.

"I'll see," she said.

He said, "What about Monday afternoon?"

"I'll see," she said again. He handed her the two books he had with him. She took them and glanced at the covers. "I can't promise. I may not be able to get away," she told him. He held up his hand with his fingers crossed and gave her a smile that seemed to illuminate his whole person, his spirit and will, and against which she felt peculiarly defenceless. Then he became very serious, and said in a low solemn tone, "You will. I know you will."

Chapter Twenty-five

In the middle of some ordinary task, folding the laundry, putting the groceries in the cupboards, watering the house plants, Catherine's mother would stop, stare at nothing, at the wall, at her hand. Then she would say she was tired, she wasn't feeling well, and she would find her way upstairs, like a sleepwalker. Catherine would go upstairs and knock hesitantly at the door to her mother's room. Are you all right? she would ask. I'm fine, her mother would say. Just give me a little peace. Instead of going upstairs to her room, her mother sometimes left the house. I'll be right back, she'd say, grabbing her sweater and purse, glancing at herself in the hall mirror, pulling her hair over her shoulder, putting on lipstick. I'm going for a walk.

Time would go by. Catherine would stand at the window in the living room, waiting. She made lunch for herself and Matt and Diane. She took Diane outside and pushed her on the swing. She tried to get Diane to play with her dolls on the living room floor, she tried to read her a story. Diane kept jumping up and running to the window. When is she coming back, she wanted to know. Soon, Catherine said. And then she would go to the front door and look down the street, as if hoping that this in itself was enough to conjure the figure of her mother on the empty sidewalk.

Once, when her mother came home she had a book with her, and it fell from her hand to the floor in the front hall. It was a thin book. Catherine stared at it. *Howl*. By Allen Ginsberg.

"What's that?" Catherine said.

"What does it look like? It's a book. A poetry book." Her mother picked the book up, wiped her hand slowly across the cover. She was wearing a white sweater, a short blue skirt, and the sandals she wore all the time, the thick straps fraying at the ends, the soles worn down at the heels.

"Is it from the library?" Catherine said, pointing at the book.

"Miss Nosy-Parker," her mother said. "What is this, the Spanish Inquisition?"

"No. I just wondered," said Catherine. "It looks interesting." It wasn't a library book, she was sure. Her mother sometimes bought second-hand books at the thrift store. Another possibility: Someone had given it to her. But who?

In the kitchen, her mother read poetry to Catherine, leaning against the counter in the kitchen. Her voice went on, breathless, reciting words like *underwear* and *dope* and *eyeball*, words that didn't make sense, as far as Catherine could tell. In any case, it embarrassed her to see her mother reading like that, dramatising, performing as if she were up on a stage. And was that poetry, was that real poetry? *Dope? Eyeball? Underwear*, for God's sake. Her mother seemed to think it was. She paused, finally, and raised her face, her eyes shining and dark, to look at Catherine. It is, it is poetry, her mother said. Of course it's poetry. It's beautiful.

One day Catherine rode her bike out to Lisa's house. Abby was in England with her parents, in England and Europe, doing the grand tour, being rehabilitated, being cured of Cal Dimitriou. Her parents wanted to show her the world, illustrate for her what she would be missing if she married a high school dropout. Abby had said, I don't care. Her parents couldn't keep her in Europe for ever. Catherine envied Abby, who didn't know how lucky she was.

Lisa gave Catherine a glass of water and apologised for the taste. The water was getting low in their well, she said. Where did the water come from, Catherine wondered. Did it come from the river? Things were floating in her glass, Catherine saw. Microscopic things. She put her glass down on the table. She thought of cholera and typhoid fever. You couldn't get diseases like that here, on Vancouver Island. Mr. Schram had told the class that Queen Victoria's consort, Prince Albert, had died of typhoid fever from London's contaminated water supply. Catherine thought of Prince Albert lifting a crystal water glass to his lips while the Queen watched from the far end of the table. He drank; microbes entered his body. The Queen smiled in her ignorance and cut into her roast beef. Catherine looked around Lisa's kitchen, which was a big room with a lot of empty space. There was a clock on the wall shaped like a daisy. Lisa's house,

with its shadows and echoing spaces and creaking floor reminded Catherine of houses in the books she liked to read,
houses where ghosts lived. Catherine's grandmother believed
in ghosts, and in an afterlife. She had told Catherine that
there was a time in her life when she used to go to seances,
trying to contact the spirit of Catherine's dead grandfather.
She had gone to tea-leaf readers and fortune-tellers.
Catherine looked at the palm of her hand: The life line had
what her Nana called a good contour; the marriage line, as
Nana called it, was fine as a hair.

Lisa took the empty glass away and rinsed it at the sink.
Light trembled on the ceiling. The tap dripped. She wiped
her hands on a tea towel and hung the tea towel on the
stove door. Then she took Catherine upstairs to her bedroom, which had a low, sloping ceiling papered with pictures torn from magazines, of John Lennon, Mick Jagger,
Eric Burden and the Animals. She liked the Beatles best, she
told Catherine, pulling her halter top over her head, throwing it on the end of her bed. Out of the Beatles her favourite
was Paul, she said. She thought it was eerie, the way his eyes
followed her around her room. On her bed there was a thin
patchwork quilt, an old pink teddy bear with blue button
eyes propped against a frilled pillow sham. There were fuzzy
blue slippers in the middle of the floor, a Kotex box on top
of a chest of drawers.

Catherine faced the wall and changed into her swimsuit,
keeping her shorts and T-shirt on until the last possible
moment. Sweat was pouring down her face. Lisa had thrown
off her halter top and her shorts, and now she was sitting
on her bed in her swimsuit, with her arms around her knees.

Catherine folded her clothes and put them in a pile on a chair beside the dresser.

"Hurry up," Lisa said. "It's so hot I could pass out. I never sleep here in the summer. I sleep out on the porch, or in a tent down by the river."

"I'm ready," Catherine said. She wasn't interested in where Lisa slept. She followed Lisa downstairs and outside in silence. They walked down to the river and waded out and sat on a rock, splashing their feet in the water. Catherine's legs appeared white, insubstantial, floating above the speckled-egg rocks on the river bottom. Water spiders spun across the glassy surface. Lisa slid off the rock and stood in the water. "Come on," she said. "I want to show you something." She waded to shore and began to walk toward a trail that led into the trees. Catherine dried her feet on her towel, put on her sneakers and followed her. Lisa walked in her bare feet. She stopped and held her foot up for Catherine to examine. "Feel that," she said, poking at the sole of her foot. "It's like leather, isn't it? Isn't it just like the bottom of an old boot? That's what my Mom says." She hopped on one leg for a short distance. "Come on," she kept saying, pulling overhanging blackberry vines out of the way. They were climbing a steep dirt trail, following the direction the river took. Lisa stopped and knelt near the edge of a cliff and motioned to Catherine to come closer. Catherine knelt; she was looking down at the river, which was wider here, a deep tawny colour that darkened to a shining blackish-green near the steep banks, where thick, lush moss and ferns grew among the trunks of giant alders and maples. And there was this silence, heavy, thick, and—what was the word she wanted?—

somnambulant, the landscape sleeping, dreaming, moving through time at the slowest rate imaginable. She thought of Africa, lions padding through a jungle until they came to a river and then paused, lapping at the water.

"This," said Lisa, "is where those guys I told you about go swimming buck-naked all the time. They dive from up the cliff. They're crazy."

"Oh," Catherine said. She drew back and sat on the ground. She wasn't interested in Lisa's stories of boys swimming naked in the river. She wet her finger with her tongue and rubbed at the dirt on her knee. She wished she'd stayed at home. Lisa got on her nerves. She was exactly what Abby had called her. A little hick. She remembered how she and Abby had imitated Lisa after they'd come out here to see her. I seen these buck-naked boys, they had said, prancing around, their feet splayed, their arms flopping around at their sides. I can whistle through this here blade of grass, they told each other.

"Get up, you lazy-bones," Lisa said. She grinned at Catherine. Her fine blonde hair was in a sort of white mist around her head, strands of hair hanging in front of her pale eyes.

"Let's go back to your house," said Catherine. "What about your Mom? Won't she be home now?"

"Oh, she won't be home yet. She had to take a bus to town. Besides, she knows I'm always around somewhere. She trusts me. She says she has no choice, she can't follow me everywhere. While my Dad's away in Cyprus, there's only her." Then she said, "This place I want you to see. It's a house. If I was rich, I'd buy it and live in it by myself. For-ever. I'd never go outside the yard."

Even in the shade of the trees it was stifling, airless. The light was green, tremulous. Once Catherine tripped over a tree root and went down on her knees and hands. Her palms were smarting. There was a little rock embedded in her skin, at the base of her thumb. She picked at it for a minute; then she got up and Lisa, unconcerned, beckoned to her. "Here," she called. "Here it is."

Catherine went to Lisa's side. They were at the edge of a cliff, looking straight down at the river. Here, the river was narrow, constricted, fast. On the other side, there was a nar-row dirt road that came down to the river. On one side of the road there was a house with a verandah, stone pillars, many small-paned windows, brick chimneys, doors, shut-ters, awnings, flowers in large clay pots. An excess of every-thing, it seemed to Catherine. And all around the house were gardens, beautiful gardens, and trees. Weeping willow trees, the branches trailing along the green lawns. And flower beds, a field of corn. It was an enchanted house in an en-chanted forest. A yellow dog was trotting across the lawn in front of the house. They were too far away for the dog to notice them. They were invisible, Catherine thought; they were just two pairs of eyes, spying on everything, disem-bodied. That was how she felt, as if she were floating above the river and the house. She was hot and tired and her legs were scratched and filthy, and somewhere along the way she had grabbed hold of a stinging nettle and her hand was burning, itching, and yet for a moment, in her innocence, in that moment of innocence, she was completely happy.

The house was beautiful. It looked a little like her house in Cayley, that same style and age, and also it looked a little like Abby Glass's house, but this house was even bigger, more splendid. Who lived here? Who had lived here, long ago? She wished she knew. Witches, magicians, elegant women in grey silk dresses, men smoking those black cigarettes. Once upon a time, horse-drawn carriages must have come down this road, ferrying people to and from this house. Who'd thought to build such a house out here? Catherine asked Lisa. Lisa said she had no idea. All she knew for a fact was that older people lived here now. They were older and they kept to themselves and worked in their garden.

Then Catherine saw something she had missed: a car, a Volkswagen, parked beneath the trees on the other side of the road from the house. And then almost at the moment she noticed the car, a man got out and went around to the other side and opened the door and a woman got out. He took her hand. It was like a play. Staged, acted, everything happening as it was intended to happen. The man and the woman walked hand in hand slowly toward the river. If they had glanced up, they would have seen Catherine and Lisa. But they were looking at the river, at the water foaming whitely as it flowed over rocks and around a tree that had fallen in the water. The man put his arm around the woman's waist, and the woman leaned her head against the man. He had dark hair; he was wearing jeans and a shirt; the woman was wearing khaki shorts and a white blouse and her long hair was floating down her back. They were blind, the two of them. Wasn't that what was said of people when they were together like that? They were blind to everything except themselves.

"Holy shit. Isn't that Mr. Schram?" Lisa said. "It is him, isn't it? He has a girlfriend. Too bad."

Catherine backed away from the edge of the cliff. The scene below seemed to her unimaginably distant, and yet every detail was precise, clear. Her face was burning. Her eyes watered and she wiped at them with the palms of her hands and her tears made the small cuts and the nettle sting hurt all over again. She stared down at the man and the woman thinking that she was mistaken, but it was true. The woman was her mother. It was her mother, her legs bare, her old brown sandals on her feet. No, she told herself. It couldn't be her mother. Her mother was at home, sitting out on the patio in the sun, reading some stupid book, drinking coffee, smoking a cigarette. She was rubbing suntan lotion on her legs. She was thinking about what she was going to make for dinner.

"We should yell, Hello, hello down there, Mr. Schram," said Lisa. "That would surprise him, wouldn't it. You want to?"

"No," Catherine said. She was whispering. "Don't." She was kneeling on the ground. On her hands and knees she was crawling backwards. Her heart was thudding against her ribs. There was a blackness floating in the air and she thought: I'm going to faint. She moistened her lips and kept her head down, looking at the ground. "We have to get going," she said.

"Isn't that the neatest old house you ever saw? I couldn't believe my eyes the first time I saw it. Do you think Mr.

Schram lives there? Maybe he bought it and he's going to live there with his girlfriend."

Lisa, Catherine realised, had never seen her mother. She didn't know what Catherine's mother looked like. So it was all right. It was all right. She felt like she was going to be sick, but there was no need to be sick. She must have a fever that was making her see things that weren't there. When I get home, she thought, I'll find out that I was wrong. I'll find out I made a stupid mistake. I know where my mother is. She is at home reading her poetry book. *Howl.* Reading that poem full of swear words and nonsense. No one else's mother would read a book with a title like that. They would put it in the trash.

When I get home, she thought, I'll find out that I made a mistake. A case of mistaken identity. Then she pictured her mother looking in her mirror, piling her long dark hair on the top of her head, stroking her white throat, seeing that she was beautiful, she was lovely, and young; she didn't look like a mother; she looked like Anna Karenina and all the other women in the books she read. Thinking, *Why not? Why not me?*

Catherine and Lisa followed the river back to Lisa's house. It was downhill going back, easier, except that Catherine slid once or twice and went down hard on her seat. She got up and kept going. Her legs were black with dirt. She was so hot she wanted to throw herself into the river.

"Wasn't that weird?" Lisa said. "Seeing Mr. Schram. That was the strangest thing."

There was a cool breeze on Catherine's face, on her bare arms. Without stopping to think, she kicked off her sneakers and walked straight into the river and began to swim. Her mother had taught her to swim when she was six or seven years old, holding her around the middle while she kicked and paddled. Her mother had taken her hands away and had said, There you go. You're on your own. Salt water was more buoyant than river water; it held you up. The river bottom was slippery, muddy. She didn't know what lived down there, in the river mud, but she was sure something did, something repulsive, slugs, leeches. She swam toward the far bank, then turned and swam back, kicking her legs hard. The water was shallow, in some places barely deep enough for swimming, but she kept going, she kept swimming, and Lisa came into the water and they swam together for a while, and then they got out and sat on the grass under the trees. Catherine was breathing hard. She felt as if she had accomplished something remarkable. An act of courage. She had washed most of the dirt off, in any case. She began to shiver. She felt very strange, as if she had just woken from a dream. In her mind she was again on the cliff edge looking down at the house, the strange beautiful monstrous house with its cultivated gardens, its flowers, the river forever moving turbulent and insistent past its doors. And the heat, the bright sun. She watched as Lisa squeezed the water from her hair. Her thin shoulders gleamed. When she turned to speak, Catherine saw that she had streaks of black mascara down her face, giving her a clownish look.

"Are you going to stay for supper?" Lisa said. "My mom told me she was going to make hamburgers."

"I don't think so. I think I should go home."

"Don't go," Lisa said. "Please stay. My mother wants you

to stay for dinner. My mother wants to meet you. I told her you're my best friend. You have to stay."

"I'll stay for a little while," Catherine said. "I don't have anything else to do," she said, and Lisa said, "Oh, well that's good."

Lisa's mother came down the drive carrying a shopping bag in each hand. She was wearing jeans and a sleeveless blouse and she had silver earrings made of tiny tinkling bells in her ears. Her face was shiny and rosy from the heat. Catherine and Lisa had changed into their clothes and were sitting together on the porch steps. For a moment Catherine thought that now things were going to be all right, because here was a grown-up, a mother, a parent, and she would make everything fine. And then she realised that this was not necessarily the case, this was not at all the case, and what was she going to do, anyway, tell Lisa's mother that she'd just seen her own mother holding hands with her Socials teacher? She got up from the steps and she and Lisa went to meet Lisa's mother. Lisa took one bag from her mother and Catherine took the other, and Lisa's mother smiled and wiped her arm across her face and held out her hand to Catherine. "Hello," she said. "Good to see you." Then she spoke in German, her eyes fixed on Catherine's face as Lisa translated.

"She says to tell you she's sorry about her English. She said to tell you she thinks her head is made of wood. And she wants you to call her Margaret."

Lisa's mother nodded and smiled, and said, "Yes. Margaret. Please."

Catherine listened as Lisa spoke to Margaret in German and Margaret kept looking at Catherine and smiling and nodding. "You have to stay for supper," Lisa said to Catherine. "She's says she'll be disappointed if you don't stay."

"Well, okay, then. If it's all right, I mean. Yes, thank you," she said, looking at Margaret, speaking slowly, as if it that would help Margaret to understand her. "I'd like to stay," Catherine said.

Later, just after five o'clock, Catherine used Lisa's telephone to call home. Her father answered. "Where is everyone?" he said. "Matt is at a friend's house and Diane is at another friend's house. At least, I think that's what the note your mother left says. I don't know, Catherine. I don't know if you can stay at your friend's for dinner. I guess it's all right. I have no idea what we're supposed to be having. There's some cold chicken in the fridge. Is that supposed to be for supper, do you know?"

"I'm not sure," Catherine said.

"How are you planning on getting home?"

"I brought my bike."

"And where did you say your friend lives?"

"On the old Cayley Road. You know. Out by the river."

"You rode your bike all the way out there? Does your mother know?"

Catherine paused. "I think so," she said.

"Well, phone when you're ready to leave and I'll come and pick you up. Hang on, here's your mother now. With Diane. Did you want to talk to her?"

Catherine pictured her mother walking in through the open French doors, picking Diane up and kissing her. At the same time she was watching Lisa's mother slicing a large white onion while Lisa cut hamburger buns in half and buttered them. No, she didn't want to talk to her mother, she told her father. "See you later," she said. Then she hung up.

After they had finished their dinner of hamburgers and French fries, they sat in Lisa's living room and watched the evening news on the television. Margaret got up to pull the curtains to keep the light from shining on the screen. Then she sat down and got up again to move the rabbit ears on top of the TV, and Lisa kept saying, Okay, there. No, move it to the left. Okay, that's good. Then Margaret kicked off her sandals and curled up in a corner of the couch with her feet tucked under her. She put her hand to her mouth. She chewed the side of her finger and said, "Oh, *mein Gott*. Oh, my." She shook her head. Then she spoke to Lisa in German. On the TV, Catherine saw, an American helicopter was landing at a US base in South Vietnam. Men leaped out of the helicopter and ran across the tarmac, heads bent, the air around them in turmoil. Then there was a scene where wounded soldiers on stretchers were being carried along a road. There was a shot of a soldier's face, his eyes open and staring, his mouth bright red with blood; his life's blood, Catherine thought. Vietnamese people in dirty ragged clothes were standing aside, their limbs rigid, staring at the soldiers, at the dying soldiers with their gaping wounds, their uniforms torn and dark with mud and blood. She looked away.

Margaret spoke quickly, interrogatively, in German to Lisa, and Lisa responded in German, drawing lines in the air with her hands and shaking her hand emphatically. Catherine tried not to stare. Was there something happening that she didn't understand? She hated these news stories from the war. Every night the same thing, these maimed bodies. Staring, shocked faces. Children burned by napalm. A war against communism, her father said. There was always some ideology, some reason to fight, he said.

"She's afraid my father will have to fight in Vietnam," Lisa was saying. "She's afraid Vietnam is going to turn into a world war, like the last one."

Catherine stood up; she had a sense of urgency, as if someone had leaned over her and whispered a message in her ear, and she thought, I must go home. She was thinking of Hazel's wedding day last winter, the snow storm, her mother being introduced to Mr. Schram. She was thinking of those books her mother brought home and left lying around wherever she happened to be reading them.

"Can I use the telephone, Lisa?" she asked. She explained that she wanted to phone her father to come and get her, and Lisa said, "Oh, please stay, please stay." They could watch TV, she said; they could stay up late, listening to her record collection. They could do whatever they liked; her mother wouldn't mind. In the morning they could go swimming again, and her mother could make breakfast for them. Her mother wanted Catherine to stay, Lisa said, following Catherine into the kitchen.

"No, I have to get home," Catherine said. "I have to." She telephoned her father, and by the time he drove up she was standing outside with her wet swimsuit in a bag. It was nearly dusk. Lisa stood in the shadows of the trees along the drive. Catherine's father got out of the car and opened the trunk and put her bike inside. Margaret had come outside. She shook hands with Catherine's father and said, "How do you do?" Catherine watched as Margaret smiled and said, "Sorry about my English."

"Your English is excellent," Catherine's father said. He thanked Margaret for having Catherine to dinner, and he said, "I hope you've thanked Mrs. McCann," to Catherine.

"Yes, yes," Margaret said. She shoved her hands into her back pockets. "Very nice," she said. "We had a nice time. Catherine is lovely."

"Why, thank you. I'm glad you think so," said Catherine's father.

"Phone me," Lisa shouted as Catherine got in the car. Catherine thought, I don't care if I never see you again. I hope I don't.

"Did you have a good time?" Catherine's father said after he had turned onto the road.

"Yes. It was okay. I went swimming."

"Is someone there when you're swimming? Does Lisa's mom keep an eye on you?"

"Yes, of course," Catherine said.

"Good. That's good. The river can be dangerous, even in the summer."

"We're very careful. We stay where it's shallow."

"No point in taking chances," he said.

When she got home her mother was outside on the patio watering the petunias. She was wearing shorts, the khaki shorts Catherine had seen her in earlier in the day, and the same white blouse; the only difference was that now her hair was in a braid. Catherine saw her put down the hose and begin to pick dead blooms off the flowers and drop them into an empty clay flowerpot. When she looked at Catherine she laughed and rubbed her thumb lightly across her face and said, "You got a little too much sun. And your hair. What on earth happened to your hair?"

"The river," Catherine said. "I went swimming." She put her hands to her head, holding her hair, which felt stiff and dirty, away from her face. The petunias were pink, white, blue. Straggly. Petunias at the end of the summer. "The river?" her mother repeated. "Is that where you were?"

"Yes," Catherine said. "Out at Lisa's house." She went into the house. The lights were on in the kitchen, and Matt was sitting at the table drawing. He had his pencil crayons spread out around him in the orderly way that he liked, erasers, rulers, pens, everything at hand, and he was bent over his paper, drawing. "That's neat," Catherine said. She looked at his picture. "That's really cool," she said.

"Thanks," he said without looking up. She sat down beside him and watched as he selected a purple pencil crayon and added more colour to a finned rear fender. Then he put down the purple pencil crayon and, after chewing on his finger for a minute, picked up a black one and drew quick thin horizontal lines behind the car to indicate the extraordinary rate of speed at which it was travelling across the white field of the page.

*

Catherine was practising the piano. This was another day, a Saturday morning. It was still August. Her mother came into the living room, where the morning sun poured in through the slats in the venetian blinds, and sat down beside her on the piano bench. Then she said, "Move over." And Catherine moved over. Her mother doodled around on the keys, playing a few bars of one song, a few bars of another, melodies that Catherine half recognised, and then she hit a wrong note and laughed and said she was no good at it anymore. She'd forgotten how to play. How sad, she said. She could stretch an octave plus two notes, she told Catherine. She once had a good friend called Iris who taught her how to have flexible pianist's hands. She spread her fingers wide, as she did sometimes when she was off in one of her trances, and then she told Catherine she'd inherited her long thin hands from her father's side of the family, from his sister, her aunt. Her aunt was still alive; she had met her a few times when she lived in Ottawa. Her Aunt Grace.

Catherine wanted to demand of her mother, Why are you telling me this? What has Aunt Grace got to do with anything? Why don't you tell me instead what you were doing at the river with Mr. Schram? Why don't you ever, *ever* tell the truth? She wanted to bring her hand down hard on the piano keys, to make as much noise as she could, and perhaps bring her mother to her senses. But it wouldn't work. Her mother was soft and quiet and unreachable. She wasn't really in the same room as Catherine.

There was a sonnet, her mother told her, by William Shakespeare. It was about the way the piano keys leaped up all in a passion to kiss the player's fingers. Well, it wouldn't have been a piano, it would have been a harpsichord, with those lovely brown wooden keys, like rotten teeth, she said. She wished she'd been born in the sixteenth—or did she mean the seventeenth?—century. She would have liked to have had all those handsome ambitious young courtiers making love to her. Poets, musicians, scholars. She would have liked life in a royal court, velvet dresses, jewelled bodices, jewels for the ears, the fingers, the hair. Secret messages being passed back and forth. Goblets of sweet warm red wine.

Catherine's mother tried to teach her how to play a duet. It was something she had memorised years ago, she said. She and her friend Iris had learned it together. It was a pretty little song about unrequited love. How did it go? She tried to sing the words for Catherine. I can't remember them, she said at last. I give up. She put Catherine's hands on the keys, then placed her hands over them and depressed Catherine's fingers, one at a time. Your hands are cold, she said. I know, Catherine said. She waited, not moving.

Her mother removed Catherine's hands from the keys. Then she played the scale of C major, two octaves very quickly. She didn't make a single mistake. Her timing seemed perfect, to Catherine. Then she slowly closed the piano and leaned her elbows on the lid. She rested her chin in her hands, like a child, and closed her eyes. Catherine stared at her, fascinated by a pulse beating in a thin blue vein in her temple, near her hairline. She didn't know what to say. Her mother seemed so fragile, so strange. What could she do? She got up, and went into the kitchen where she stood for a moment, her fingers nervously picking at the seams in the sides of her jeans, thinking, What was I going to do in here? What was it I came in here for?

Chapter Twenty-six

After the children had left for school, Arlene sat at the breakfast table alone. She had a glass of orange juice, a slice of toast, no butter, no jam. Coffee. A cigarette. A Beatles song was playing on the radio. She put her hand in the pocket of her bathrobe, where she was keeping a note from Brian. It had been tucked inside a book he'd left for her at Caroline's house. Caroline was a co-conspirator. An intermediary. Arlene took the note out of her pocket and looked at it for perhaps the tenth time. *Lib. Wed. 7.* That was all it said. When she closed her eyes he was what she saw, his mouth, the long thin upper lip, the lower lip fuller and indented slightly at the centre. When he had left in August to go to Toronto, she'd told herself whatever it was, a flirtation, a friendship, a literary society composed of two earnest readers, it was over. Smarten up, she'd told herself. Smarten up, take a good look at what you're doing. Aunt June doesn't exist. In reality it's not his Aunt June he's gone to see, but some gorgeous girl, a twenty-one-year-old university student called Debby or Tracy. She tried to make herself believe in Debby or Tracy, or whatever her name might be, but she didn't really believe he had a girlfriend. She believed what he'd told her, that there was no one.

That day, in August, by the river. Had Catherine seen her with Brian? It was the worst luck that Catherine had been out there at all. She hadn't asked for Arlene's permission to ride her bike out to the river, she hadn't asked if she could see that girl, Lisa. Was that her name, Lisa? Catherine had come home sunburned and dirty, scratches all over her legs and hands. I rode my bike out to Lisa's house, she had said in a cold, flat voice. A look of contempt on her face. Perhaps Arlene had imagined the look, the tone of voice. If Catherine had seen her, she would despise her mother. She would never, ever forgive her.

The thing was, Arlene would drive herself mad if she kept worrying about what Catherine knew, what David knew or guessed, because he was bound to suspect there was something wrong. Wasn't he? He wasn't stupid. They all knew and suspected and were beginning to mistrust her. To hate her. She went upstairs and made the bed and showered and dressed and then she went downstairs and got out the vacuum cleaner. In the first place, she hadn't wanted to go with Brian to look at the house by the river. Or perhaps she had wanted to, but had known she shouldn't. It had taken all kinds of planning. She'd had to arrange for Julia to look after Diane. She'd told a lie about having a dentist's appointment. Then she'd walked half a mile down the old Cayley Road and had waited near the railroad tracks, where people waited for the bus that went down the Island to Victoria. The side of the road had been littered with chewing gum wrappers, cigarette butts, broken glass. She had thought that if the bus arrived before Brian, she might get on, pay her fare, spend the day in Victoria. She remembered thinking, when she had seen his car approaching, this can't be me waiting here like this. It can't be. What if someone saw her?

After he'd picked her up, Brian had driven out to this house, or cottage or whatever it was, that he was thinking of renting, and they'd taken a look at it. They'd walked through the rooms, pretending it was going to be their house. Where would they put a sofa? Where they would put the table and chairs and bookshelves? What kind of pictures would look best on the walls?

She was damp-mopping the hardware floor in her own house, pushing the mop in behind the chairs and around the legs of the coffee table, and what she was seeing was the hardwood floor in the living room of that other house. As it turned out, it hadn't been what Brian had expected. It had looked like a rather quaint cottage on the outside; inside it was a bit of a dump. There'd been some nice things about it, but mostly it had been old and dirty and neglected. The fireplace was pretty, white plaster with a curved oak mantelpiece, but the black slate hearth was chipped and cracked. Brian said, Well, that would be easy enough to repair, or to replace. They had gone into the bedroom and he had opened the closet door and looked inside. The bedroom floor was covered in dark green linoleum; the window frame was skewed in the wall; there was an unmistakable odour of damp. She'd been imagining a double bed in the room, with a comforter smoothed over it, and pillows in ruffled pillow shams, lamps on either side of the bed, a rug on the floor. She was imagining waking in that bed. The room was dark, cold. The whole house was chilly, even though it was a hot day, and Brian had said, Do you think it's haunted or something. I think it might be, she had said, and she had shivered. And then they had kissed. It was the first time they'd kissed, ever.

"Let me look at you," Brian had said. "Let me get a good look at you."

"Don't look at me," she had said.

"I have a good idea. Live with me here, in this house."

"This house?" she had said. "No, thanks."

"We'll have an exorcism," he had said. "We'll get some fumigators in, and paint the walls. We'll buy ant traps." She had gone to the window. A tree pressed its leaves like hands against the glass, which was cheap, old, flawed. The garden had been let run wild. There were rose bushes growing all over the fence along the front of the yard, and in front of the house there were clumps of giant lupines with purple blooms. There were other wild flowers, too, mostly yellow and white, all stalk and nondescript straggly leaves. It would, she thought, be possible to live an anonymous life out here. Who would see; who would care? The land had no shape, it was all green, lush, wild; houses sprouted randomly from the earth like toadstools and then almost at once began to moulder and collapse in on themselves. The river was like a long, slippery, transparent backbone holding the hills, the forests, the rocks, in some kind of order. Sometimes it overflowed its banks and took in the soft flesh of the countryside. She remembered coming out here with David one spring after a heavy snowfall followed by days and days of heavy rain. They had walked down from the road into the little graveyard beside the bridge. Some of the graves had been under water. The water had been absolutely clear. Grape hyacinth and yellow and purple crocuses had been blooming beneath the surface, astonishing and pure. Resurrection. Rebirth. The life everlasting. A feeling like sorrow or grief or woe had come over her. Someone else's faded ancient grief; supportable. She had wanted to stay there, in sight of such beauty, such strangeness.

After they'd driven to the owner's house and returned the key, Brian turned back and drove to the end of the road, to the banks of the river. She'd never been there before. It was hot and bright and the reality of the little house in the wild garden was already extinguished. Next to the river there was an unexpected sight: a grand house, a sort of English Tudor manor house, huge, with mullioned windows and a shady verandah and four or five tall chimneys. Brian said, "That's the house I'd like to take you to." There were hollyhocks in a row along the fence. There were roses, tiny red roses, trailing over a trellis. A yellow dog came walking down the drive. It did not see them, or did not care to see them. Imagine that such a place as this existed, Arlene thought, and she had never seen it before, or known of it.

They got out of the car and walked toward the river. The road was dry and dusty, the trees and bushes were covered with the lightest coating of pale dust. She leaned her head on his shoulder. He put his arm around her waist. There was the feeling that they had reached some new understanding, had come to some kind of an agreement. They were closer to one another, bound together. And yet they were still children playing a game of make-believe. This could never, Arlene thought, be anything other than make-believe. It couldn't, could it? They were hidden from the windows of the grand English manor house by an old weeping willow tree. On the opposite side of the river the land rose up steeply; there was a rock face with the tangled roots of trees growing down it, ferns growing in the crevices of the rock, and dried brown moss. The river was rushing past; there was a piece of wood caught in the current, and she had watched it, fascinated, waiting to see if it would be carried away or if it would get snagged on something and stay there forever, the water flowing around and over it, white and pure and restless.

CHAPTER TWENTY-SEVEN

Catherine got a ride with Cal Dimitriou. She had been walking along the old Cayley Road, and he stopped and she got in and he drove her to her house. There was an icon stuck to the dash, a little picture in a fancy frame of a pale stern saint, and a crumpled Mars Bar wrapper on the floor. Catherine put her hand on the door handle; then she stopped. "Can we go for a drive somewhere?" she said. It seemed to her she couldn't bear to go home. "If you're not busy," she said.

"Sure, we can go for a drive," he said after a moment. He pulled away from the curb and drove to the end of the street and turned to the right, heading back the way they'd come, toward the old Cayley Road. His style of driving was determined, delicate, pushy, as if the car was in need of flattery and cajoling. After a while, he leaned back and propped his elbow in the open window. He told her to open the glove compartment. There was a postcard in there from Abby. A picture of Carnaby Street, London, England. A skinny girl in a mini-dress leaping in the air, all surprised eyes and mouth and a Mary Quant hairdo. Cal said, "Doesn't she look like Abby? Isn't she the image of Abby?"

It was a warm day, a beautiful day, fluffy white clouds in a blue sky, the wind smelling of pine needles and roses, or some other perfumed flower Catherine couldn't identify. Cal had the car radio on. He tapped his fingers on the steering wheel. "You have to be anywhere special in a hurry?" he asked, leaning over to adjust the volume. "No," Catherine said. "Well, then," he said. He asked her what she was doing for the summer, if she was going away anywhere, and she said she was trying to get a tan and that was about it. "Oh, that and baby-sitting my little sister," she said.

Cal fished a packet of Export A cigarettes out of his shirt pocket. "I've done my share of baby-sitting," he said. He picked a thread of tobacco off his lower lip and wiped it off on his jeans. "Baby sisters, baby nieces. I'm already a family man, it seems. No peace for the wicked," he said. Then he smiled at her. "Well, where would you like to go? Las Vegas? Hollywood? Tijuana? Just say the word and I'll take you there."

Cal drove past the river. He drove through a small town where there was a pulp mill. The air smelled of sulphur. Cal told her it was the smell of money. He turned onto Osborne Bay Road, a narrow dirt road that wound up a mountain. He was wearing mirrored sunglasses, and when he turned to look at her she could see herself in them, a distorted shimmering image: bare legs, white shorts, yellow top, her hair held back with a white hair band. "You want to drive?" he said.

"I don't know how to drive," she said.

"Well, you should learn. You should learn how to drive. Come on, I'll give you a driving lesson," he said. He stopped in the middle of the road and put the car into neutral.

"I can't drive your car. What if I wreck it?"

He got out and walked around the car. He opened her door and said, "You won't. Go on, move over." And she did move over. The engine was running. The steering wheel was red; it was a beautiful red steering wheel. The upholstery was red. The car was red and white, with chrome trim. It was a '57 Chevy hardtop. It had a sticker on the rear bumper that said, *No Free Rides, Blondes, Brunettes and Redheads Exempted.* The first time Catherine and Abby had seen it, they had said, Are we exempt?

Catherine gripped the steering wheel with both hands. Cal said, "Okay, you know where the brake pedal is, right? Good. Now put your left foot on the clutch and your right foot on the brake pedal. I'll change gears. Now release the parking brake. Good. Terrific. Now bring your foot up slowly on the clutch and give it some gas." He kept telling her what to do, how to turn the steering wheel firmly, letting the car know who was boss, a little to the right, a little to the left, not too much in either direction, no abrupt movements, easy, easy. And she followed his instructions. He moved over and sat close to her, his thigh touching hers, his shoulder against hers. He put his hand on the steering wheel, next to her hands. Easy does it, he said. He told her to depress the clutch, and he changed gears. She drove along Osborne Bay

Road at twenty-five, thirty miles an hour, through the hot summer air, heat waves coming off the hood of the car, a stippled pattern of light and shade falling on the windshield. She got up a little more nerve, pressed her foot harder on the gas pedal. She could feel the rocks, the small pebbles and rocks, under the tires. She could taste dust in her mouth, feel it on the steering wheel. Cal leaned across her and tossed his cigarette butt out the window. "Aren't you worried about starting a forest fire?" she said. "Not especially," he said. "Do you think Smokey the Bear is watching?"

He told her about a friend of his who had been travelling along this road, this very road, at about this time of year, on a Honda Super 90 motorcycle, when he had disappeared. It was a true story. His bike had been found a few days later in the bush, not a scratch on it. Cal was one of the first to volunteer for the search party. He had hiked straight up to the top of the mountain, but he'd seen nothing to suggest anyone else had been that way. No broken branches, no footprints. The guy's parents kept his bike in the garage for about a year, Cal said, waiting for him to turn up, and then they sold it for some piddling amount, two hundred bucks, nothing near what it was worth. Cal wished he'd bought it himself; he wished he'd known it was going cheap. Anyway, Art, his name was Art, he had been seventeen, eighteen, when he disappeared; he didn't have any enemies, he was a good kid, innocent as hell; whatever happened, it probably wasn't a dope deal gone bad, or suicide, nothing like that. "The cops figured he slipped climbing the mountain and broke his neck. He's here somewhere, still. His bones. Poor Art. So there you go: a short sad story."

Cal had taken his hand from the steering wheel. She was driving on her own. Cal was wearing a black T-shirt, white jeans, white socks, black loafers. His hair, his black curly hair, was glistening with some kind of sweet-smelling cream. She took her foot off the gas pedal. What if she met another car, coming in the opposite direction? She was suddenly nervous, unsure of what she was doing. "Cal, what do I do now?" she said. She felt for the brake pedal, she put her hand on the gear shift, the clutch pedal, but her foot slipped, it was too late, the car shuddered and bucked, the engine coughed and died. Silence. She kept her hands on the steering wheel. "Sorry," she said.

"That's okay," Cal said. He reached over and turned off the ignition. Then he put his hand on hers. "You did fine," he said. He put his arm behind her, along the back of the seat, and he touched her neck. She knew that he was going to kiss her, and he did. He put his hand under her chin, and turned her face toward his, and then he kissed her. She thought: This is the first time I've ever been kissed, this is my first kiss. She kept her eyes closed, and let him kiss her. He kissed her and touched her closed lips with his tongue and she parted her lips and he ran his tongue over her teeth. She opened her eyes and there, on the side of the car, on the other side of the road, she saw a figure in the shadows. And it seemed to her that it was the boy Cal had talked about, the boy named Art, the one who, on a summer day much like this day, had ridden his motorcycle up this mountain road and then disappeared. She had the impression of someone thin, with blonde hair. His hands were hanging at his sides. He had such a look of hunger about him, and sorrow,

loneliness. She closed her eyes. She knew what she was doing. She was trying to make too much of this moment, of
this kissing Cal, being kissed by him. There was nothing at
the side of the road, other than trees, branches, leaves. Cal
stopped kissing her. He put his hand on her throat and
rubbed his thumb along her jaw. She swallowed. She didn't
want him to stop kissing her. He could do anything he
wanted to do, as far as she was concerned. Anything. She
wanted him to. She saw that there was nothing at the side
of the road, only the shadows beneath the trees, the empty
dirt road, the red car, Cal, staring at her, saying, You okay?
Catherine? You okay?

Chapter Twenty-eight

If you broke something, a teacup or a mirror, say, or even a fingernail, you had to break two matches or two toothpicks because bad luck happened in threes. So her grandmother told Catherine. Bad luck could be changed into good luck by this simple expedient. For example, if you walked under a ladder you had to recite your name backwards three times. Could this, Catherine wondered, work under other conditions? She wasn't superstitious, but her Nana was. There were more things in Heaven and Earth than Catherine could imagine, her Nana said, and besides, it didn't hurt to be on the safe side. Catherine wrote her name on a piece of paper and held it up to the mirror in her bedroom. Matt and Diane watched. Catherine was supposed to be looking after them. It was summer and they were bored and fed up. All afternoon, they had been waiting for their mother to come back from the store, or the post office, or wherever she had gone this time. They had played checkers and Snakes and Ladders until Matt and Diane began fighting over the rules and who was cheating or should take an extra turn, and then Catherine had put away the board games and set the sprinkler going on the front lawn, so that they could run through the water. When they got tired of that, they came back inside, shivering and soaking wet, and got dried off and dressed in clean clothes. And now they were watching Catherine write their names backward, which seemed to her a suitable enough activity, since everything in their lives felt backwards, or upside-down; wrong.

When Catherine held the piece of paper she'd printed her name on up to the mirror it became enirehtaC. Eni-reh-tac, Matthew said, sounding out the syllables. Diane laughed and pushed her hair out of her eyes and said, "Now do my name."

"In a minute," Catherine said. She wrote down their grandmother's name, Eunice, which, in the mirror, became ecinuE. Matthew was wehttaM. Diane laughed. Wehttam, she kept saying. Matthew Wehttam pants. Very funny, Matt said. He told her she was Enaid, the Greek goddess of leftover spaghetti sauce. Diane chased him out of the room. Catherine could hear them scuffling and shrieking in the hall. Catherine couldn't wait for the summer to end. She didn't want to go back to school, though, where she'd be forced to see Mr. Schram every day of the week. Her Nana always said to her, Don't wish your life away, Catherine. But that's what she did wish for. She wished she were old, and far, far removed from this summer and this house.

She tore a fresh sheet paper from her notebook and printed her mother's name on it with a blue felt pen. She held the page up to the mirror. Arlene was enelrA. Catherine thought: Of course. A sorceress or a witch in a fairy tale would have a name like that. She knew how the story would go: The wicked witch Enelra would place a spell on all the people of the town, who would fall into a deep eternal sleep. A princess would eat a poisoned apple. The king's youngest son would venture out to slay dragons and he'd never be seen again. Mirrors would crack. Storms would ravage the land. Beware, beware, the townspeople would say. *Enelra approaches.* Catherine crushed the paper in her hand. She felt tired and sad and frightened. It was nonsense to think there was any kind of power in writing backwards, or repeating a name three times. Then she thought: How could she be so cruel, so unfair to her mother, who was not Enelra, but simply Arlene.

That evening Cal drove Catherine, Abby and Lisa to the beach, where they went swimming. Abby was back from England. She sat next to Cal and she held his hand as he drove. "You should grow your hair, Cal," she said. "No one in England wears their hair in a crew-cut. You'd just get laughed at."

"This isn't a crew-cut," he said.

"Whatever it is, it looks gross," Abby said.

"It doesn't look gross," Lisa said. "It looks nice."

Catherine and Lisa were sitting in the back seat. Lisa's father had sent her a silver ring from Cyprus, for her birthday, and she kept taking the ring off and playing with it. Then she dropped it on the floor of the car beside Catherine's foot and Catherine picked it up and put it on her finger. "It looks good on you," Lisa said. "It's too big," Catherine said. She took the ring off and gave it back to Lisa. Abby started fiddling with the car radio. She said she was trying to find a station that didn't play music that was twenty-five years out of date. Leave it alone, Cal said, slapping at her hand.

They went to the beach near Cal's family's restaurant. The sea was a pale blue, and where it wasn't blue it was silver. Cal called it the pond. The beach was coarse dark sand, pebbles, broken oyster shells. Abby had brought rubber thongs to wear, but Catherine and Lisa had to tiptoe gingerly in their bare feet down to the water. The water felt cold at first, then, the longer they were in it, the warmer it got. There was a raft pulled up close to shore, in the shade of some trees, and Cal climbed up on it and then Abby, then Lisa and finally Catherine. They sat in the shade dripping with water and shivering and looked out at the silver sunlit sea. Catherine had thought she'd feel awkward around Cal with Abby back, but she didn't. He didn't seem to her the same person as the Cal who'd let her drive his car, the Cal she'd kissed. He didn't seem even remotely the same. Was this always the case? Was memory so unreliable events could be erased or turned into what seemed fragments of an old, half-remembered dream? If so, life was scandalous, Catherine thought. It was a scandal.

There were some friends of Cal's out on the water with a speed boat, water-skiing. They brought the boat in close and cut the engine and shouted at Cal: Did he want to ski? The wash from the boat was making the raft go up and down, and Lisa kept jumping around and screaming that she was going to fall in. The boy who'd been skiing was climbing into the boat. He stood up and shook water from his hair. Cal shouted back at them, "No, I don't want to go water-skiing." He sounded amused by the idea; a little bored. Catherine said, "I do. I'd like to try it." Her words took her by surprise, and she laughed, nervous, excited. Cal's friends brought the boat in closer to the raft. They were Greg, Jonathan, Mike, Cal said, introducing them quickly. The boy called Jonathan climbed from the boat onto the raft. Some-one handed the skis to him and he put them on the raft.

"They're big for you. You'll have to sort of curl your toes to hang on," he said to Catherine. The skis were home-made, flat clumsy slabs of plywood rounded off at the ends, with rubber foot bindings made, according to Jonathan, out of old truck tire inner tubes. He took hold of her foot and helped her put them on. "You want to change your mind?" Cal asked.

"No, it's okay," she said, even though the skis felt like fence posts strapped to her feet. It seemed to her that it would be a good idea to change her mind, right now. The skis didn't fit; Jonathan was right. And the rubber was cold, it felt aw-ful, like the flesh of some kind of dead sea creature. She'd only been water skiing once before in her life. "Catherine?" Abby said. She had her arms wrapped tight around her chest. "Catherine? Are you sure about this?" "Yes," Catherine said. "I'm sure. I think I am." Then it came to her that if she pictured herself floating across the surface of the water on the skis, if she thought of the water as being solid as a sheet of glass, which was how it appeared, she would be all right. She could do this. Why not?

Jonathan got back in the boat and the guy called Greg started the engine, and Cal kneeled beside her on the raft. They were both giving her instructions, saying, Hold the rope like this, keep your legs straight, don't turn your feet in, keep the ends of the skis out of the water. You can do it, they said, patting her on the back. And indeed for the first few seconds she was fine. Jonathan gave her a thumb's up sign from the boat. Greg increased the boat's speed. She was skiing, she really was. And then the blunt ends of the skis seemed to get caught in the water, and she was pulled under, and it felt as if she were skiing underwater. She was still holding onto the tow rope. It didn't occur to her that she could let go. One foot was still stuck in a ski, and the ski was pulling her down deeper. The ski was pulling her in one direction, and the tow rope was pulling her in another. She was able to understand what was happening, and at the same time she was able to notice that the sea down here was a clear radiant green. It was beautiful, shining with light. She was surprised that she could see as well as she could, and she became captivated at the sight of the bubbles rising from her mouth toward the surface. They were silver, and enormous, propelled by a weird energy. It seemed to her that she had always known this was going to happen, and she thought, *so this is what it's like to drown.* She was surprised how quickly she became reconciled to the idea. It seemed that this was a replay of something that had happened to her before. If she concentrated, the memory would come back to her. Her arms and legs were white, languid, estranged from her, one of them ending incongruously in a heavy clumsy wood contraption. She admired the whiteness of her limbs, their easy grace. She opened her mouth as if to hasten the process of drowning, the inevitable process of giving in to the water. If the water wanted her, wanted her so much, it could have her. She was willing. She was giving everything up, giving herself over to the water. What was it but dreaming, this slow descent?

Then she panicked. She thought, I can't drown. I can't. Then she saw that someone was with her in the water. Someone thin and as palely transparent as the long strands of seaweed that spun slowly through the water. And she thought, It's Myrtle. Myrtle Kriskin was beside her in the water, saying, Catherine, here's the thing. You have to let go of that stupid old tow rope. Catherine did what Myrtle told her to do, she let go of the tow rope, and then she used her hands to get her foot free of the ski. That's the way, Myrtle was saying. Good for you. Myrtle was waving her long white arms in the water, she was drifting further from Catherine. *Don't go*, Catherine wanted to say. Her chest hurt. She felt enormously heavy and it seemed to her it would be a whole lot easier to sink than to try to make her way up toward the light of day. She was going to die, she thought. There wasn't anything else she had the energy to do. She pushed against the water with her arms. She kicked and moved her arms and somehow made it to the surface, to the clear air, which, unlike the water, was kind, forgiving, an effortless medium. She treaded water. The boat was circling back to her. It was going slow and people were reaching toward her, helping her into the boat. Her throat burned from the salt water she had swallowed. There was a long strand of dark seaweed on her arm and it startled her. She peeled it away. The boat took her back to the raft. Abby and Lisa kept saying, Are you all right?

Lisa put her arm around her. "You could have drowned."

"Oh, Lisa," Abby said. "She didn't drown."

Catherine kept seeing the green water, the bubbles rising from her mouth. She kept thinking, Well, it's true, I could have drowned. But she made herself sound as if nothing much had happened. I'm okay, she said. I need a few water-skiing lessons, that's all.

They went up to Cal's house and got changed out of their swimsuits, and Cal gave them each a Coke to drink, then he drove them all home. He dropped Catherine off first. As soon as he pulled up outside her house, Lisa opened the door and got out. "So this is where you live!" she said. "I never knew before. I've never been to your house. Is that your mother in the window?"

"Yes," Catherine said. She got out of the car and said good-bye. She ran up the steps to her front door and opened it just enough to slip inside. Then she closed and locked the door and went straight into the kitchen. Her mother was following her, saying, "Catherine, where have you been? Do you know what time it is?"

Catherine got a glass out of the cupboard and turned on the tap. She was thinking: Lisa would have forgotten by now. She would never connect Catherine's mother, at home in her own house, a face in the window, scarcely seen, with the woman who'd been standing with Mr. Schram, holding hands with Mr. Schram, beside a river tumbling silver and dark and mysterious between the cliff and that strange old house. And yet, Catherine had to be careful. For all she knew, Lisa had a photographic memory, the kind of trick memory that never forgot a single thing, that kept the past pure and simple, absolutely reliable. There were people like that, Catherine was sure. Lisa must never get the chance to say: But I've seen you before, Mrs. Greenwood. I saw you down by the river, near that old house. Wasn't that you? Wasn't it? How come you didn't *tell* me that was your mother, Catherine?

Her mother came and stood beside her and said, "Catherine. Where have you been? Who was that, Catherine? Who drove you home?"

"No one. Just Abby. And Lisa, this girl I know from school, and Cal."

"Cal?" her mother said. "Isn't he a lot older than you and Abby? I thought Julia didn't want Abby seeing him anymore. Anyway, I'd rather you didn't start riding around in cars with boys."

Catherine drank a glass of water and still felt thirsty. She opened the fridge and took out the milk. She felt like saying, Well, *frankly*, I don't want *you* riding around in cars with boys at *your* age.

Catherine thought of Myrtle Kriskin, and her children, her two little boys. They had all died, drowned, trapped inside a car, and they were buried in the Cayley Cemetery, in a row of grassy graves marked with little grey stone crosses and the date they'd died: 04 August 1957. The same date on each cross. They'd all been there for more than ten years. Sleeping. No, absent. They didn't exist anymore. Or were they in heaven? Had Myrtle Kriskin looked down from heaven, down through the surface of the sea, and had she seen Catherine in the process of drowning, and rescued her? Had Myrtle appeared in the water, like a mermaid, saying, *You can do it, Catherine, I know you can.* You sweet little thing, you're the spitting image of Marilyn Monroe when she was young. Here, honey, Catherine imagined Myrtle saying. Let me just give you a hand up from that cold ocean floor.

Catherine's father had built a darkroom in the corner of the basement where he had once had what he'd called a bomb shelter. Up until he started work on it, no one had wanted to use the basement for anything but storing stuff, like Matt's sled, her father's set of snow tires for the car, and a few boxes of old books, a shelf of ancient canned food that her mother kept talking about throwing out. It was a dark musty basement with four high windows, two at either side, and a cement floor that sloped in odd directions. Catherine's father started to spend his weekends down there, putting up plywood walls and a doorway and a door that locked. They hardly ever saw him upstairs. He converted the old cement laundry tubs into a double sink, and installed a counter and set up work tables and arranged timers and light switches and shelves for his bottles of chemicals. He went around town taking pictures with his 35 millimetre camera, and then he exposed the film in his darkroom and developed prints from the negatives. When the prints were dry, he brought them upstairs and showed them to everyone. They were all black-and-white photographs, and they had all been taken in Cayley. He was just practising, he said. He knew he wasn't any Ansel Adams. Still, they had a surprisingly interesting quality, about them, didn't they? he said. He was really pleased with some of them, he said, spreading the photographs out on the kitchen table. In some cases, the paper hadn't dried perfectly flat, and he had to weight the corners with the salt and pepper shakers and the sugar dish. Catherine looked at the photographs from a distance, and then she went right up to the table and examined them up close. She thought they were extraordinary. She loved the way the light fell upon the most ordinary objects and transformed them into something of importance. Her father had captured Cayley exactly the way it was, the way she herself saw it. Here were the backyards, the unpainted picket fences, the rusted-out burning barrels next to the compost piles, the narrow paved walks leading to neatly cultivated vegetable gardens. The carefully pruned apple trees, the wooden bird houses stuck on top of poles. Here was the Hamilton's front yard, overgrown with juniper shrubs and uncut grass, the front gate hanging from one hinge, because Angus Hamilton couldn't mow the lawn anymore, or do any repairs. He'd injured his back in an accident at the mill, and now he stayed indoors, playing solitaire at his kitchen table. The doctors evidently kept telling him his back had healed and the pain was all in his head, but Mrs. Hamilton said it was real enough, and Catherine could certainly see Mr. Hamilton's pain in this photograph, in the long black shadows beneath the neglected junipers, in the spikey seed heads on the dandelions growing in what had once been flower beds, in the peeling and blistered paint on the front door of the house. And here was Miss Caroline Bluett, wearing a frilly blouse, a gathered madras cotton skirt, her tiny waist nipped in with a wide patent leather belt. She wore hoop earrings, and barrettes in her snow white hair, and dark lipstick. Every line etched in her heart-shaped face had been captured by the camera. Her mischievous little-girl eyes were sunken in her head. She was standing in front of her house, looking as if she was just setting off somewhere, her white clutch bag held in the crook of her arm.

And here was a picture of Catherine's house, the steps leading up to the front door, the leaded-glass windows with small diamond-shaped panes of glass, the steep roof, the chimneys stark against a sky streaked with high, thin cloud. The front lawn was neatly edged, the oval leaves on the laurel hedge pruned and glossy, the shadows long and thick across the lawn. The geraniums along the front walk were in bloom. Diane's new tricycle was propped against the side of the garage, and the garbage can, dented from the time Catherine's mother had backed the car into it, was standing on the curb waiting for the garbage collection truck to arrive. So the photograph must have been taken on a Wednesday, an ordinary day, Catherine and Matt and Diane home from school, her father for some reason home from work and walking around with his camera.

Here was a picture of Catherine's mother, in the backyard, beside the star-shaped Belle de Crécy roses. She was standing in front of the apple tree. Diane was behind her, sitting in the swing. One second after this picture was taken, Catherine's mother had said, "You and that damned camera, David." Catherine had stepped through the French doors and had hesitated, seeing her father raising his camera to his eye. Catherine's mother had, up until that moment, been gazing at some distant place, her eyes dark, luminous, a faint smile on her mouth, as if, Catherine thought, her own pretend people from long-ago had suddenly gathered at her mother's side with their dream-stories, their whispered fragments, their promises, their pale solicitous fingers.

Now Catherine's father turned the photograph slightly on the kitchen table, so that Catherine's mother could see it better. "It's a good picture of you, don't you think?" he said. "You look happy. I like it."

"Do you? I think it's awful. Give it to me."

"It certainly isn't awful."

"I hate having my picture taken."

"Arlene, Julia Glass is always showing me photographs of you that she took. She must have about a hundred by now. I've never heard of you shouting at Julia."

"She has to take those pictures. She's painting my portrait. And I'm not shouting at you. Anyway, Julia always warns me before she takes my picture. She doesn't sneak up on me. Here, let me see that, please, David."

Catherine watched as her father first handed over the photograph, then took it back, then held it out to her mother again. Her mother, who was laughing as if she were at the same time close to tears, grabbed the photograph and held it as if she was going to tear it in half.

"Don't you dare," her father said. "Don't you dare rip it up."

"I can if I want," she said. "It's a picture of me. I can rip it up if I want."

"Arlene. Don't. Give it to me."

"Well, take it downstairs with you then. Put it someplace where I don't have to see it again."

"Don't always fight, you guys," Matt said. He came and stood beside Catherine.

"We aren't fighting," his father said. He ruffled Matt's hair. "Ask your mother. We aren't fighting. We're doing fine."

Catherine opened the glass doors of the bookcase in the living room and removed her mother's copy of *Anna Karenina*. She was alone in the house; her parents and Diane had gone out for a drive and Matt was at a friend's house. Catherine took the book upstairs to her bedroom, and sat down on her bed with it. Then she opened it and read the opening sentence. *All happy families are like one another; each unhappy family is unhappy in its own way.*

Catherine read a little further. The Oblonsky family was unhappy because the wife had discovered that the husband "had had an affair with their French governess . . . ." The husband was Prince Stepan Arkadyevich Oblonsky; he was called Stiva by his friends. Out of curiosity, Catherine turned to the last page, to the end of the novel, where she read the words: *My life, my whole life, independently of anything that may happen to me, every moment of it, is no longer meaningless as it was before, but has an incontestable meaning of goodness, with which I have the power to invest it.* These words belonged to someone called Levin. Catherine was not sure of their exact meaning, except that they gave her a sensation of strength and weakness combined, a feeling as sharp and sudden as homesickness, a sense of loss, a yearning for the impossible, things she couldn't even picture in her mind.

Anything that may happen to me. . . is no longer meaningless as it was before . . . . She turned back to the beginning, to the family that was unhappy because of terrible, loveable Oblonsky, who had a "plump, well-cared for body" and eyes that "sparkled gaily." He was truthful "in his attitude to himself."

Perhaps she would read the book. It was very thick book, and heavy, and the print was small, but she loved the way it smelled, like chocolate and dust and dried pine needles. There were stains on some of the pages, small stains left behind by her mother, who read while she ate breakfast, while she drank coffee, when she was having a bath. Here was what Catherine's mother did: She opened her book and disappeared from sight. An astonishing, exclusive trick, and one that Catherine remembered fearing and resenting and envying when she was a small child.

Catherine went to her desk and sat down and laid her head down on the open pages. When she was little, she had been crazy about the smell of books. She had believed the words themselves had a smell, like flowers after rain, like candy. Different words had different smells, of damp grass, of burning leaves, of peppermint, of wet dirt. She closed her eyes and at once, without consciously willing it, began to dream the story of the book.

Oblonsky is standing behind her. He is dressed in a dark suit, ready to leave the house. His hair smells of sandalwood, of cedar, of jasmine. He wears several heavy gold rings on his plump, carefully manicured fingers. Lightly, he touches the back of her neck. His hand is warm. He lifts a lock of her hair, then lets it fall. He strokes her head as if she were a cat asleep on his lap. She is not a cat; she is his children's governess. She speaks Russian with an accent that amuses Oblonsky. He laughs at everything she says. He brings her little gifts: chocolates, face powder, bookmarks with scalloped gold edges. In his presence, she is timid, meek, obedient. She is absolutely in his power. Whatever Oblonsky asks of her, she will do. She knows she will.

Catherine shut the book and left it on her desk, which she had cleared of everything except a pencil holder in the shape of a white china Persian china cat. She would, she decided, read a minimum of twenty-five pages a day of *Anna Karenina*, until she had progressed from the war in the Oblonsky household to the incontestable meaning of goodness on the last page.

She changed from shorts to a pair of blue cotton pants. She brushed her hair and put on some lipstick, pale pink. She was getting ready to go out with Abby and Lisa and Cal. She didn't know where they were going. It didn't especially matter. They were just going out to have a good time. She took a nail scissors out of a drawer and tried to trim her bangs, just a little, because they were getting in her eyes. Oblonsky's substantial form lingered in the centre of the room, watching her eagerly, his eyes bright, telling her not to ruin her hair, not to spoil her looks. He bunched his fingers to his lips and blew her a kiss. Then he began to dissolve until all that was left were the shining gold buttons on his waistcoat. Then those too went out, like little suns.

CHAPTER TWENTY-NINE

Not only the acorn barnacle but also the goose barnacle began its life as a free-swimming *nauplius* larvae. This was another fact Arlene picked up in her book on marine biology. According to the book, the goose barnacle—*Mitella polymerus*—didn't look much like the acorn barnacle; they were, however, closely related. *Mitella* occurred in clusters, like a constellation of stars or a handful of wildflowers. From its chalk-coloured plates protruded six pairs of delicate feathery appendages. With these, it fed itself. Its thick, fleshy, purplish stalk, one-half the length of the entire goose barnacle, was considered a delicacy by the Spanish and the Italians.

Arlene had never heard of John Gerard before now, but she liked the sound of him. Born in 1545, Gerard was an English botanist and a barber-surgeon. He gave the goose barnacle its common name. This "woonder of England," enthused Gerard, who seemed to love all living things and the telling of fabulous lies in equal degree. *This wonder of England.* He knelt in the waves, the hem of his cloak dripping wet. He knelt, and fell in love with the goose barnacle, with its mystical and wondrous guises, the strangely tender and amorous-looking flesh of its edible stalk. Goose barnacle, goose-tree, Barnakle tree, tree-bearing goose: Gerard's canticle, his taxonomic Song of Songs.

John Gerard discovered the goose barnacle in this way: One day, walking along the coast of England between Dover and Rummey, he came across a rotting tree trunk adrift in the water. With the help of some women waiting for their fisher husbands to return (Arlene could imagine herself as one of these women, her feet in wooden clogs, her sea-stained gown the colour of the earth, her gaze fixed on an illusory speck in the farthest distance), Gerard dragged the log to shore. To his astonishment and delight he observed growing on it "long crimson bladders . . . verie cleere and shining." And at the end of each crimson bladder there grew something like a shellfish, resembling, to Gerard's mind, a limpet. Inside each limpet-like shell Gerard further discovered:

> living things without forme or shape; in others which were neerer come to ripeness, I found living things that were very naked, in shape like a Birde; in others, the Birds covered with soft downe, the shell halfe open, and the Birde readie to fall out, which no doubt were the foules called Barnakles.

The foules called Barnakles, Arlene repeated aloud, dazed by the strange beauty of the words. "They spawne as it were in March and April; the Geese are formed in Maie and Iune, and come to fulnesse of feathers in the moneth after."

There was a drawing done by Gerard, of the goose barnacle in the act of giving birth to its offspring: The limpet-like shell at the end of each stalk had opened in an act of voluntary charity and maternity, and the living creatures within, "in shape like a Birde," had tumbled out and at once taken flight.

Who could know where their birth-flight took them? Who could track their passage across the heavens, over the wide seas of the planet? From microscopic *nauplii* to a flock of snow-white wild geese: a lovely completion, a circle, part biology and part fairy tale, part history and part practical joke. From freedom to fixed, sober adulthood, and round again to freedom. They "come to fulnesse of feathers in the moneth after," which would, of course, be July. It was August now, nearly the end of August, and Arlene was walking quickly down a lane between high wood fences overgrown with blackberry vines on which the fat overripe berries glistened like jewels and exuded a sweetish volatile musky incense. Arlene thought: I will always associate this smell with this day. I will always remember this. She was on her way to see Brian at his apartment, which was on the corner of Oak and Third. When she got to the end of the lane, she ran across the street and up the walk and slipped in through the main door of the building. And there she was, in a poor sunless front hall with a dingy floor and smudged fingerprints all over the walls. No one was about. No one ever was. She ran up the stairs to the second floor and rapped lightly at his door.

What she liked about Brian's apartment was its simplicity, which made up for its shabbiness. It had large rooms, big windows, high ceilings. If Arlene were Brian, she'd rather live here than in the house by the river, which he had, in any case, decided against renting, saying that she was right, it was too damp, too dark, too cheerless. He was in the kitchen, putting the kettle on for tea, and she was standing near the open window. She could hear children's voices, cars going past, the thump and slap of wood being stacked at the sawmill. There was such a bright, white, truthful light at the window. The whole town was bathed in this light. She had to turn away to ease her eyes. She had to concentrate on the room, its green walls and shining floor. Another thing she liked: his makeshift furniture, the bookcases constructed of boards and grey cement bricks, the coffee table that was really a wood box upended and covered with a length of Indian cotton, the old sagging couch, a plaid flannel blanket, like the ones used to cover an invalid's knees, folded across the worn cushions. She liked the posters he had hung on the walls: pictures of white buildings against intensely azure skies; a matador in a red cape; a painting that looked like a Jackson Pollock; a Matisse, although she didn't know it was a Matisse until she admired it, and then he told her the name of the artist. She nodded and went over to look at the houseplants lined up in red clay pots at the edge of the room. He was always apologising to her, saying he really ought to buy some proper furniture, so that she'd have somewhere comfortable to sit. Now that he saw everything through her eyes, he said, he realised how truly inadequate it was, what a jumble. "Well, you're not seeing it through my eyes, then," she said, "because I like it. I envy you. It's peaceful here, restful." She sat down on a cushion and smoothed her skirt tidily over her knees.

"No, you don't envy me," he said. "Of course you don't. You're one of the tidy house-proud bourgeois, aren't you? You're used to your nice department store furniture mixed in with a few well-cared-for old pieces passed lovingly down through the generations. Isn't that so? Only the best for Arlene?"

He was standing over her, his hands in the back pockets of his jeans. His tone was unexpectedly sharp and critical, and she was unsure how to respond, or if she really wanted to respond. Was he trying to tease her? Was he being deliberately cruel? What had she done to be spoken to like this? Or was she being too sensitive? "I don't think I'm what you'd call house-proud," she said at last in what sounded to her like the small apologetic self-condemnatory voice of a boring bourgeoisie. (Who did he think he was, Levin, full of theories and uncompromising ideals?) Or was there something false in her home, her very existence, detectable not to her but to Brian?

"Oh, Arlene," he said at last. "Forget I said that. I don't know what I was talking about. I'm an idiot. I didn't mean to make you angry."

"I'm not angry," she said. "And I do envy you."

He knelt on the floor in front of her and took her hand and folded her fingers against her palm. "The truth," he said, "is that I envy you. I envy everything that belongs to you, everything that you touch and own and see, or scarcely notice because it's so completely familiar to you. I even envy your children because they have your company whenever they want and they can adore you openly, and—wait, there's more—I envy the sun because it shines down on you and illuminates the simple objects you see every day of your life."

"Is that from a poem?" she said, laughing.

"It's a poem for you," he said. "For Arlene, with admiration. And adoration." He stroked her hand. "Forgive me?" he said. "Yes," she said. She looked at him doubtfully, then she smiled. "Of course," she said. "There's nothing to forgive."

"I'll tell you what. I'll make tea," he said, and placed her hand on her lap, and kissed her on the mouth and got up and left her.

It didn't seem in the least believable to her that her own house was only a few blocks away. It was a Saturday, and they were all at home, her husband and her children. She'd told them she was going for a walk, maybe to the library, and that she'd be home soon, in time to get lunch for them. She'd told these outright lies, and then she'd said goodbye. She'd thrown her jacket on, catching sight of herself in the hall mirror, the pale distracted oval of her face. And then Diane, for some reason dressed in the Halloween costume Arlene had made for her the year before, had run after her. She'd stood on the front porch in her black satin witch's dress, its wide Medieval sleeves held out like the wings of some exotic little bat, calling, "Wait for me, Mummy. Wait up!" Such a heartfelt cry! Little child of the bourgeoisie, calling to her mother. Arlene had called that she'd be back soon. "Go in the house," she'd said, then she'd waved again, and had turned and kept walking, faster and faster, her heart racing, her mouth dry, all nerves, all nerves and will, the will to do what she wanted to do, until she'd reached the corner of the street, where she'd paused for a moment to try to calm herself.

Now Brian came in from the kitchen and put a tray down on the wood box and sat down on the floor beside her, cross-legged. Boyishly, he thrust a hand through his thick brown hair. Then he sneezed, and said, "Oh, excuse me." He wiped his nose, and said it was his neighbour's cats. His neighbour was an old man who had about four cats, and cat fur was everywhere. He couldn't get rid of it.

Arlene thought to tell Brian the story of Gerard and the goose-bearing tree: They come to *fulnesse of feathers*, she thought of quoting to him. She studied the table in front of her. Herb tea in a Chinese teapot, fragrant steam, honey in a clay pot, little handleless cups to drink from. A plate of cookies baked by Brian, a sort of dumpy health-food cookie, made, he told her, with molasses and sunflower seeds and raisins. "Go on, they're quite good," he said, and she took a cookie and held it in her hand without tasting it. Another image lingered at the edge of her mind, and it also had to do with geese. Geese flying against a cold northern sky. And then it came to her: the image originated in a fairy tale she had read long ago, or that she'd had read to her when she was a child. In the fairy tale a witch cast a spell over seven brothers—was it seven? She thought so. Seven brothers turned all at once by the witch's potent magic into geese. Only their sister could undo the enchantment—that was the way the witch set things up—and so she set to work, knitting garments out of thistles, seven identical garments, that, when thrown over the geese, would reverse the spell and purchase their release. The sister worked faithfully for years and years, the story went, gathering thistles, weaving them into coats. Her fingers were raw and bleeding from the thistles. But she didn't mind; she didn't mind if her fingers dropped off, as long as she could complete the task. And she did. At last the garments were completed, all except for one, which lacked a sleeve, and that was how the youngest brother ended up with a wing in place of an arm. In a story of such devotion and fidelity, Arlene wondered, why couldn't the ending be perfect?

"You look very serious," Brian said. He put his teacup down and said, "What are you thinking about? No, that's not fair. I shouldn't have asked. Don't tell me."

"I was thinking of geese," she said. "Wild geese. That's all." Immediately he took her cup from her and put it on the Indian-cotton tablecloth. He put her uneaten cookie back on the plate. He took her hand in his. "Geese," he repeated. "You're wonderful. You looked so sad," he said. "And then you come up with something like that. Geese."

"It was something I read once," she said. "In this old book."

"My parents kept geese for awhile. They had a little farm, in Ontario. I was really young, only four or five, when we lived there. There was a pond, and these white geese. They fascinated me, but I was afraid of them. I threw a rock at them once, and my father smacked me. I think I had the idea the geese hated me, that they thought I was an inferior life form. Then the farm got sold, and the geese, too, I suppose. I can't remember where the geese went."

"They flew across the sea," Arlene said.

"These were domestic geese," Brian said. "I don't think they'd ever flown anywhere."

"I have to go," she said. She glanced at her watch and saw that it was twelve-thirty. If she'd gone to the library, as she'd told her children she was doing, she'd be home by now. She drank the last of her tea.

"I have to go home and make lunch," she said. "They'll be wondering what happened to me."

"Surely your family can get themselves lunch once in a while," he said.

"Yes, they can," she said. "They can." She started to bite her thumbnail, thoughtfully. Here she was, sitting on the floor, her empty tea cup beside her. Brian was running his fingers languidly through her hair, combing it out, letting it fall into place around her shoulders. His touch was tentative, light, reverent. She moved slightly, so that she was closer, so that her hair was falling free and he had easier access to it. David, she recalled, thought her hair was too long; he thought she looked like a hippie, which was ridiculous; she didn't. Brian had told she must never cut her hair. Arlene didn't want to speak or think of David, or of the children. She wanted to pretend they didn't exist, which was very wicked of her. She had turned them into geese.

They were flying in distracted circles above the roof of the building. *Come back, come back,* they were calling to her.

The sun was shining through the leaves of a tree outside the window. Dappled light danced on the linoleum floor, which Brian had washed and waxed until it actually shone, old and worn as it was. It all seemed, for as long as she was here, in this room, a grand mystery to her: the vagaries of the light, the old floor upon which it shimmered and faded and reasserted itself. This too was mysterious: his breath on her face, his nearness, his touch, which was illicit, unlawful, full of wrong-doing and sinfulness. No, that wasn't true. Brian said that love erases the possibility of sin, that there was no sin in the heart, there was only truth. If so, then she did have the notion that her love, if it was love, perhaps she should say her *affinity* for him, was regenerative: she had taken up habitation in a new body, like those molluscs that moved from shell to shell, a process that must have as its eventual by-product the eradication of past scars, old failings. This new body of hers had no history whatsoever; furthermore, she could do with it what she pleased. She was no longer bound by promises she had made while inhabiting her former body. Everything, as Brian maintained, was in a state of flux: The way people looked at life, the way they existed in the world, the social structures they upheld, all of it was changing. He thought all history, personal, cultural, global, was a natural, organic process, like the Reformation and the Counter-Reformation and the Industrial Revolution. There was no mechanism that could stop these events from taking place. At such times everything formerly dormant suddenly bubbled to the surface. That was why, every time you looked at a newspaper or watched the television news there were riots in the streets, and people dressed in bizarre costumes, and everyone travelling to distant places, and soldiers putting flowers in their guns and walking away from war zones. These were all good clear indications, Brian said, that the old, outmoded order was reaching its limits, and a new order was in the ascendancy. Each individual had one responsibility, and only one, which was to attain his or her full potential. His voice was cold and triumphant, as if he was pleased to see humanity finally falling into line behind him. He saw no paradox in this, or in his injunctions to her. He didn't mind what use he put his theories to, it sometimes seemed to her. As in: There is nothing astonishing any longer in infidelity. If that's the word you choose to use. In radical change at the human, individual level. Change is everywhere in any case, he implied, or in fact boldly stated; it is under the very skin of the planet, and cannot be avoided. She must, he said, come to a decision soon, before next spring, at the latest. But the decision was, of course, entirely hers to make.

"There's only one solution to this," he said. "Don't you think so? We have to find some way to be together."

"I wish you wouldn't say that," she said. "It's not possible. It just isn't. I can't leave my children. I can't leave David."

"You can, Arlene. I mean it. I think it's a miracle I've met you and you can't walk away from a miracle, can you? Until I met you, I couldn't imagine what in the world had brought me to this town. I hated it here. I decided a few years ago that I would just go wherever I felt I was destined to be. Like the wind. The wind doesn't wish for anything other than to be the wind. Isn't that what Montaigne said? *The wind, wiser than we, loves to make a noise and move about.* . . . And Jesus, too, said the wind bloweth where it listeth, or something like that. If you keep resisting, you'll end up with nothing, you'll be nothing. You'll have lost your sense of destiny, you'll falter."

"Don't," she said, putting her hands to her ears. "You make it sound so desperate. I don't have a sense of destiny, anyway. I never have had."

"It's time you acquired one. And it is desperate, Arlene. It is."

They would go somewhere where no one knew them, he said, and they would start over. They'd build a plain little house in the middle of green fields. They'd get a dog and plant a garden. He'd make their furniture himself, out of pine wood, carving hearts and flowers and birds in it. They wouldn't need a great deal. He told her he had some money; he had some money coming to him from relatives of his mother. He would teach and they would have enough to live on. Every summer they'd visit a different country: England, France, Morocco, Italy.

He also told her that they didn't exactly choose this, did they? They didn't set out to fall in love, but it had happened; it was meant to happen, and they couldn't turn away, they couldn't destroy or cast aside a gift that life, or fate, or whatever, had freely, without prejudice, given them, could they?

In the grocery store Arlene took a can of black olives from the shelf, thinking, oh, he'll like these, and then she stopped dead, uncertain for a moment who she meant, David or Brian. They both liked black olives, didn't they? In tossed green salads. In pasta dishes. In her mind she saw David getting out of his car and walking toward the house. Then she saw Brian waiting for her in the shadows in the lane behind the library, his face in profile, the pure sweet lines of his face and throat. Then the two separate forms melded together and she couldn't tell them apart—*living things without forme or shape; in others which were neerer come to ripeness.* But her husband didn't look anything like Brian; they weren't anything alike. She put the can back on the shelf. There was a stopped-up sensation in her ears; the corners of her vision swam with blackness. She bent over for a moment, her hand to her forehead. When she straightened up, she thought, am I the only one in this store who has done this terrible thing, fallen in love with a man who is not my husband? The only one? She felt dizzy, disoriented, nauseous, almost. By the time she got to the parking lot she was completely paranoid; she was imagining people pointing her out. She thought, I can't do this, this is making me crazy. She made up her mind that never again would she meet Brian; she'd never call at Caroline Bluett's house again, as Brian had instructed her to do, to pick up one of his books, one of his precious books with their words, words, words, insightful passages, directions for ways and methods of being. And a note tucked inside the pages, a crisply folded piece of paper that Arlene couldn't believe Caroline would be able to refrain from taking out and reading. What did Caroline have to do with this, anyway? Why had Brian bothered to involve her? Nobody will find out, he told her, and then he sabotaged himself by practically making Caroline an accomplice. Arlene had to end it; she had to finish the whole thing, the relationship, the friendship, whatever it was.

When she was at home, however, she felt quite differently. She was visited by a lovely composure that allowed her to get out of bed every morning and dress and clean the house and serve meals and spend a little time reading at the kitchen table with her morning coffee. She sat with Diane on her lap and whispered endearments in her ear: baby, sweetheart, darling one. She brushed her daughter's hair and braided it tight, a rope of hair as smooth and warm as silk. She cut up an apple the way Diane liked it, served on a plate with a sprinkling of cinnamon, and later, when Diane had finished eating, Arlene sponged off her hands. She tended her as if she were still a baby. Diane didn't mind; she was an amenable child. Catherine and Matt stood at the counter pouring cereal into bowls, passing the milk carton and the sugar bowl back and forth. Matt had this strange habit of evening out his cereal with the back of a spoon, tamping it down. He did it with potatoes, rice, almost everything he ate. Arlene and David told him he was part squirrel, part racoon. Catherine carried her bowl over to the table and sat down. She picked up her spoon and started talking to Diane. Arlene had the impression that lately Catherine was less cautious, less wary around her. She hoped she was right. Part of her didn't see any reason why anything had to change. She imagined a day in the fall, when school had resumed and her children were coming home after school to be with her, to tell her everything, their words all chaotic and rushed in their eagerness: what they'd got on their tests, their homework assignments, what they did at the meetings of the clubs they belonged to, the sports they played. In her mind she could see this picture clearly, serene and lovely and *exactly the way it was supposed to be.*

Brian had painted his entire apartment, including the insides of the cupboards and closets, which he proudly showed her, opening the doors and standing aside so that she could look inside. He'd stripped the old wax from the linoleum floors and applied new, buffing and polishing. She thought about this sometimes, when she was at home alone. It wasn't important; he could do what he liked with his own apartment. He took her into his bedroom and removed her clothes and made love to her on his bed, which was a mattress on the floor, and there was a thin length of fabric stretched over the window through which the light came softly, softly, and everything was delicate and forbidden and otherworldly and nothing mattered outside the door of that secret room.

But then she thought: He talks about being like the wind, unfettered, but he isn't like that, he's finicky, obsessive, a stickler. She couldn't imagine David trying to get old linoleum to a shine, or cleaning the baseboards in those hard-to-get-at corners behind doors. What would it be like to live with someone who did? What would it be like to give up everything and go away with someone whose stated desire was to carve hearts and flowers in handmade furniture? What would be any different from the way her life was now? Nothing ever changed, not really. Men and women came together and formed a unit of two individuals and it all ended up involving living space and money and bank accounts and furniture. She liked to think she was a practical person; she was a realist. Growing up Eunice's daughter had done that to her. She believed she had developed the ability to see through people. She saw through the romance of life and glimpsed the everyday beyond. This, she believed, was the source of her pain and her strength.

It was half past ten in the morning. She lit a cigarette, her first of the day. She was outside, on the patio, and she had to cup her hands around the flame to keep it from going out. It had taken her forever to acquire the knack to do this, and it always gave her a sense of accomplishment. Brian didn't want her to smoke; he kept taking her cigarettes out of her hand and throwing them in the garbage. It was kind of him to think of her health, but there you were: It was in reality his own health he was thinking about, his allergies, his childhood asthma. She tossed the spent match into a plant pot and gathered her sweater around her and put the cigarette to her lips and inhaled deeply, and then slowly exhaled a thin blue stream through her nostrils. The lawn had been recently mowed. It was lush and green in the shade of the house and the trees and burnt dry everywhere else. David had started cleaning up the garden, taking out the dead bean plants and the row of lettuce that had gone to seed, turning over the soil. Apart from the peas and the scarlet runner beans, which were still producing, the only crops left to be harvested were a few tough old zucchinis and the pumpkins, seven or eight big fat orange pumpkins lying in a welter of leaves. All at once a flock of starlings took off from a cedar tree at the end of the garden, their anxious startled song rising in the air, a slipshod aria. Arlene remembered how, when they'd first moved here, she'd felt like a complete vagabond, always packing up the china and the linen and moving on. And now look: this was the twelfth summer they'd lived in this house. This was their home. They'd settled down here because of the children; children needed stability, David said. They needed a home and parents and schools and friends. If she did anything precipitate, she knew the whole structure would turn out to have been illusory, a lot of wishful thinking. But wasn't it true, as Brian said, that she had some kind of responsibility to herself, a responsibility to whatever glittering unknown landscape lay beyond the trees at the back of her yard, the cities she'd only read about, full of people whose faces she'd encountered only in dreams. Soon it would be autumn. She always felt like this at this time of year, haunted by the thought that there was some other life she was entitled to, some other place she was meant to be and had to reach before winter came. She dropped her cigarette butt on the patio and ground it out with her foot, then kicked it into the flower bed. She went back into the kitchen and filled the sink with hot water and started washing the breakfast dishes. And while standing there at the sink, the clock ticking on the wall in front of her, the sharp scent of late summer wafting in through the open French doors, Gerard's words came to her, his lovely antiquated words, their sweet undercurrents of sense, of meaning, their dangerous, absurd music. *And the Birde readie to fall out, which no doubt were the foules called Barnakles.*

CHAPTER THIRTY

Arlene found herself going through a sort of rehearsal, to see what it would feel like if she were actually getting ready to leave. She went through the rooms, trying to decide what she would take, what few small things she couldn't bear to leave behind. And also what she wouldn't be able to take and would have to get used to living without. Her children's school pictures, for example, lined up on the piano and the bookcase. All these versions of her children, an archive of children with gaps in their teeth, with braces on their teeth, their faces changing yearly as they assembled themselves into the adults they would become. Catherine had the darkest hair, the lightest eyes. Matt had a freckled nose. Diane looked most like her. The truth was, all three of them looked a lot alike. But then, how much genetic variation could there be in the offspring of second cousins, or whatever she and David were? In any case, there were too many photographs for her to pack up and take with her, and they would make her sad, anyway; they would be a constant reminder of what she'd given up. If she gave anything up. And she wouldn't. This was just a rehearsal; a game of make believe: What if? What if? And what else would have to stay, under the mysterious conditions of her departure? Her good china, which had belonged to her Grandmother Myles. She couldn't pack along boxes of china, and it wasn't the kind of stuff she'd ever use again, anyway. Not in the kind of pared-down simple life she and Brian would share. She wasn't a bourgeoisie, not that she was entirely sure what the word meant. But she wasn't concerned with the value of property above all else. She never had been, never. Although here was a white porcelain horse with a beautiful, flowing sculpted mane—a present from Matt and Catherine on her birthday, the year before Diane was born. She did value this. It was too fragile, too large, unfortunately, for her to remove it from its place on the mantelpiece. It would have to stay, and every time David or one of the children saw it, they would be overcome with sadness. Or with anger. They would think of her, and curse her name. No, it wouldn't come to that. She wouldn't let it.

Sunlight was coming in through the front windows and falling across the floor and the wall, these lovely lazy bands of the most benign-looking placid yellow light. And it was quiet in the house, which made her move softly, her feet bare, her hair, damp from the shower, covering her shoulders like a cold heavy cape. She felt a little like a tourist visiting a museum. Inspecting the exhibits. She imagined a running commentary: The family that occupied this house. Typical middle-class family—petit bourgeois, if you wish to use such a term, and some do—there are individuals who think in such a fashion, Arlene thought, smiling inwardly—two parents, three children. Average in most respects. Privileged. Note the colonial-style furniture, heavily in vogue during this era. The rock-maple coffee table and end-tables, the frilled lampshades. Overall the effect is a little much, isn't it? The walnut dining-room suite clearly doesn't match; you have to wonder what the owners were thinking of when they chose their furniture. And look—a lacquered Chinese bowl on the dining-room buffet, with three keys in it. What could the keys be for? One key, as far as Arlene knew, was for the door to the cellar; one was for the freezer. And the third? She couldn't remember. Oh, yes, she could. It was for the suitcase David had bought when he went to an accountant's convention in Vancouver just before Christmas. It was an expensive leather suitcase, and he'd said it was a good investment, because one day they were going to take a real vacation and go to Europe. She could have gone with him to Vancouver; he'd wanted her to go, but she'd made some excuses about the kids and school Christmas events. She picked up the key to the cellar door and then dropped it back into the bowl. The bowl was a gift Eunice had brought back from a holiday in San Francisco years ago, when she was returning from a trip to see Grandmother Myles in San Clemente. Grandmother Myles was no longer alive. She was buried beside Grandfather Myles in the Episcopal cemetery in San Clemente. Arlene's family was getting smaller all the time. All she had, beside Eunice and an aunt she scarcely ever heard from, was David, the children, and David's family. All those wholesome, rock-solid Gamlins and Green-

420

woods who thought the best of a person, no matter what, and refused to listen to gossip or smutty stories.

Last week, Eunice had spent a few days with them. She'd brought her new Buick Skylark Sports Coupe over on the ferry, and she'd driven down the Island Highway and surprised them by pulling into the driveway and leaning on the horn. They'd all run outside to see who it was. The new car was red, and Eunice had been wearing red slacks and a white-and-red striped blouse. She was so proud of her car; she sat in it with the windows down and waited for everyone to go outside and admire it. She demonstrated how everything in it was electric, the windows, the doors, the seats. Then she'd taken the children off for a ride to the Dairy Queen in Duncan, where she'd bought them each a soft ice-cream cone. They told Arlene later that they'd had to eat standing beside the car in the parking lot, even though it was cold and starting to rain, so that they wouldn't get the interior of the new car messy. In any case, Eunice had wanted to tell Arlene and David in person that she and her business partners had put the dress store on the market. It was getting harder all the time to keep up with changing trends in the ready-to-wear trade, Eunice had said. No one wanted to pay for quality anymore. No one even bothered to dress properly, half the time. People were getting terribly lax. You saw it everywhere, she said. It was all jeans and T-shirts, long cotton skirts, hippie outfits. She'd noticed the trend on the ferry, coming over to the island. Clothes were becoming practically disposable items, things you wore once or twice and then discarded. And besides, the regular customers at Natalie's Dress Shoppe were intimidated by the hippies and panhandlers who had started to congregate in front of the dress store. They littered the sidewalk and made a lot of noise and generally pissed everyone off, Eunice said. She'd go outside and try to shoo them away politely, and they'd tell her to keep cool, hang loose, and then they had the nerve to ask her if she had any spare change. She'd never had to contend with anything like it before. But, apart from all that, she and Rosemary and Olive were getting tired of being tied to the store. Rosemary wanted to travel and Olive was going to move in with her daughter and start a home craft business, whatever that was. That's all right, you can relax, she'd said to Arlene. I'm not about to move in with you. Later, before she left, Eunice cornered Arlene in the kitchen and asked her if she was all right. "You're awfully thin," she said. "You seem all on edge. I hope your nerves are all right. Bad nerves are a family failing. I know, I've suffered all my life. Maybe you should get a tonic to build you up. Or, better yet, come back home with me for a few days. We can order in Chinese food and pizza and watch late movies on TV and go shopping. It would make a nice break for you."

Arlene had told her mother she couldn't leave, she had too much to do, the children needed her. And now here she was, going through her own house with a calculating eye, trying to think what she'd take with her if she were leaving forever. She didn't consider taking her children. It hadn't even entered her mind to take them. She couldn't envision a place for them. In any kind of life she might make for herself beyond this house, this marriage, this family, she couldn't find a place for them. They would have to remain behind with their father. Like Anna Karenina's little boy. What was his name? She tried to remember. She'd read the book so many times, she must know the child's name. She went to the bookcase to get her copy of *Anna Karenina*, but it wasn't there. The book would have to come with her if she ever went away. It was one thing she definitely wanted to keep. Her book, and what else? A few items of clothing, her pearl necklace, the one David had given her for her twenty-fifth birthday.

How could her book be missing? What if it was lost? She would have to replace it, but it wouldn't be the same. She wanted the book her Grandfather Myles had given her. It had been her companion all these years, whenever she was lonely and unhappy and had nothing else to read. Why was it that reading was better than life? she wondered.

At last she located the book in Catherine's bedroom, on her desk. Obviously Catherine was reading it. Arlene remembered how, when she was a little girl, Catherine had wanted to know what all the words meant. Tell me what this means, she'd say, stabbing at the page with a stubby finger. Arlene had said, Go away, leave me alone. She'd been cruel, she supposed, but she hadn't meant to be; it was just that Catherine had been the most exasperating child. Arlene sat down on the edge of Catherine's bed with the book, and, by coincidence, it fell open at a passage where Anna and Karenin were arguing over the child, whose name was Seryozha. Karenin was saying that he had *lost his love for his son*, because of Anna. Everything was Anna's fault. This was the point in the book where Anna told Karenin that soon she would give birth to another child, which he of course knew was not his. *I cannot change anything*, Anna had whispered to Karenin. It was what Anna believed.

Out of the most untenable situations at least one thing could be salvaged. By at least one individual. This was something Arlene believed with all her heart. It was true in real life as much as it was in fiction. Consider this scene: Ann Karenina had given birth to her daughter. She was very ill. She was in her husband's house; Karenin's house. Karenin stood at her bedside working out what seemed to him the intricacies of Christian forgiveness and how they were to be applied in this difficult case. He himself felt calm and at peace. Anna, poor Anna, was burning up with fever.

It will pass, it will all pass: Words of comfort, spoken by Anna's seducer. This was earlier, before the birth of their child. Anna regarded him without emotion. His "cold cheeks." His "cropped hair." Poor Anna. Why was she never able to stop and think what she was doing? The problem was, she hadn't ever learned to think of herself first, to put her own interests first. Instead, she did what she thought was right in terms of the human heart, which she elevated in her mind to the position of a divinity. Passion. Romance. She was so defenceless. Foolish. Vulnerable. Extraordinary.

So. Here was Anna, sick, febrile, not expected to live for another day. She had puerperal fever, an infectious condition that occurred in the nineteenth century with alarming frequency following childbirth, and that, as the doctor announced to Karenin in a matter of fact way, was fatal in ninety-nine percent of cases. Anna was a wretched figure, pitiable, lying there in her husband's well-run house. And who, really, had given birth? Not Anna, when you thought about it. No. It was Karenin. It might as well have been Karenin; he was glowing, magnanimous, forgiving, solicitous, indeed nearly maternal in his solicitousness. Even Anna, in the state she was in, was aware of these qualities in Karenin. His kindness, thoughtfulness. The child is not getting enough to eat, he said to her, out of his great concern. The wet nurse is no good; I will have to look for someone else. He was viewing everything, the situation, the illegitimate child, his wife's lamentable indiscretions, the silently suffering, shamefaced lover, who was slumped alone on a chair in Anna's sitting room—even the lilac ribbons on the nurse's cap—Karenin viewed all these things with the same graceful acceptance, the same benign, sustaining sense of charity and temperance. He was real, he had discovered his real self, and Vronsky was not real because he had, so far in his life, acquired nothing that was valuable or of use.

Arlene lay down on Catherine's bed with her head on the pillow and the book on her chest. In this position, she began to imagine she could share her daughter's thoughts, her dreams. There was an optimistic, serene quality to her daughter, Arlene thought. Catherine was nothing like the little girl she'd been, full of energy and a wild, irrepressible insistence on getting her own way. Catherine was mature for her age; dependable. In some ways, that was. In other ways, of course, she was remarkably immature. Arlene could sense that she wanted to remain a child a little longer. But she couldn't. She would have to grow up, just as Arlene had. What would it be like to be seventeen again? Arlene wouldn't have the courage to find out, even if it were possible. She had been seventeen the summer she met David. Only seventeen, and the only thing she could think to do with her life was to get married! Eunice had made a ceremony out of showing her the things she was going to give Arlene: Grandmother Myles' cast-off blue-flowered china set, silver sugar tongs, a silver cruet set, a lace tablecloth. The way Eunice had spread these items out on the kitchen table at their house had seemed like a challenge to Arlene: I dare you to do better with your life than I've done, she seemed to be saying. I dare you to have as happy a marriage as George and I had. What Eunice in fact said was, I wish you luck. It had seemed to Arlene, at the time, more like a threat. It occurred to Arlene that Eunice had been almost exactly the same age then as Arlene was now. To her, at the time, Eunice had seemed old, her life more or less finished, and yet in reality she'd still been young enough to marry again, even to have children. Why hadn't she? Arlene wondered. Perhaps she'd been waiting for Duff to return, but he never had. A few years ago Eunice had told Arlene she'd had some bad news: she'd heard Duff was dead. She wasn't able to find out how he had died; she had just got a brief note from his daughter. The last time she'd seen him had been in California, when she was visiting her parents. She'd telephoned him and they'd made a date for lunch. She had dabbed at her eyes and held onto Arlene's hand. "Isn't it strange how someone can be so much a part of your life, and then simply disappear? For a while, we were like a real little family, weren't we?" she had said. "The three of us. We were happy, though, weren't we?" she persisted. "We had fun, didn't we?" If Arlene had said as far as she was concerned it had been the worst time of her entire life, Eunice would have been shocked. Her blue eyes would have filled with tears, the tip of her nose would have reddened in dismay. And so Arlene had merely said she was sorry to hear about Duff. And Eunice had sniffed and said, Oh, well, he was years older than me, you know.

Arlene thought she might stay like this, prone on her daughter's bed, for the rest of the day, or at least until Catherine got home. Asleep, she wouldn't have to go on trying to decide what she would take with her if, when, she left. Asleep, she would be free of the endless repetitive thoughts in her brain, the insoluble problems she'd given herself to work out. Then, just as she was beginning to drift off to sleep, she heard the kitchen door open. She made herself get up and, holding onto her head, which was starting to ache, she went to the top of the stairs. "Catherine, is that you?" she called. There was no answer, but she could hear someone moving around in the kitchen. When she got downstairs, she found David with the fridge door open, looking for something to eat.

"I was upstairs," she said. "You scared me. I must have fallen asleep for a minute. I was beginning to think someone had broken in."

"Oh, sorry," he said. He held up a plate of leftover roast beef and lifted the waxed paper wrap to take a look at it. "Is this still good?" he said.

"I think so. We just had it for supper the night before last." She was looking at the dirty dishes piled up on the counter, the crumbs littering the floor, the newspapers and discarded pages of someone's math homework on the table.

Her skirt was crumpled; her hair was unbrushed. She didn't think she'd even washed her face yet. She started to pick things up. She carried a plate to the kitchen counter and deposited some toast crusts, sticky with marmalade, in the garbage can under the sink.

"Just leave that stuff," David said. "I'll get it later."

"Didn't you take a lunch with you this morning?" Arlene said.

"I left it at the office," David said. He was standing next to her, wiping off part of the counter, so that he could make his sandwich. He opened the bread box and took out a loaf of bread. He put two slices of bread on a plate and started spreading them with Dijon mustard. "I just got offered a promotion," he said. "I came home to tell you about it. It's a senior management job at head office in Vancouver. In the accounting department. A good job. More money." He filled the kettle with water. "Is tea okay with you?" he said. She saw that he was staring at her hands, at the way she was gripping the counter, her fingers white with effort. She was holding on so that she wouldn't fall over. "And?" she said. "What are you going to do?"

"It's done," he said. "I've already said yes. It was the only answer I could give, under the circumstances. Do we have any lettuce?"

"In the fridge," she said. "In a bowl." She let go of the counter and walked over to the glass doors. He'd got it wrong; he was making a mistake. She was the one who was leaving. Not him, not the children. She was leaving them behind. They were staying put, where they belonged, in this house.

CAROL WINDLEY

"What about the children?" she said. "What about school? Catherine's graduating in June."

"I know. But she'll adjust. I think it would be a good idea to put the house on the market pretty soon, though. And we'll have to go house hunting in Vancouver. That'll be exciting, won't it? All these years you wanted to move to Vancouver, and now you get your chance."

He cut two slices of roast beef and placed them on the bread. He added a lettuce leaf, a slice of tomato.

"But David, I thought you liked it here. I thought you wanted to stay."

"This seems like the right time, I guess. It's a good job, a wonderful opportunity. Not the kind of thing you can turn down. I had an interview when I was in Vancouver just before Christmas. I didn't tell you about it, because frankly, I thought my chances of getting the job were slim. Do you want a cup of tea? Sit down and I'll bring you one."

She sat down. He put a cup of tea in front of her and then he sat down with his sandwich. "You don't seem very happy," he said.

"I'm surprised," she said. "That's all."

"Well, to tell you the truth, it's a position Howard sort of wanted, although as far as I know, he never got around to doing anything about it. Poor Howard. He wasn't very happy when he heard I'd got it. I thought it was a good idea if I stayed out of his way for a couple of hours."

Two days later, on a Friday evening, Arlene went to Caroline's house to get something Brian had supposedly left for her. Not a book, he'd told her on the phone; just something he'd like her to have. She had called him, using the phone in the bedroom, trying to dial quietly, praying no one would pick up the phone in the front hall. She had to whisper. Brian kept saying, Arlene, I can't hear you, are you there? Can't you speak up just a little, please? No, she said, I can't. She had thought, impatiently: Where does he imagine I am when I'm not with him? Does he have any idea what my life is like?

On one occasion when she was talking to Brian, David had walked into the bedroom and she'd slammed the receiver down hard and turned to him, her heart beating ridiculously fast, and had said, Wrong number, I guess. Or else it's another one of those nuisance calls. She had laughed, a false idiotic laugh that had remained awkwardly in the air, and she had picked up her hairbrush from the dresser and started pulling it through her hair as hard as she could. She felt like a stage actress with a starring role in a farce. She could see David in the mirror. He looked faded, sad, worn. It was difficult not to compare him to Brian, who was full of a wild romantic kind of energy that seemed salvaged from a previous and more imaginative age. After a moment, David had said, I wasn't aware we were getting nuisance calls, and walked out of the room. She hadn't had the slightest idea why he'd come in in the first place. Unless he'd heard her pick up the phone and start dialling. Unless he was watching her, which wasn't likely, was it? David wasn't that kind of person. At least, he had never seemed like that kind of person. Perhaps he had changed. Perhaps he was moving them all to Vancouver because of his suspicions, because of jealousy, envy, wild surmises—except they weren't surmises, were they? What was she to do? She had picked up the phone again as soon as the door closed. "I can't talk," she had said to Brian. "But I have to see you sometime soon. I have some news to tell you."

At Caroline's house she sat close to the fireplace, hunched forward, her elbows on her knees, her chin resting on her knuckles. She was staring at the flames, the brilliant heart of the fire, and then she heard herself saying the most extraordinary things—how for years she'd felt like a prisoner in the town, she'd been frightened of the town, as if it had a personality. As if it hated her, and how could that be? The things that had happened to her since she moved here. "You know how some people talk about lines of energy passing through a certain place, and how these lines can affect what happens," she said to Caroline. "And they affect different people in different ways. Am I making any sense? It was something I read somewhere. I don't even know what I'm talking about, do I? You must think I'm out of my head. Anyway, I've been quite happy here lately. Everything's changed." She glanced up at Caroline, and then looked away. She rubbed her knees with the palms of her hands. How much did Caroline know, she wondered.

Caroline put the tea tray down on a hassock in front of Arlene and poured her out a cup and said, "I'm going to put sugar in your tea. I think it'll be good for you. When was the last time you had anything to eat, dear?"

Caroline took a Kleenex out of her coat pocket—she had kept her coat on, she was cold, shivering—and wiped her eyes. She said, "I had dinner. I'm fine, really. This is ridiculous. I do apologise. I'm not usually an emotional person.

To tell you the truth, I'm cold as ice. I have no real feelings whatsoever. Ask my mother. She'll tell you. She used to shout at me when I was a girl—You're no daughter of mine, she'd say. Where'd I get a pasty-faced daughter like you?" She stopped, horrified, and stared at Caroline. "I'm sorry, Caroline," she said. "I should have stayed at home. I'm upset about something. Just ignore me."

Caroline gave her a package wrapped in white tissue paper. "Why don't you open this?" she said. "This should cheer you up. I love getting presents. I'll leave you on your own. I just finished making an orange loaf. We'll have some in a minute. Go on, Arlene, dear. Drink your nice hot tea and relax."

"Thank you, Caroline," Arlene said. She smiled. She was grateful; she was full of gratitude. The fire was warming her face, her hands. She felt human again. It was wrong to give in to despair, she knew it was.

Alone, Arlene removed the wrapping paper from a small box. She folded the tissue paper neatly and set it on the arm of the chair. Her fingers were trembling. She took the lid off the box and there, inside a great mass of crumpled tissue paper she found a miniature crystal sailing ship, an exquisite little thing. A tall ship, its delicate masts and glass sails and the delicate prow turning blood red when she held it in her palm, in front of the fire. The ship seemed to dance in the light of the flames. There was also a note inside the box. She put the crystal ship down on the tea tray and read: *I thought this would make a suitable—and certainly elegant!— means of travel for those of us unafraid to put our whole faith in the power of the wind! I don't know how old it is, I found it in an antique store and it immediately reminded me that we must—we owe it to ourselves!—to be as pliable and as eager as the wind. Keep this, Arlene, and follow only the truth that is in your heart.*

She read it again. It reminded her of the notes she and Iris Shaw had written to each other when they were school girls. It reminded her of the books she used to read when she was a girl. It made her think of the sentiments she had tried to write in the journal her father had urged her to keep. She felt as if the crystal sailing ship had long ago, perhaps in a dream, taken her off to a frozen sea, like the ship in *The Ancient Mariner.* She read the note a third time, searching for a word, a phrase, she had overlooked, although she didn't know what she hoped to find, what it was she wanted. She got up and put the note on the fire. The flames warmed her. She felt like kneeling on the hearth and waiting patiently until she'd turned into a pillar of salt. Then she sat down and stared hard at the crystal sailing ship.

"It's lovely," Caroline said when she came back into the room. "Don't tell me anything about it, dear. Don't talk about it. It's meant for you. It's yours." She was rubbing almond-scented hand lotion into her hands. She was, she said, waiting for the kettle to boil so that she could make another pot of tea.

"Oh, you shouldn't bother, not for me," Arlene said. She laughed a little and held up the crystal sailing ship. "Do you like it? Do you really think it's lovely? I wonder if you could keep it here for me? Would you mind?"

"Of course I wouldn't mind. We'll put it right here, shall we, next to my lamp? I have a picture that dates from the 1880s, of sailing ships like that one at anchor in the harbour. In those days, and for a long time afterwards, the sawmill here was the most productive in B. C. This town was a hub of commerce."

Arlene couldn't think of a response. She couldn't think of a thing to say. She'd been planning to leave everything in her house behind, all the furnishings and books and most of her clothes and just walking out. She'd meant to do it for love. She'd considered leaving her children behind, for God's sake. Was a crystal sailing ship delivered to her through a third party supposed to compensate for that? And what was Brian really trying to say about her, about the kind of person who would want to receive such a pretty, decorative, fragile gift, such a symbolic gift, as he seemed to intend it? She remembered an expression she'd heard: He who travels fastest travels alone. Something like that. Who had said it all the time? Who had repeated it to her? She remembered: It had been Duff. He'd been speaking of himself, his way of life. She got up and reached for her coat. Caroline said, "Oh, you can't leave. Aren't you going to stay and have another cup of tea and some orange loaf? Don't go yet."

"Thank you so much, Caroline, but I have to go," Arlene said. "I have to make sure the kids are getting ready for bed." This wasn't true. The kids could get themselves to bed. And besides, David was at home with them. Nevertheless, she wanted to get home. She stood up and gave Caroline a kiss on the side of her face. Caroline would look after everything, she thought; she would make sure no harm came to anyone. Arlene did have the sense that Caroline was a sort of beneficent fairy godmother, always at work arranging events, offering sanctuary of a sort, keeping evil at bay.

Chapter Thirty-one

Catherine was in the kitchen when Abby called by on her way to work. Abby had a summer job as a cashier at the grocery store on Ashlar Street. She wore a skimpy black skirt and a red smock with her name stitched on the pocket. Her hair was in a stubby braid. She had painted her nails scarlet and wore big gold hoops in her ears. Why not have a little fun? That was her attitude, she said. Catherine had seen her at work, perched on a stool at the checkout counter, her fingers flying over the keys of the cash register as she chattered in a breezy off-hand way to the customers. "How's it going?" she'd say. "Hot out, isn't it?" and "My what a little cutie," to the babies propped up in the shopping carts. She chewed gum, partly, she said, because she wanted to emulate the head cashier, Laura, who was noted for sticking pencils in her permed hair and constantly shifting a wad a gum from one side of her mouth to the other, and partly to disguise the fact that she, Abby, was smoking cigarettes and occasionally doing a little dope in the evenings, or in the afternoon, before work, just a little weed, she said, if she happened to run into her friends. She had a whole collection of friends who lived in an old farm house in Valenzuela Bay, people in their late teens and twenties, male and female, who had migrated over from Vancouver. They scared Catherine half to death and fascinated her, at the same time. Catherine had the feeling they put up with her because she was Abby's friend, but she could tell they thought she was weird, square, completely out of it, and she guessed it was true, she was. Next to Abby, Catherine felt like a dumb kid, an amateur, a know-nothing. Abby said all she needed was some different clothes and a different attitude. When Abby left work, she said, she ducked into the phone booth outside the post office on Ashlar Street, and presto change-o, just like the man of steel, she had herself a different personality. It was easy for her, she said, because she was a natural-born actress. Her friends didn't know whether she was a freak or a total dipstick, which was fine with her. It was her policy to keep people off-balance. "I didn't mean you, Catherine," she said. "You like me either way, don't you?"

Catherine dumped the packet of powdered eggs into a bowl and added lukewarm water and stirred the mixture with a fork. She was remembering that Abby had run away from home two times. At least, she called it running away. Once, she went to Vancouver on the ferry and ended up spending the day with Catherine's grandmother at her dress store, and the second time, one day after school in March, she walked up River Road to Hazel Kavanaugh's house and begged Hazel to let her stay. She told Catherine she put her head on Hazel's shoulder and cried, and said she couldn't take it, her parents did nothing but shout at her, she lived in a house filled with hate, and finally Hazel gave her dinner and let her sleep on the bed-chesterfield in the living room. Abby described to Catherine how she lay awake all night, trying to adjust herself around the lumps in the mattress, listening to the sound of Norm snoring in the bedroom, traffic going past on the Island Highway, truck drivers applying their air brakes as they approached the lights at the intersection of the highway and River Road. A neon sign above the gas pumps at the garage where Norm worked cast a dire blue glow through the Fiberglas drapes onto the walls and ceiling. Ghosts and shadows. Pale tense wraiths that resembled her mother and father pacing through the rooms of their house, waiting for her to come home so they could scream at her. At last she'd got up and gone into the kitchen and searched through the cupboards until she found a bottle of red Okanagan wine, and she'd opened it and consumed about half, then left the bottle open on the kitchen counter and went back to bed. Finally, at about four, she'd fallen asleep and almost immediately, at six-thirty, she had been woken by the sound of a car pulling up on the gravel outside. Catherine could picture it: the front yard at Hazel's was nothing but gravel. There were three wood steps going up to a front door someone had once painted yellow. Hazel and Norm rented the house from Norm's boss, who owned the garage. In any case, it was Abby's father at the door. She heard him say, "Have you seen anything of my daughter, Hazel?" Hazel, who had rushed to the door holding her housecoat together, little pincurls all over her head, said,

"Oh, Mr. Glass, I'm so sorry. I tried to get her to phone you last night but she didn't want to disturb you." Abby imitated Hazel being apologetic and obsequious. She imitated Norm poking his head around the living-room door to see what was going on, the collar of his pyjamas sticking up around his ears.

That morning, Abby said, her father drove her home in silence. It was still dark. When he stopped the car in front of their house, he said, "As long as you're living under my roof, Abby, I want you to treat your mother with respect. You know she worries herself sick about you. God knows why, but she does." Abby told this part of the story with relish. She sat on the stool beside the kitchen counter and watched Catherine finding bowls and measuring cups to make the Angel Food cake. Abby described how her father had unlocked the door of the house and waited until she'd walked inside. She had her parka on over the night-dress Hazel had lent her; she was carrying her clothes and school books in a paper bag from the store where she worked. Her father slammed the door shut and put his hand around her neck and practically slammed her up against the wall and said he'd wring her neck for her if she didn't shape up. He'd said, Good God, your breath reeks. What in the hell have you been drinking? She'd dropped the paper bag smack on the floor at his feet and he'd jumped back and called her a slut, a pig, and said, pick up your mess and get ready for school. Meanwhile, in the kitchen, her mother was listening to the radio and frying bacon. She had her hair tied up with a yellow ribbon. When Abby walked in, she'd said, "Hello, darling." "Can you imagine? said Abby. She told

Catherine her family reminded her more each day of an Ingmar Bergman movie.

Abby told Catherine that as soon as she'd saved enough money from her lousy part-time job, she was going back to England to live with a guy she'd met there called Nigel. Nigel worked on a fashion magazine. She had met him in a park in London last summer. He was eating his lunch out of a paper bag and staring at her. She was sitting on a bench opposite, having escaped from her parents for a brief, wonderful time. So she told Catherine. Imagine, she said, if Nigel got her a job working for the magazine. All he needed, he said, was a word from her and it would be arranged. Abby had a photograph of Nigel striding toward her. He was wearing a jacket with no collar and ultra-skinny trousers. He had a neck like the watery stem of a tuberous plant, a thin face with the features all crowded around a pointed nose. He looked to Catherine both predatory and needy. He was twenty-three. Abby, who thought he was "cute," wrote to him once a week, ending each letter with a little heart beside her name. Catherine could see that Nigel was meant to rescue Abby from the prospect of going to some boring college to acquire what Julia Glass called a good grounding. Catherine, on the other hand, couldn't wait. Her idea of paradise was to go to school forever, to live alone, alone with books and ideas. She would acquire reading glasses and wear tweed suits and spend her days at a library, a mode of being she understood—from reading her mother's Tolstoy book—was essentially *antinihilistic*, a word she loved and couldn't stop repeating in her head. Antinihilistic. She didn't even know if she was pronouncing it correctly. In any case, a life of reading, a classical education, would enable her to take up the duties and responsibilities of a rigorous life, even though—as some of Tolstoy's characters insisted—even though she was a girl and therefore suited to a future as a wet nurse at a foundling hospital in nineteenth-century Russia.

Catherine had looked up the word nihilism in a dictionary. A thin cold word, dangerous, a sharp needle stitching a silver letter "i" all through it. It seemed to her that the word antinihilistic must carry within it a negative force capable of repudiating an even more powerfully negative force. This brought to her mind a scene in which she, her sister and brother and her parents were standing in an open field looking up at the sky. The sky was empty of everything except itself, its clarity and vastness. They stood aghast and chilled to see that this was so, this was where they'd found themselves, unendingly, at that moment and forever after. Then she pictured her mother reading, the familiar pose her mother adopted when reading at the kitchen table, her head resting on one hand, her eyes taking in the words on the page at some ferocious lightning speed, her free hand turning the pages until the entire book was consumed.

Catherine wanted to go away, she wanted to grow up and free herself from her family, from the exhausting work of being part of this family, and yet at the same time she was afraid to leave. Everything was changing. There was a For Sale sign outside on the front lawn, although no one, so far, had shown any interest in buying their house. Diane had pulled the sign out of the lawn twice and dumped it behind the garden shed in the backyard. Her father had told her if she did it again, she'd suffer the consequences. He was smiling as he spoke, of course, because no one ever got really angry with Diane. "I don't care," Diane said, stamping her foot. "I'm not moving." Catherine had tried to console her by saying, "Maybe it won't happen. Maybe we won't have to move." Her father said, "Look, we are going to move. You should think of it in a positive light. It's a chance to start fresh. It'll be exciting for all of us." He hadn't sounded entirely convinced himself. He turned away from them. He broke off speaking practically in mid-sentence and went downstairs to his darkroom. What Catherine heard in his voice was doubt, uncertainty, pain. She thought they had lived in this house for so long it belonged completely to them, as if it were a living thing they'd fed and loved and coaxed into existence. The trees and shrubs in the garden had grown until the house was nearly invisible from the road, and the neighbours seemed to have vanished behind a thicket of greenery. And it was getting quieter every day, a silent house. This morning, for example, it was absolutely silent, or had been, until Abby arrived. A tense, suspicious silence that made Catherine want to drop something on the floor or slam a cupboard door shut. This was because she was waiting for her mother to get back from another one of those trips she made, ostensibly to pick up milk and bread at the store. Diane was upstairs in her room, playing with a friend of hers called Shelley. Matt had gone out to play touch football at the elementary school. Her father was upstairs working at his desk. At least, she'd thought he was, but here he was, walking into the kitchen, not paying any attention to her and Abby. He went directly to the French doors and looked out. "Whose car is that in the driveway?" he said.

"Mine," Abby said. "Want me to move it? Is it in the way?"

"Oh, Abby," he said. "I didn't see you there. No, you don't need to move your car." He turned and stared at Abby, then said, "Catherine, your mother didn't take the car to go to the store?"

"No, she walked," Catherine said.

"She's been gone a long time, hasn't she?" he said.

"She left around ten, ten-fifteen," Catherine said.

"And now it's what, eleven forty-five," he said. "Since when does it take an hour and half to walk to the store and back?"

"I don't know," Catherine said, re-reading the directions on the cake mix box. The cake was to go with fresh strawberries she and Matt had picked the evening before. The berries had dropped from their stems into her fingers, perfectly ripe and firm, filling the air with a sweet upwelling of fragrance that had caught at the back of Catherine's throat and had, mysteriously, brought tears to her eyes. This was the first summer these plants, planted a couple of summers ago, had produced berries. Who was going to be eating them next year? Who would pick them on a warm summer's evening and the next morning eat them chilled with fresh cream in *their* kitchen, in the house that had once belonged to the Greenwood family.

"I have to get going," Abby said. "If I see your Mom, want me to tell her you're looking for her?"

"That's all right," Catherine said. "You don't need to." She couldn't help noticing how intently Abby had watched

Catherine's father as he walked out of the kitchen. Wasn't it true that Abby envied Catherine's family? Hadn't she said often enough that she wished Catherine's mother was her mother? Abby adored Catherine's mother. She called her Arlene and discussed fashions and hairstyles with her, and exchanged the names of cream rinses and face creams, because, Abby said, she and Arlene had the same kind of complexion, a normal complexion with slightly dry areas around the mouth and eyes. She thought there'd been some kind of mistake and she was the one who was Arlene's daughter, she'd say, smiling at Catherine in her evil concentrated fashion, trying—and succeeding, at times, Catherine had to admit—to make Catherine feel jealous, as if she was not pretty enough or sophisticated enough to be Arlene's real daughter. Abby would trade families any day, she'd said. Did that still hold true, Catherine wondered. Or was Abby's interest now confined to taking in all the details of what must look like a movie, a TV melodrama, as Eunice called it.

Two minutes after Abby had left, two boys, friends of Matt's, came to the front door to say that Matt had hurt himself playing touch football. Catherine told them to wait, and ran up the stairs and told her father. He was sitting at his desk with his hands clutching his hair, staring out the window. He stared at her blankly for a moment and then jumped up and ran downstairs. He told the boys to get in the car with him and they'd drive over to the school yard. He told Catherine to wait at home with Diane. What else was she going to do? She kept going to the window, looking out to see if her mother was coming down the road, but there was no one. Diane had come downstairs with her friend

Shelley. They were both holding onto their Barbie dolls and trailing little glittery doll costumes along with them. Seven-year-old girls with pigtails and knee-socks and skinny arms. Catherine wanted to gather them to her and hold onto them, and tell them to take her advice and not get any older. Diane asked Catherine if she and Shelley could have something to eat, and she made them a plate of graham crackers spread with butter and honey from Joan Mullis's bee hives. There wasn't any milk, so she gave them each a glass of orange juice. She sat at the table with them and listened as they invented lives for their dolls: Pretend my Barbie goes to California, Shelley said. Pretend my Barbie rescues a dog from a burning house, Diane said. A burning house? Catherine thought. She could tell Diane wasn't really concentrating on her dolls; she was waiting for their Dad to come home with Matt; she was waiting for their mother to come home and restore the situation to normal. Catherine, on the other hand, was afraid this was just the beginning of a whole series of disasters. She thought of all the terrible things that could have happened to Matt, like a concussion or a broken neck. Then her father phoned from the hospital to say that Matt had torn a muscle. Nothing was broken. When Catherine's father brought him home, he had an elastic bandage wrapped around his knee, and the doctor had given him a shot of some kind of pain killer that he said was making him feel mentally fogged out. Catherine's father helped Matt through the house to the living room, where Matt lowered himself onto the sofa.

"Does it hurt?" Catherine said.

"Sort of," Matt said. "I'm thirsty. My mouth is dry. Do we have any Coke?"

"We don't have anything," Catherine said. "Except some orange juice."

"I'll get you some Coke," Catherine's father said. "I'll go to the store and I'll try to find your mother. If she's on the same planet as the rest of us, which I doubt, to tell you the truth."

"I'd rather have Cream Soda, actually," Matt said. He lay back against a cushion and closed his eyes. "If you don't mind. Cream Soda instead of Coke."

Catherine's father had been to the store by the time Arlene finally walked in the front door, her hair all tangled by the wind, her face flushed from the sun. She closed the door quietly and then stood there in the dim hall light, blinking like some kind of small cornered animal, with a childish, vulnerable, guilty look on her face that had made Catherine want to laugh out loud in spite of the tension in the room. Her father had been sitting in a chair beside the sofa Matt was lying on. He had stood up very quickly and looked at Arlene for a moment without speaking. Then he said, "Where in the hell have you been, Arlene?"

Diane ran to her mother and Arlene looked down at the top of Diane's head as if she had no idea what she was supposed to do next. At last she put her arms around Diane and hugged her. Then she said, "Matt, what on earth has happened to you? Are you all right?"

"We've been to the hospital," Catherine's father said. "I don't know if you're interested in this or not. You never seem to be here when anything goes wrong, do you Arlene?"

Arlene was smoothing her hands over Diane's hair, petting her, soothing her. "Please, David," she said. "Don't be like that. Anyway, it's not true. I'm here, I'm always here." She took Diane's hand, and they went over to where Matt was lying on the sofa with a pillow under his knee. Arlene sat down on the edge of the coffee table and leaned over Matt, gathering her hair in one hand to keep it out of the way. Catherine heard her say, "Tell me what happened, darling. Tell me everything." She was patting his hand and murmuring, "You just rest, just lie there and rest. Have you had any lunch? I'll get you a sandwich. Would you like cheese or tuna fish?"

"I'm not hungry, Mom," Matt said. "Maybe later."

"Well," Arlene said, twisting part of her skirt in her hand. "I didn't mean to be gone for such a long time. I walked farther than I meant to. Well, I actually called in to see Caroline, and more time went by than I'd thought. You know how Caroline is when she starts talking."

"I don't, actually," Catherine's father said.

"She's lonely, I guess," Arlene said. She put her hand on Matt's forehead and Catherine could see how tender her touch was, how gentle. And they forgave her. They all forgave her, Catherine knew they did, and they believed every word she said and felt fortunate to have her back with them.

Matt was fourteen years old and nearly six feet tall. He was thin, pale; he tired easily; he got mysterious pains in his legs, in the joints of his arms, in his lower back, all of which were attributed to his having outgrown his strength. He had torn a muscle playing touch football, and the only cure was rest and keeping his weight off his leg. He had the use of a pair of crutches from the hospital, but he spent most of the first few days lying on the sofa in the living room reading a book by H. Rider Haggard that Eunice had given him for his birthday. Catherine knew he'd get better, there was nothing seriously wrong with him, and yet she worried that the torn muscle was a fabricated diagnosis, and that he really had some awful illness, bone cancer or something. She kept seeing in his willingness to succumb to his injury an almost cheerful pliancy, as if he'd come to terms with his fate. But if this were true, wouldn't she know? Wouldn't someone tell her? Her father believed in the truth. He said the truth was more important than anything else, it was the one constant against which everything else was measured. The truth was, she supposed, *antinihilistic.* She sat on the floor beside the sofa and Matt set his book aside and told her he'd been thinking, and maybe it would be a good thing for all of them if they moved. It would be kind of neat, wouldn't it, he said, to start over again at a new school. He'd had the same friends since he'd started grade one, he said, and it was getting to the point where he had hardly anything in common with most of them. And it might be fun to live in a city after living in a small town for most of his life. "You could go to university in Vancouver," he said. "You could live at home. And we could see Nana whenever we wanted. There would be lots of good things about it." His voice trailed off. Catherine looked at him. He was sitting at the kitchen table with a glass of milk and his book, and she was at the counter, filling the hollow centre of a stick of celery with

Cheez Whiz. Matt said it had occurred to him that it might be a natural process to uproot yourself every so often and move to a new location. It would be similar to the way the cells of the body renewed themselves every seven years. It would be like country music: you just gotta travel on. His eyes, as he spoke, were dark and lustrous and difficult to read. He cleared his throat and picked up his book without looking at it, and Catherine imagined that the real reason he wanted to make moving away sound like a good idea was that he was aware of how close their mother was to leaving them all. Like their father, Matt thought they could forestall her; they could scoop her up and move her to a different time-frame, a different universe, one where events could be replayed and fiddled with until everything ended up the way it was supposed to be.

Once Arlene made a cat's cradle from a length of blue wool. This was long ago, when Catherine was younger than Diane was now. Catherine remembered how her mother had held the wool up for her to see, and then she had wound it quickly around her fingers and pulled a loop up and through, and brought her hands apart, and there was the length of wool transformed into a seamless complicated pattern without beginning or end. But how was it a cat's cradle? It was full of holes. Her mother had laughed at her. Use your imagination, she had said.

This was something else Catherine remembered: at school, when she was in grade four, her friend Phoebe Sceats used to sit on the floor of the girls' patio at recess folding a piece of paper into triangles. She diligently printed fortunes inside each flap, pausing every now and then to expertly lick a finger. Then she added her own system of numbers to the outside edges of the flaps. Lots of girls knew how to make paper fortune-telling games, but Phoebe made them faster than anyone, and better. Her little blunt fingers manipulated the device at top speed until someone was given the chance to choose a number, and then Phoebe stopped and read out in an important, emphatic voice: *You will be rich! You will marry three times! You will have twelve children! You will climb Mt. Everest! You will live to a hundred! You will be a movie star!* In Phoebe's hands the future was never bad, nothing bad could happen to you no matter how long you lived or how far away from home you got. Every day, Catherine remembered, every day at school your fortune was different, and you had this amazing guarantee: You'd accomplish whatever you wanted, your heart's desire, your dearest wish was certain to come true. All you needed was a certain amount of time and luck.

That summer her father secretly made arrangements for Diane to spend two weeks with her grandparents in Summerland. He didn't tell Arlene until one Monday afternoon, when he came home from work. He threw his jacket over the back of a kitchen chair and immediately started saying that it seemed to him Diane should get to know her grandparents better. His parents were getting older, and his mother hadn't been well this past winter, he said, and he wanted Diane to spend some time with them while they were still able to enjoy her company. And while they were still living in the family home. His mother was going to give Diane his old bedroom.

Catherine was shredding iceberg lettuce at the kitchen counter, and her mother was standing beside her, removing the skin from an economy-sized package of chicken breasts. Catherine saw her go absolutely still, as if an electric shock had passed right through her body, and then she heard her draw her breath in sharply, and for a moment she was afraid her mother was going to do something drastic, like stab her father with the knife she'd used on the chicken, and Catherine couldn't help thinking how unhygienic that would be. But Arlene let the knife fall with a clatter onto the cutting board. Then she turned around and held out her slimy chicken-fat smeared hands like Lady Macbeth branded with incriminating, imaginary blotches of blood she couldn't wash away. Catherine almost laughed, imagining her mother suddenly reciting in a quaking voice, *all the / perfumes of Arabia will not sweeten this little / hand . . . .*

David stared at Arlene, his face impassive. It seemed to Catherine his expression was sending one message to her mother and his voice, which was cheerful, managing, good-natured, was sending another. He was telling her that he was going to take Diane over to the Vancouver Airport on Friday, and put her on a flight to Kelowna. The stewardess would look after her, and his parents would meet the plane and drive her to their house. It was all arranged, he said; he'd made most of the phone calls from work.

"You bastard," Arlene said.

David blinked. "I beg your pardon?" he said.

Arlene turned away from him and began rinsing her hands at the sink. She picked up a tea towel and dabbed her hands dry, and at the same time she said, "You can't make plans like that without talking to me first, David. What were you thinking of? Wait. I don't have to ask, do I? I know what you're thinking of, and how dare you try to get at me by sending my children all over the goddamned countryside?"

"Arlene," David said. "Calm down. You're talking nonsense." He glanced uneasily at Catherine, and said, "Would you excuse us, Catherine?"

"Stay right where you are," Arlene said. She came over to Catherine and grabbed her arm and held on tight. Catherine stood there, wanting to free herself from her mother's grip but afraid to move, and listened to everything her parents had to say to each other, her father trying to be conciliatory and reasonable; her mother so angry her voice was shaking. Diane was too young to travel alone, she said. Diane was shy, a baby, still; she needed her mother. She'd die of homesickness at David's parents' house, sleeping in his goddamned bedroom with those stupid pennants all over the walls, and soppy pictures of cocker spaniels and men fishing for trout.

Catherine could see that her father was trying not to laugh. He was angry, and he was close to laughing at the same time. Then he said, "Oh, come on Arlene. Diane is a normal seven-year-old girl. She's anything but shy; where did you get that from?"

"She's my daughter," Arlene said. "I know what she's like."

"She's mine, too," David said. "She's my daughter as much as she is yours."

"Stop it," Catherine said. "Please stop fighting. Can't you two stop fighting?"

Arlene became quiet suddenly. She let go of Catherine's arm. She said in a low voice, "You're trying to sell my house and get rid of my children. I know what you're doing." Then she reached out and picked up a plastic tumbler from the counter and threw it at the sink, or at least Catherine thought she was aiming at the sink. But the tumbler hit the window and shattered the glass. Suddenly there was glass mixed in with all the clean dishes in the draining rack, and glass lying beside the chicken breasts and the knife. Who would have thought there was so much glass in that old window, Catherine thought. Who would have thought? The jagged vacant space seemed to let in an unusual amount of light, a cold hurtful light that forced Catherine to see her parents more distinctly than she normally did. Her father looked unexpectedly old; his hair was getting thin, she saw; there were lines around his eyes and mouth; he'd gained a little weight around his waist, and the way he was standing, his shoulders slumped and his chest caved in as if something had knocked the wind out of him, made him look vulnerable, almost frail. She'd always known her father was ten years older than her mother, but for the first time she was able to see what the difference in age meant. Her mother looked terribly young. She was skinny and distracted, wringing her hands and looking down at the glass around her feet. She raised her hands and covered her face, then took her hands away and said, "I didn't mean for that to happen."

"Jesus, Arlene," David said. "Was that necessary?"

"I'm sorry, I'm so sorry," Arlene was saying.

David said, "Being sorry isn't much of a help, is it, Arlene? Just—let's clean this up. We'll just clear up this mess."

"Yes," said Arlene. "We'll just clear it up. It was an accident."

She lifted one foot then set it down tentatively, glass crunching beneath her shoe. She stood there, watching Catherine as she helped her father sweep glass up from around her feet.

"Look, Arlene," her father said. "Why don't you go upstairs and have a bath or something. Make sure you don't have any glass on you."

"Decontaminate myself, you mean?" Arlene said. She took a few steps, then stopped and examined the soles of her sandals, grasping an ankle in her hand and brushing at each one before she walked out of the kitchen, not hesitantly, as before, but briskly, leaving Catherine and her father in silence amid the debris.

CHAPTER THIRTY-TWO

Joan Mullis, gowned and veiled, gloved and booted, walks across a field of couch grass and buttercups toward her city of hives. It is a hot, cloudless summer day. The air is filled with the hypnotic late-summer sound of cicadas. When she approaches her bees, Joan tells Catherine, she imagines herself drawing inward, becoming as narrow and as fine as a beam of light. Her mind empties itself of distractions. She feels, she says, like an acolyte in a mysterious cult, or at least as she imagines such an acolyte would feel. And, in a way, beekeeping is like belonging to a cult, she tells Catherine: beekeeping takes over your life. Whereas before she had only herself to worry about, really, and the changing seasons were merely noted in passing, now, as a beekeeper, she has to think about what is coming up, inclement weather, whether or not pesticides are being used on neighbouring land, and, if so, what kind, and what damage they could do, potentially, to her bees. Is there going to be a drought, a long period of rain, a hard, cold winter? Everything is more difficult, and more important. In addition, Joan says, bees make you poetic. I know it sounds silly, she says, laughing, but it's quite true; bees somehow endow you with a sense of the poetic. Because of their strangeness. For example: Inside the hive, a worker bee newly returned from finding a source of nectar, clover, say, or a clump of sweetly-scented wildflowers, performs an elaborate ritualised dance for the other bees. This dance is not something a bee learns; it's part of the bee's biological makeup, like its size and the sound it makes when it's airborne, and the marvellous shape of its eyes. The distinctive choreography of this dance is designed to convey precise information as to the distance from the hive to the source of food, and the location of the food, its precise angle from the position of the sun. The dance is not performed for pleasure, or for entertainment. Oh, no. It is entirely serious and purposeful. It has to be: a honeybee can starve to death in the space of a single day. A single day! Imagine a life so fragile, so ephemeral, and yet so sturdy and productive, and, indeed, full of poetry. Would Catherine like to know more? Well, a colony such as this one contains about 10,000 worker bees, a single queen, and as many as 3,000 drones. The drones are male. The queen bee is nothing less than a factory, with nurse-bees feeding her and feeding her, stuffing her full of sweetness and energy at one end while she lays her multitudes of eggs at the other end. The domestication of the honeybee began only a little over a hundred years ago, with the invention of the movable frame. Ten frames to a hive. Watch, and I will show you a frame, a frame of comb, I will show you how honey is extracted from the comb, by centrifugal force. Magic, says Joan. At first, it all seems magical, she says. And it is. But it can be learned. I will show you, she says.

Catherine is standing beside Matt, and they are both looking at the city of bees. Catherine is acutely aware of everything that is going on; she is ready to start running for the back door of Joan's house, if she has to. Joan may believe that her bees are harmless, mild-tempered and easy-going, but Catherine does not. A bee is a bee, in her opinion. And she's been stung before, and it hurts.

Arlene and Diane are sitting on Joan's back steps. Arlene is wearing a sun-visor, shorts, a T-shirt. Her presence is another reason to be on guard, as far as Catherine is concerned. She looks harmless enough, but things happen whenever her mother is around. If anything is going to go wrong, it will be in the presence of Arlene. Lately, Catherine has been having nightmares, in which her mother is in danger. Her mother is wounded, hurt, sick, and she is dragging herself around the house trying to pretend that nothing is wrong. Her feet are dirty and bare, her face is smudged with grime. She has to keep stopping to rest, her hand pressed to her temple, and Catherine wants to go to her, but she is afraid. Something prevents her from helping her mother. What can such dreams mean? What is wrong with her, to have such awful dreams about her own mother? This is her first thought, when she wakes. She imagines herself going downstairs, greeting her mother as if nothing has happened— and what has happened, really?—saying good morning, giving her a kiss. She imagines her mother smiling, her eyes tired, not herself at all, grateful that Catherine has shown her some affection, as if she too has been caught in a strenuous and terrifying dream and now all she wants to do is forget and start over.

They wait to see Joan take a frame from one of the hives. Catherine's father stands off to one side with his camera. Photography, it occurs to Catherine, is for him the equivalent of beekeeping. It's practically a compulsion with him, as far as Catherine and Matt can see. Their father embarrasses them by stopping on a street corner to peer through the lenses of his camera, and then making complicated adjustments and backing into strangers, nearly knocking them off their feet, or climbing up onto something, a park bench, the edge of a planter full of tulips or petunias, to get a better view of his subject. This happened in downtown Vancouver, when they were visiting Eunice. They pretend they don't know him, at such times. They walk away, and leave him to himself. And then, when he gets home, he's down in his darkroom for hours, making prints on eight by ten sheets of glossy photographic paper. Pictures of trees and of people, of flowers and of cats, of barns and cars and even, once, the blank sun-washed side of a house in another town, a house he had never seen before, a plain house with nothing in the least unusual about it. He must have a hundred pictures of Catherine and Matt and Diane. Candid shots, he calls them. Her father believes in sneaking up on people. The unaware subject is his ideal, he maintains. This is so unlike his usual forthright, unsubtle approach to life that Catherine likes to pretend she's even more astonished—or annoyed—at the result than she really is. One photograph shows her sitting on the edge of the sandbox where she used to play as a child. Her feet are in sand up to her ankles. She is reading, a book open on her knees. Her hair is a mess, tangled curls casting weird shadows on her face. Shade from the apple tree falls across the background of the photograph, across the long wild spear grass that grows near the garden shed and always gets missed by the lawnmower. In the shade, in the darker pools formed by the shade, there is a vague blur hovering just above the ground. Eunice was intrigued by this blur, when she was shown the photograph. She believes in spirit photography. That is, she believes that partial or even complete images of ghosts can be caught on a strip of film even when they are invisible to the human eye. So what is this? Catherine wonders. What is this blur? Is it a ghost watching her as she reads? It must have been a bold ghost, to get so close. If Catherine had reached out a hand, she would have encountered it. Her hand would have passed right through its cold, misty form, if it had a form. She doesn't believe in ghosts, but every time she looks at the photograph the blur in the background begins to look more and more like a figure, like someone waiting in the shadows.

Catherine wonders at these adult obsessions, beekeeping, photography. Abby's mother paints in oils. She has painted several portraits of Abby, not one of which looks especially like Abby, as far as Catherine can see. She painted a portrait of Catherine's mother last year, and she's started another one this summer. It seems to Catherine that these hobbies, if that's the proper word, are simply ways in which adults try to justify their existence, or perhaps ignore the fact that they exist. As if their lives are not enough, and they know it; as if they fear that what they see each day with their own eyes is not enough. She feels a sense of cold self-righteousness. She will work as hard as she can, and become something, a teacher, and then she'll come back here, to Cayley, and for a while she'll live alone, live a splendid modern life, with a few friends, a car of her own, nice clothes, and after a few years of this she'll get married and have two or three children, three, ideally, and she will be happy, calm, serene, devoted, imperturbable. This is a blueprint for her life, and one she'll follow without being side-tracked. Definitely, she won't make the kind of mistakes her mother is making.

And then it occurs to her, as a random thought, that if she's right about these adult obsessions, then her mother is more honest than most adults, and more courageous, because she at least discovered for herself an obsession that was real, that existed. A person, an individual, flesh and blood, with a brain and a soul and an intelligence.

In June, when she got her new high-school yearbook, Catherine asked Mr. Schram to sign it. The yearbooks had just arrived that day from the printer and had been distributed to each classroom. Inside the front cover was a black and white picture of Cayley, taken from the air. There was the sawmill, and the harbour, a freighter tied up at the dock. And there was the school, the flat tar and gravel roof of the school, the rows of windows, the long oval of the cinder track, the baseball diamond, the leafy canopy of young maple trees planted by Catherine's biology class the year she was in grade eight. And there, right there, was Alma Avenue, and the roof of her house, and the sea. She traced the streets with her finger, along all the usual routes she took to get to her friends' houses, to her piano lesson, to Abby's house, the road that led out to the river, and Lisa McCann's house. The more she stared at the aerial photograph, the more entranced she became. It looked perfect, a perfect town, lost in the trees, the forests, a small lost town at the very edge of the sea. It seemed to her a shame that she was about to ask the person she hated most in the world to touch her yearbook. Her photograph was there—one of forty-two students in the grade twelve graduating class at Cayley Secondary—with a caption that said she was always smiling, a true, loyal friend. Ambition: *To return to Cayley as a primary school teacher.* Last Will and Testament: *I leave my algebra exams for the advancement of mankind.*

When she saw him, he was coming out of the staff room, and she stopped him and held out her yearbook, open at the page of staff photographs. "Mr. Schram? Excuse me, sir? Please?" she had said. "Would you sign this for me? Would you please be so kind?"

He had taken his pen from his pocket, an expensive-looking black and gold fountain pen, uncapped it and signed his name. Regards, B. Schram, he had written. His hand must have been shaking; the letters were uneven, uncertain. *Regards,* what does that mean? she thought. She'd known he'd write something dumb. She had watched him pocket his pen and then nervously touch the knot in his tie, and he had raised his hand and rubbed at the corner of his eye. Then he had dared to look directly into her eyes. And she could see that when he looked at her he didn't see her, not the real Catherine. He saw certain similarities between her and Arlene, in the colour of the hair, the shape of the eyes, the manner of standing. He saw a pale image of Arlene, and beyond that he saw nothing. And this, it seemed to Catherine, diminished both of them.

Catherine's father steps closer to Joan, adjusts the settings on his camera, begins snapping photographs, advancing the film, shifting his weight slightly to get another angle. And there are the bees, clinging to the frame in clusters, like over-ripe, decaying fruit. Catherine stares, fascinated, repelled. The bees, crowded together like this, seem to have become another kind of organism, a single, grotesque and powerful organism, potentially dangerous. Matt moves to the back steps of Joan's house, where Arlene is sitting. He and Diane sit on either side of Arlene, and she places her hands protectively on their shoulders.

Joan Mullis serves them iced tea on the deck at the back of her house. They all sit around the patio table facing the field, which is lit with the sun and a golden agitation of bees. Joan tells them the bees will settle down, that honey-bees almost never sting unless provoked. But haven't they just been provoked, Catherine thinks. She imagines the bees seeking some kind of revenge for the stolen honeycomb, which Joan has carried down to her cellar. Later, she tells them, she'll extract the honey from the comb. "Do you know how the honey is made?" she asks, directing her question at Diane, who opens her eyes wide at being singled out, and then shakes her head emphatically: No, she doesn't know. Joan tells her how the bees gather nectar from flowers, and carry the nectar and pollen to their hives and store it in cells made of beeswax. "When there is only a very small amount of water left in the nectar, the worker bees cap off the cells and the nectar is turned to honey.

"And do you know," she then says, turning to Matt. "The night your sister was born, you and Catherine came out here and saw the hives. You weren't very old yourself, at the time. Do you remember, David?" she said, and Catherine's father said that, yes, he did; he remembered very well. And then he looked out toward the field, and Catherine looked, too, and all she could remember of that night was the frost on the grass, the slick glassiness of the ground, the stars overhead, the emptiness that remained in her mother's absence.

"Joan," Arlene says. "Do you mind if I smoke?"

"No, not at all," Joan says. Then she says, "The ancient Egyptians evidently kept bees in hives of woven rushes. They used honey in their medicines and food. Only the wealthiest Egyptians could afford honey, of course. Did you know honey used to be used as a preservative. It's true. You'd be surprised at the things honey can preserve. For example, Lord Nelson's corpse came home from the Battle of Trafalgar in a vat of honey. Did you know that? The honey kept him from decaying until he could be properly buried in Westminster Abbey."

Arlene looks at Joan. She's sitting back in her chair, a cigarette in her hand, the sun visor obscuring the expression in her eyes. "It wasn't Nelson," she says. "It was Alexander the Great who was preserved in a vat of honey."

"Oh," says Joan. "Are you sure? I thought it was Nelson. Lord Nelson."

"Nelson," says Arlene, "was sent home in a barrel of brandy."

"I read a biography," says Joan. "Of Nelson."

"Well, the biography must have got it wrong," says Arlene.

"Well, I don't suppose it makes much difference," says David, looking startled. "Does it? After all this time?"

After the visit to Joan Mullis's house, Matt draws a picture of bees on a honeycomb. Matt gives each bee a face, a face that is close to human, that is, in fact, human. Some of them are recognisable, to Catherine. There is Joan herself, as a bee, a short fringe of hair framing her small, precise features, her eyebrows raised in a kind of perpetual surprise. And there is Catherine's father, as a bee. He is smiling, that polite slightly eager smile he always has, his eyes mild and somewhat sleepy looking, his outsized bee head propped on one thin bee leg. And here is Diane, a bee with pigtails, smiling hugely, her eyes large, dark, shining, her rear-end waggling as she roars around the honey-comb. Catherine's mother is a nervous-looking bee with fine, very delicate features, her glance directed at some distant object, oblivious, it seems, to the activity that surrounds her on all sides.

And there she is: Catherine Greenwood, a bee with its legs going in several directions at once, a teenage-girl bee, with pale lipstick and dark hair curling around her face, and too much eye makeup and a look of anticipation, tinged with dread, with fear. Is that what Matt has caught, in the bee's expression?

"Can I have this?" she says to him. "Can I keep this? No, I mean it. I'd like to have it."

"What for?" he says. His hands are smudged from his pencil, his oil pastels. He rubs his nose and tells her the picture isn't finished yet, he's still working on it. You like it? he says. He gives the picture an appraising glance, gets up from the table, stands back from it. He's working at the kitchen table, and the doors to the patio are open. A breeze comes in, ruffling an edge of the paper and there is the illusion that the bees are dancing.

On Abby's right wrist there's a small thin scar where she cut herself with a razor blade. She lets Catherine touch it. It's slightly raised, inelastic and cold, pale as a sliver of wood. Abby hadn't seriously intended to hurt herself, she says. She was fooling around, trying to see how much she could take, what the real thing would feel like. She wanted to scare her mother. She wanted to scare herself. In any case, she's wearing a wide silver bracelet on that wrist. It's a new bracelet she bought herself with her pay check, from her job as a cashier at the grocery store.

Abby and Catherine are driving out to Lisa's house, to pick her up, and then they're going to drive around and maybe go out to Valenzuela Bay, to see Abby's friends—the people who are living in the old farmhouse at the edge of the mudflats. As she drives, Abby tells Catherine that certain scientists in the nineteenth century figured out how to remove the skin from a corpse in one piece. With a little slice here and there, in just the right places, and a few careful tugs, they could take the skin off nearly intact. They ended up with the empty shape of a person, which they hung out in the sunlight to flap around like a nightgown.

Abby swears it's true. She shifts to a higher gear, then turns to look at Catherine and shakes her head a little. It is true, she says. Catherine doesn't know whether to believe her or not. The idea gives her an empty sensation, a sinking in the pit of her stomach. Along the side of the road the leaves on the alder trees tremble and glow with light. She and Abby are nearly there, at Lisa's house, beside the Cayley River, where, last summer, Catherine saw her beautiful dark-haired mother walking as if in a dream. But was it her mother? What if the woman she'd seen had been merely a spirit-shape, a representation of Arlene, as fluid and disconnected as mirror-writing, or one of those ghostly pale images that can be captured and studied only on a roll of film?

Chapter Thirty-three

When Arlene was eleven years old her father George Francis May had given her a notebook and had told her to fill it with the details of her life, her hopes, her aspirations, and she'd put the notebook aside and had, out of timidity, written scarcely a word in it. That was what she'd always believed. But it was a lie.

The truth is, the journal is full. Its green carapace cover is dented and scuffed and the gilded pages are dog-eared from use and here and there patched together with sticky tape. Every page is covered in her round clear handwriting. There are notations in the margins, and tucked between the pages for safekeeping are the program from her high-school graduation ceremony and a newspaper clipping dated May 7, 1950 announcing the engagement of Arlene Clare May to David Philip Greenwood. There is also a pressed flower from her wedding bouquet and a card announcing Catherine's birth. All the years of her life are accounted for, right up the present and even beyond. She is perfectly aware that the notebook contains contradictions, false leads, half-truths, but as far as she can see it has to be that way if what she writes down, if what she has already written, is going to approximate real life, or whatever this is she's working her way through. It seems to her it was all set out in advance like a blueprint, in any case, all the possibilities, and as a result a strict limit has been placed on what she can chose to do or not do.

She recalls having seen Matt playing football with his friends the day he got hurt. She'd taken a shortcut through the school playing field, on the far end, near the softball diamond. He hadn't seen her. He was running, head down, in a sort of crouch, and the other boys were running after him, getting ready to tackle him. She didn't stay to watch. She exited the school yard through a trail the kids used and came out on Third Street. From the crest of the hill, she had a good view of the sea, which that morning had been a pale, shimmering vastness toward which she was drawn irresistibly. It had been in every respect a beautiful morning, a soft wind gently stirring the bright leaves, small clouds racing across a clear blue sky. And when she got to Third Street, she turned onto Esplanade, near the park, and immediately she saw Brian riding a bike toward her.

"Where did you get that thing from?" she said, laughing. He rode up to her and stopped, keeping his hands on the handlebars. It was an old black bike with fenders painted a blunt dull aluminium colour. He said the bike belonged to his landlady's son. His landlady, he liked to say, was good to him, a real friend. She baked him bread and sometimes brought him a cup of hot coffee and a home-made biscuit if he was in his apartment on a Saturday or Sunday morning marking papers or term exams. Arlene had met the land-lady once or twice, as she was letting herself in the front door of the apartment building. Her name was Elise. A big woman with dyed blonde hair in a chignon. She wore cotton dresses and white sandals with intricate ankle straps that only made her stout legs look more stout, in Arlene's opinion. She and Arlene always smiled at each other and said hello, but having nothing in common with each other whatsoever, as far as Arlene could tell, they never ventured into conversation. Elise, with her bundle of pale hair and her fresh baked bread, her mugs of steaming coffee, her subdued mostly unseen tenants, who nevertheless left their garbage in overflowing containers on the door stoop, and let their cats sit precariously on the window sills, and tied a fat wiggling golden lab puppy by a rope to the tree in the yard. All the incidental background things that made up Brian's life. That was the only reason she had to take note of any of these things.

And here was Brian, riding Elise's son's bike. Arlene said, "Well, look at you!" The playground equipment in the park, the bright blue and red roundabout and the swings and slides, all set out on the green grass above the sea, gave the moment a festive air, although the park was oddly empty for such a fine warm morning. Out on the water there was a green and white tugboat pulling a log boom. A seagull was sitting on the red buoy in the harbour. The sea was flecked with whitecaps. Arlene walked with Brian up the street to his apartment. Anyone who happened to glance out a window would see them together. Brian pushed the bike, which he said he had to get back to his landlady's son. The rear wheel made a tickety-tick sound, like a clock. After he'd dropped off the bike, Brian said, perhaps they could drive somewhere out of town. He did want to talk to her, he said. They had to talk. Yes, she said, I think that's a good idea.

This is something she will write in her notebook: The day I meant to go straight home, I meant to go for a walk and then go home, but I met Brian on Esplanade Street, and then we drove out to the house out by the river. He kept saying we had to talk, and the house by the river was still empty, it seemed no one wanted to live there, which was lucky for us: It was the one place where we could be fairly sure no one would see us. Brian parked down the road, and then we walked back, and went in through the gate and along the path to the back garden, picking our way through the long grass and weeds. There was a sort of concrete bench in the garden to sit on. Beside the bench was a neat stack of bricks, as if someone had once intended to build a wall or a paved area and had then abandoned the project. There were flowers everywhere, roses and hollyhocks, snap dragons and daisies, as well as a wild tumult of ivy creeping up tree trunks and spilling along the ground. Fir and cedar seedlings were sprouting up like weeds among the paving stones. At the end of the garden the true forest began. A squirrel was running up and down a fir tree, scolding us continually. If we listened carefully, we could hear the river. We talked about everything, about the past. We were born six months apart, and when we compared what we were doing at different stages of our lives, I could see not only how different we were, because, after all, I was married with a child when he was still going to school, but how much alike—more like complementary phases of one organism than two separate people. We were, we agreed, both introspective and solitary. We preferred reading to socialising. We had what I would term a fastidious approach to life, a natural wariness combined with an unfortunate inability to foresee danger or understand what we needed to watch out for. We were cautious but on the other hand we seemed determined to take risks. When I tried to explain to him exactly what I meant, he spoke of the two Chinese forces of energy, yin and yang, negative and positive principles, male and female. I said, Yes, something like that. I had something much more personal and even more indivisible in mind. One day, I expected, the words I wanted would come to me. I'd find some way of making myself clear. I felt emptied out and purified; beyond logical thought. He told me that the future could be divined using oracle bones and the eight trigrams of the *I Ching*, the Book of Changes. The eight trigrams came from patterns on the back of a river creature, meticulously copied down long ago by a Chinese Emperor. When in an obliging frame of mind, the river creature was capable of carrying a weary traveller on its back across a swiftly flowing river to safety on the far bank.

We sat in the garden and talked, and then it began to rain. Neither one of us wanted to leave. We had so little time together, as it was. I knew that I should be at home, that my family would be waiting for me, but I chose to stay. That was what I was like, at this time. Brian tried the win-

dows at the back of the house, to see if one had been left
unlocked. Then he took a brick from the pile beside the
concrete bench and, wrapping his jacket around his hand,
used the brick to break a pane in the bedroom window. I
watched as he plucked the remaining shards of glass from
the pane. There was a sad smell of dampness and decay coming from the house. Brian reached inside the broken window pane and opened the window, and then climbed inside,
and that way we gained access.

We sat on the bedroom floor of the cold house by the
river and held our hands up, palm to palm, our fingers in-
terlaced. We stared into each other's eyes—the game children play, daring each other to be the first to look away. His
glance faltered, and then mine. We held our hands tight
together until my fingers began to ache. What had brought
me to such an unlikely place? I felt like a pilgrim who had
made her way to the necessary destination and must now
wait patiently to see what the result would be, and if she
had the strength to bear it. Never leave me, he said. He stared
at me steadfastly. Let's make a pact, right now, he said.
Arlene? Let's decide right now. That this is going to end well
for both of us. I looked away, unable to speak.

Julia Glass is painting Arlene's portrait on the beach below
her house. It is a summer of improbable occurrences, Arlene
has found. She has to sit on a rock at the edge of the water,
while Julia sits on a log a short distance away, beneath an
overhanging cedar bough, with her paints and her easel. It
is the first time in Arlene's life that anyone has painted her
portrait, and there are times when she wishes the process

could go on forever. She likes knowing that every line and angle of her body, the features of her face, her eyes, nose, mouth, all distinctly hers and unlike anyone else's features, are being depicted in oil paints on a sheet of canvas. She feels as if Julia's palette knife is, in a tender, painless, absolutely precise fashion, peeling the skin away from her bones, revealing something about her that is essential and pure and unknown even to her.

Julia climbed up on this rock first to demonstrate how she wanted Arlene to pose, with her ankles crossed and her hands resting lightly on her knees and her chin raised so that, Julia said, she would appear to be staring out to sea, as if waiting for a ship under full sail to come by and rescue her. A sailing ship, Julia said, and Arlene thought of the crystal sailing ship Brian had given her, the gift she'd left at Caroline's house, for safekeeping. When she assumes the pose herself, in any case, that is indeed how she feels, just as Julia described. She's waiting for a ship to come by and rescue her. A miniature ship, its glass sails on fire in the sun, sailing on a painted sea.

The wind wiser than we are, loves to blow about. . . . She can't remember the rest of the words. She's never read anything by Montaigne. She doesn't know half the things Brian knows. She has that feeling again, of being almost formless, as if she's floating above the rock, above the sea, like the figure in an impressionist painting, or a cubist painting, whatever they're called. A painting by Picasso, say. A painting in which a three-dimensional figure that ought to have weight and substance appears to defy all natural laws in order to delight the eye.

She looks out at the water, which dances with light. A seaplane takes off, a yellow dragonfly-shape trailing its cartoonish pontoons, banking sharply as it ascends into the air. In the harbour the massive black hull of a freighter looms. She can see heat waves shimmering above its decks. It arrived here from some distant foreign shore and will soon be gone again. Although, from this vantage point it isn't easy to believe that there is a wider world beyond this small town, with its spoon-shaped pewter-coloured harbour, surrounded, it appears, on all sides by dark, forested land. It doesn't seem as if there is a way out at all. The tide is coming in. The water laps around the rock and the sound seems to put her into a trance. The strangest thing happened to her the last time she posed for Julia. She was looking out at the sea, as she was supposed to do, and she saw them again. She saw the two little boys on the rock. She saw the way they clung to each other, the sun glistening on their hair and skin as on the wings of a bird, and she knew what it was they meant—that everything can be lost, that the human soul can become as cold and as transparent as water. She wanted to reach out her arms to them. She wanted to swim to them and gather them to her. She wanted to feel their arms around her neck, their breath warm against her face.

Myrtle is still twenty-five years old. For her, it is still 1957. As far as Myrtle is concerned, Arlene is still shut in her new house, unpacked boxes stacked in the closets, reading her way through *Anna Karenina* for the hundredth time. Half in a dream, half-asleep, reading, oblivious to everything around her. It comes to her that Myrtle tried to speak directly to her when she painted Catherine's face. Is that such a strange thought? Perhaps not. Imagine that Myrtle painted Catherine's face and sent her indoors as a cautionary message for Arlene: Don't take yourself so seriously. For once, get up, put down the book, go outdoors, go out into the glorious sun and the light of day. Take a deep breath. Lift your face to the light. Don't waste a minute.

When she climbs down from the rock, the tide has started to rise, and she finds herself standing up to her knees in water. In a little while, the rocks just a short distance out will be covered. The rock the little boys were sitting on will be completely submerged. Here, close to shore, sea anemones nestle like eggs among the brown rockweed that grows on the rocks. And there are a few purple starfish, which she loves to touch, to feel how warm they become in the sun. For a moment, she pretends she's a freshly hatched barnacle goose, flicking moisture from her downy wings, preening herself, getting ready to take flight. *They come to fulnesse of feathers.* She told the story of Gerard's geese to David. He listened in silence and then asked to see the place in the book where she'd found it, and he'd read the account himself. "If only it were true," he'd said. "Then this Gerard would really have discovered something."

"But it is true," she'd told him, taking the book from him. "Don't tell me you've never seen a barnacle goose?

She once saw a painting of a woman in just this pose— leaning over slightly, as if hoping to catch sight of her reflection in the uncertain surface of the sea. Perhaps Julia should paint her like this, instead. Arlene doesn't need to see herself in a portrait to know who she is. She can tell everything about herself by placing the fingers of one hand around the opposite wrist. She can feel her pulse. At the base of the palm there's a dab of blue oil paint, the colour of the ocean, or the sky, which she must have got when she helped Julia carry her painting equipment down the stairs. Arlene's wedding ring fits more loosely now than when David put it on her finger nineteen years ago, on the morning of June 6, 1950. Eunice sat in the front pew and delicately dabbed at her eyes with a lace hankie, pretending to be sad when really she was overjoyed: her daughter was off her hands, nothing left to worry about; she could hold her head up in the company of other women who had marriageable daughters. Eunice with her face powder the colour of peach skin, her faded-lilac perfume, her ropes of pearls.

Arlene wades back to shore, and puts her sandals on and begins to help Julia gather everything up, the paints and easel and the canvas, and a bottle of suntan lotion, and Arlene's cigarettes and the chocolate bars and thermos of coffee they'd brought with them. And then they make their way up the rickety steps to Julia's house. This is the fourth afternoon Arlene has posed for Julia. Julia says it's going to take another two or three sessions to get the painting to where she wants it. "If you're able to spare the time," Julia says, and Arlene says, "Oh, I'm not going anywhere." She has told Julia she doesn't want to see the painting until it's completely finished. The truth is, she's not sure she wants to see it at all. The idea scares her, a little. She thinks she knows herself, but what if the painting shows her someone she doesn't expect to see?

When they get to the top of the steps, Arlene pauses for a moment to catch her breath. She puts her hand on the wood railing beside the steps and looks out at the calm blue water and the blue sky. She sees two gulls sitting on a rock, and then one rises into the air, and soon after, the second follows. They fly toward the islands, flying forever, past the islands to the open sea, and she's following them, she's taking it upon herself to enter that strange, wilful territory where nothing is named or certain.